A Prince to be Feared

A Prince to be Feared

THE LOVE STORY OF VLAD DRACULA

MARY LANCASTER

A PRINCE TO BE FEARED

ISBN-13: 9781910245101

DEDICATION

*To Harriet and Dorothy,
who joined in my first pursuit of Vlad through Transylvania.*

The Principality of Wallachia around 1450–1475

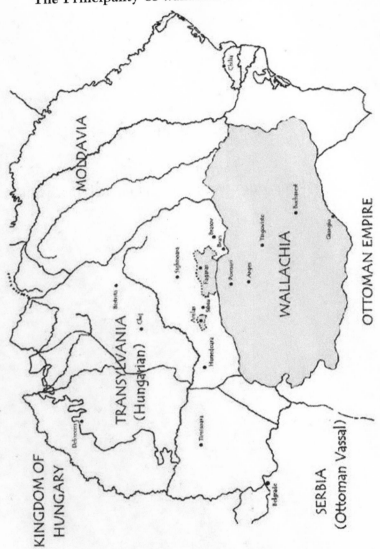

"it is much safer for a prince to be feared than loved..."

Niccolò Machiavelli, *The Prince*, 1513.

The Characters

The Wallachians

Vlad Dracula, son of Vlad Dracul, Prince of Wallachia.

Vlad Dracul, Vlad Dracula's father, Prince of Wallachia

Prince Mircea, Dracul's eldest legitimate son, Vlad Dracula's elder brother

Prince Radu, Dracul's youngest son, Vlad Dracula's younger brother who shared his imprisonment in the Ottoman Empire.

Vladislav, Prince of Wallachia, who deposed and killed Vlad Dracul and his son Mircea.

Besarab Laiota, another ruling prince of Wallachia from an alternate family line

Dragomir, minor Wallachian boyar, Maria's husband, supporter of Prince Vladislav

Carstian, Wallachian boyar, friend of Vlad Dracula

Tacal, Wallachian boyar, supporter of Vlad Dracula

Radul, Wallachian boyar, one time supporter of Prince Vladislav

Stoica, Wallachian boyar, friend of Vlad Dracula

Dan, a pretender to the Wallachian throne

Mihnea, son of Vlad Dracula and Maria

Turcul, Wallachian boyar, friend of Vlad Dracula

Cazan, Wallachian boyar

Pardo, Wallachian boyar, enemy of Vlad Dracula

Gales, Wallachian army commander

The Hungarians

Ilona Szilágyi, daughter of Count Mihály Szilágyi, niece of John Hunyadi and cousin to László and Matthias

Count Mihály Szilágyi, Transylvanian nobleman and soldier, loyal supporter of his brother-in-law, John Hunyadi

Countess Szilágyi, his wife

Miklós, their son, Ilona's younger brother

Katalina, their daughter, Ilona's elder sister

Count John (János) Hunyadi, viceroy of Hungary, known as The White Knight, Ilona's uncle

Countess Erzsébet Hunyadi, his wife, sister of Mihály Szilágyi, Ilona's aunt

László Hunyadi, elder son of John Hunyadi, Ilona's cousin

Matthias (Corvinus, King of Hungary), younger son of John Hunyadi, Ilona's cousin

Ladislas the Posthumus, King of Hungary

Count Cilli, Hungarian nobleman, supporter of Ladislas, opponent of John Hunyadi

Margit, Ilona's gently bred attendant

Count Szelényi, Hungarian nobleman and courtier, official Keeper of the prisoner Vlad Dracula.

Helena, Count Szelényi's mistress

Maria Gerzsenyi, member of minor Transylvanian nobility, Ilona's friend, first encountered as Countess Hunyadi's attendant.

Josef, Maria's married ex-lover.

Mihaela, wealthy resident of Sibiu, Transylvania, family friend to the Szilágyis

John of Capistrano, Papal legate to Hungarian lands.

György Baráth, minor Transylvanian nobleman

The Moldavians

Bogdan, Prince of Moldavia, Vlad Dracula's uncle

Stephen, his son, Vlad Dracula's cousin

Petru Aaron, Prince of Moldavia, who deposed and killed Bogdan; Stephen's opponent

The Ottomans

Zafer Bey, Ottoman Ambassador

Mehmed "the Conqueror", Sultan

Hamza Pasha, Ottoman soldier and representative of the Sultan

table of Contents

Chapter One

Visegrád, Hungary, 1474

He made a perfect villain. Even after years of imprisonment and the loss of all he'd once won, even with the prospect of regaining his country and his crown being dangled before him like a carrot, Vlad Dracula still looked fierce, arrogant, and utterly unrepentant.

From his shadowy position in the gallery above the exercise chamber, Stephen, Prince of Moldavia, watched the long, hard fight reach its inevitable conclusion. Both men wielded their swords with skill and with such force that without the protective padding they wore, and the presumably blunted blades of their swords, there would have been blood everywhere. But although his opponent was younger and this was sword play rather than battle, Vlad, the one-time Prince of Wallachia, always fought to win.

Stephen would have been disappointed if defeat and hardship had dimmed the ferocious gleam in his cousin's eye, if the humiliation of his long imprisonment had managed to bow him. If it ever had, and Stephen couldn't really doubt it, he was back with a vengeance, and the knowledge made Stephen smile involuntarily as the pleasure of memory overcame the dull pain of loss.

At heart, surely, he and Vlad were still the same men who'd set out together as youths, shoulder to shoulder, to win the world for themselves and each other. Young and invincible.

The swords, flashing in the streaming sunlight, clashed together, screeched painfully, and suddenly the younger man staggered backwards, his sword falling to the floor.

At the same time, the door into the exercise chamber flew open, and a crowd of young men strode in. They stopped in their tracks, staring, as Vlad dropped his padded jacket on the floor and said something to his erstwhile opponent. It might have been gracious or taunting. Stephen couldn't tell, and neither could the noisy youths at the door who exchanged low-voiced comments in an excited sort of way as Vlad walked across the room.

He still moved like a large cat, quick and dangerous yet peculiarly graceful, sure in the knowledge that whoever was in his path would swiftly get out of it. But the youths, clearly, had never met Vlad Dracula, only heard of him, and they were looking for easy glory.

Behind him, on his feet once more, the man he'd just defeated watched in silence. Vlad himself, finding his way blocked, stood very still. Stephen, his heart beating unaccountably fast, eased backwards to observe better as the prince looked around the four bristling youths.

"If you wish to address me," he said haughtily, his voice sending shivers down Stephen's spine, "you must stand at least a foot away from my person."

"I was here first," the largest blustered with unforgivable rudeness. Vlad's age as well as his rank entitled him to far greater courtesy. But with a flash of rueful insight, Stephen saw what his old friend was up against: boys who imagined it was safe to bait the monster of Wallachia because he was a helpless prisoner. And he would be a magnet for the young glory hunters. Stephen's guilty heart wrenched as if the humiliation was his own rather than Vlad's.

But Vlad appeared to be used to it. Without warning, he seized the young man by the throat and hurled him across the room.

Before the others could react, he rattled his sword between the heads of the two on either side, knocking them apart.

"Let me help you with your manners,"Vlad said contemptuously and strolled out of the room.

His recent fencing partner grinned, somewhat to Stephen's surprise since the half-strangled youth on the floor was choking and clutching his throat, and blood oozed down the faces of the two who'd come in contact with Vlad's sword. Clearly it wasn't so very blunt after all.

Vlad's fencing partner sauntered across the floor, tutting. "That's no way to pick a fight with His Highness," he observed. "I'm sure your parents taught you better."

Stephen didn't wait to hear more. Judging it was now safe to descend from the gallery without encounteringVlad, he made his way to the stairs just as a servant appeared at the top with the news that the king awaited him in the garden.

"Well, did you see him?" the King of Hungary demanded almost as soon as Stephen stepped into the fresh air. Slightly disoriented as much by his own churning emotions as by the sight of the royal retinue spreading around the terrace, Stephen took a moment to focus on King Matthias Corvinus.The king beckoned him away from the rest of his following, and Stephen obediently fell into step beside him.They appeared to be walking alone in the direction of the king's formal garden.

"Yes, I saw him."

"Did he look pleased with himself?"

A breath of laughter escaped Stephen. "No more than usual."

"Well, Ilona's here, so our plan is almost complete."

Stephen breathed a sigh of relief.With the Ottomans threatening the borders of Moldavia, he needed the Hungarian alliance. And the Wallachian one.

"Have you told him which marriage you intend for him?" Stephen asked.

"Of course."

"What did he say?" Stephen asked curiously.

The king shrugged. "Nothing."

"I thought he'd be pleased." Stephen couldn't help his pique. He'd done Vlad a rather selfless favour promoting this marriage, considering he'd once coveted Ilona Szilágyi himself—even before her cousin Matthias had become King of Hungary. And in Stephen's eyes, the existence of his own beautiful wife did not detract from this generosity.

"The alliance is good, and he knows it," Matthias said comfortably. "Let's go and find her. A private, informal meeting will be kinder."

She moved among the bright spring flowers like a wraith, grey and dull against the carpets of yellow and orange and white spread out before her. Although her steps were quick and light, almost gliding, she made slow progress, stopping frequently to bend and examine the blooms in minute detail. As she crouched down, her grey veil, which was the only head covering she wore, fell forward over her face. One slender, elegant hand pushed it back absently, revealing a tired, almost emaciated face, the skin stretched taut across the high, broad bones of her cheeks and the narrow, almost pointed chin below. With a little more animation, she might have resembled a peasant child's idea of a witch. As it was, she just looked worn-out, vague, and very badly dressed.

Stephen blurted, "*That* is Ilona Szilágyi?"

"You are shocked by my cousin's appearance?" The king sounded amused. "You can't have laid eyes on her in ten years!"

"More," said Prince Stephen. "The Ilona I remember was not afraid to speak her mind to anybody. This one looks terrified of her own shadow."

"All to the good," said the king, just as the woman caught sight of the two men approaching along the path and rose to her feet.

Suddenly uncertain, Stephen touched the king's velvet-clad arm. "Are you sure about this?"

The king lifted one interrogative eyebrow at him. The rest of his attention and the gracious smile beginning to form on his lips were for the woman in grey.

"You would truly give your cousin to him?" Stephen felt obliged to check now that he'd seen her. "In all her...frailty?"

"Well, damn it, man," said the king through his smile, "what else is she good for? Cousin Ilona!" The grey lady extended one ungloved hand, and the king, who had clearly meant to embrace her, deftly clasped it between both of his instead while she dropped a faint bob of a courtesy. "Are you enjoying my gardens?"

She mumbled something in return, drawing her hand free and casting a glance up at Stephen before returning her patient gaze to the king.

"You do not recognise an old friend?" the king said jovially. "Prince Stephen of Moldavia."

Her eyes came back to him with curious reluctance. "What a surprise," she said vaguely, "to find you here. Now."

Stephen blinked. Was that sarcasm in the calm, indifferent voice? Did she actually understand why he was here at Visegrád, on such obviously friendly terms with his one-time enemy, the king? The doubt kept him from noticing till later that it was the only greeting she gave him.

Her eyes moved on to the newly planted trees at the far end of the walled garden. She said distantly, "What is it you want, Matthias?"

Clearly unused to being so addressed these days, the King of Hungary frowned, as if searching for a suitable reply. His ageing cousin dragged her eyes back to him. "I want to go home," she explained. "I don't care to live in palaces anymore. Tell me what you brought me here for so that I can do it and leave. Please," she added by way of an afterthought.

King Matthias beamed at her. "I brought you here because I have found you a husband."

"Thank you," she said. "I don't want one." She might have been refusing an apple or a sweetmeat.

"Nonsense," the king said robustly. "Every woman wants a husband, and you have been widowed, what, nine years? Ten?"

"I have grown comfortable as I am. I don't need your favour in this." After a pause, her wandering eyes came back to his, and she added with some difficulty, like a forgotten rhyme or prayer, "Though I thank you for thinking of me."

"To be frank," said the king, "I am thinking of myself too."

A hint of amusement flitted through her dark brown eyes, like an echo of the youthful beauty Stephen remembered. She was still only, what, thirty-six or thirty-seven years old? She didn't need to look such a damned fright.

She said, "Matthias, I am no prize—a mere cousin, widowed and ageing. Surely we have better relatives with whom to buy allegiance. Unless you wish to appease with a well-born prize of no value?"

She must have seen the truth in her royal cousin's face, for a breath of ghostly laughter escaped her pale lips. "Give him a castle instead," she advised, reaching down for a yellow daffodil, whose head was drooping much like her own.

"I'll give him a castle—lots of castles—*as well*," Matthias said with the first hint of impatience. "Don't you want to know which bridegroom I have chosen for you?"

"No." Frowning over the impossibility of the task; she was trying and failing to stiffen the flower's neck.

"It's an old friend of yours—the Prince of Wallachia."

As if she couldn't help it, her gaze flew up to the king's. But, straightening, she only said sardonically, "*Which* Prince of Wallachia?" Her eyes alighted on Stephen, some of their vagueness falling away like petals in a breeze. "You can't be trying to buy Radu. He already has a wife. And Besarab…"

Abruptly, she broke off. Her eyes fixed on a point beyond his head, and, turning, he saw that it was on the lowering building known as Saloman's Tower. Some distance downhill from the main castle, almost on the bank of the Danube, only the top of the tower was visible from where they stood. It was where the king imprisoned rebellious nobles and other high-ranking enemies. She knew *he* was here; she had always known.

She said, "No." The word came out no more than a strangled whisper. Backing away from them, she clutched at her veil with trembling fingers, tugging until it sat askew on her head. Beneath it, her hair was still burnished red-gold, though Stephen could glimpse traces of grey streaking through it. And suddenly she was speaking again, with an intensity she hadn't looked capable of seconds before. "No, Matthias, not that. Please… ! Don't put me back on that *sleigh ride*, not with *him*…!"

"You're not making any sense," Matthias said coldly.

A sneaking compassion entered Stephen's guilty soul, drowning whatever brief suspicion had arisen about her pretending this ridiculous new character Perhaps these were not the amends he should be making to his cousin. He had been right when he first saw her—she wasn't capable of dealing with Vlad now; time had not been kind to her. Nor fate, he acknowledged, remembering belatedly the awful execution of her father at Ottoman hands, then the sudden death of her mother and the suicide of her closest friend barely a year later—almost at the same time, surely, as she'd fled Wallachia before the invading Ottomans. No wonder she looked like a ghost of her own past.

Matthias said sternly, "I need Wallachia on my side. It's unstable. Neither Radu nor Besarab can be trusted, either to hold out against the Ottomans or to remain loyal to me. I need him back there. And his price is you."

"*His* price?" she exclaimed. "*His? He doesn't *have* one for freedom after twelve years! He doesn't have a price for taking back his own country! Just send him there, and he'll hold it at your back as he always did, as he always would if you hadn't—"

Breathless, she broke off, whirling away from them as if trying to hide the agitation she had already betrayed. Matthias and Stephen exchanged glances.

The king said, "It's your duty, Ilona. And the man has a fondness for you; he won't hurt you. He asked for you before, remember?"

Her hand flapped helplessly. She mumbled something that might have been, *"Fourteen years ago."* And ruefully, Stephen had to agree that the bridegroom might well be a little shocked by the changes those fourteen years had wrought in his old friend.

He wasn't in Saloman's Tower. He was honourably confined in the main palace. The discovery terrified Ilona as the possibility of his more distant presence in the tower had not. If she attended dinner with the king, as she was bidden, she might be forced to meet him, even sit beside him. So she sent her well-born attendant, Margit, with a message pleading a sick headache, which was not so far from the truth.

For a long time, she just paced the comfortable apartment she had been given, wringing her hands and wondering how this had happened, how to stop it. The woolly covering she had deliberately grown over her once sharp mind got in the way of political analysis, but even she grasped that Stephen of Moldavia must be here because he wanted to loosen his allegiance to the Ottomans, and he mistrusted the present ruler of Wallachia. Without Wallachia to help him against the Ottoman threat, he needed powerful Hungary behind him. So was Stephen or Matthias considering the restoration of the deposed prince held prisoner in this palace? Which of them was making it a condition of their alliance? And how had she become a pawn in any of it?

For her, a woman, there was no way out—except death, and despite the poetic justice of committing suicide as Maria had, she could not quite bring herself to that sin. He would put it on his conscience too.

Abruptly, she sank down on the nearest stool. Caught by her own gaze, she stared into the Venetian glass mirror so unkindly placed upon the table, forced to look full into her ravaged face. She would have laughed if she could. All their plans, all their alliances would founder because of this face…

And this mind.

Ilona gazed into her large, hollowed dark eyes. For a moment, they looked unfamiliar, like someone else's—because they weren't vague and dull. They were…wild, fearful.

Is there a way? Can I find a way out of this? Can I think?

Erzsébet Szilágyi had grown used to holding her head high. Widow of the greatest Christian knight in Europe, sister of the bravest of soldiers, mother of the king of Hungary, she had not allowed age or grief to dampen her pride. Even entering the private apartment Matthias had given to her niece—somewhat overgenerously in Erzsébet's opinion—alone and being greeted by no one more important than Ilona's gently born attendant, she kept her habitual, regal posture.

Ilona sat on a stool before a large mirror, absently brushing at the same greying streak of hair among her unexpectedly luxuriant auburn tresses. However untidy, her hair had always been beautiful, thick, and shining, and of such a rare shade of auburn that sometimes it had seemed like dark gold.

Erzsébet blinked away the memory. The present Ilona was no longer a young girl. She wore unrelieved grey, both gown and undergown of the same uninspiring hue. One wide oversleeve flapped like a bird's wing with every stroke of the brush.

Though Erzsébet stared at her back, Ilona didn't turn or acknowledge her aunt's presence in any way, even when Erzsébet said loudly, "What is she doing?"

"She's not feeling well," the woman excused her.

"So I heard." Erzsébet didn't trouble to keep the disbelief out of her voice or her face as she strode forward and took hold of her niece's shoulder.

Annoyingly, Ilona didn't jump or cry out. Instead, the faintest of smiles stirred her lips. She leaned her head to one side, actually touching her cheek to Erzsébet's hand.

The old lady snatched it back. The affectionate gesture reminded her too much of the past. A very different past.

"How are you, aunt?" Ilona asked, as if they'd parted just last week.

"Better than you, by the look of you."

"True." Ilona reached out for the ugly grey veil lying on the table in front of her and began to pin it in place. She didn't trouble with any kind of frame or crespine.

"What's the matter with you?"

"I have a headache."

Erzsébet curled her lip. "For twelve years?"

"No." Ilona didn't sound angry or ashamed, just tired. "Only since coming here."

"Only since the king, my son, explained your duty to you?"

Her mouth twitched at that, as if she would deny it. But her gaze still avoided her aunt's. "Yes," she said. Her slender, almost transparent hands fluttered down to her side, leaving the veil in place, slightly askew but covering all that was left of brightness in her. Erzsébet remembered her hair flashing in the sunlight like exotic, burnt gold as she whirled about, laughing in some childish game.

Erzsébet knew an instant of pity, not unmixed with contempt. "It's time you pulled yourself together, girl!"

"Yes," Ilona agreed.

Surprised by this easy victory, Erzsébet peered round into her face. "Then you accept the inevitable?"

Ilona smiled, the first true smile her aunt had seen on her countenance in many years. It might have broken a less stony heart than hers. At the same time, Ilona looked into her eyes.

"We both know my acceptance doesn't matter. It isn't mine you need, is it?"

Erzsébet searched her face, looking for insolence, for rebellion, for any spark that would reveal the old Ilona still inside this faded shell.

Understanding dawned slowly, along with renewed pity that the girl had lost her grip on reality to this extent.

"You think he'll reject you? Because you've lost your youth and beauty, you think he'll turn down the offer of the King of Hungary's cousin? For God's sake, you can't actually imagine this is about *you*? You know it was *never* about you! It's about alliance! Alliance with your family. Alliance that will regain him a country and a throne after twelve years in effective prison. Do you really imagine he cares if your hair is grey or your lips red? He isn't marrying you. He's marrying *us*."

Curiously, Ilona's face seemed to whiten. And yet those pale lips curved upward. Light definitely glimmered in those dark, opaque eyes. Not a spark, but something.

She said, "Ask him, Aunt Erzsébet. Ask him if he'll take the deal without me."

Without her, without a marriage alliance to cement it, he wouldn't believe in the deal, wouldn't trust Matthias—and frankly, who could blame him?

"Why, in the name of all that's holy, would he do anything so stupid?"

"Because I wish it," Ilona said vaguely. She stood, tugging at the ugly veil as if to check it was secure. "Have them tell him that…if you like."

Seething with indignation and incomprehension was no way in which to face him. Countess Erzsébet Hunyadi knew it and yet, after ignoring his presence for twelve years, she couldn't stay away one more hour.

Count Szelényi, his official jailer, was easily summoned and conducted her without question to the prince's apartment. Erzsébet watched with curling lip as he pushed the key into the lock. He couldn't be ignorant of the dreadful reputation of his prisoner; he must have heard all the salacious and chilling tales, including the latest, that he trapped birds outside his chamber window and impaled them. Hardly the act of a gentle or sane man.

"Aren't you afraid to enter his chamber so casually?" she enquired.

Count Szelényi smiled. Although he didn't appear obviously afraid, neither did he seem surprised by the question. "No, madam. But if you wish, I can wait inside with you. Or outside the door, if you prefer."

"That won't be necessary," Erzsébet said drily. What had *she* to fear from him?

"As you wish." Szelényi turned the key, withdrew it, and knocked.

"Enter."

The voice from inside sent a shiver down Erzsébet's spine. Not of fright but of…memory. His voice was as it always had been, just as deep, just as vigorous and commanding.

Szelényi swung the door wide. "Sir, you have a visitor. Countess Hunyadi."

Though her heart had begun to beat unaccountably fast, Erzsébet sailed into the room, registering as she did that it was comfortably furnished with cushioned chairs, and rugs on the floor. His bed had green velvet hangings, and a closed, ornately carved chest stood beside it. The prince might have been detained here, but his imprisonment was not arduous.

And then all peripheral thoughts vanished as a shadow rose from the desk under the darkening window and moved forward into the lamplight.

She'd had a nice speech prepared, a little condescending, a little pitying to remind him of his place, but not unkind. And yet now that those strange green eyes clashed with hers for the first time in twelve years, it all flew out the window. Her mouth was too dry to speak.

Dear God. She had forgotten the force that blazed out of those fierce eyes, the way he dominated a scene just by being in it. He had been the same even as a boy come boldly to her brother's house in Transylvania to plead for the aid no one had any intention of giving. Supplicant or sovereign, János, her husband, had mocked him. And it was the same now. There was no gratitude, no remotest surprise in his face as he regarded her.

On the other hand, she could have sworn *he* mocked *her*. Though, of course there was no obvious disrespect in his stance, in his elegant bow. Vlad Dracula had always possessed exquisite manners.

"Countess Hunyadi," he said, taking her nerveless fingers and just touching them to his lips. "I am honoured."

She stared suspiciously at his bent head. Was that sarcasm? Was he chiding her for never visiting him before? What in God's name did she owe a deposed prince of Wallachia?

The man who, whatever his motivation, had served her husband and her son so far beyond the call of duty.

She shut off that line of thought. She had learned long ago never to reveal weakness, and it was doubly important in the company of this unpredictable and too-perceptive creature.

"Yes," she agreed. "You are."

A genuine smile curved his full, sensual lips. Above them, his moustache, longer and thicker than she remembered, was as perfectly groomed as ever. His black locks were loose, his head uncovered, but otherwise he was dressed as formally as if he had just attended the court dinner. Which he hadn't. He wore black hose with light leather boots and a black, high-necked doublet with short leather tassels dangling from the shoulders. A pristine white collar showed at his throat. Rings adorned both hands.

Relinquishing his light, cool grasp on her fingers, he straightened. "Will you sit down? I can offer you excellent wine—a gift from the king, your son."

"Thank you, no. I cannot stay. I merely came to congratulate you that your fortunes appear to be looking up at last."

"I have new hope," he allowed.

Had his hopes ever sunk? How had this active, turbulent man coped with twelve years of confinement? Because, despite his pleasant surroundings, that was what it was. She hadn't believed Vlad could tolerate such curtailment of his freedom. She'd almost expected to find him faded. Like Ilona.

But this, this was definitely the same, arrogant man who had stood before her in his own castle and assured her with perfect self-belief that he would defeat the Ottomans and bring about a new era of peace for Wallachia, Hungary, and all their neighbours. Failure, even after twelve years, seemed to be a temporary matter.

"Perhaps you have," she allowed. Then, unable to resist taunting him, she added, "Now that you are to become a true Christian."

He didn't say anything to that, merely inclined his head. But his gaze never wavered. She had the impression he was waiting for something.

"And so your old betrothal to my niece is resurrected."

He stood very still. She could almost imagine he didn't breathe. "I am so honoured," he said, still waiting.

"Would it surprise you to know that my niece does not consider herself honoured by this match? That she does not wish it?"

Still those eyes didn't waver. Erzsébet began to feel her own watering with the effort of holding his gaze.

"No," he said. "We have not met in twelve years, and I am sure she has heard nothing of me but tales of cruelty and carnage."

"Twelve years," Erzsébet marvelled. "They have not been kind years to Ilona."

Something moved in his eyes then, a flash of some emotion suppressed before she could even begin to recognise it. His lower lip clamped over his upper in an old gesture she remembered well. Once, as a boy, it had betokened nervousness, until he'd adopted it as a pose of pride.

He said, "What has happened to Ilona? The king told me only that she was well and unmarried."

"Twelve years have happened to her! She is old," Erzsébet said unkindly. "And has been since she escaped from your castle."

His eyes dropped. Erzsébet knew relief because at last she could blink, and also an upsurge of triumph because she was right. Something had happened during those last days of Vlad's reign, something that *could* have affected Ilona so deeply that she'd turned into the poor, empty creature she'd just left staring blindly into her mirror. Erzsébet and her family were innocent of this.

"Is she here?"Vlad asked. And that, at last, was simple, genuine.

"Yes. She seems to think that if you know her wishes, you'll take the alliance without her."

Vlad's lips curved, separating once more. They both knew that the king held all the cards. The terms of the alliance were his to deal. Marriage alliances were important, yet was it not unnecessarily unkind to give a damaged, gentle being like Ilona to the Impaler now? Perhaps there was a different option, a different relative…? A different way to assuage unreasonable and unnecessary guilt.

"I won't,"Vlad said."I will change my religion and swear new oaths of allegiance to the king. But I will have Wallachia, and I will have Ilona."

Ilona rose with the dawn. She'd had little rest, less sleep, unable to think of anything except whether or not Erzsébet had gone to Vlad and explained that she didn't want the match.

Wearing only her night shift, she pushed the heavy blankets off and slid out of bed. The floor was icy under her feet, and she shivered. But she needed air. She felt she'd been suffocating all night. Padding over to the window, she unlatched it and threw it wide. A rush of blessedly cool air caressed her cheeks, surrounded her head and shoulders. The smell of newly made bread filled her nostrils, reminding her she hadn't eaten yesterday. Her stomach rumbled, comfortingly normal.

It was a good sign. Everything was going to be fine now. It was a beautiful dawn, the sky just beginning to glow pink and orange around the peeping sun. From her window, she could see the garden that had attracted her out of doors yesterday—only to be bearded by the king and Stephen.

Had Stephen seen him yet? Had they met since Stephen had betrayed him at Chillia? Perhaps he understood, now that his anger was passed. Perhaps he would even have done the same.

No. Pragmatic as he was, as a prince had to be, nothing would have induced him to betray Stephen.

She could smell the flowers now, their sweet, subtle scents drifting over the bread, reminding her that she needed to be home to care for her own garden. The servants would neglect it without her to nag them.

Perhaps I can go home today…if she's spoken with him. How will I know?

One didn't order Countess Hunyadi. One could only suggest and hope curiosity would do the rest. And if she had gone to him, if she had passed on Ilona's wishes, what did he say, how did he look? How did he feel? Relieved. The Vlad she remembered would always honour old promises, but now she'd released him. He could marry, or not, some other cousin.

Whom?

It doesn't matter to me, or to him…

And she, Ilona, could go home to Transylvania and live out the remainder of her days in the quiet domesticity she had finally found. Great lives and great events would go on, uninfluenced by her, unaware of her existence. And in time, she'd get the peace back. She would…

The castle was stirring. Not just the servants baking and cleaning and lighting fires. She could hear the gentle clip–clop of horses being exercised across the courtyard. Not the king at this hour, but perhaps one or two of his more active courtiers.

Yes, there they were, two of them, with servants and soldiers riding behind. In silence, the two courtiers rode side by side, skillfully controlling the natural exuberance of their mounts, forcing them to a sedate walk at least as far as the castle gates.

They sat very straight in their saddles, one in particular presenting an eye-catching posture, at once graceful, proud, and strong. If you could tell so much from one broad, erect back. Ilona frowned, blinking in the dim dawn light as if that could help her see more clearly. Her heart began to thud against her ribs.

Is it Vlad? Is it him?

He wore a round black hat with a red feather at the side, and from under it long black curls flowed around his shoulders and partway down his powerful back. Ilona swayed, her fingers gripping the sill for support.

Just so had she watched him ride away from her after their very first meeting. The horse had been different—her uncle's, not her cousin's—and his garments had been rough and worn, but he had held himself with the same pride, ridden with the same perfect confidence so that she'd almost imagined he was as splendid as he'd wanted to be.

The rider stopped. His horse snorted, and his companion paused too, glancing back at him in quick interrogation. The man who could have been Vlad—*please God, don't be Vlad*—began to turn his head.

Frozen, Ilona couldn't move, couldn't run, couldn't even fall out of sight onto the floor. Panic held her paralysed.

His head continued to turn, his neck twisting so that he could look upward. Unerringly, he gazed at her window.

Holy Mary, Mother of God.

Vlad Dracula, exiled Prince of Wallachia. Even over this distance, vitality blazed out of his face.

He won't see me; he can't recognise me…

The full lips didn't smile. But his gaze, rooting her to the spot, didn't move on. His head dipped, acknowledging her, and at that, she grasped her hair in despair. Her other hand flew to her throat, and she fell back so that she couldn't see him, couldn't visualise his failure to recognise her, or worse, his horror at what she'd become.

Her mouth opened in a soundless cry of loss. She pushed herself up against the wall under the window and, for the first time in ten years, let the past consume her.

Chapter Two

Horogszegi, Transylvania, 1451

The summer had passed without war or the threat of it. To Ilona, thirteen years old, it always seemed like a time of permanent sunshine, when the adults were not too occupied to play, when the children themselves played without fear and without the pall of politics waiting to engulf them as it would do all too soon. In some ways, it was her last summer of innocence.

She had spent most of it on the family estate at Horogszegi, with her mother, brother, and sisters. With the autumn, her father, Mihály, came more frequently, as did her uncle, the great White Knight, John Hunyadi, viceroy of Hungary, and his family.

Of course Hunyadi was married to Mihály Szilágyi's sister, but even then Ilona was aware that the ties between the two men went far beyond the loyalty of duty or family.

With war temporarily in abeyance, Hunyadi himself was merely harassed by recalcitrant noblemen. He allowed himself the occasional bouts of rest and healing at the Szilágyi's home and always departed in better humour than he'd arrived.

The day that changed everything for Ilona was an unseasonably warm one toward the end of October. After receiving a messenger, John Hunyadi emerged into the garden and threw himself down on the wooden bench beside her father. Mihály Szilágyi, from his comfortable seated position was playing a vigorous four-cornered game of catch with Ilona, her brother Miklós and little Matthias Hunyadi, who was only about eight years old.

John Hunyadi said, "The wretched boy is here now!"

Ilona, who had learned early to pick up the difference between threat and mere annoyance, wasn't worried, just interested in the strange combination of amusement and frustration in her uncle's voice.

"Who?" her father asked lazily, hurling the leather ball well above Ilona's head.

It was too high, but she refused to give up. Miklós began to run in from his corner, sure he would catch it before she did. Ilona leapt, one hand stretched up to its limit while she used the other to balance. The ball slammed into her hand, and she gave a crow of triumphant laughter, dropping back to her feet with the ball secure.

Her father smiled.

"Dracula," said her uncle, with a wave of his hand that was not quite disparaging. He regarded the "son of the dragon" as a nuisance, but even he couldn't quite dismiss the boy who had, at the tender age of seventeen, walked into the country which had deposed and killed his father, and simply taken the throne while its legitimate prince was occupied in war elsewhere. Without spilling a drop of blood, he'd made his presence felt all over the region. Even though he'd been ejected a couple of months later, he'd warned the world that Vlad Dracula, son of Vlad Dracul, was out to get his throne back.

Ilona liked the nicknames by which father and son were popularly known. It gave them a sort of mythical glamour that appealed to her, even though she knew the actuality was rather more mundane: the late Vlad Dracul had once been made a member of the Empire's Order of the Dragon—*dracul* in Romanian—sworn to oppose the infidel, which he'd done off and on for much of his turbulent life. Conversely, the son, Dracula—son of the dragon—had used infidel Ottoman troops when he'd briefly snatched the Wallachian throne.

"What's he doing here?" Mihály asked, watching indulgently as Ilona's throw to Matthias was intercepted by the larger Miklós.

"Well, when I say 'here,' I mean he's in Transylvania. He crossed the border two nights ago with Stephen of Moldavia, who wants my help to restore him to his throne."

"Yes, but what does young Vlad want?"

"Your guess is as good as mine. Rumour says he blames me for the death of his father and wants my blood. I'm afraid he's doomed to failure there too. I've told Brasov and the other cities not to harbour either youth."

"Probably safest," Mihály agreed. "Vlad's father was unpredictable, to say the least. From his career to date, I imagine this son is cut from the same cloth."

Unfortunately for Ilona, who rather admired the daring tactics of the young, one-time Prince of Wallachia, Matthias chose that moment to fall over Miklós's feet, and she had to stop listening in to the adults in order to pick the boy up and rebuild his wounded pride in the face of Miklós's blatant laughter.

"Come, let's go and find László," she suggested, restoring peace at once to the two boys who had only their hero worship of Hunyadi's elder son in common.

László was then about twenty years old and handsome enough for Ilona's sisters to flutter around like moths to a flame. It occasionally bothered their mother, since they were full cousins to László, but Ilona suspected that half the attraction of such a crush was its safety. They could practise flirting with impunity—and so, to be fair, could László.

But that afternoon, the amusements were more childish: a boisterous game of tag, at which Ilona excelled, even against the athletic, long-legged youths like Miklós and László. At thirteen, she had no compunction about picking up her skirts and leaping over fences and younger children, dodging and swerving to avoid being tagged, hurling herself onto benches, boulders, or tree trunks to be safe. And since her mother and aunt had begun to groom her for staid adulthood, it was doubly exhilarating.

Flying across the slightly wilder, bumpier ground that led up to the high garden wall, with László ever closer to her heels, she swung around the big oak tree, feinted to the left, then, when László fell for it, she dashed back the way she'd come. At least, she tried to, but without warning, an obstacle dropped into her path as if from the sky, and she cannoned into it with enough force to rattle her teeth.

Somewhere, she recognised that the obstacle was a person, but it didn't give or fall or even allow her to. Hands at her back and shoulder steadied her, and she found herself gazing breathlessly up at a handsome stranger.

He was young, no older than László. Large, dark green eyes framed by long, black lashes stared back at her with blatant curiosity. They seemed to flash in the sunlight, blinding her.

Then he moved, urging her behind him as László stumbled to a halt.

The stranger drawled, "Are you in need of assistance?"

Even then, his voice did something to her. Deep and low, it seemed to reach far inside her and turn her awakening body outside in. And in her confusion, it took a moment for her to realise what he meant, that he was addressing *her* rather than László.

As the stranger's hands fell away from her, she blinked from him to her glaring cousin and back again. A touch of hysteria bubbled up with the laughter. László, flushing with all the embarrassment of a young man being caught in childish pursuits by a possibly dangerous contemporary, took an aggressive step forward at the stranger's implication. His hand even reached to his hip for the sword that wasn't there.

In response, something leapt in the stranger's eyes. Though his hand never moved, he *did* wear his sword. A rather fine one, with an elaborately carved hilt that sat oddly with his worn and dusty clothes.

Ilona said hastily, "Of course not. We're playing tag. László is my cousin."

The stranger took a quick breath and bowed as though to an equal. "I am delighted to meet your cousin."

László frowned, clearly as flummoxed by the change of manner as by the greater mystery of who the devil this man was and where he'd come from. And why. The other children were running over to join the crowd, Ilona's older sisters hastily gathering their dignity back around them as the stranger bowed to them.

His cloak, hanging off one shoulder, was spattered with mud. Beneath it, his tunic showed signs of mending. His long boots, reaching up over his knees, were good quality but looked well-worn. He wore no jewels. There was certainly nothing about his dress to impress, and yet no one doubted his importance.

"Won't you introduce us to your friend, László?" Katalina said, gazing modestly up at the newcomer from under her eyelashes. Ilona wanted to slap her.

"Can't," said László baldly. "I've no idea who he is."

"Forgive my oversight—I have been most remiss," drawled the stranger. Even then he had a way of turning the most civil or even bland statements into insolence. Only you couldn't put your finger on how or why. He bowed with unsurpassed elegance. "I am Vlad, son of Vlad Dracul, Prince of Wallachia."

The air crackled. The dangerous stranger smiled around his stunned audience. It wasn't a nice smile, and it was aimed, mostly, at László, who saw the threat as quickly as Ilona. László's eyes dilated. Before he could suppress it, he made one quick instinctive movement to place himself between the children and Vlad.

But he couldn't. Vlad still stood close enough to Ilona to be touching her, and Matthias, unaware of the stranger's history, had given in to natural curiosity and was fingering the carved hilt of the prince's sword. László stilled.

In some trepidation, Ilona turned her gaze up to Vlad. She could feel tension thrumming through his body. This was the son of the man who had once had the nerve to imprison John Hunyadi himself. A young man with many grudges and scores to settle, a man brought up from the age of eleven by the cruel, infidel Ottomans. Only minutes ago, her father had called him unpredictable.

With his eyes still locked to László's, he moved one hand, brushing Matthias's stroking fingers aside, and drew the sword from its scabbard.

Ilona, afraid to look away, held her breath and prepared to hurl herself in front of the child. She sensed rather than saw László sway forward as if desperately gauging his time to strike.

But she was watching Vlad's face; she recognised his fierce joy in thus holding them all in his power. Relief poured off her in a cool sweat. He wouldn't hurt them. If he'd wanted to, he wouldn't be taking this much pleasure in their fear of it… Would he?

Vlad drew the sword free. László launched himself forward, but, ignoring him, Vlad turned the sword away from Matthias, pointing it straight up so that he could display the full glory of the carved hilt and glistening blade to the younger boy. Oh yes, he was enjoying this.

"Beautiful, isn't it?" he said.

László skidded to a halt.

"Ooh yes," breathed Matthias.

Vlad said, "It was my father's. A gift from the Emperor Sigismund, along with the Order of the Dragon."

Rumour said one of his father's loyal boyars had ridden from Wallachia to Adrianople in only five days in order to pass these gifts to his heir. Presumably along with the news of the death of

Vlad Dracul and the terrible murder of this youth's older brother, Mircea.

Ilona regarded him with increasing fascination and saw, among other things, that she'd been wrong. He wasn't actually handsome at all. The strong bones of his face were too prominent, providing too many shadows and hollows for openness. His eyes were too heavily hooded, the lashes too long and thick for manliness, his nose too long and sharp, his lips a little too full with the faint outline of a long, dark moustache above. She thought he began to smile at Matthias, but a movement beyond him distracted her, and she saw that László, taking advantage of Vlad's distraction, was about to make a sudden attack.

Several thoughts chased instantaneously through Ilona's mind, not least how tragic—and damaging—it would be for László and Vlad to kill each other here. Especially when the Wallachian presented no real threat, whatever impression he was trying to create. And yet she couldn't say, *Leave him alone, László, he's harmless.* She was well aware how insulting that would be to both of them.

So, from more desperation than she hoped appeared in her voice, she blurted, "You might want to take that off to play." She waved one hopefully careless hand at his sword and the scabbard at his hip.

Again, László paused. Vlad's intense gaze flickered to her in some bafflement.

Well, I've started now. "Last one in the game is It," she said serenely. Without looking, she knew both her sisters and László now wore appalled expressions.

The menacing Dracula, however, drew in a breath that might have held laughter. At once his lower lip clamped over the upper, as though to hide it. But his eyes still glinted with something that looked like amusement. They held hers, considering, while he slowly resheathed the sword.

At least some of the tension in the air vanished.

"It," he repeated.

Had he never played tag, then? This serious, desperate prince… There seemed to be a storm in his dark green eyes, a brief battle of dignity versus temptation. Ilona began to smile.

"It?" Vlad's hand lifted, forefinger extended, and poked her in the arm. "Not anymore."

"That's cheating!" Ilona objected, feeling her face flush with genuine indignation. Before he could expect it, she lunged at his chest, but he sidestepped, avoiding her touch and dodging hastily the other way as she tried to compensate. When Ilona leapt at him, he stunned her by jumping backwards over the bench behind him. Matthias and Miklós began to laugh.

Ilona regarded him from narrowed eyes. Either he was a stupid player—the smart move would have been to jump *on* to the bench, which was "safe"—or a contemptuous one, and she would not permit the latter. Hoisting up her skirts, she flew after him.

Vlad Dracula, the would-be Prince of Wallachia, turned tail and ran. Ilona's siblings and cousins howled with glee, all except László, who stood still and bewildered as the younger ones raced around him both for a better view and to avoid Ilona's tag. Ilona, however, had no intention of tagging anyone but Vlad. It had become a point of honour, all the more appealing because of the hilarity involved in trying to catch him. Ilona, it seemed, had met her match.

He wasn't just quick but agile, even with his long cloak and cumbersome sword swinging against his hip and legs. Within the space defined by the erratic, weaving circle of children, he leapt and dodged, feinted and swerved until finally she cornered him in front of the bench that backed onto the old willow tree. Ilona never used that bench to be "safe" except as a last resort; the roots of the willow sloped down to the river, and she knew from experience that it was just too difficult to get off the bench until whoever was It got bored and went after easier prey. Ilona had no intention of getting bored. She grabbed for his arm, just as he jumped onto the stone bench and safety.

"He's beaten you, Ilona," Katalina crowed, her new adult dignity forgotten once more in the fun of the game. "Give him up!"

"Not I." Panting for breath, she smiled at Vlad Dracula and flexed her fingers significantly. "I'm good at waiting."

Vlad twitched in the direction of the river, and since she didn't put it past him to get wet just to win, she followed immediately, only to discover it was a feint and he was already lunging the other way. Ilona didn't hesitate. She hurled herself after him, knowing she'd fall hard but knowing too that she could reach some part of him as she went down.

It was his boot, encountered in midair as she tumbled and rolled. But, frustratingly, his other foot remained firmly on the bench, so it didn't count. She was still It.

"Ilona! Come here."

Her father's sharp command froze her as she sprawled on the ground. Vlad, finely poised to leap off the bench, managed to retrieve his balance and hold still. The tolerant half smile on his lips died. The gleam in his blazing green eyes, which was part teasing and part pure fun, became something else entirely. She almost saw him gather an invisible cloak of splendour about his shabby person, and yet he didn't move at all. His gaze went beyond her.

Ilona rose from the ground to face not only her father but Count Hunyadi, striding across the grass toward them, a gaggle of excited servants and men-at-arms streaming out in their wake. Obediently, she walked toward them, resigned to a lecture, at the very least, on the behaviour expected of a daughter of the Szilágyi family.

But although she slowed as she met the two men, they strode past her as if she didn't exist. Both pairs of anxious eyes were on the stranger.

László, unable to keep the excitement out of his voice, said, "Let me introduce you to Vlad, son of Vlad Dracul, one-time Prince of Wallachia. Sir, Count Hunyadi, my father, the viceroy of Hungary and governor of Transylvania. And your host, my uncle the lord Mihály Szilágyi."

Ilona turned to watch the spectacle, avidly curious to see how it would fall out, now that the insolent if fun trespasser was faced with the ultimate earthly authority in these parts.

Vlad Dracula stepped off the stone bench as if it were a raised dais supporting his throne, and bowed with impeccable grace and faultless respect.

"It is a great honour to meet the famous Count Hunyadi."

Absolute civility, of face and voice and posture. So how come Ilona sensed an edge to his words? Just because she knew the history? Because Vlad's father had once held Hunyadi prisoner? Because Hunyadi had been responsible for Dracul's deposition? It was more than possible that the son held Hunyadi personally responsible for the death of his father. And of course, Hunyadi still supported the present Prince of Wallachia, Vlad's enemy.

"You must excuse my not being present to receive you," Mihály said coldly. "My people omitted to inform me of your arrival. I'll have them flogged."

Vlad couldn't have been expected to care. It was interesting, though, that Ilona's father presented him with the polite myth— perhaps to save his own face more than Vlad's.

"That would hardly be fair," Vlad observed, "since they didn't know of my arrival. It is I who should be flogged for abusing your hospitality."

Again, his voice held civil apology, his expression regret, and yet Ilona thought his eyes flashed a challenge. *Dare to flog me; just dare.*

Whether it was the words or the unspoken challenge that held both older men speechless, the silence grew.

"I climbed over the wall," Vlad explained.

Hunyadi stirred. "May one know why?"

"Because I was fairly sure I wouldn't be admitted through the front door."

Hunyadi blinked. But her father's lip twitched. "There's a hint in that knowledge that you failed to follow," Mihály Szilágyi observed.

Vlad transferred his difficult gaze to the speaker. "I think we all understand the adage, 'needs must.'" He smiled faintly. "Besides, if I had taken the hint, I would never have had the honour of meeting two such great soldiers. And your charming children."

László made a sound of irritation in his throat.

Ilona's father said, "I trust my daughter didn't injure you?"

"Your timely intervention saved my skin."

Ilona tried to swallow the rising giggle. It was as much released tension as amusement, and it didn't help that Vlad's gaze flickered to her as he spoke. Or that one of his eyes closed so speedily that it might have been merely a twitch.

"And did you walk alone into this lion's den?" her father enquired.

"I did. Although my cousin may well be at the front door as we speak. Stephen of Moldavia," he explained, as though anyone had any doubts.

"We regret the death of Prince Bogdan, his father," Hunyadi said formally.

"I'd hoped you would say that," Vlad confessed.

The two older men stared at him. Ilona's father began to smile in a lopsided sort of a way.

Hunyadi said faintly, "You broke into my brother's castle to ask for my help in restoring Bogdan's son Stephen to the throne of Moldavia?"

"And Vlad's son to that of Wallachia."

Hunyadi exchanged glances with Mihály Szilágyi. Amid the astonishment, there might have been a hint of humour. Mihály said, "For so bold—if ultimately useless—a stroke, the least I can do is offer you refreshment."

It was only later it struck Ilona that Stephen, Vlad's companion, never appeared—whether the servants forbade him entry at the door or whether he simply gave up and went away when Vlad failed to return. It left Vlad alone to be entertained, the centre of all curiosity, whether veiled or blatant. The air of Horogszegi seemed to crackle that day. The images, the conversations stayed with Ilona in vivid detail long after.

Taking full advantage of her childhood status, Ilona lurked and observed without any of the burden of conversation or the need to impress.

Of course, Vlad's need in that field was greatest, and he managed to impress without apparent effort. Despite the shabby clothes, he held himself with a pride that should have been laughable and yet wasn't. Whether he stole the centre of the stage or accepted it from the wily Hunyadi was hard to tell, but he certainly retained it—and shone.

Without raising his voice or veering from his respectful attitude, he conversed in perfect Hungarian on all manner of topics thrown his way, from the current weather to learned treatises. He seemed to have acquired more than a smattering of education in the classics along with vast stores of knowledge from doctors in the Ottoman lands where, of course, he had been a hostage for many years.

"Then you acknowledge an affinity with the Ottomans?" Countess Hunyadi enquired. She alone maintained her barbed attitude to her brother's uninvited guest for most of the day. In her middle years, Aunt Erzsébet was formidable, authoritative, and still beautiful. She bore her power as the great Hunyadi's wife not with lightness but with regality.

"Affinity?" Vlad repeated, surprised. "No. Though I like many of them, there are some I hate with a loathing. Others, I learned a great deal from."

"And into which category do you place those who helped you invade Wallachia?"

"Under a separate category," Vlad said serenely. "That of 'useful.'"

"Needs must?" murmured Ilona's father.

Vlad smiled.

"I take it the sultan is no longer of that category," Hunyadi said. "When you have not received further help."

"I did not ask for further help. The price would not have been right."

"There is a price for loosing the infidels in a Christian land?" Aunt Erzsébet sounded outraged.

"And if you didn't ask," Hunyadi pursued, "why did you return there when you lost the throne?"

Vlad's lower lip claimed the upper for a brief instant. He stretched out his hand to the goblet on the table and took a sip before he answered. "My brother was still there."

It wasn't the answer they'd expected. They didn't even know if it was true. But Ilona knew, just because she understood his difficulty in saying it.

And her mother picked something of that up too, for she leaned forward to say with compassion, "Do they treat him well?"

Did they treat you well? He'd been younger than Ilona when his father had been forced to leave him and his brother as hostages with the sultan. Had they beaten him, mistreated him? At the very least he must have been terrified, especially when his father had broken his word and aided the Christian army against the Ottomans. For no greater a crime, the similarly hostaged sons of the Serbian, Brankovic, had been blinded. And their sister was the sultan's wife!

Vlad laid down the cup. "He has no complaints."

"But they would not let him leave?"

Ilona had the impression that only massive willpower stopped him wriggling with discomfort. Interestingly, this was one subject he did not wish to discuss.

Ilona's father said, "I'm sure they wish to hold on to at least one possible candidate to the Wallachian throne."

Mihály Szilágyi had given him a way out, but again, just as he'd refused to blame the servants for his stealthy entrance, he wouldn't take it.

He said, "My brother did not wish to come with me." It was careless, spoken with a shrug. Only the stillness of his mobile face betrayed him. "Radu," he explained to Countess Hunyadi, "believes he *has* discovered an affinity with the Ottomans."

With surprising gentleness, Hunyadi said, "I'm sorry."

Vlad flicked one hand to dismiss the whole issue. "He is young, barely fifteen when I saw him last." He switched the conversation then, but Ilona didn't notice the subject. She was too intrigued by the discovery that Vlad was secretly hurt by his brother's refusal to join him in exile. In Wallachia, a brother was more likely to be a rival than a friend, and surely this formidably intelligent young man was aware of it.

So what then of that other brother? Mircea, whom he couldn't have seen since he was eleven years old, who was buried alive by Prince Vladislav's noble supporters. They said Mircea had been Dracul's favourite. What did Vlad feel for him?

His restless gaze shifted suddenly and discovered her staring at him. Just for an instant, she felt paralysed, unsure whether to smile, drop her eyes, or continue to stare with defiance. Before she could decide, he looked back at Hunyadi.

It was left to the women to tell her off.

"What were you thinking of?" fumed her mother when the men had gone for a walk in the gardens, no doubt to talk politics and possibilities. Ilona would rather have been with them, but this was one scolding she couldn't escape. "A lady does not play tag with her uncle's—or anyone else's!—visitors! One certainly does not do so with an uninvited stranger who could easily be a dangerous enemy!"

"I'm sorry," said Ilona. She had no choice but to plead guilty to unladylike behaviour. "It was just a—distraction."

"To take his mind off killing us all?" Aunt Erzsébet said drily.

"Well, László," Ilona corrected.

Both women stared at her, mouths ajar. "He was going to kill László?" Erzsébet demanded.

"Well, he might have, if László had attacked him," Ilona said reasonably. "You see, László didn't know he wasn't a threat."

Her mother closed her mouth, clearly still speechless. Erzsébet, without any of the expected sarcasm, said, "And you did?"

Ilona nodded.

"How?"

Ilona sighed. "Lots of things. If he was going to kill anyone, he'd have done it quickly, before he could be discovered. Also…" She broke off, trying to find the right words. "He wanted László to *think* he was a threat. To frighten him. Why would he want that if he actually was one?"

"Why would he want it anyway?" asked her mother faintly.

Ilona shrugged. "Because he's powerless and hates it; because László's father killed his. Indirectly," she added hastily, flushing under her aunt's unblinking stare. She swallowed and wished she'd kept her mouth shut.

Countess Hunyadi's eyes narrowed. "You're not just a pretty face, are you, Ilona?"

"I wish," muttered her mother.

Ilona smiled tentatively and took a step nearer the door. The women exchanged glances.

"Oh, go on, get out!" snapped her mother, and Ilona grinned, blowing both ladies a kiss as she ran.

She could hear the voices of the younger children playing in the garden. Hunyadi had just gone inside to speak to the women, leaving her father and Vlad alone on the terrace. Ilona, sitting on the ground behind a low wall, unseen and unthought of, imagined herself drifting on the breeze. She wondered how far it would take her. Was there only one wind, constantly circling the Earth in ever-changing direction and force? Or were there lots of little ones that were born and died like people?

Her father said, "He won't help you, Vlad. He can't."

Who wouldn't help him? John Hunyadi, of course…

"Without considering how I can help him?"

"He doesn't know you. We have a friend on the Wallachian throne. Of course he won't replace him with a young, untried prince he doesn't know well enough to trust."

"You believe the usurper Vladislav is trustworthy?"

For the first time, Ilona shivered at the tone of his voice. When he spoke the name Vladislav. Vladislav had killed his father, at best had allowed the horrific murder of his elder brother Mircea.

"No," her father agreed. "But better the devil you know. Besides, you should be aware that we are negotiating a truce with the sultan. The terms are likely to maintain the present state of affairs in Wallachia, forbidding interference from either side should Vladislav fall."

Vlad's cause was lost before he even came to Horogszegi. And his silence said he knew it.

Mihály Szilágy said, "It's not yet your time, Vlad. My best advice to you—for what it's worth—is to prove yourself while circumstances change. As they will."

"My country and my family are the play things of circumstance."

It was unfortunate. Ruling a small state, buffered between the might of the Ottoman Empire and the encroaching Hungarian crown, Wallachian princes needed the goodwill—or at least the toleration—of both to survive. At least the strange young man understood that. But impatience surged beneath the even temper of his voice. He wanted to live, to *do* now, not when circumstances dictated.

"You have done yourself no harm here today," her father said gently.

"And no good." There was a short pause, then, "Apart from the pleasure of your acquaintance and his. Which is better than wealth."

He'd made himself say it, to cover the ungraciousness of his previous words. And yet Ilona could find none of the hidden insolence she'd detected at various stages of the day. For some reason, she wanted to hug him.

Then the swishing of skirts heralded her mother's voice, kindly inviting her guest to dine.

To Ilona's disappointment, he turned her down. "I have abused your hospitality for long enough, lady. Tempting though your kindness is, I shall impose no longer."

"Then wait one more moment," Hunyadi said. "I have something for you."

Ilona heard them move away and laid her head back against the wall. There came the sound of someone exhaling. Clearly, someone still lurked in the garden. Quick, light footsteps sprang across the terrace, and before she could register their direction, someone vaulted over the low wall and landed right beside her.

Vlad Dracula paused in midstride. "You again."

"Are you leaving?" she asked.

He didn't answer. Instead, he said, "You have a good family."

"You sound surprised."

His lips curved. "I didn't expect to like them."

"I imagine they can return the compliment."

For an instant, his eyes searched hers. "You'll dirty your dress and get into trouble."

"I'm in trouble already."

Unexpectedly, he stretched down his arm to help her up. Ilona gazed at his capable, long fingers, her breath catching.

She took his hand and allowed him to pull her to her feet before she grinned with blatant triumph. "Tag."

Vlad Dracula blinked. Then he threw back his head and laughed. He was still laughing as he walked away.

Count Hunyadi's gift was a horse, but Vlad would accept it only on the terms of a loan, promising to return it. And all the Hunyadis and Szilágyis, including a sizable portion of their servants, stood around the doorway and steps to watch him ride out of the front gate—an upright and proud young man in shabby clothes and a borrowed mount, with no home and, surely, very little hope.

"It's a pity in some ways," Aunt Erzsébet murmured. "But that boy will ride straight to the devil. That's the last we'll see of him."

She couldn't have been more wrong.

Chapter Three

Visegrád, Hungary, 1474

Matthias Corvinus, King of Hungary, glanced up as his mother made her regal entry into his reception chamber. Waving away his secretaries, he rose to greet her.

"Mother. You are abroad early this morning."

"I'm always abroad early. You just don't normally see what I do." Matthias's eyes narrowed. "And what do you do this morning, Mother?"

An alien expression flitted across Erzsébet's paper-skinned face. So alien that it took Matthias several seconds to recognise it as uncertainty.

She said, "I need to talk to you about Ilona."

Matthias waved one impatient hand. "She'll do her duty as we all must."

Erzsébet drew in her breath. "Find a solution to the problem of the principalities that doesn't involve him."

When he realised his jaw had dropped, he picked it up. "Believe me, I've looked. Stephen and Vlad are not just the best solution. Right now, they're the only one. Why are you against it all of a sudden? I thought you went to talk sense into Ilona last night."

"I did. And I realised what an unnecessary cruelty it would be to give such a pathetic, damaged creature to him."

"She isn't *damaged*," Matthias said derisively. "She's merely ageing badly. Let herself go, if you ask me. But if Vlad wants the alliance, I'm more than happy to accommodate him. She won't be the help to me I'd once hoped for in that position, but since he's determined to stick to the bargain we made fourteen years ago…"

"Matthias, she's your cousin! You were almost brought up as brother and sister! I am all for duty as you know, but I cannot countenance forcing my niece into this marriage. Not after what she's been through. In our position, there is duty and there is politics—and there is sheer inhumanity."

"Don't be so melodramatic, Mother. She always liked him. More than she should have, if you ask me."

"Sometimes you are obtuse," Erzsébet accused. "Do you really think that when she looks at him now she'll see the engaging youth who dared to climb over her garden wall under the sentries' noses, just to speak to your father? If he was ever truly that boy we imagined him to be, he certainly isn't now, and she knows it."

"You're being ridiculous," Matthias said coldly. "In danger, one would suspect, of believing your own propaganda." From the corner of his eye, he saw Stephen of Moldavia enter the room. "She was agreeable enough to the match fourteen years ago—in fact, as I recall, she was reluctant to give it up, even when commanded by her entire family! She should be doubly grateful for it now."

"Maybe," Erzsébet interrupted. "But fear could have motivated her then as it does now. Fear of him if she didn't stand by him. And now, with the passage of time, fear of going back to him. Something happened to her in Wallachia, when the Ottomans invaded. She was never the same after that, was she?"

Something he didn't want to think about prickled Matthias's skin. His mother *wanted* to believe in Vlad's evil as the alternative to her own guilt, to his. Neither suited Matthias at this moment. "Her mother died. Her friend died. You can't blame that on him." Deliberately, he summoned Stephen closer.

"Can't I?" demanded Erzsébet, turning to glare down whoever Matthias was trying to shut her up with. Recognising Stephen, she simply carried on. "Something happened there that showed her what the rest of the world already knew. Tell me, Prince Stephen, would *you* give a female of your family to the Impaler?"

Count Szelényi's duties were not arduous. There was a certain cachet in being the official keeper of such a notorious prisoner as Vlad Dracula, yet the task itself was far from unpleasant. He accompanied the prince on riding expeditions each morning, partnered him in sword practice, conducted him to the king's very fine and constantly growing library whenever he wished, and to whichever social functions the king wished his "guest" to attend. In between times, he occasionally remembered to lock the captive's door before going in search of his mistress or other amusements to be found at court.

It was a recent appointment, but he was hoping it would earn him another piece of land to add to his growing estates in Hungary and Transylvania. He thought about that, and about his wife and children at home, as he left the palace and stepped out into the midday sunshine, making his way to the formal gardens where he had an assignation to keep.

The left-hand path was usually deserted. Any parties out to enjoy the flowers tended to stick to the central path, which led to a charming, open summerhouse. But today he was sure someone followed him. The hairs at the back of his neck prickled. If it was his mistress, she was early, and he could look forward to a longer than expected dalliance. If it was her suspicious husband, he might well have to postpone it.

With careful nonchalance, he paused to inspect the red tulip on his right. With his attention on the path behind him, he was surprised to hear hushed male voices drifting on the breeze over the nearby hedge. Alarm bells began to ring in his head. Had Helena's husband truly discovered their affair? Had he hired someone to teach Szelényi a lesson?

Uneasily, Szelényi strained his ears and caught a furious, intense whisper: "…damn it, we tried! But he's not an easy man to pick a fight with!"

"I never heard he was a coward," came a different voice, and one that made Szelényi frown, because although it spoke Hungarian, the accent reminded him of an occasional inflection he noticed in his prisoner's. Wallachian?

"I never *said* he was a coward!" came back the angry, Hungarian whisper. "He just sneered at me as though it would insult his sword to cross it with mine. Before throwing me across the room by the throat!"

And abruptly, the overheard conversation was far more important that petty intrigue. For Szelényi was sure it related to the incident in the exercise chamber this morning. He and the prince had been practicing sword play as usual when a group of young courtiers had come in and tried to pick a fight with Vlad. It wasn't such an unusual occurrence. Young bullies trying to make an easy name for themselves by besting the ageing prince with the fearsome reputation. If the prince had ever risen to the bait, it hadn't been in Szelényi's time. He wasn't going to risk his freedom and his throne for the pleasure of humiliating a stupid young man. And Szelényi had fought often with Vlad. Provoking him for self-gain was incredibly stupid unless you wished to die.

Vlad had dealt with them leniently by his own lights and anyone else's. Szelényi had then murmured a few words about the king's displeasure and their own narrow escape, designed to frighten them. He'd thought no more about it. But now… The young men from the morning had been Hungarian natives. Now it almost seemed they'd been put up to it by a Wallachian who wasn't best pleased by their failure.

He needed to warn the prince that someone didn't want him free. Presumably the agents of the present incumbent of the Wallachian throne, Besarab Laiota. Or even Vlad's brother Radu...

Szelényi wondered ruefully if he could still fit in his assignation. Then his eye was caught by a drifting grey figure gliding along the path toward him. The person he'd imagined was following him. A woman. Definitely not his mistress, unless she was in heavy disguise.

Szelényi blinked. *Good God.*

Straightening, he bowed to the princess. The voices drifted away, no longer audible.

The lady stopped in her tracks as if surprised by his courtesy. A nervous smile flitted across her face and was gone before he could acknowledge it.

She took a step nearer him. "Count Szelényi?"

"At your service, my lady."

"I'm Ilona Szilágyi."

"I know," he said gravely. "And I'm honoured to meet you." He found himself speaking gently to her, as if to a nervous horse. Her restless eyes sought his once more, searching.

"Are you?" she asked vaguely, and yet he had the uncomfortable feeling that those eyes weren't vague at all but distressingly perceptive.

He swallowed, and found himself dropping both the courtly manner and the condescension behind it. "Actually, yes. I have the honour to attend the exiled Prince of Wallachia."

Her tongue flickered over her lips. Her gaze dropped once more. "I know." She reached out with odd blindness, touching one soft white petal at random. "And you are—conscientious in your duties?"

"I hope so," he said, frowning with incomprehension. "To be honest, they don't tax me. I find the prince most amiable."

Again the fleeting smile skimmed across her lips. "Amiable," she repeated with blatant disbelief. "And biddable?"

Since she caught and held his gaze once more, he found himself smiling back. "No, not biddable. But then—"

"And is he well?" she interrupted. She blurted the words as if they wouldn't wait any longer, and yet as soon as they tumbled out, she waved one slender, surprisingly elegant hand as if to dismiss her own question. A delicate flush brightened the pale skin of her cheeks.

Fascinated in spite of himself, Szelényi chose to answer. "Yes, he is very well. Not unnaturally he has suffered bouts of frustration and melancholy in the past, but I am happy to say he looks to the future now with hope. I'm very glad that his fortunes are improving."

Her gaze pierced him once more. She nodded as if believing him. Then, abruptly, she turned. "Thank you," she said over her shoulder. And Szelényi, oddly reluctant to let her go, fell into step beside her.

"My pleasure," he said. "I can also tell you he's very much looking forward to meeting you again."

Her gaze flickered up to him, hunted, distressed. He would have pitied her had he not become distracted by the delicate beauty of her bones. Ilona Szilágyi had once been a lovely woman. In fact, now that the vitality or emotion, whatever it was, consumed her face, she still was. Too thin perhaps, and grey was not her colour. Her dress was ugly, but the lady was not.

Or perhaps that was the illusion. As she turned away and quickened her step, he saw once again the grey, ageing frump.

She said, "Did my aunt, Countess Hunyadi, visit him yesterday? In the evening?"

"Yes."

She nodded. Her mouth opened as if to ask another question. Then, apparently deciding against it, she closed her lips.

Szelényi's mistress, inexplicably shocking to his eyes just then, tripped along the path toward them. In a charming, heart-shaped headdress and a blue overgown with ridiculously trailing sleeves, she couldn't have presented a greater contrast to the colourless princess.

Ilona seemed to regard her with even less interest, merely nodding to the other woman's elaborate courtesy. Helena's eyebrows danced in Szelényi's direction, her blue eyes glinting as she walked gaily past them.

Szelényi could hardly compromise her by following just then. But neither, he found, did he want to. There was some mystery about his prisoner's proposed nuptials that he wanted to get to the bottom of, some help this frail lady needed that he wanted to give.

She said, "He spoke to you about meeting me."

"Well, it was hardly a discussion," Szelényi admitted. "But he said it once. And in any case, I can tell. I know him quite well now."

"Then you would know if he changed his mind."

Szelényi stared at her averted profile. "Changed his…?"

"You must tell me at once. Good-bye, Count."

Perplexed and dismissed, he stared after the ghostly figure until she whisked round the corner of the path. He was free now to go to Helena. But his thoughts were still with the other, very different woman. And he found what he most wanted to do was to go and ask questions of his formidable prisoner.

Count Szelényi didn't feel at ease as he knocked on his prisoner's door later that afternoon. Mostly, he didn't feel at ease with himself. For the first time in months, despite his hectic and delicious interlude in the shrubbery with Helena, he wanted to go home to his family.

"Enter," came the prince's familiar voice. And it struck him as he unlocked and opened the door that the person he would miss most when he left court would not be Helena or even the king or any of the high-ranking noblemen who called themselves his friends. It would be this strange, isolated prince with his formal manners and veiled humour.

Vlad Dracula sat at his desk, writing busily, his long, still-black locks falling around his broad shoulders, half hiding his face. Without looking up, the prince greeted him civilly and invited him to take some wine.

Szelényi went to the table and poured two glassfuls from the silver jug. He laid the first by the prince's elbow and received as always a murmur of thanks. Taking his own to the carved wooden chair by the empty fireplace, he sat and sipped his wine.

He waited until the prince began to fold his letter. Like all his correspondence, it would he handed to Szelényi before he left, but never by word or deed had the prince acknowledged that he knew his jailer was expected to read them.

In fact, Szelényi rarely did. These days he had a list of Vlad's acceptable correspondents, and he simply sent on all such epistles. Most of them were addressed to noblemen of Wallachia, old friends and supporters, exiled and otherwise. Once, when he'd first come in trepidation to this post, it had surprised him that there were so many of those who kept in touch with him. He'd assumed the boyars would have been delighted to see the back of so cruel and unpredictable a lord.

Szelényi quickly explained his suspicions about the men trying to provoke him in the exercise chamber this morning. The prince merely sighed and nodded as if unsurprised. Leaving the matter to Vlad whether or not to take the matter further, Szelényi took a deep breath. "I had the honour of meeting your lady today."

Vlad made his second fold in the paper with precision. "You are to be felicitated."

Szelényi inclined his head and waited. But it seemed Vlad was too indifferent—or too proud—to ask for any further information. The prince reached for the wax. "I trust you found her well," he said at last.

"Well? I believe so. To be frank, I found her a little—perturbed."

The ring seal paused just a little too long in the wax. Vlad lifted his hand, then turned deliberately to Szelényi.

"In what way?"

For the first time since his original meeting with Vlad, fear coursed through Szelényi's veins. The prince's green eyes darkened until they were hard as agates, relentless. His lips thinned to a cruel line. Szelényi couldn't help remembering the stories, the legends that had built up around this man, the ones he had discounted over the months of what he had taken for growing friendship. But this, this man was one you would never cross. Christ, you wouldn't even spill his wine.

But you bloody *would* answer his questions.

Even when you floundered.

"I'm not sure." It was an effort simply not to stammer. "I don't know the lady, so it's very hard for me to judge. But I couldn't help seeing that she was..." Szelényi cast around for the right word.

"Perturbed," Vlad supplied. "We've established that part. What can have perturbed her?"

"I don't know," Szelényi said miserably. "I can't—you," he blurted. "Something about you. She came up to me especially, I'd swear, to ask how you were."

The prince's eyelids swept down over his hawklike eyes, granting Szelényi a brief respite. He let his breath out and continued. "Only when she'd asked, she seemed embarrassed. And then, when I said you looked forward to meeting her again, she looked *very* perturbed."

Vlad's gaze flickered back up to him. The anger still lurked there, cold and terrible, but Szelényi began to believe it wasn't aimed at him. In fact, the large green eyes didn't appear to be seeing him at all. He found himself hoping the fury wasn't aimed at poor Ilona Szilágyi.

"What else," Vlad said with such deliberation that Szelényi realised how difficult this was for him to ask, "did she say?"

Szelényi cudgelled his memory. "She asked if Countess Hunyadi had visited you and then…" He trailed off and swallowed. But under that commanding gaze there was no way to avoid it. "She asked if you had changed your mind."

Vlad nodded, slowly, as if it made sense to him.

Encouraged if even more mystified, Szelényi added, "And she said I should tell her at once when you had. She didn't seem to doubt that you would." The last sentence was aimed more at himself, stating yet another tiny mystery, for he'd never encountered anyone less likely to change his mind about anything than Vlad Dracula. But having said it aloud, he blanched, not least because something sparked into life in the prince's eyes, something blatantly dangerous.

After a second, his lower lip moved, clamping on the upper in an attitude of thought.

"The king," he said, "has arranged for our formal betrothal to take place tomorrow evening."

"Congratulations," Szelényi said automatically.

A glint of sardonic humour lit the prince's eyes. "Thank you." He stood up. "I feel a visit to my promised bride is in order before then. It is not my intention to be betrothed to a perturbed lady."

"You would like me to arrange something tomorrow?"

"No, I'd like you to take me there tonight."

"I can't!"

"You've been forbidden?"

"No, but—"

"Well, then. You needn't come. Just tell me where to find her."

"Sir, please, you must allow her time to prepare—"

"Wrong," said Vlad, silencing him without raising his voice. Lifting his glass, he tossed the contents down his throat and strode toward the door. "The trouble is, she's had too much time."

Margit had served Ilona Szilágyi for more than eleven years. In that time, she realised, she had never really learned anything about her. She had first met her in the Szilágyi family home at Horogszegi, dazed and shocked, after her miraculous escape from the Ottomans in Wallachia. The rumour was she had been betrothed then to Wallachia's hero prince, but she never spoke of it and neither did anyone else in the family. Presumably, when the prince turned out to be not only homeless but unheroic to the point of traitorous, the family called it off. Even Vlad Dracula couldn't be married in prison. Not to a member of the king's family at any rate.

Yet here she was, all but betrothed once more to the same imprisoned prince. Although Margit had seen him move freely enough around the palace when she had been exploring in her own time.

Margit had been delighted to come to court, to escape her pleasant but dull existence in Transylvania. She'd then been appalled when Ilona maintained her modest, excruciatingly drab dress. There were two fine court gowns in the trunk and a particularly pretty new silk dress for day wear, but the lady ignored them all.

Margit had hoped court and marriage would brighten her fading lady, had been ready to encourage her in all kinds of entertainment and fun. But frustratingly, her lady was wasting both their lives. Margit was aware she should be angry. And yet when she saw Ilona sitting on the floor, her back against the raised bedstead, her awful grey veil askew on her troubled head, what Margit chiefly felt was a surge of protection.

In sudden pity, she sank down before Ilona and took her hands. "My lady, what is it?" she pleaded. "Are you ill?"

Ilona's eyes came back into focus. She looked guilty. "No. No, I'm not ill."

"Won't you go down to the king's supper?"

She began to shake her head. "No—" She broke off, staring at her attendant. "Or perhaps I should?" she said uncertainly. Her gaze moved beyond Margit. "Will *he* be there?" she murmured.

"Who? The prince?"

Ilona flushed and drew her hands free to stand.

"You're to be betrothed tomorrow," Margit reminded her. "Perhaps it would be more comfortable—"

A spurt of laughter, halfway to a sob, escaped Ilona. "*Comfortable?*"

With compassion, Margit racked her brains. There was no way out for her lady. It was decreed she should marry a monster, and so she must. Surely even a monster would not be unkind to so gentle a wife? Perhaps the king would immediately send him off to win back Wallachia, and she—and Margit—could simply live out of range of his attention. After all, it was a political alliance, not a mere love match, and Vlad already had an heir. Ilona too was hardly in her first flush of youth for a bride.

But she had no idea how to say this to Ilona without insolence or offence, how to lighten the lady's despair.

A knock on the outer door made them both jump. Margit tried to smile. "Someone's come to take you to supper," she said lightly. "I'll help you to change," she added, leaving the bedchamber to answer the door.

Ilona, who thought on the whole she'd rather keep the frumpish grey dress, stood in the connecting doorway to see, mainly, if her escort was someone who'd let her away with it. *Not Aunt Erzsébet*

Margit opened the door and revealed Count Szelényi.

Ilona's heart lurched painfully. Had he brought news, a message? She couldn't breathe. With one trembling hand, she tugged at the neck of her gown. Then Margit fell back, Szelényi stepped aside, and Vlad Dracula walked into her room.

Chapter Four

Hunedoara, Transylvania, 1454

He walked into Countess Hunyadi's hall as if he had been there many times before. He didn't swagger, like many young men, but strode with purpose and unexpected grace, his sword clanking at his hip as if to remind everyone that he was still dangerous to someone.

Ilona, standing behind the countess's throne-like chair, beside Maria, Aunt Erzsébet's other attendant of the day, was conscious of the strong, steady beat of her heart. It had been nearly three years since her first glimpse of the strange Wallachian prince, and she'd been looking forward to seeing him again with an urgency that surprised her. Perhaps curious to know if he could still impress the more mature woman she'd become at sixteen. Perhaps just curious to know *him*, who was still an enigma to her father and to Hunyadi himself.

This time, he came by formal invitation. The venue was not Mihály Szilágyi's more informal home, but John Hunyadi's impregnable castle at Hunedoara. And he'd ridden over the bridge ahead of several well-dressed attendant noblemen and men-at-arms. Ilona knew, because she'd watched from the upper window above the main hall.

"Is it he?" Aunt Erzsébet had demanded from her stool by the embroidery table.

"Oh yes. With quite an escort."

"Hmm," the countess had grunted. "Naturally, he's collected a following from the exiled and dispossessed boyars. He's their hope of going home."

He sat very straight in the saddle, in a brave red cloak, holding the reins in one ungloved hand, resting the other on his thigh, just above his long boots. Ilona glimpsed, beneath a red velvet hat, the strong features she remembered, his expression untroubled by so much as a frown. He was acting again. Which made her wonder, as often before, what he was like when he didn't act, this young man who had told her that, reluctantly, he liked her family? Or had even that been said in the knowledge that she'd pass it on? Just another man who'd say anything, do anything in pursuit of power.

The prince himself had looked neither to the left nor right as he crossed the bridge into the castle, but the man riding closest to him did. Perhaps even younger than Vlad, this youth had openly scanned his surroundings and inevitably come to Ilona, hanging precariously out of the window. At once, he grinned. And sweeping off his hat, he bowed low in his saddle. She saw him speak to his companion, who didn't react, and then they'd ridden out of sight.

When Ilona, in her capacity as Countess Hunyadi's official attendant, had accompanied her aunt to receive the Wallachian guests, they'd found Maria already waiting for them in the main hall—the Council Hall, they called it.

"I saw him!" Maria crowed. "At least I think I did. Do you suppose he's the gentleman—"

"Stop gossiping and straighten your hair, Ilona," interrupted Erzsébet, who was still keen to suppress all knowledge of the previous encounter with Vlad three years ago. If news of that had ever got out, it could have caused Hunyadi all sorts of problems, not least with his puppet prince Vladislav, the current Prince of Wallachia. "You look like a peasant."

"It blew in the wind," Ilona pointed out. She didn't need to add that this had occurred when she'd been spying on Erzsébet's orders. They all understood that.

Erzsébet made a derisive sound that in anyone else would have been a snort and glared at her niece. Ilona smiled serenely and submitted to the more skilful Maria's ministrations. However, the sound of the men approaching caused her to brush the other girl's hand aside, and she simply dragged her own fingers once through the tangled, copper clump. Since she wore her hair loose, it couldn't look *too* bad...

There had been no more time, for the door was flung open to admit the Hunyadis' guests. Ilona had simply dropped her hands to her sides and prepared to observe. It was a long walk to the countess's throne. She'd designed it like that, the better to size up her visitors. As a result, a stately progress across the room could be a mistake. Even great men begin to look a little silly with a smile of greeting fixed on their faces for so long. On the other hand, advancing at Vlad's rapid if splendid pace still allowed plenty of time for visitors to observe the magnificence of their surroundings on their way to the lady of Hunedoara.

Vlad himself looked neither right nor left. Nor did he smile or appear remotely uncomfortable with his long walk or the forbidding scrutiny of his hostess. As he drew closer, Ilona could see that his clothing, though still austere, was no longer shabby. Under the red cloak, pushed back now over one shoulder, he wore a black silk doublet with silver buttons and what seemed to be plain black hose beneath his long boots.

Above his full lips, the long, thin line of his moustache was a little more pronounced than before, his unusual green eyes piercing but veiled, with no frown between. A serious man, but not a desperate one. In this situation, impression was all. And Ilona was secretly pleased to see he was carrying it off so well. But then, she suspected she'd have been disappointed if he hadn't.

Behind him, his noble following gazed around with blatant awe, taking in the fine portraits of the White Knight and his wife, the fine silver plate on display, the ornate carved benches with bright, beautifully embroidered cushions.

Of course, John Hunyadi himself had greeted the visitors downstairs and now walked among them to introduce them to his wife.

"My lady, allow me to present to you the lord Vlad, son of Vlad Dracul, Prince of Wallachia. And the lord Stephen, son of Bogdan, Prince of Moldavia."

Erzsébet nodded graciously. Both young men removed their hats and bowed with synchronised elegance. Stephen, however, remained clutching his black hat. On rising, Vlad carelessly held his red velvet one out to his left, and one of his followers took it. Ilona wondered if he'd simply have dropped it on the floor if no one had troubled to catch it.

Vlad spoke, saying all the civil things expected of him, presenting each of his followers in turn. After which he at last raised his gaze above the countess's head and encountered Ilona's.

Prepared as she was, the clash of his dark green eyes still shocked her. Those eyes could never be bland, but they contained not one iota of recognition, not even the most secret glint of memory at that silly childish game. She should have been pleased. She had grown into a civilised young lady, far removed from the Ilona of three years ago, and she was glad of it. And yet, perversely, she felt the loss of the attention won by the child she'd once been.

"My niece, Ilona Szilágyi," said Aunt Erzsébet. "And the lady Maria Gerzsenyi."

She received a bow, but it was Maria who was honoured by his smile, faint and tantalising. Piqued, Ilona spoke to Stephen. She could never afterwards remember what she said or what the Moldavian replied, but the flash of appreciation in his eyes stayed

with her while wine was served to the travellers. And then, before
the odd tension in the room could begin to evaporate, a servant
appeared at the door.

As if it were a signal, which it probably was, Hunyadi said,
"Ah. Count Szilágyi has arrived."

Ilona, who hadn't been informed her father was expected,
made an instinctive dash from behind the countess, past Stephen,
only to be brought up short by her indulgent uncle.

"Later, my dear," he said, catching and patting her arm. "We
need him first on matters of state. He'll send for you."

Flushing with embarrassment as much as disappointment,
Ilona returned to her stony-faced position behind the countess.
She didn't look at Vlad. Maria squeezed her hand.

Hunyadi said, "Gentlemen, I'll leave you for a little in the
gracious company of my lady wife. Vlad, if I may have your
presence…"

It was why he'd come. His very tension spoke of his anxiety
for this moment, and yet his bow to the countess, to herself, and
Maria was unhurried, his gait as he departed the hall more leisurely than that with which he'd entered.

Stephen's gaze flickered after him. So did the Wallachian
boyars'. A few glances of hope or interrogation were exchanged.

"What's going on?" Maria whispered in Ilona's ear.

"I'm not sure. I think the count may be considering Vlad as
the new Prince of Wallachia. They'll be negotiating, finding a way
to make that work for both of them before they get to *how* to
make it happen."

"What happened to the old Prince of Wallachia?"

"Nothing—yet," Ilona murmured. "But everyone's jumpy
since Constantinople fell to the Ottomans, and there's a suspicion
Vladislav of Wallachia is growing too close to them. If the Ottomans
are allowed free passage through Wallachia, then Transylvania and
Hungary itself are in far more danger."

But Maria's eyes had glazed over. Politics didn't interest her. Personalities did.

"What do you think of him?" she murmured.

Ilona shrugged, watching the Wallachian boyars.

Maria crowed, "He smiled at me—I think he likes me!"

At that, Ilona couldn't help nudging her friend. Fortunately, the countess's eyes were pointing in the opposite direction. "Of course he does. Everyone likes you."

It was true. Beautiful, soft-hearted, and fun, she was justly popular with both the men and women of the Hunyadi household. A couple of years older than Ilona, she had quickly become a valued friend and confidante, although, to be fair, it was usually Maria who had anything worth confiding. Her betrothed, an old childhood friend, had died two years ago, and, grieving done, she was eager to be married to another. Ilona didn't imagine this would be difficult. Although Maria's family was not particularly wealthy or influential, she had a powerful friend now in Countess Hunyadi, and her personal charm would go a long way to securing which ever husband she chose.

"No, I mean *likes* me." Maria pressed Ilona's hand significantly.

Ilona glanced at her with a hint of irritation. Maria's infatuations were just too impractical. The last, barely two months ago, had been a visiting Hungarian nobleman whose main fault was that he was married already. It hadn't stopped him *liking* Maria. And now…

She swallowed her annoyance, because at heart she sometimes wished she was more like her friend, able to flirt while waiting for marriage. Ilona had never mastered the art of flirtation. She either got into serious discussions that convinced men she wasn't flirting material or became tongue-tied, appearing overproud, thus convincing them of the same thing by a different route.

Fortunately, her father seemed in no hurry to make an alliance for her. His fortunes fluctuated with Hunyadi's, and although her sisters were well married, Mihály was biding his time for Ilona. She was in no hurry either to tie herself to a stranger or to bear children.

Although she *would* like to have her own household and manage her own life. And, perhaps, her husband's. He would be a great man who would value her insight and advice...

Of course he would, she mocked herself. *Just see how the great men here all hang upon your every word.*

It was two hours before her father sent for her. By then, the visitors had gone to inspect Hunyadi's horses, but under Aunt Erzsébet's eagle-like eye, she still forced herself to walk sedately as far as the hall door, before she picked up her skirts and flew downstairs to the knights' hall, which was where the servant had informed her she would find Mihály Szilágyi.

She saw him through the half-open door, his shoulder leaning casually on the mantel above the fire. Her heart lifted as it always did at the sight of him, an echo of the intense childhood pleasure she'd known whenever he had come home safe from the wars that were his life.

Without hesitation, she ran across the room, swerving to avoid the corner of the table. Her father saw her at once. A smile lightened his austere face, and he opened his arms. By then Ilona had seen there was another figure in the room, one resting his hip on the table facing her father, but in the momentary joy of the reunion, she didn't care.

Mihály Szilágyi hugged her close, and she kissed his rough cheek.

"I see my sister still hasn't made a lady out of you," he said.
"Thank God."

"Well, don't tell her or she'll turf me out," Ilona said happily.
Her father's arms relaxed, and she turned, frowning, to face the
interloper, who should have had the tact and sense just to go away.

Her stomach gave a lurch that was only half-unpleasant. Vlad
Dracula straightened, easing his hip off the table, and inclined his
head.

Her father said, "Vlad tells me your earlier greeting was so
distant, he thought you really didn't remember him."

Ilona met the mocking green eyes with defiance. But she was
a lady now. She extended her hand to him with elegant, slightly
bored civility.

Vlad took it between his cool, firm fingers and bowed with
equally practised politeness. His lips parted in a provoking smile. "Tag."

Which was when she realised how remarkable it was that
he should remember the childish incident in that day of important encounters, especially amid all that had gone on in his life
since. Secretly, she'd hoped he would still be impressive; she hadn't
expected to find him so…human. The discovery was enchanting.
A responsive smile tugged at her lips.

Her father said, "I must make my bow to your aunt. Vlad, my
daughter will show you around the castle, conduct you back to
your friends, or to the Council Hall, whichever you prefer. In any
case, we'll talk again over dinner."

That, more than anything, told her they had done a deal with
the exiled prince. The contrast with the fear in her father's voice
three years ago when he'd shouted her name across their own
garden, when none of the children had been allowed too close to
him, was marked.

As Mihály Szilágyi strolled from the room, Ilona asked politely
where the prince would like to go.

"Outside, if you can bear it," he said. "I need fresh air."

It was only just spring, and the day was sharp and cold, but Ilona moved at once toward the door, and he fell into step beside her. She observed, "You prefer outdoor life."

"On the whole," he agreed, but she had the impression he wasn't really listening. His mind was elsewhere, no doubt on the agreements he had just made.

As they emerged from the castle's great doors, the biting breeze cooled her overwarm cheeks. She had no cloak with her, but she found herself glad to step out into the cold, fresh air.

Only when she heard him exhale beside her did she realise he'd been holding his breath. For an instant, she thought he would leap down the steps in one bound. She wished he would, so she could do the same. But he didn't, merely ran down them lightly before turning, hand held out as if to help her to the bottom. As if he'd just recalled her presence.

But she was already beside him. She saw another faint tug of his lips before he began to walk. With each stride, she saw the tension in his body ease. His shoulders sank almost imperceptibly lower, his mouth relaxed, and he actually smiled.

Ilona said, "Either you *really* don't like being cooped up, or you're very pleased with yourself."

It wasn't the sort of thing she should have said. Especially not to *him*. Even as the words tumbled out, she was aware of it, but he didn't seem to mind.

A breath of silent laughter escaped his lips. "Both," he said.

"Did the Ottomans keep you in close confinement?" She shouldn't have asked that either, and his quick glance confirmed it. A frown twitched across his brow and vanished.

"Some of the time," he answered. "The worst time."

"How did you bear it?"

"I really don't think you want to know that."

"Don't I?" she asked doubtfully. Then, answering herself, "Yes, I do."

The green eyes glinted; whether with amusement or annoyance, they were too veiled for her to tell. "Then I dreamed of fresh air—and revenge."

She continued to withstand his gaze, but it wasn't easy. Her heart was thudding. "Against the Ottomans?" *Or against my uncle?*

His eyes moved, looking beyond her. "Against the world, I expect."

She said nothing while he continued to gaze out over the peaceful Transylvanian countryside. It wasn't always peaceful, of course, but you wouldn't suspect so from the quiet brown and green fields spread out before them and the tiny figures working them. The oak forest spreading up the nearby hill looked as if it never harboured anything more dangerous than a few hedgehogs. Even the blue-green mountains, looming over everything, looked benevolent today.

He said, "Don't you want to know why I'm pleased?"

"If you want to tell me."

"Count Hunyadi has made me an officer in his army, given me a post and residence at Sibiu."

Keeping him close—and safe. Stringing him along. Drawing the Wallachian's teeth...

"Is that what you wanted?" she asked as neutrally as she could.

"It's an opportunity," he said, "which I would be foolish not to take."

An opportunity to learn warfare under the greatest commander of his day. An opportunity to shine and win support. And he would. She knew that he would.

Almost to herself, she said, "Of course, you already have military experience."

"With the Ottomans," he agreed shamelessly. "And I had the honour to serve under my uncle, the Prince of Moldavia, when we drove out the King of Poland's soldiers."

She could feel excitement thrumming through his body as he walked beside her. For an instant, it blazed in his eyes too before he had them safely veiled again. When he turned them on her next, they were incalculably lighter. "And what of you, Ilona Szilágyi? You serve the countess now?"

"Well, I annoy her and stand behind her at formal receptions."

"And are you happy?"

Surprised, Ilona blinked. No one had ever asked her that. "Happy? Yes, I suppose so... What a strange question—why do you ask?"

He shrugged. "I don't know. You just make me think—this time as last—that you're like me. Waiting. You said you were good at it."

She stared at him, incomprehension struggling against some half-understood truth.

"And then I wonder," he pursued, "what does a fifteen-year-old girl of good family wait for?"

"Sixteen," Ilona corrected, affronted. But it was an easy question. "For a husband and family, if she doesn't already have one. What were you waiting for at sixteen?"

"For the sultan to free me and give me an army to win back Wallachia."

"You didn't need the army," she remembered.

"True. Your uncle was kind enough to take Vladislav out of my way. On the other hand, I doubt the sultan would have let me go without the army to keep its eye on me."

"My uncle took Vladislav to war," Ilona protested, "not on some expedition of pleasure!"

Since his only response to that was a subtle wink she wasn't even sure she saw, she added, "Weren't you afraid to go back? After you lost Wallachia again?"

He shrugged. "I was in no danger from the Ottomans. They'd no reason to keep me anymore. My father was dead." And even before he died, the fact of the sultan holding his sons hostage hadn't prevented the elder Vlad from fighting the Turks. How in

God's name had that felt to young Vlad? Betrayal. Terror, surely. No wonder he'd raged against the world. "And the sultan had already decided I was best causing trouble here instead."

Maybe, Ilona thought. And maybe not. He hadn't been sure what would happen, but he'd gone anyway.

"When did the sultan decide that?"

"After he saw me fighting, of course."

"Are you boasting?"

"I thought I'd give it a try. See if it impressed you."

She smiled. *I like you, Vlad Dracula.* She was so used to speaking her thoughts as they occurred that for a moment she was afraid she'd actually said the words aloud.

"So who's the husband you're waiting for?" he asked. "I hope he's a good man."

"So do I. But nothing has been arranged."

He nodded thoughtfully, though exactly what those thoughts were remained a mystery. His head turned upward to the nearest tower. "I hope it's worth the wait." She no longer knew if he meant Wallachia or her marriage. And before she could ask, he said, "Take me back to the fray, Ilona Szilágyi."

"And don't tell anyone you used such a word to describe my aunt's hospitality?"

A quick smile crossed his face, lightening the care. "I like frays," he said.

Dinner turned out to be an emotional sleigh ride. For the occasion, she was regarded not merely as the countess's attendant but as Hunyadi's niece and Szilágyi's daughter, and so she found herself placed next to Vlad. The excitement of that was new to her, as was the physical disturbance when he sat down next to her. Unfamiliar butterflies fluttered around her stomach, and for some time, she found it difficult to breathe properly, let alone think of anything interesting to say to him. Instead, stupid anxieties rippled through her mind, mostly to do with her appearance, how mature she looked, and how pretty.

The green gown was new and worn over the simple white underdress, showing puffs of contrasting white between the silver buttons of the green sleeves. She rather liked it. She'd fastened it at her breast with a pearl brooch given to her by Countess Hunyadi. She should have felt important and regal, but she didn't. She felt ridiculously tongue-tied and totally confused.

Fortunately, at the beginning, most of his attention was given to Countess Hunyadi on his other side, allowing Ilona time to gather herself. Although he was not a particularly big man, he seemed so when he was this close, the physical manifestation of his forceful personality. Vlad Dracula was just a little too overwhelming to be comfortable. In fact, so strongly did she feel this that it took her some time to connect her powerful response to Vlad with those far fainter flutterings of attraction she'd felt for one or two of Hunyadi's handsomer knights. And then she didn't know whether to be appalled or excited. For an instant, it felt more like *agony*.

So she did what had always helped her over difficult or embarrassing situations in the past. She laughed at herself.

"Are you fasting?"

His deep voice broke into her self-mockery, but at least her panic was manageable now. She dragged her full plate into focus, along with the ineffectual meanderings of her fork.

"Perhaps I should be."

"Atoning for some dreadful crime? What did you do? Run in the hall? Lose the countess's favourite earring?"

Ilona's lip curled. "You think my life is very trivial," she observed. *Isn't it?*

She cast a quick, defiant glance at him, caught surprise in his face. "Nobody's life is trivial. Only the use to which it is put. In this household, I would say very little is trivial. Even the fact that you do not enjoy this excellent duck. What's wrong? Do you miss your home?"

It was equivalent to asking if she was happy. "You're a very curious man," she observed.

"You mean nosy." He placed the last of the duck into his mouth in one neat movement.

"No, I mean strange."

His eyes gleamed, but he waited until his food was swallowed before he responded in kind. "You're rather strange yourself." He lifted his glass, clearly about to tease her some more, but his observant gaze caught on something farther down and on the other side of the table. His eyes seemed to darken, but his lips flickered into a curve, and he raised his glass almost imperceptibly to someone else.

Ilona turned from curiosity and saw Maria blushing a pretty shade of pink and smiling.

It was like a blow in the stomach. Ilona had never known jealousy, not like this.

Now she truly had a reason to laugh at herself.

It was the pattern of the meal. He spoke to her because he had to, because he was placed beside her, while the majority of his attention was given to the countess, because manners as well as ambition dictated that it should be so. Pride and defiance forced Ilona to hold her own in each of their conversations, and she couldn't suppress a surge of fierce satisfaction each time she managed to surprise him with the depth of her own knowledge, whether of politics or of classical philosophy and literature. *How trivial am I now?* she thought unfairly. And then unbidden, *What's it all for? For waiting…?*

To give him his due, the prince appeared genuinely to enjoy her company. While more than once Ilona lost herself in his alternative, often Turkish-oriented knowledge, his opinion, and the insight she *almost* gained into his contradictory character. He was an actor who seemed to value honesty above all else, a trained warrior prepared to use the most ruthless violence to bring peace and prosperity. She caught fleeting glimpses of ambition, understanding, casual brutality, compassion, austerity, a love of luxury at odds with his proven capability of thriving with none at all. It all added to her fascination, her enchantment to call it no worse. And she wouldn't have swapped her agonising place at his side for the largest palace or the best, most powerful husband in Hungary.

And yet each time, it seemed, her happiness in his company was brought up short by discovering his gaze again shifting down the table. She never looked at Maria at these times, but later, when his attention was once more on the countess, she would glance at her friend and find her watching Vlad—with something very like her own fascination.

Once, Maria caught her gaze and smiled, dazzlingly.

I think he likes *me…*

Chapter Five

Hunedoara, Transylvania, 1454

*I*n a good-natured sort of a way, Maria envied Ilona her place
at dinner beside Vlad Dracula. She was glad Ilona had someone so exciting to talk to, and there was no point in grudging
Ilona the reality of her close relationship with the Hunyadis. Maria
loved her friend and wanted her to shine socially and marry a
good and rich man. But she couldn't help wishing that it was she,
Maria, that the prince turned to so frequently, sometimes with a
teasing gleam in his amazing green eyes that melted Maria's bones.

Sometimes he looked stunned, as if Ilona had said something outrageous—which she probably had—and Maria wanted
to laugh. Especially because he never appeared offended. On the
contrary, he seemed to like talking to her, which was, Maria con-
ceded, something else in his favour.

That and the fact that he liked looking at her, Maria. She caught
his attention several times, knew from her infallible instinct that he
liked the way she flirted with only her eyelashes. As dinner progressed,
she grew increasingly more certain of an assignation that night, and
her heart beat and beat. Because this could be her salvation; she could
turn disaster into triumph, into something wonderful for her whole
family by becoming, eventually, Princess of Wallachia—if what Ilona
had told her was true. But mostly and increasingly, it beat because in

just a few hours she could be held in those strong arms, know all the
passion of his ruthless yet surely sensitive body...

She rose with alacrity when the countess did because it
brought the moment closer. As she tripped along the length of
the table, she saw Vlad bowing to his hostess, blocking Ilona's path.
Straightening, he stepped back and turned. Since it was impossible
to bow to Ilona in the space now left to him, he smiled and took
her hand instead. He raised it to his lips, politely, barely touching
her skin at all with his mouth before releasing her, and yet Ilona
blushed—not a faintly pink, flirty blush, but a fiery red one. Poor
Ilona, she still hadn't quite grasped the social niceties, especially
where men were concerned.

Vlad stood aside, and she brushed past him in the wake of the
countess, who was already sailing regally toward the stairs. Maria
hurried after them, but not so quickly that Vlad didn't see her. She
lowered her gaze modestly and smiled under her lashes.

Another few minutes, Maria thought. *Just a few, and then I'll go downstairs to the hall, pretend to search for my earring. He's bound to be there...*

"So do you like him? Is he nice? Did he mention me at all?"
she asked Ilona, not for the first time.

The two girls were in the tiny bedchamber they shared. Fully
dressed, Maria sprawled on top of the bed, one hand under her
head while excited dreams whirled through her mind and her
body buzzed with anticipation.

Ilona, already in her nightgown with an old shawl around
her shoulders for warmth, sat in the deep window bay, her knees
under her chin, her gaze fixed on the window, not on the sky, but
something vaguely downwards. Maria doubted she saw anything.
She was gazing into space again. In fact, Maria doubted she'd even
heard her questions and was about to repeat them when Ilona, as

if she couldn't remembering answering before, said vaguely, "Yes, but he's a bit strange. And no, he didn't mention you to me. It would have been bad manners."

"He has good manners, then?" Maria asked eagerly. "I like that in a man. What did he talk about? What will he do for Count Hunyadi?"

"Guard the border, apparently," Ilona answered dreamily. "From Sibiu."

"That's not so far from Hunedoara... Ilona, we *will* always be friends, won't we?" She wasn't sure why she asked, where the sudden attack of anxiety came from. Not given to self-analysis, she nevertheless knew that she would miss Ilona in another house, another town. But Transylvania wasn't a massive country. Unless her parents married her to some distant lord—and the Szilágyis could look high these days, to any nobleman in Europe—they could surely meet frequently. And in the meantime, Countess Hunyadi wouldn't grudge her niece for a few days, would she?

Almost to her surprise, Ilona turned her head to look at her. She even smiled. "Of course, idiot. Why wouldn't we?"

"Oh, I don't know. If our husbands were enemies..."

"Then it would be our business to make them friends," Ilona said, as if it would be as easy as baking a cake. For her, perhaps it would be. Her gaze moved back to the window, and she let her head drop back against the wall as she stared down into the night. A shadow passed across her face, making Maria think of hunger and pain and incredible sadness. None of which she normally associated with Ilona, but which were so familiar to her right now that she sprang up and went to hug her friend from pure empathy.

She never did. As she knelt beside Ilona, some movement through the window caught her eye. Two young men in the darkness of the narrow courtyard below, lit only by a sputtering torch in a wall sconce. One who stood, gesticulating—Stephen of Moldavia—and the other, seated on the wall around the well, one knee under his chin, smiling with amusement at the antics of his companion. Maria's breath caught. Her heart thudded. She would never have a better opportunity than this.

"Forgive me," she gasped, already springing down to the floor and bolting across the room. "I'll tell you everything later. Wish me luck!"

She was so worried that they'd be gone before she arrived that her soft cry of surprise on seeing them still there was entirely genuine. As she stood, gasping, on the step, the heavy door swung shut behind her, and both handsome young heads turned toward her.

Stephen bowed. Vlad unwound himself and stood.

"Lady Maria," Stephen said. "Are we disturbing you?"

"Oh, not at all. No, I often come here in the evening—it's peaceful." She smiled at each of them in turn and walked toward the well—and Vlad. "I make wishes to the well."

"How very pagan of you," Vlad murmured, and Stephen smiled. Maria sank onto the wall and gazed down into the darkness of the well.

I wish that he wants me, that I make him happy, and it all ends well...

She glanced up at Vlad. "Have you made a wish tonight?"

"I have many wishes, but I'm afraid I'm too cynical to expect a mere well to fulfill them."

Stephen laughed. "You are a wise man, my friend. Lady Maria, I bid you good night. Vlad, I'm going back to the knights' hall."

Stephen, thought Maria with approval, was a perfect gentleman. Leaving them alone, discreetly informing Vlad that the bedchamber she knew they shared would be vacant awhile yet.

But Vlad, Vlad had still not resumed his seat on the wall of the well. She patted the stone beside her, and he finally sank down, close but not touching. Not too pushy, then—she liked that too.

"Are you not cold?" he asked.

"Not for a little." She smiled. "Actually, I'm glad of the chance to talk to you alone. It's so—constricting in a formal situation."

He inclined his head but said nothing. Vlad Dracula, tongue-tied? He hadn't struck her as the shy type. But then, she was a noblewoman, one of the countess's ladies, and it would be fatal for him to make a mistake. She had to show him her willingness before they ran out of time.

"May I be frank?" she asked, glad of the hint of huskiness that had entered her voice. It was induced by nerves as much as by desire, for his eyes, so compelling, were disturbingly bright.

"Always," he returned, and with relief, she reached out and daringly touched his cheek—a little rough with new stubble, and warm.

"I hoped to find you alone," she whispered. "Ever since I first saw you this morning…"

He took her hand and rose to his feet. Heart thudding, she rose with him, felt the spark of pleasure as his lips brushed her knuckle.

"You are very beautiful, and I am very honoured. And weak enough to wish not to be so tempted. You must go back inside now."

Not quite understanding, she said, "You will come to me?" How? Where?

He shook his head and began to speak, but shock had made her desperate. She could feel the heat from his body, knew he wasn't indifferent. She would not allow him to reject her. Swaying against him, she simply reached up with her mouth and took his.

Full and hot, the feel of his lips inflamed her. She pushed closer, felt the leap of his body, the hardness that spoke more volumes than mere words. Triumph made her bold, and she laid both arms around his neck.

His body shuddered. Without warning, his mouth opened wide, bore down on hers, hard, and his tongue plunged inside, swept once around her mouth and caressed the length of her tongue with such sensuality that she knew beyond doubt that he would be the best lover she had ever known or ever would.

And then, just when she thought she'd won, he lifted his head and drew back, breaking her grip around his neck.

"Good night, Lady Maria. I wish you well." His voice didn't even shake.

And turning away from her, he walked back inside.

Vlad was still awake when Stephen scratched on the door.

"Come in, you idiot."

"Alone?" Stephen enquired as his head poked round. He sounded disappointed. He came in and closed the door behind him, quizzically regarding Vlad, who sprawled on the bed with a cup hanging loosely in his fingers.

Vlad curled his lip. Though the wine had blunted the sharp edges of his lust, enough frustration remained to ensure a short temper. "Don't be a fool. Of course I am."

"*I'm* the fool? You managed to alienate that beautiful girl? She was so hot for you it almost dripped out of her eyes!"

"There's more to life than beautiful girls." There were inconvenient rules of hospitality. And, somewhere only half grasped, the understanding that seducing Maria Gerzsenyi would show disrespect not only to the dragon countess but to that other, younger girl he'd met before—Mihály Szilágyi's daughter who, for no reason he could fathom, appeared to be his friend.

However, his body did not appreciate his mind's scruples. Neither did Stephen, who reminded him, "That's not what you said last week with those gypsy sisters."

Vlad threw the cup at him. Fortunately, it was empty. Stephen caught it, smirking. Then, as the smile died in his eyes, he regarded Vlad more seriously. "So you are content with this?"

"For now. It's an opportunity and puts us in a good position for the next."

"It's less than I hoped."

Vlad shrugged. "More than I feared. We're part of his plan now."

"What plan?"

"To kick the Ottomans out of Europe. Constantinople is too close—the Ottoman conquest there has put the wind up everyone. More than ever, Wallachia and Moldavia have to be safe Christian bulwarks. Vladislav sees the power of the Turks and grows closer to them to save his skin—thus alienating Hungary and the Christian powers. His time is up."

"Then why doesn't Hunyadi just give you an army and send you to get Wallachia? Doesn't he trust you?"

Vlad gave him a lopsided look. "Why should he?"

"Do you trust him?"

"As long as I'm useful to him."

"So in the meantime, you get to watch the Ottoman border. From a nice comfortable house in Sibiu."

"Could be worse."

"Is there space for me to lodge?" Stephen asked casually.

"Of course. You'll come in useful polishing my boots and procuring women."

Stephen threw the cup back at him, and this time Vlad caught it and refilled it from the jug on the bedside table.

Stephen sat down on the bed and watched him drink. "There are other candidates for any vacancy in Wallachia," he pointed out.

"There always are," Vlad agreed. "My family breeds like rats. But I have one advantage—I know the Ottomans. I know how their collective mind works, and I know the sultan."

"And you invaded Wallachia with them," Stephen pointed out dryly. "How the hell did you make him forget that?"

"He hasn't forgotten," Vlad said, surprised. "He just knows his offer has to be more attractive than anything the Ottomans might come up with."

"Then he doesn't trust you at all! He's just keeping you where he can see you."

"Partly," Vlad allowed. "And partly—he understands pragmatism. We all have to do what we must to survive. Or to achieve a greater good. I can do that for him." He lifted the cup in a toast to Stephen. "So can you."

Ilona was asleep when Maria returned, drooping, to their chamber. A single candle burned on the table under the window. It was enough for Maria to undress by. Then she blew it out and crept, shivering, into the bed.

She wanted to die. It wasn't just the humiliation of rejection when she had been so sure of him. It was the feeling that this was her last chance and the alternative was...

"Oh Mary, Mother of God, help me," she whispered, and the tears came in great, racking sobs that shook the whole bed, however hard she tried to suppress them.

Behind her, she felt Ilona move and lean over her. "Maria?" she whispered. She sounded frightened. "Maria, what's wrong?"

Only then did Maria remember that she'd left Ilona at the window from where she could have watched the whole scene.

"Didn't you see?" she gasped.

Ilona shook her head in the darkness. Her loose hair brushed against Marias's cheek. "I went to bed as soon you left. See what, Maria? Oh God..." She took Maria by the shoulders, turning her, staring into her eyes. "My God, am I wrong? Did he—*hurt* you?"

"Hurt me? He's broken my heart." Maria sobbed. "He sent me away, rejected me…"

Ilona hugged her. "Of course he did," she whispered, as if to a child.

Outraged despite everything, Maria pulled back. "*Of course? Why of course?* Am I so ugly, so unacceptable to a man?"

"Oh, my dear, anything but!" She had the indignant feeling that somewhere Ilona was laughing at her. "Don't you see, it doesn't matter how beautiful you are or how much he wants you—he couldn't dishonour a girl in the care of his hostess, under the protection of his patron. I told you he's well-mannered."

Maria gave a shaky giggle. "You're laughing at me," she accused. She peered up at Ilona in the darkness. "You mean I still have a chance with him?"

Of course, Ilona didn't understand. "In time," she said vaguely. And Maria felt her slipping away again.

Clutching her to keep her there, Maria said desperately, "I don't have time. I need him *now*."

"You've only known him a few hours! Even you can't fall in love so fast!" There was a rare irritation in her voice that made Maria answer in kind.

"Of course I can't! But I *could* have, Ilona, I could, with him. When he kissed me, I sensed such passion, such *hunger* that I thought I could die for him. It was so wonderful… But I don't have the time anymore, do I? This was my last chance!"

"Last chance? Maria, what are you *talking* about?"

"I'm talking about…" She was shouting, and realization brought her up short. Even in the darkness, she turned away from her friend and squeezed her eyes shut. "I'm talking about the baby. I'm going to have a baby."

The silence enclosed her. Ilona was such an innocent. She knew Maria made assignations with men, sneaked off to meet them, but it never entered her naïve little head that this meant more than kissing in dark corners. Or perhaps that was how she thought babies were made. And now she would despise her, cast her off. Right now that seemed the ultimate tragedy.

She heard Ilona's breath come out in a rush. "A baby," she whispered. "Oh, Maria…"

Maria sat up and threw herself into her arms. "I don't know what I was thinking." She sobbed. "I've been mad with worry this last month, and then today I saw *him*, and I wanted him, and I thought that if only he wanted me and took me, then he'd marry me when I told him about the baby."

"Pretend it was his?"

She felt Ilona's hands take her by the shoulders, pull her back. She could imagine the shock in her friend's face. She didn't need the light to see it.

"Oh no, you couldn't do that."

"It's been done before," Maria said bitterly. "Trust me, when you're desperate, your standards drop."

Unexpectedly, Ilona seemed to understand that. "Not just women's either," she said ruefully. "But seriously, you mustn't, not with Vlad. Apart from anything else, Wallachian princes don't see any particular need to marry the mothers of their children. Vlad himself has several illegitimate half siblings. Besides, if he ever found out you'd lied…" She broke off and shivered.

She was right, of course. Vlad Dracula was not the man to bear lightly any such humiliation.

Maria sighed. "Well, it won't arise, will it, because he wouldn't lie with me. And to be honest, my heart quails at approaching anyone else."

"Oh, Maria, there must be another way. Who *is* the father?"

"Josef." She caught Ilona's inadvertent squeak and added with defiance, "Yes, married Josef—you see my problem?"

Ilona tugged at her hair. Even in the dark, Maria knew she was frowning. Eventually, she sighed. "We can't do this by ourselves. We need to tell Countess Hunyadi."

Maria shook her head violently. "Are you mad? Of course we can't! Ilona, you must promise me not to say a word to her, to anyone!"

"Then what will you do, Maria? Wait until a bump starts appearing beneath your gown and people start sniggering and asking questions? She *will* dismiss you then, and if your family… Oh, you've thought of all this before; you must have. How long do you have?"

"Seven months, maybe—I've missed two courses now."

"That's time enough, I'm sure. She'll stand by you, Maria, I know she will."

"Why should she?" Maria said miserably. "She'll see it as that I betrayed her trust, as I suppose I did, and brought disgrace upon her house. My family is not worth placating. We all know she did us a favour taking me into her household in the first place."

"And for that reason, she'll cover it up. In her own eyes, she's failed you by not protecting you. She doesn't want the world to know that. So she'll find you a husband and make it right."

Maria wiped her streaming eyes. "It won't be the husband I dreamed of."

"Who knows? He might be." Ilona put her arms around her. "I wish you'd told me sooner. You must have been in hell."

I am. I am in hell.

"It will be better now," Ilona said gruffly. "We'll tell the countess in the morning. I'll speak, but you must come with me, for she despises cowards. And she'll find you a haven."

Against all sense, hope of something better than disgrace and destitution began to rise once more. "And if she doesn't? If she throws me out?"

"Then my mother will help. But it won't come to that. Trust me."

And curiously, despite Ilona's youth and innocence, Maria did
trust her. That night she slept more peacefully than she had for
weeks.

Ilona wasn't looking forward to the morning. Having slept badly,
she rose early, put on her cloak, and went for a brisk walk around
the castle grounds. The necessary interview with the countess
loomed large in her mind, and she spent much of her walk rehears-
ing the precise words she should use to enlist the countess's sympathy. The support she would give anyway, Ilona was convinced,
but the quality of that support could make a huge difference to
Maria's future. Maria should be married. She needed a husband to
give her love and attention instead of seeking it from unprincipled
and opportunistic young men who should know better.

The countess would say some nasty things to Maria. There
would inevitably be insults and accusations of betrayal and loose
behaviour. And the trouble was they were true in one sense. Only
Maria wasn't *loose*; she was just—loving. Ilona suspected she'd
been taken advantage of several times, and Ilona would not and
could not judge her. Sitting in the window last night, gazing down
at Vlad and Stephen by the well, how much had she longed for
the courage to do what Maria had done? Only Ilona had had the
sense to know that she'd be rejected—and for more reasons than
Maria had been.

She was the precocious child who played tag, and it was no
longer enough.

And so she walked in the cold light of dawn to ease her pain
and need, and bent her intellect to Maria's problem, which at least
she knew she could solve, with the countess's help. It wouldn't be
perfect for Maria, but it would be something she could make the
best of. Any husband would adore her. And Maria...

The sounds of horses' hooves broke into her thoughts, brought her back to reality. She was approaching the front of the castle as several horses rode out from the direction of the stables. Vlad Dracula, Stephen of Moldavia, and their following.

She raised her hand in farewell, unsure that she'd be seen and even half hoping that she wouldn't be. But he pulled up, holding in his wild, snorting horse with one strong hand and the pressure of his knees. She could do nothing but go up to him and play the scene honestly.

He bent from the saddle, holding down his hand. She laid hers into it and looked up into his blazing green eyes.

"I wish you well, Vlad Dracula. I hope your waiting is soon over."

A faint smile tugged at his lips. "And yours."

"Oh, in my case I've decided waiting's not so bad. Especially when I don't know what or whom I'm waiting for."

"Then I wish you all you want from life."

A choke of laughter fought its way out. "No, you don't," she said ruefully. "But I thank you all the same."

He smiled again, releasing her hand and straightening in the saddle. "You intrigue me, Ilona Szilágyi. One day you must tell me what it is you wish for."

She stepped back, and he released his anxious horse, plunging away from her in a cloud of dust. His boyars paused only long enough to bow to her before galloping after him to the bridge. Only Stephen of Moldavia bade her a more formal farewell, bending from the saddle as Vlad had done, to take her hand. Then, outdoing his cousin in gallantry, he kissed it respectfully.

"Thank you for making our brief stay so pleasant."

"If it was pleasant, I regret not having more to do with it," she said dryly.

"You're as modest as you are charming."

Ilona drew her hand free, making a derisive hoot before she remembered how unladylike it was. Stephen, however, merely grinned, and a teasing gleam appeared in his fine eyes. "No, I insist that you are."

"Will you join your cousin in Sibiu?" she asked hastily.

"Probably. We are sworn to help each other. I hope we shall see you there, now that we're respectable again."

It crossed Ilona's mind then, somewhat belatedly, that Stephen was flirting with her. The idea made her laugh, which seemed as good a time as any to end the conversation. Stepping back, she watched Stephen gallop after the others. No one looked back.

With reluctance, Ilona turned her feet toward the castle once more. It was time to seek out the countess and negotiate for Maria.

However, when she entered the castle, the sound of her father's voice coming from the knights' hall, gave her pause. Because he spoke Vlad's name. Ilona hesitated, but as ever, curiosity won over good sense. To say nothing of manners. Since there was no one else around, she trod quietly across to the half-open door and listened.

Mihály Szilágyi said, "You've given him a difficult task, with very little authority. Vladislav will pressure Sibiu to defy you and eject him. He'll have to deal with that as well as any incursions from Wallachia."

"You think he's not up to it?" Count Hunyadi asked. His voice was more mocking than doubtful.

Her father sighed loudly. "On the contrary, I think he's a most unusual and able young man, but none of us can do the impossible."

"It shouldn't be impossible."

"You're testing him," Mihály observed. Impossible to know if he approved or not. Probably, he would have done the same. In any matter of importance, Vlad Dracula was untried.

Hunyadi said, "We know the sultan thought highly of his military prowess, and we know he fought with distinction in

Moldavia. But I need him to grow quickly into this task if we're to face the Ottomans in Serbia. As we will, very soon. We know they're coming for Belgrade, and when they do, he must be capable of holding Transylvania for us. At the very least. We can't trust the King or the Hungarian nobles to act, so we must take care of it ourselves. And Mihály…"

Footsteps from inside had made Ilona draw back, preparing to dash across the passage and upstairs, but since everything seemed to pause inside the hall, she did too.

Her uncle said, "I'll want you to hold Belgrade for me."

Ilona's gut twisted. It was an honour, of course, proving once again the governor's trust in her father's loyalty and ability. But to hold a city under siege by the conquerors of Constantinople, with neither support nor relief certain from any of the bickering states and factions of Europe—that was something of a poisoned chalice, and both men knew it.

However, her father said only, "When?"

"Hopefully not till next winter, but if our spies bring different news, we'll have to move a lot faster."

It felt as if something was running through her fingers, slipping away. The security and safety of the last few years, her old, privileged life divided between Horogszegi and Hunedoara, her old companionship with Maria. All about to be ripped apart by events over which she had no control. And nothing would ever be the same.

But at least she could do her best for Maria. With determination, she turned toward the stairs and prepared to face the countess.

Chapter Six

Transylvania, 1455-6

The sky was filthy, promising more snow before night-fall. The maid in the carriage with Ilona kept up her vocal hopes that they would at least make it as far as Sibiu before then. Ilona was sure they would. They were making good progress, despite the difficulty of the snow-covered roads, and it was only just midday.

Wrapped in furs and muffs and the countess's own blanket lent for the occasion, Ilona was cozy enough to appreciate the white beauty surrounding her. Snow capped the thick forest of trees on either side of the road, and when, occasionally, she could glimpse the more distant hills, they too were covered. It made the countryside she knew so well look unfamiliar and exciting.

Although much of the excitement came from inside. It had been a difficult year at Hunedoara, where tension and frustrations had run high. Not just over the business with Maria—although Aunt Erzsébet still bore a grudge about that, despite the Hunyadis now having an effective if insouciant spy in the house of one of Prince Vladislav's loyalist supporters in Wallachia.

It had become Ilona's job to trawl through Maria's letters and separate the barrage of news and gossip from anything useful to do with her new husband's or Vladislav's policies toward the

Ottomans and toward Hungary. And although the task made Ilona grit her teeth with discomfort sometimes, she guarded it jealously so that the good-natured Maria's private chatter remained just that. The odd passages that revealed Vladislav's treachery she was glad enough to pass on.

In some ways hardest to bear was John Hunyadi's fall from grace. In truth his standing had never fully recovered from the defeat at Varna, but to watch his enemies, the unspeakable Cilli family, who had neither the brain nor the heart to achieve a fraction of what Hunyadi had, gradually close in on the king and work against a far greater man was galling in the extreme. The countess was permanently enraged, and Hunyadi himself had grown so disgusted with the intrigue and lack of trust that he'd resigned virtually all his influential positions.

Not that this had altered his determination to find any way he could to meet the inevitable Ottoman threat that his enemies denied existed…

If she had been her uncle, Ilona thought she would have pulled all her hair out by now. Who could live like that? It was bad enough observing from a safe distance.

But for a week or two, she could put all that aside. She was going to Sighisoara to spend Christmas with her family. One of her brothers-in-law had a big house in the town, and it had been decided that this was the best place for the whole family to meet up for the holiday celebration. It made her feel like a child again, reminding her of past Christmases, of the wonder of gift giving, and the sense of goodwill that had always seemed to go with it. And of course the fun and games and the joy of having her father home.

She had all that to look forward to, and before it, a night in Sibiu with trusted family friends of both her parents and the Hunyadis. And a letter from John Hunyadi to put into the hands of Vlad Dracula—a duty that created an equally powerful if secret excitement.

As the day wore on, she had to wrestle with the insane urge to throw off the blanket and leap out of the carriage to run through the snow beside the horses, making her own deep footprints in the pristine snow. She wriggled again, because she couldn't be still. And then the carriage stopped.

Ilona and the maid exchanged glances. Was the snow impassible after all? As one, they stuck their heads out of either window. She could hear voices, low but urgent. The men of her escort were gazing about them, swords drawn.

Her heart lurched. They only had a small escort, enough to deal with any wild animals and frighten off any hardy, enterprising robber, but this was not a dangerous road, especially at this time of year. Although there had been a few Ottoman raids from Wallachia toward the end of autumn, the Ottomans never fought in winter…

The men seemed to loom out of nowhere, black, menacing, and terrifyingly silent in the muffling snow. They sprang out of the trees, armed with javelins and bows, and then stood perfectly still, covering each of the helpless men-at-arms and, by the look of it, her drivers too. More men ran beyond them, quickly and just as silently surrounding the carriage.

"Oh my lady, my lady!" wailed the maid. "What's happening? What can we do?"

Her voice cut through the dreamlike silence like a knife.

One of their attackers spoke, low and irritably. "Somebody shut that wench up."

Ilona dragged her head back inside the carriage, urgently pressing her finger to her lips. It made excellent sense not to annoy their captors until it would help their cause. But before she could speak to warn the maid, the door was wrenched open and a man said, "Be silent, or you die."

The maid moaned, and Ilona didn't blame her. His words were hardly comforting. He held a sword in one hand and a dagger in the other. But this paled into insignificance beside one other fact.

Ilona frowned at him. "I know you."

"You'll know me a damned sight better if you don't..." He broke off, his eyes widening with recognition. His name still eluded Ilona, but abruptly he fell into place. "Lady! Oh the devil. I beg you, be silent and shut the woman up. No one here will hurt you. Sir," he hissed over his shoulder, "it's Hunyadi's niece."

Ilona's hammering heart lurched. Through the carriage door, she saw the legs and body of a horse, flanked by stirrups and long, leather boots which pressed the animal farther forward. She saw a tangle of black hair as the rider bent in the saddle, and then the face of Vlad Dracula. His eyes blazed in his vital, arresting face.

"Ilona Szilágyi. Come to fight the Ottomans?"

The Ottomans, it seemed, had crossed the border from Wallachia to set a trap specifically for Vlad. But forewarned, Vlad was surrounding them before he rode openly into their trap. Ilona's carriage would not only have drawn Ottoman attention in the wrong direction but driven straight into a nightmare she didn't even want to think about.

"The Ottomans have come in winter? Especially for you?" Ilona repeated as she walked with Vlad through the snow into the cover of the trees. He moved like a wolf, covering the ground efficiently, silently, speedily, his eyes never still. Behind them, the carriage wheels grumbled softly; the horses' hooves were muffled.

"There may be Ottomans there," he allowed. "It's a myth we keep up for national pride. Most will be Wallachians, and both come on the direct orders of Vladislav."

Of course, Vladislav must fear this pretender to his throne now he was the openly preferred candidate of John Hunyadi, who'd even taken him to meet the Hungarian king and reswear the Dragon oath of his father.

Casually, Vlad said, "He's been trying to attack Sibiu for months, to punish the town for 'harbouring' me. In fact, once we've dealt with the ambush, we need to return quickly to Sibiu in case their forces split to draw me away. I advise you to accept my escort but warn you it will be an uncomfortable ride."

Energy seemed to surge through him. He spoke briskly, his eyes and his mind clearly busy on the forthcoming fight. Ilona, unused to war at quite such close quarters, felt her stomach churn and twist. And yet the excitement wasn't all unpleasant.

"Do you have enough men to defeat them?"

He didn't laugh at the naïvety of her question. He simply said, "Yes." And stopped. "Don't come closer than this. Keep as silent as you can."

The drivers were hooking nose bags to the horses, feeding them to keep them content, at least until the fighting started, when any more noise would scarcely matter.

Vlad nodded to her and spun on his heel, searching for his horse. Someone gave him the reins, and he vaulted lightly into the saddle.

"Be careful," Ilona urged, and this time he did laugh, briefly, soundlessly.

His men surrounded him once more, almost like some silent, magical materialization. Attuned to his deep voice, low yet commanding, Ilona heard him give his final instructions. Most of the words were lost, but she did hear the clearly spoken, "No mercy."

"For the Ottomans," one of his men amended.

"For anyone. Kill them all."

Kill them all. The words stayed with her, chilling her to the bone as the cold could not. While the maid stayed huddled in the carriage,

Ilona paced around the outside of it until she had worn a ring of snow almost completely away.

What exactly had she expected of him? A stranger, an exile by his own admission bent on revenge. She lived in a ruthless, war-torn world, but it had always seemed an honourable one before, at least on the side of good, where men who surrendered to greater odds or to better men were treated with mercy. Vlad, it seemed, had none of that particular commodity. Infidel or Christian, Ottoman or one of his own people over whom he hoped to rule one day, all would die.

Unless he did.

For the first time, she began to understand her aunt's misgivings about him, her father's ambiguity. Hunyadi, it seemed, had unleashed a terrible weapon in his war against the Ottomans and their collaborators.

And yet if he lost, would the Ottomans or their Wallachian allies show any more compassion? If Transylvania fell, what then would happen to the Christian world? What would happen to her home, her family?

She had lived with this issue for so long that it had become a background to her whole life. It came as a shock now to be actually *thinking* about it—the possibility of losing everything to the Ottomans. The old childhood belief that neither her father nor Uncle John Hunyadi would ever let it happen no longer rang true. And that made her feel very small and very cold. The possibility was suddenly real, frightening, compelling, brought powerfully home by those three callous words. *Kill them all.*

"That's it," said one the men-at-arms suddenly. "Listen."

Ilona paused in midstep. In the distance, muffled by the trees and the snow, men's voices shouted. She couldn't distinguish war cries from the screams of soldiers or horses. The men-at-arms listened intently, visibly torn between conflicting desire to be in the thick of the fight and relief to be well out of it, guarding their charge in safety with all honour.

Is he dead or victorious? She knew it had to be one or the other. It would be such a tragic way for him to die, so young, before he had even done more than wait.

Pain gripped her stomach like a claw and squeezed until she forced herself to breathe and loosen it. Men died all the time. It was one of the things women endured. And in her heart, she knew he'd survive. He'd set out like a hunting wolf, with such confidence, such brisk efficiency that he couldn't lose. Could he?

Which meant the forest would be full of the dead.

He rode back into their little makeshift camp at the head of his victorious troop. A little bloodied, a little torn around their clothing, the men buzzed with excitement and triumph, their laughter occasionally too boisterous but never undisciplined. Vlad himself didn't laugh. There was blood on the knuckles of his right hand, trickling between the fingers which so effortlessly held his agitated horse in check. His eyes still flashed with the same restless excitement, and Ilona soon realised why. His task was not done until he returned to Sibiu and saw it safe.

She didn't know if he read the relief or the accusation in her eyes when he met her gaze. Certainly, he didn't appear to care.

Dismounting, he said, "We must leave now. We travel at speed, so the carriage may get stuck behind. Either way, it will not be a comfortable ride. I suggest alternative transport."

Frowning with incomprehension, she followed his gaze to his men—and the two vehicles they guided.

Vlad said, "This is how they covered the ground so quickly."

"Sleighs," said Ilona, stunned.

"I haven't driven one of these since I was a child playing on the hills of Sighisoara," Vlad said happily.

It couldn't be resisted. In spite of everything, fun bubbled up from her toes as the horses were quickly harnessed to the sleighs.

Ilona found herself seated on the bench of one while the prince in person laid the countess's blanket over her knees.

He winked at her, more like the boy who'd climbed the wall at Horogszegi than the man who'd just slaughtered umpteen other men in battle, and climbed onto the bench beside her. There was an instant when she remembered exactly who and what he was, and excitement spiked through her, overwhelming the sudden, unspecific fear. Then Vlad yelled a challenge to the sleigh on the other side and let his horses go.

It was exhilarating, swishing through the snow at high speed. Sometimes they moved off the road and swerved among the trees to avoid the carriage, which careered along beside them. Ilona clung to the side, ridiculously happy to be thrown from side to side, sometimes unable to avoid bumping against him. Vlad's attention was necessarily on the road and the horses, but she caught an occasional flash of his teeth as he grinned.

The emphasis was on speed, though Ilona noticed the frequent arrivals of lookouts and their reports yelled to the prince without stopping.

"I think we're clear," he called to her once. "No sign of any other parties. We can slow down if you want."

"Oh, no," said Ilona, and he laughed and urged the horses faster. He was like some god of ancient legend, and yet giving her more fun than she'd had in years.

Her stomach twisted with inconvenient protest. "Vlad?"

He glanced at her.

She blurted, "Did you kill them all?"

He twitched the reins, and the horses swerved left. The sleigh flew between two trees with inches to spare.

"Yes," said Vlad. "I killed them all."

It felt like pain, only she didn't know where. "Why? Why no mercy?"

It was none of her business. Even from the privilege of marriage, her mother had never questioned any of her father's military decisions. She wasn't even sure why it mattered so much, except that it was he who'd done it. In her mind, foolish and childish, she'd made him into something he wasn't. Because she'd understood him once, she'd forgotten she didn't really know him at all.

The hooded lids swept down over his eyes, veiling whatever he didn't wish her to see. His lashes, long and thick, curved over his cheek. Unerringly, he guided the horses through the trees at high speed and spilled back onto the road.

He spoke conversationally. "What do you want me to say, Ilona? That they deserved to die? That they were only a few infidels and traitors, no loss to the Christian world? That I did it for God or for John Hunyadi? To teach my people to fear thwarting me? Or just that I wanted to, because I'm a cruel and callous bastard?"

She swallowed. "Whichever is true."

She couldn't even be sure he heard her over the rushing air and the whisper and crunch of the sleigh over the snowy ground. His breath streamed out, long and steadily.

"All of them." His glance was like a knife stab, and yet for some reason she thought the mockery there was aimed not at her but at himself. "Apart from the God bit. Let me not take his name in vain."

As if God heard, there was a sudden jolt as the harness snapped and they were thrown backwards. Ilona gasped. One of the horses whinnied as if struck by flapping leather, and then both animals began to draw away from their slowing sleigh, which skidded off the road once more. The coach and the other sleigh and the troop of riders got smaller.

For an instant, Vlad stared straight ahead. She thought he would say something more, prayed that he would. And then he jerked forward, hard, and she realised the sleigh was picking up speed once more. His hand caught at a passing tree. It was only later she realised he wasn't trying to slow them down, but pushing them faster, and now, alarmingly, they were on a wooded incline, which was turning into a steep slope.

Ilona squeaked with sudden fear. "Vlad!"

Vlad laughed. "Hold on to my belt," he said and pushed himself forward to grab the wooden bar along the front. The sleigh gathered speed, bumping and sliding faster and faster toward a tree which filled Ilona's vision. She closed her eyes and grabbed at Vlad's belt. Beneath her knuckles, she could feel his warmth, the movement of his skin and muscles as he wrenched his body forcefully to the right.

Ilona opened her eyes. The tree was no longer there. Just yards and yards of snowy hill descending sharply before her, and beside her, Vlad who let out a huge, exhilarated yell.

Ilona couldn't help it. Her stomach was still somewhere at the top of the hill, her heart surely wrapped around the tree. But she laughed aloud and held on as the sleigh careered down the hill, controlled only by the weight of Vlad's body, drawing hers with it to left or right to avoid bushes and boulders.

At the foot, although the sleigh began to slow again, it still came to rest with a jolt that threw Ilona hard into Vlad's shoulder, winding her.

He didn't move, didn't turn to look at her.

She gasped, "You did that deliberately!"

"Yes."

She dragged her fingers free of his belt to punch his shoulder. Something caught at her breath—fury, joy. "Can we do it again?"

His body began to shake. Turning at last, he flung one arm around her and hugged her to him. It lasted only an instant, but still there was time to register the shock of his strong, hard body, to fear and to rejoice in his closeness.

"Another day," he said, still smiling. She imagined his lips in her hair, felt her own leaping response—and then his arm fell away to wave to his men approaching from around the foot of the hill. "We won!" he called with satisfaction.

Sibiu looked different. Even through the freshly falling snow, Ilona could see that Vlad had strengthened the town walls. But mostly, she thought it seemed different because *she* was.

Somehow, like last year's dinner at Hunedoara, she couldn't simply enjoy his company for the remainder of the journey. There was an edge to his companionship that churned her up, disturbed her beyond belief, and yet she wanted the journey to go on forever.

Reharnessed to the recovered horses, it didn't take long. Vlad didn't say much, and Ilona, lost in thought and feeling, spoke even less. Mostly, she watched him surreptitiously from the corner of her eye. Either he himself changed like the weather, or her perception of him did, for in the fading light he seemed sterner, more austere, a faint frown between his thick, black brows. For much of the time, he even forgot to tease her.

But once in Sibiu, he brought the sleigh to a sliding, gentle halt in the correct street. With perfect civility, he handed her out of the vehicle and conducted her into the house of her hosts for the night. Miserably, she sensed his desire to be gone as he bore the half-alarmed, half-gratified greetings of her parents' friends.

"Oh!" she cried, remembering only when she caught sight of her trunk being carried upstairs. "I have a letter for you from my uncle! One moment!"

"Let the maid...!" began her hostess, almost outraged, but Ilona could not be still.

She almost expected him to be gone when she returned with her uncle's letter, but he still waited patiently in the cramped hall, refusing all offers of refreshment. He even inclined his head to her as he reached for the letter.

Placing the crumpled paper into his hold, Ilona glimpsed again the dried blood on his knuckles. But now she saw something else too—the fresh trickle that came from his sleeve, that had already stained the white cuff of his shirt a bright red and continued to drip down his wrist and along the back of his hand.

Her eyes widened. "You're hurt!" she blurted. No wonder he'd been so silent in the second part of their journey. Looking back, she should have recognised the pain and the growing weakness in his secretive face, in his very silence. The signs had been there, only she, in her confusion, had been too wrapped up in her own foolish concerns.

"A scratch," he said distantly.

"I didn't know…"

"How could you?" He sounded amused now, until his hostess bustled over, demanding to see and treat his wound. Then he drew himself up until he seemed far taller than his actual average height.

"That won't be necessary. My own people will deal with it. Thank you for your kindness."

Cowed, poor Mihaela stepped back. Vlad bowed to Ilona. "Until tomorrow morning. We'll conduct you beyond the danger area and set you on the way to Sighisoara."

"There's no need," Ilona protested.

"It will be my honour," Vlad said implacably and waited for no more before sweeping from the room.

"Goodness," whispered Mihaela. "What a very alarming young man!"

"Hush!" said her husband, flapping his arm.

Ilona's laughter was decidedly shaky.

The morning brought not Vlad Dracula but a messenger with the bad news that rock falls and bad weather were blocking much of the road between Sibiu and Sighisoara, and that the prince suggested postponing her departure until tomorrow.

Ilona, anxious to be with her family, and convinced there would be a way round such obstacles, was all for travelling immediately, with or without her military escort, but her hosts absolutely forbade going against the advice of the governor of the city—especially now that they'd met him. And before Ilona, laughing in spite of herself, could talk them round, she had another visitor—Stephen of Moldavia who came, he said, to show her the city.

Mihaela, clearly seeing a distraction from Ilona's determination to leave, bundled her into fur cloak and muff, all the while pretending to be outraged. "My goodness, the Szilágyis have come up in the world. I remember when you were ordinary like us, and now you have princes at the door every day."

"Only exiled ones," Ilona pointed out.

"I don't think there's very much of the 'only' about these two," Mihaela said shrewdly.

Stephen seemed flatteringly pleased to see her, and asked all the questions Vlad had not, about her family and the health of the Hunyadis. He looked very dashing in a fur-trimmed blue hat and matching cloak, and it occurred to Ilona that he was actually more handsome than his cousin. It was just that something about Vlad tended to grab one's attention and keep it…

"I hear you've been sleigh-riding," Stephen teased as they paused on the stone bridge to watch the skaters on the frozen river beneath. "Not to say impromptu sledging!"

"He did that deliberately."

"I know, and he's sorry for it. Unfortunately, in some ways, he's a creature of impulse."

Ilona regarded him with a spark of curiosity. "I think you know him very well."

Stephen smiled slightly. "He's the best friend I'll ever have."

"You trust him."

It was hardly civil, implying as it did, that neither she nor anyone else did, but Stephen only said, "Yes." Then, as if feeling her gaze still on him, he turned and slouched against the bridge wall. "He came to us an exile, already a veteran fighter at the age of seventeen, offering my father his sword. We took him in because he was family, but he repaid us a hundred times over. He fought beside me in Moldavia, protected me at the risk of his own life many times when my inexperience would have got me killed; and again against Petru Aaron, who seized my father's throne. We lost that one, but he stayed with us."

He straightened and began to walk on over the bridge. "I've seen enough ambition and intrigue to know that such loyalty is rare in this world."

It was so much what she wanted to hear that, perversely, she argued, "I would not say your cousin is a stranger to ambition or intrigue."

"Lord, no, he's full to the brim of one and a past master of the other! That doesn't negate his other qualities. What I'm saying is—and I know Hungary trusts neither of us fully—Vlad doesn't give his loyalty or his friendship easily, but when he does, it's unchangeable."

"And who is he loyal to? Apart from your family?"

Stephen shrugged. "Memories, mostly. His father's and, especially, his brother."

"Radu?" He whose "affinity" for the Ottomans kept him with them still, despite the fact that he'd been freed years ago.

"No," Stephen confessed. "Not that I think he'd turn Radu away from his door. He protected him from the Ottomans when they were children, took his punishments, and kept him from harm when things were tough. The kind of 'tough' he'll never tell you," he added quickly, no doubt catching sight of the intended question forming on her lips. "But it was Mircea, his older brother, that he loved. Beyond even Vlad Dracul, I sometimes think. To be honest, that's why I sometimes fear..." He broke off, shrugging.

"Fear what?"

"I fear for him when he goes home. Too many ghosts. Too much revenge."

"*When* he goes home," she repeated, smiling faintly.

"Oh, he will, and within the next year. I don't doubt that."

"You don't grudge him it either," Ilona observed.

Stephen glanced at her. "How could I? His throne is the first step to my own. And why am I here with you talking about him?"

"Because I asked."

"He'll like that."

She cast him a quick, uncertain glance. "Why do you say that?"

"Because I would, in his shoes."

Understanding dawned, along with the laughter. "Are you flirting with me?" she asked, more pleased with herself for recognising it than anything else, and he grinned.

"I'm trying to."

"But why?"

"Maybe I'm hoping your father will entertain me when I'm Prince of Moldavia."

Ilona blinked. "My father is a great soldier, but the Szilágyis are not great nobles. We do not entertain princes!"

"When I'm Prince of Moldavia, who knows what will be true?"

Although she doubted the governor of Sibiu would come in person, especially since he was injured, he was the first person she saw when her kind hosts conducted her outside the following morning. Wearing a black cloak with a black fur hat, he stood by his horse's head, idly stroking the animal's nose until she emerged. His hands were gloved, and she could see no sign of his wound.

It was difficult to look at him, remembering that brief intimate moment in the sleigh at the foot of the hill. Although, curiously, it helped in the cold light of a new day to realise that to him it had been a mere instant of amusement, perhaps even relief that he hadn't hurt Hunyadi's niece by his insane action. He'd already confessed as much to Stephen.

In some ways, he's a creature of impulse…

No mercy. Kill them all.

The sky was brighter today and travelling beyond Sibiu not too difficult. Shut up in the coach once more with her maid, Ilona saw very little of her princely escort. Only as he prepared to leave her in the company of her original men-at-arms did they finally exchange more than politenesses.

Emerging from the inn where they'd changed the carriage horses and where she'd been given a bowl of warm, tasty soup, she found him in the courtyard instructing her men. He turned as she approached, saying, "You should be perfectly safe for the rest of the journey. If your father knows more, he'll send men from Sighisoara to meet you."

Ilona sighed. "It's all so uncertain these days."

"Hopefully it will be calmer after this coming year."

"How?" she demanded. "Everyone expects war with the Ottomans now."

"Oh, there will be war," Vlad agreed. "There has to be to restore any sort of security. Not just to prevent the Ottomans from taking Belgrade but to push them back. I doubt they'll leave Constantinople very easily, but we can certainly keep them out of Wallachia and Moldavia and reduce the threat to Hungary. Maybe then Europe will unite to push them out once and for all."

"Another crusade?" Ilona said doubtfully. "John of Capistrano is not the best recruiting officer."

"He's a little sh…swine,"Vlad said with unexpected feeling. John of Capistrano, the papal legate had come as inquisitor to root out heresy. His recently adopted cause of crusade against the Ottomans was having little success, largely because of the ill feeling he had already stirred up among Orthodox Christians—many of whom looked on the infidel Turks with more sympathy than they accorded Roman Catholics. "He doesn't even speak any useful language. But we need the Roman church if we're to have help from the west."

"We," she repeated.

His eyes glinted. "You will, of course, report my wholehearted adoption of Hungary's cause to your uncle?"

It was a challenge she could answer. "You don't care whether I do or not," she observed.

He inclined his head. "Actions speak louder than words."

No mercy. Kill them all. She shivered.

"You're cold," he said, opening the carriage door to hand her in. He paused, gazing down at her hand, which looked ridiculously small in his gloved one. He said, "Count Hunyadi bids me to Hunedoara next month. If you return then, my escort is at your disposal."

"Thank you," she managed. She began to step up, adding, "It's to be a council of war, I expect."

She thought his fingers convulsed briefly around hers, an uncontrollable spurt of excitement. And when she glanced at him, she saw his lower lip clamped over the upper before he let it go to smile.

He wanted war. He needed war, to win back Wallachia and to keep it.

"We need to be thinking of your marriage," Mihály Szilágyi said lazily as he watched her sisters and their husbands dance. The main hall of Katalina's house in Sighisoara was festively decorated with greenery and berries, the table pushed back to make space for games and dancing. They'd even hired a gypsy fiddler, whose music soared to the rafters, pulling everyone's spirits with it.

Ilona, still seated on the cushioned bench beside Mihály, smiled, because even her mother danced, and because this was a rare moment of quiet companionship with her father, in the midst of rushing children and noisy celebrations.

"We've been lax," Mihály said. "You're eighteen years old now. Perhaps after this summer, when things are more certain…"

When you're not in Belgrade, facing the lions. To distract herself from that line of thought, she teased, "Stephen of Moldavia was flirting with me in Sibiu."

"Was he indeed?" said her father, straightening with disapproval. "Stephen?" He frowned. "Not Vlad?"

She could feel the warm blood suffusing her face and neck. To cover it, she said hastily, "I don't believe Vlad does flirt."

Her father gave a bark of laughter. "That's not what I've heard. If we call it no worse. Stephen, you say?"

"Only very mildly," Ilona excused. "And respectfully. He must know that if and when he ever wins Moldavia, he'll look down his nose at the Szilágyis."

"No one looks down his nose at the Szilágyis."

Ilona blinked at him. Her father had certainly consumed more wine than normal, but it rarely addled his brains. "Even princes?"

Mihály shrugged. "Your sisters all married well, above their own rank. There's no reason why you shouldn't do even better. Especially…" He broke off.

Especially if John Hunyadi defeated the Ottomans at Belgrade and re-exerted all his old influence? Or did he mean more than that? She opened her mouth to ask, but before she could, she was pulled to her feet and swung into the hectic dance. And once again, politics and marriage and war faded into the distance.

"What will you do?" Ilona asked.

Vlad said, "I'll build myself a palace of gold and live there with my treasure and ten thousand exotically dressed servants who will feed me delicacies whenever I snap my fingers. And I'll hold banquets every night. Until I die of overeating."

Ilona regarded him. They rode side by side on horseback since the weather was better and the roads clearer. On either side of them, the snowy hills rolled back as far as the eye could see. In front and behind streamed Vlad's men, and somewhere in among them, her carriage, with the maid and her trunk.

Ilona watched his breath steaming patterns in the cold, dry air and kept silent until he glanced at her to see, perhaps, if she was offended by his mockery.

"So it's all about food?" she challenged.

"Of course. And palaces and costumes. I promise you, I will be a *gorgeous* prince. You're laughing at me," he added with mock indignation.

"No, no, I fully believe in your gorgeousness, Your Gorgeousness. I'm just wondering where you'll find the time to fight the Ottomans."

"I won't. They might tear my clothes."

Ilona laughed, and reached out to catapult snow from an over-hanging branch onto him. Just how she'd got from the discomfort of Sibiu to this easy, bantering companionship, she still wasn't sure. But she thought it had to do with him and his mood. He liked that Mihály Szilágyi had voluntarily entrusted him with his daughter. He liked going to Hunedoara to receive Hunyadi's orders for the coming season. If the truth were known, she was pretty sure he liked the Ottomans' war preparations providing the shake-up that could bring him back to Wallachia. And as his attitude dispelled her unease, she remembered why she'd always liked him.

But she hadn't forgotten Stephen's remarks in Sibiu.

While Vlad brushed snow off his shoulder, she said, "Then it's not really about revenge?"

His hand paused infinitesimally, then gave one final brush. "Food."

Ilona frowned. "Won't you be serious?" Why should he be? She was an eighteen-year-old girl who wouldn't understand men's concerns of government and policy.

"I am serious," he insisted. The heavy lids of his eyes lifted fully, allowing the green blaze of his eyes to dazzle her. "Food is vital. I want to clear vast swaths of the forests for arable land, so everyone can grow food, and we all eat and prosper. I'll endow the churches which use their land properly and guide the people spiritually. I'll encourage trade and manufacture to develop the towns. And everywhere, the rule of law will be paramount—no exceptions. Without crime and corruption, we'll prosper some more."

Ilona felt her eyes widen at the sudden flurry of quiet words, spoken quite without mockery. He waited for that, for her surprised admiration before he spoke again directly into her eyes. "And I will take my revenge on those who murdered my father and my brother, and on all those who oppose me. No mercy, Ilona Szilágyi. I will kill them all."

He thought, he really thought she would gasp in horror and ride away from him, perhaps scuttle back into her safe carriage. But although the words wrenched at her, she held his gaze without flinching.

"You're saying that to shock me," she said calmly.

"Why would I do that?"

"Because I questioned you. For the same reason you forced the sleigh down the hill when the harness broke."

This time it was his eyes that widened. It gave her some satisfaction. Then he threw back his head and laughed, a clear, ringing sound, rare enough to turn the heads of several of his men.

Chapter Seven

*V*lad had seen her that morning when he'd ridden out with Count Szelényi. The back of his neck had prickled as it did when he was under observation, and he'd turned and seen her at the window, watching him.

For an instant, the world stood still. She seemed like part of the pale, grey-and-gold dawn, an insubstantial wraith conjured from the morning air or his own imagination. A wraith in an ugly grey shift with a halo of stunning auburn hair tumbled around her white shoulders and the delicate blades of her clavicles. For an instant she stood perfectly still, framed in the palace window like a painting, and he'd been afraid to breathe in case the vision vanished.

Then her arms jerked upward, perhaps to cover herself, but one hand caught and dragged at her hair in a gesture so achingly familiar that the years of pain and fury rolled away. Her face, her whole person seemed to crumple, and she disappeared. As if the picture had fallen off the wall.

The metaphor had stayed with him throughout the day, reminding him that his mind's image of her was twelve years old. More uncomfortable to contemplate was her image of him. He could not doubt that her first glimpse of him in twelve years had upset her. He could not doubt that for whatever reasons, she wanted—*expected*—to be excused this marriage. Erzsébet Hunyadi and Count Szelényi had both told him so.

He didn't understand what was going on in her head. But he knew one thing: all was not well with Ilona Szilágyi. She couldn't stop the marriage—women never could—but she could destroy a great deal of what he was building.

And so when Szelényi told him of his conversation with her in the garden, he made up his mind. They'd been living in the same building for days, and at this rate they wouldn't even meet until the betrothal. Patience was a virtue he had cultivated over his years of imprisonment but with indifferent success, and Ilona's avoidance had gone far enough. It was time to end it.

And so he strode with some purpose through the palace corridors, forcing Szelényi to quicken his pace, ignoring his jailer's whispered pleas that he think again before acting. Since it was the formal dinner hour, they encountered only a few straggling courtiers rushing along corridors to further their ambitions. Most took the trouble to bow to him on the way past, a respect which he acknowledged briskly. Only as they entered the female quarters did he encounter curious stares from well-dressed women who clearly wondered what the devil he was doing there. Sooner or later they'd put two and two together, and that would pile yet more pressure on Ilona. Well, he'd no objection to that either.

Count Szelényi paused at the foot of two steps on the left, which led up to a closed door, and glanced at him. "Sir, won't you reconsider?" he asked again.

The corridor was empty. Pity, Vlad thought savagely.

"No," he said and reached past his jailer to knock on the door.

"At least permit me to announce you," Szelényi pleaded. "Your position and hers demand that."

Smart bastard, Vlad thought with a flicker of amusement, because the man was using Vlad's own insistence on his rank against him. With exaggerated graciousness, he stood aside once more, just as a woman opened the door. A pretty woman, still young. Her bright blue eyes suggested intelligence, the softness of her mouth, good nature. Lines of anxiety surrounded both pleasing features.

Szelényi said, "Prince Vlad is here to speak with Countess Ilona, if the lady is here…"

The lady was here. Vlad could *feel* her. He moved, forcing Szelényi to step inside. The woman fell back in alarm, and Vlad strode past them both.

He saw her at once, wide-eyed with shock, her pale lips falling open. She stood the length of the room away from him, framed in the doorway of her bedchamber. The grey wraith of the morning had become a grey frump. Ugly clothes, an unbecoming veil askew on her head, revealing a clump of straggling grey hair, and behind it, one strand of dark red-gold.

Vlad drank her in, saw what she'd become, what she was hiding. Her beauty, her *life*. Behind the dull, ugly garb of the penitent. *No, oh no, I will not allow that.*

He kept walking, ignoring the moan of fear that escaped her parted lips, the squeak of protest from her attendant. She jerked once, as if trying to back away, but she seemed paralysed, unable to move. Her eyes grew huge, racked with pain and memory like his, surely like his.

He didn't stop until he was right in front of her, could feel the trembling of her body. In one swift, deliberately startling movement, he raised his right hand and swept the grey veil from her head.

As it fluttered to the floor, she made an instinctive grab for it and missed. Through the tangle of her lovely, burnished hair, streaked now with grey down one side, she returned her gaze to his. Huge and wet, her desperate, dark eyes stared at him—with shame, it was true, but also with an echo of the old defiance.

"Tag," he said. "What now, Ilona Szilágyi?"

Her eyes widened impossibly. Her trembling lips parted.

"*Now*," said Countess Hunyadi's furious voice from behind him, "you leave the room until you can meet in a more appropriate place!"

Damn the woman, she had always had ears like a dog's, and old age seemed only to have sharpened them further. And of course, the attendant was there too, a protective arm around her lady's waist.

"My lady is not well," she said, clearly intending, despite her own fright, to help Ilona back into the bedchamber. Ilona, however, appeared to be still rooted to the spot.

As Countess Hunyadi swept across the room, ordering, "Take her inside!" Ilona's hands lifted. For an instant, Vlad thought they were reaching for him. And then her eyes closed, as if to hide the tears she couldn't stop. But her eyelids only squeezed them down her cheeks faster. She swallowed once, like a gulp.

"I want everyone to leave." Though her voice shook, the words were clear enough.

Vlad, who knew he could clear the room in one short sentence, was forestalled in doing so by Countess Hunyadi, who said fiercely, "I will not go until he does."

"Oh God." That was Ilona, halfway between desperation and hysterical laughter. "Then I will go." And instead of retreating backwards with the force of her woman's urging, she stepped forward, brushing past him, clearly with every intention of leaving the room.

He could stop her, physically. The thin body which touched his so briefly was pathetically frail. He could eject everyone else and do what he came here to do. Only this was not how he intended it to happen—reinforcing every word of his terrible reputation. And somewhere, somewhere he didn't even want to acknowledge right now, he couldn't do it because she didn't wish it.

"There is no need," he said, in his most distant, princely voice. "I shall leave until you—feel better." She paused, her back to him now. "You *will* feel better in the morning?"

Everyone in the room seemed to hold their breath. Then Ilona nodded, once.

"In the gallery," Countess Hunyadi ordered. "It is a good place to talk."

In public. Under a thousand eyes.

"I will ensure your privacy," she added regally.

Privacy of speech, perhaps. A few yards of space. And still the thousand eyes beyond. It was not what he wanted, but at least he could talk enough to calm her, make her allow him the space he needed to do this properly.

"Very well," Vlad allowed. "Ten o'clock." It felt more like arranging a duel. He walked past her this time, careful not to touch her. When he turned to bow from the doorway, he half expected her to be safely bolted behind her bedchamber door. There were enough people fluttering behind him in that direction as he walked. But she still stood where he'd last seen her, flanked by the attendant and the countess. She held herself rigid, as if she would shatter if she let anything go for an instant.

Jesus, what have they done to her?

What have I?

The questions stayed with him, nagging unendurably as he strode back to his comfortable prison and let Szelényi lock him in. It was a formality, one that would be over with his betrothal tomorrow. But somehow, this massive step on his road to freedom and restoration had sunk to the realms of trivia.

His plan had got stuck on the vague but desperately troubled face of what should have been its joyful centre.

Don't do this to me, Ilona Szilágyi... Don't do this to yourself.

It seemed to be too late. Whatever it was had already been done to her, and he had no idea if he could undo it.

As darkness fell, he threw himself on the bed. He hadn't allowed the servant to light the lamps as he usually did, so there was little to distract him from his own thoughts. Only a blank darkness in which to conjure up a thousand images and memories of Ilona. What had happened to the triumph of winning her once more? It was lost in the ghosts, and he was haunted by images of the Ilona he'd just seen, tired, frightened, and unworldly. Images of her mother, sick and dying, of Maria, distraught and broken. Ilona, wild with grief and love and guilt. And himself, Vlad Dracula, villain of a thousand stories and legends. Vlad the Impaler, a fierce and terrible tyrant.

He wanted to impale Countess Hunyadi on a very high stake. Second only to bloody Matthias's.

How in hell did he go about making that right? He couldn't undo the past; he'd always known that. All he could do was build a new future. And for the first time, he doubted that that would be enough for her...

A knock sounded at the door, breaking into his boiling, unpalatable thoughts. A very faint knock, nothing like Szelényi's cheery tattoo or the servant's dull thudding. Frowning, Vlad swung his legs off the bed and stood. He still wore his boots.

"Enter," he commanded.

The soft knock sounded once more. But there was no way whoever was outside wouldn't have heard him. Years of such encounters had taught him precisely how to pitch his voice to avoid confusion.

An unlikely idea caught at his breath. His heart beat and beat as he walked toward the door. A light shone underneath it, shadowed by the swishing of a skirt.

The women who assuaged his bodily needs came at his command, not at their own whim. Erzsébet Hunyadi would not knock like a thief in the night. Which left...

The woman? Had she sent her faithful attendant?

No, Ilona Szilágyi possessed too much pride for that. Or, she had once...

Vlad laid his cheek against the cool wood of the door and closed his eyes, trying to sense the presence on the other side, listening in vain for the sound of her breathing. Afraid to be wrong. And yet if he didn't speak, she would leave, and he would have lost this chance too.

"Ilona?"

Then at last he heard her breath, a gentle shudder as she drew nearer the door.

"Vlad Dracula," she whispered.

How has it come to this?

The words sliced through her pain as she drove them all finally from her apartment, and stayed with her through the darkening of the lonely night.

How had she, the most private of people, who had hugged that privacy ever more tightly around her with the passage of years, come to be seen in this condition by so many? Her aunt, a total stranger, her faithful Margit, and *him.*

Above all, him. Why in God's name had he come?

Because he doesn't know what's going on. He has the chance of free-dom, of restoration, and you're pulling against his plan.

And he didn't know why. He was fulfilling his old promise without understanding that if Matthias wanted him in Wallachia, he'd put him there with or without Ilona. She was an easy gift, and Vlad's pride would make him take it. Even now, when he'd seen her in all her "glory."

Ilona closed her eyes, laying her forehead on the cold glass of the darkened window. How long ago was it she had watched from another window as he'd come into view below? With Stephen, once his best friend… And Maria, once hers, had seen him too and fled down to them to make her pathetic attempt at seduc-tion and save her reputation by trickery. Ilona hadn't been able to watch. Knowing he would reject Maria, riddled with jealousy in case he didn't.

Tonight there was nothing to see, but she closed her eyes anyway.

It didn't take away the image of his face, the fierce gleam of mockery in his blazing green eyes. *"Tag. What now, Ilona Szilágyi?"*

So like the man she remembered that even now the pain in her chest caught at her breath. He had come to her, to talk. He had tagged her, and she was It. The next move was hers.

"He remembered," she whispered, wrapping both arms around herself and hugging. "He remembered." And she wanted to weep again, because it was no longer enough. There was what he remembered, and there was *this*. This Ilona she was now.

But even this Ilona would not spoil his plan, and she had to tell him so. Tomorrow. In the gallery. Under the watchful eye of her aunt, possibly even the king himself. And behind them a thousand others. It was what he had tried to avoid by coming here tonight.

Maybe he was right. Maybe it would have been the best thing. Only Aunt Erzsébet had come in, snarling for a fight, and Count Szelényi, the amiable stranger she could never look in the eye again, was there too. And Margit... What did Margit think of her now?

Do I care?

She opened her eyes, staring out into the night. The sky was clear and black, showering a million stars down on the world. On her.

She was It, and it was her time to act. Not tomorrow. Now.

Her breath caught at the boldness of the idea. It had been a long time since she'd done anything more outrageous than missing mass to care for her garden. But she knew where he was, where they kept him. She'd made it her business to find out, so that she could more easily avoid him. Well, she couldn't avoid it anymore.

Her stomach twisted, her heart drummed in her breast, but her mind was made up. Pinning the ugly veil back onto her hair at last, she left Margit asleep on her pallet and crept through the dark, empty corridors to go to him.

She knew the door was his. In an otherwise unlived-in passage, it was particularly stout. And when she lifted her lamp, she could see the heavy lock holding it in place. On the other hand, no light shone under it from inside. He must be asleep.

The disappointment was like a blow. She knew she should go back to her room before she was discovered here. People wouldn't think less of her for visiting her betrothed—until he no longer was. But it would be embarrassing all the same. Especially with a locked door between them.

Mocking herself, she lifted her hand and knocked softly. Over the beating of her own heart, she heard a faint, rustling sound. His voice said, "Enter!" loudly enough to make her jump. And so, unable to speak, she knocked again.

She heard his footsteps, measured and firm, cross the floor. Then, silence.

Speak, Ilona, tell him you're here! But her throat had closed up. "Ilona?"

It was little more than a breath, so close he might have been speaking against the door itself. Her throat opened.

"Vlad Dracula," she whispered.

There was a pause, then, "I'd offer you a seat, but there is this obstacle between us."

She didn't know whether to laugh or cry. Instead, she lifted her hand, placing it over the spot his voice seemed to come from, and closed her eyes. *Vlad. Vlad.*

"I can still manage to stand." She swallowed. "I'm sorry. There were too many people before. And I couldn't wait until tomorrow."

"For what?"

"To talk to you. I tried to tell you before…"

"That I can change my mind and not dishonour you or me?"

"Yes," she said, relieved as so often in the past by his quick understanding.

"Why would I do that?"

The abrupt question threw her, but only for a moment. "Because you don't need me. Matthias will support you with or without me."

"Circumstances will always determine Matthias's support, or lack of it," he said impatiently. "It isn't about Matthias or honour. Yours or mine. It never was."

Gladness rose up, swift, aching, unendurable. Without meaning to, she laid her cheek on the door. "I know," she whispered. "But that was before. I'm not the Ilona you remember. You've seen me, I am—*old...*"

"I am still seven years older. When did age come into it?"

"Don't be obtuse, Vlad. You need a young wife who can give you an heir."

"I have an heir."

"A legitimate heir would please the Church better."

"Then we shall marry quickly."

"Oh, Vlad, don't be so stubborn!" Her fingers curled into the door, as if embracing the stubbornness her words reproved. "Have you learned nothing in these twelve years? There is too much between us. Too much tragedy, too much guilt. I can't live with that. I can't live with *you* because of it."

She could hear his breath through the door, as if he held her. Her arms ached.

His voice husky, he said, "Can you live without me now?"

"I've lived twelve years without you," she whispered. Tears gathered in her throat, threatening to choke her all over again.

"I said *live.*"

Oh Jesus, did he still see everything? "As I did then? Without a thought for the hurt or the care of others? Something died in me after that, and now I don't know which I want more—my own peace, or your happiness."

"I'll give you both."

She couldn't help smiling till her mouth ached. Probably there was only an inch of wood between her lips and his. "Peace with *you*, Vlad? Don't make me laugh."

"I want to make you laugh. I want you by my side."

"You want Wallachia." *But thank you, thank you for saying it…* She touched her lips to the door, a last kiss and one he would never know about, let alone feel.

He said, "I can't have you without Wallachia. You're the king's cousin."

Her lips froze against the wood. Her heart beat and beat. She gasped. "Vlad, stop, I'm old and tired—you've *seen* me…"

"And you're twelve years more beautiful. Though your dressmaker should be impaled."

A sob that was more than half laughter spilled out of her mouth, and this time, she heard unmistakable relief in his voice. "I was afraid they'd turned you against me. Irrevocably."

"I stopped paying attention, Vlad, but I was never stupid."

"Then smile when you promise yourself to me. And mean it."

She could have sworn his breath touched her through the warm wood. She could smell him, taste him on her lips. Like wine after a long thirst. Her body stirred, remembering.

She whispered, "Is that the solution after all? Back on the sleigh ride…with you?"

A door slammed somewhere farther along the passage, and she jumped, gasping. "Someone's coming! I have to go."

Yet she'd only dashed a few paces when, on impulse, she turned and ran back. "Vlad?" she whispered. She thought he'd have gone, back to bed perhaps, at any rate too far away to hear her.

But his voice returned at once, so close it made her shiver. "Yes?"

"I'm glad your waiting is over."

King Matthias was grumpy at being wakened so early just to receive a messenger. Sitting up in bed, he snatched the accompanying letter from the silver tray with ill grace and tore it open.

After a moment, he began to laugh. The messenger looked shocked.

"Good news for my mother," he said jovially. "My sister is a widow."

His chamberlain picked up the dropped letter. "I cannot imagine it will cause the countess great joy."

"Of course it will," said Matthias flippantly. "Her precious Ilona's off the hook. We'll stick my sister on it instead. At least she'll be some use to us."

Chapter Eight

Wallachia and Transylvania, 1456

Under the boiling sun, Vladislav fought with surprising fury. He'd been defeated by a small army of exiles and mercenaries, and the country had risen up against him. Vladislav had lost, and he must have known it, yet, here at Targsor, surrounded by his halfhearted men-at-arms, he alone fought with conviction.

It was how Vlad recognised him and was able to force his way through the melee to meet him. Shoving aside the two who already engaged him, Vlad raised his father's sword and looked into his kinsman's eyes.

Neither of them wore helmets.

Vladislav smiled. "At last. I've been waiting for you."

"Anxious to die, like your sorry supporters?"

"You're my last hope, Vlad Dracula. You've taken my country, but I can still get it back by one simple act."

He lunged at Vlad, his stroke powerful and unexpectedly quick, managing to draw blood from Vlad's shoulder, slicing just outside the breastplate. But Vlad's sword had largely deflected the blow, and the sudden despair in Vladislav's face said that he knew it was the only chance he'd be given. Nevertheless, he fought fiercely and could have done considerable damage against anyone else. But Vlad, who hadn't slept in three nights and was living on a volatile combination of determination and nervous excitement, with destiny on his shoulder and no possibility of failure in his heart, was invincible.

Vladislav knew it too. The deathblow seemed almost to come as a relief to him in the end. Vlad's cut to his arm had already ripped tendons, and he could no longer hold his sword, which fell to the ground with a dull thud. It was all Vlad needed. With one mighty stroke, he severed his kinsman's head.

Vlad gazed down at the broken, fallen body of his enemy, waiting for the inevitable triumph, for the sense of fulfillment to invade him and let him rest.

Vlad had wanted this for so long, played the scene so often in his head, his final victory over his father's killer. And yet there he lay, just one more death in the greater struggle for power. While John Hunyadi engaged the Ottomans at Belgrade, Vlad had won this smaller war for him. There would be no Ottoman attacks through Wallachia and Transylvania. Vlad had given his word, and he would keep faith. It didn't interfere with his own agenda.

Stephen stood beside him, nodding slowly. "It's over," he said, something approaching wonder in his voice. "You've done it."

Vlad lifted his gaze beyond the fallen men and the cheering victors. Before him lay the nervous little town of Targsor and the majestic countryside of his homeland, spreading out through low hills and valleys, over gentle lakes and rushing rivers to the mountains that must keep it safe.

"Oh no," he said softly. "I haven't even begun."

John Hunyadi was dead.

For Maria, the news was more devastating than the loss of her own husband. As Ilona had prophesied, she'd grown fond of Dragomir, but her grief at his passing was not unmixed with annoyance, because he'd backed the wrong horse. Even when so many of the other boyars left Prince Vladislav, either secretly or blatantly, to support the exile, Vlad Dracula, Dragomir had thrown everything behind Vladislav in the belief that the prince's alliance with the sultan would bring most benefit.

And though she didn't pay much attention to political matters, Maria could see why he might think so. No one really believed that the Christian states of Europe, not even the White Knight, John Hunyadi himself, could organise any kind of viable resistance to Ottoman invasion.

And when the Ottomans finally made their long-expected attack on Belgrade, even the brave heart of its commandant, Mihály Szilágyi, Ilona's father, must have quailed to see the tiny size of the force John Hunyadi led to his aid. If it hadn't been for the crusading rabble which appeared out of nowhere thanks to the no longer quite so awful Roman churchman John of Capistrano, Belgrade would surely have been lost.

Or so she'd heard people say. At any rate, Hunyadi had won his last great victory and died three weeks later of the plague which the Ottomans carried everywhere in their wake. The same plague had done for the papal legate.

But she hadn't known any of this when Vlad Dracula swept into Wallachia and ruthlessly took back his throne. Dragomir had died fighting him, as had Prince Vladislav himself. She hadn't known about Hunyadi when she'd dressed this morning, and presented herself as bidden in Vlad Dracula's public hall at Tîrgovişte. She'd come to plead for her stepson's life and estates, and people had said John Hunyadi was dead. The countess would be devastated…and her children…and Ilona.

Someone called her name, impatiently, as if it had been said several times before. She moved forward in a dream, not thinking as she should, *I'm about to meet Vlad Dracula, who holds the power of life and death over me and the boy,* but thinking, *John Hunyadi is dead.*

And then the gaggle of lawyers and clerks and noblemen parted to let her through, and she thanked God she'd taken the trouble to dress well for the occasion.

Before her, on a high, ornately carved throne, sat Vlad Dracula. Not the young soldier who'd let her kiss him before he rejected her. But the Prince of Wallachia in all his splendour. He wore a red silk hat encrusted with rows of pearls and jewels, a red velvet mantle with golden buttons, and a snowy collar of the finest lace, and he looked every inch the stern, implacable ruler.

Her legs began to shake as she took the final few steps to the throne and knelt. Someone may have told her to, but mostly, she thought, her knees just gave way.

She couldn't look at him. Those dark green eyes were like shards of ice, hard and cold and piercing. His face was so haughty, she could only pray he didn't remember her from Hunedoara.

"I know you," he said, and she shivered as much at the sound of his voice as at his words. Only later did she realise it was the first time she'd heard him speak Romanian. Slowly, knowing the game was up, she lifted her head and met his gaze. "You attended Countess Hunyadi."

"Is it true he's dead?" she blurted.

The green eyes darkened. His eyelids dropped like hoods, and when they lifted once more, she read nothing more than the original ice. And yet she could have sworn there had been a storm of pain and fury. Certainly he didn't ask who she meant. He knew.

"Yes, it's true."

"That is…awful."

"Yes," he said again. "It is." And surely there was a hint of amusement in there now. She didn't dare risk a smile, but she didn't look away either. "And yet I think you would have been better staying at Hunedoara."

"It was the countess who arranged my marriage."

"You have not brought your son," he observed.

My son. That was one loss she would never get over. Dragomir had agreed to marry her, to gain Hunyadi's valuable friendship as well as a beautiful young wife—but not to bring up another man's son as his own, even though he already had an heir. And so she had given birth in secret on one of the Hunyadis' smaller estates, and the child had been given to a well-to-do free farmer and his wife. Part of her heart had stayed there when she'd come to Wallachia as Dragomir's bride.

But of course, the prince did not mean that son. He meant Dragomir's.

"My husband's son is only eight years old. It didn't seem fitting to bring him."

"Or safe?" asked Vlad.

Maria's eyes flickered. They said he'd already butchered entire families to punish those who'd stood against him.

Vlad's lips twisted. "In the absence of trustworthy relatives to care for his estates, we shall do so. In the meantime, upon swearing allegiance to me, he—and you—may live on them."

Someone almost dragged her to her feet and out of his presence.

I've done it, she thought in wonder. *I've done it…*

Ilona clung convulsively to her father. Beyond words, they both knew that it could so easily have been his body brought home by John Hunyadi. There were many—probably including Mihály Szilágyi himself—who believed that would have been a better outcome for the world. But Ilona wasn't one of them. If there was guilt in her fierce joy at her father's survival, it couldn't overwhelm it.

Her father's arms loosened. She knew why. Slowly, she drew herself out of his embrace and stepped back.

Countess Hunyadi stood in the doorway, the wind catching at her veil. Erzsébet's wailing was done. Not her weeping, but the basic, uncontrollable element of her grief. White-faced and drawn, she stood poker straight, forcing herself to look at the carriage which brought her husband to her for the last time.

Mihály Szilágyi said, "Forgive me. I never thought to have such unhappiness in bringing him to Hunedoara. Like the rest of the world, I thought he would live forever."

Erzsébet nodded. "Thank you for bringing him here and not…"

Not to Hungary, not to the king, who had done so little to help but who would now take credit for the victory of Belgrade. But she broke off, unable to continue.

"It was one of his final wishes."

"László?"

"In command of Belgrade. He feels the loss of his father deeply, but he'll do his duty."

She nodded again. She didn't say she wanted him here instead, but Ilona knew. She thought her heart would burst from pity, from her own grief.

But more than that, who would look after Hungary and Transylvania, who would pull the strings and wield the sword to keep the Ottomans at bay now that the White Knight of Christendom was dead?

"I will," said Mihály Szilágyi.

It was when they heard the news that László Hunyadi had nearly destroyed everything. Left with the awesome responsibility of governing Belgrade, he'd invited the young king to visit the scene of the great victory. And when King Ladislas had graciously arrived with his favoured followers among the hated Cilli clan, László had pulled up the drawbridge before his men-at-arms could follow. After that, Count Cilli had been killed—whether by László himself or one of his henchmen was unclear.

Ilona knew why. Furious with grief, László was avenging the many slights and insurmountable obstacles placed in the way of his father by this self-serving and much lesser man. He'd probably even enjoyed his brief power over the surely terrified young king, though in the end Ladislas had left the fortress unharmed and László continued as governor of Belgrade and of Transylvania in his father's stead. But for how much longer? If the Cillis had been enemies before, how much was the feud aggravated now? Worse, whatever things appeared on the surface, he must have made an open enemy of the king. And that meant the whole family was in danger.

And if the Hunyadis fell, what would become of Hungary and the network of alliances and balances that had kept the kingdom safe for so many years? Strong hands were needed at the helm, to placate the king and to guide him. In the long term, it would be László and young Matthias. Right now, it had to be Ilona's father.

"And I will," said Erzsébet in a small, hard voice, and when her brother glanced at her in surprise, a sour smile curved her thin lips. "For twenty years I have been the consort of the man who effectively ruled Hungary. I may be a woman, but I am not no one. János rose high—with our backing, my sons will rise higher yet."

Ilona, forgotten in the background as she often was, lifted her head, struck by something in the countess's voice.

"Higher than John Hunyadi?" she blurted in disbelief. "Why that would make them…"

"Hold your tongue, Ilona," said Mihály.

Ilona closed her mouth and swallowed. She understood, finally, that they'd talked about this before, that John Hunyadi himself had not ruled out the ultimate promotion of his son—to King of Hungary.

She had a bad feeling about it.

Mihály said, "We must consider our position, strengthen all alliances, make new ones. First of all, László and Matthias must be kept apart at all times. I'll leave at once to see the king and try to mitigate what László has done, but you must make László understand the danger he's now in."

Erzsébet nodded. "Perhaps it's time I too went again to court. You'd like that, wouldn't you, Ilona? We might even find you a suitable husband at last." Ilona, feeling slightly hunted under both pairs of eyes, looked from one to the other. Erzsébet said consideringly, "She's quite an attraction in her own right, Mihály. She can only help our cause. And if she can just learn when to keep her mouth shut and stop asking the wrong questions, she'll be a positive asset."

"What cause?" Ilona asked. Her deliberate provocation went over Erzsébet's head, busy as she was in her own plans, but Mihály frowned at her.

"We need you, Ilona," he said briskly. "Go and prepare your own and your aunt's things for court. We travel immediately. Prepare for a long absence. After Hungary, I may take you to Wallachia."

Ilona tugged once at her hair, a tiny gesture of agitation, but she'd already stood to obey.

"Keep young Vlad on the straight and narrow," Erzsébet approved. "No slipping back toward the Ottomans."

"There's that," Mihály allowed. "And also that if it comes to a struggle, we're going to need him on our side."

"What the hell is he doing?" Stephen asked.

He'd come in search of Vlad that evening, imagining there would be some kind of celebration. In Dracula's first major diplomatic victory of his reign, he'd managed to convince the Ottomans that Transylvania was too strong for them to attack it this year. Very cleverly, he'd enlisted the help of the major Transylvanian towns to do this, having them send major, powerful-looking delegations to Tîrgovişte while the Ottoman ambassadors were there. And so Transylvania also saw how the new Prince of Wallachia protected them and prevented the Ottomans attacking them through Wallachia.

It had come at a price, of course—the inevitable one of swearing allegiance to the sultan and promising tribute. Despite the fact that he'd already sworn allegiance to the Hungarian king. Balkan princes had to preserve a highly precarious balance to maintain the independence of their countries and Stephen was well aware he'd just received a masterful lesson from his cousin. When he ruled neighbouring Moldavia, it would be beyond useful.

But now, the Ottomans had gone home to report to the sultan the unwisdom of raiding Transylvania this season, and the Transylvanians had gone home with renewed friendship for Vlad. It seemed to Stephen that everyone had won. And yet when he came to join in the celebrations of the court, Vlad was nowhere to be found.

Finally, Stephen had tracked him to an open piece of ground outside the palace walls. It was dark, the good citizens were mostly in bed, and the nobility celebrating either in the palace or in their own homes. Even those who had once opposed Vlad's succession were coming round to him, having been granted a glimpse of his brilliance and determination. Like Carstian, whom he'd recently made governor of the fortress of Tîrgovişte, an act of trust in this newly sworn vassal that Stephen hoped would not come back to haunt him.

Vlad was not given to instinctive trust, of course. Carstian must have proved himself in some way. If this was a risk, it was a calculated one. For in this quiet little field, some yards away from

Vlad, stood Carstian himself, watching unhappily while Vlad dug a hole in the ground.

It wasn't the first hole either. The field looked as if it had a plague of giant moles.

"What the hell *is* he doing?" Stephen repeated.

In his shirtsleeves, the Prince of Wallachia was efficiently and steadily digging, his upper body bending and straightening, his arms working the spade without respite.

Carstian stirred. "You remember that his brother died in Tîrgovişte?"

"Mircea?" For the first time, a twinge of unease twisted through Stephen's half-amused amazement at his cousin's behaviour.

"Rumours say he was buried alive."

"I heard that rumour. So did Vlad."

Carstian nodded. To Stephen's relief, Vlad flung down the spade, but instead of striding across to his friends, he crouched down and reached into the ground.

Carstian said, "I wasn't here. I was with Vlad Dracul until he was killed, and then I returned to my estates. The prince knows that. But he asked me to find out."

"Find out what?"

"Where Mircea is buried."

Stephen swore. "He can't do that. He can't rule his country now from the perspective of the past! He'll ruin everything, *lose* everything..."

Without waiting for Carstian, to whom he'd probably said too much anyway—the man had that effect on people—he strode across the field toward Vlad, who sat back on his heels, staring into the hole he'd just dug.

"Vlad you have to leave this obsession. Now."

Vlad didn't glance at him. He didn't seem to be even remotely surprised that he was there.

"What obsession would that be?"

"Mircea!" Stephen stepped forward, laying his hand on his cousin's shoulder. Forcing his voice to greater gentleness, he said, "You have to let your brother rest in peace."

"Does that look like peace to you?"

"What?" Instinctively, Stephen glanced in the direction of Vlad's gaze, into the hole. By the light of the lantern placed beside it, he saw what looked, stupidly, like a smooth, pale, misshapen ball. The back of a skull.

Stephen swallowed. "That could be anyone."

"It's Mircea."

"He spoke to you?" Fear made him sarcastic; a need to jerk Vlad out of it made him unkind.

"Yes," said Vlad. "He spoke to me. He said, 'They threw me into this pit, facedown, and piled soil on top of me until I suffocated. My mouth and nose and eyes were full of dirt; the weight was unbearable. I couldn't breathe in anything but mud until my heart burst and my lungs...'"

"Vlad, stop it!"

Vlad lifted his head at last, gazed into Stephen's frightened face. His eyes were opaque, not weeping as Stephen had feared.

"You can't know that," Stephen said.

"I can."

"What will you do?" Carstian spoke the words Stephen was too afraid to ask.

When Vlad didn't answer at once, Stephen blurted, "Don't burn the bridges you've built here, Vlad. If this is true, the crime wasn't committed by one man."

"I know who was responsible."

Stephen said, "You made him find that out too?"

"Carstian? No. I listened and I looked and I learned."

"Don't do anything hasty," Stephen begged.

Vlad stood. "I told you years ago. Revenge is a dish best served cold. Go and fetch a priest."

"It's a bit late for that!"

Vlad turned on him. Though his limbs never moved, Stephen felt as though he'd been struck. As if Vlad's pain had somehow slammed into Stephen's body.

"Fetch a priest. My brother will have a proper burial." Picking up the spade, he began to uncover the rest of the body.

While Carstian moved swiftly and silently in search of the nearest priest, Stephen watched helplessly as Vlad uncovered the bones of his dead brother, lifted them, and placed them faceup in his cloak for a shroud. Only then, when he laid his brother back in the ground, did something fall into the grave. A drop that glittered like rain from the clear sky.

Vlad dashed his dirt-spattered arm across his face, as if wiping sweat away, and turned to face the priest.

"Say the words," he whispered.

It was Vlad's birthday. He used the occasion to hold his first formal reception purely for entertainment. Previous affairs had been designed to receive the homage of his vassals or the ambassadors of foreign countries. This would be a more relaxed event, an opportunity to know his boyars better and let them know him, the man behind the splendour. Or at least as much as he chose to reveal.

Using the gold he'd found in Vladislav's coffers, he served them fine wines from Hungary and Italy, the best local meat and poultry, cooked to perfection, and the most elegant of sweetmeats and pastries prepared by his Italian-trained cook. He hired the best musicians that could be located, and after the banquet, there was dancing.

Vlad didn't care to dance, but he'd been taught in his childhood, along with all the other princely arts, and he knew his duty. To open the occasion, he led out the wife of Lord Tacal, his most senior boyar, and set out to entertain her. It wasn't difficult. At least the woman danced well and possessed a sharp intelligence that made it easy to converse. Although she was an experienced and well-mannered lady, she couldn't quite hide that he surprised her.

Vlad wanted to laugh. Which was when he caught sight of Maria, Countess Hunyadi's old attendant and informant. Presumably she was still informing, though on him rather than his predecessor. She was dancing some distance away, but as if she sensed his brief scrutiny, she glanced up and cast him a quick, surprised smile from under her lashes.

Unexpected memory wakened. Seated at John Hunyadi's table, catching something very like the same glance. Several times. While he'd been talking to Ilona Szilágyi, the girl with the laughing brown eyes that had no right to look so soft when they pierced like a sword point. Of course, Ilona was Mihály's daughter.

Maria was not high on his list of people to entertain, but he didn't forget her. Later in the evening, he approached her and asked if she was enjoying herself.

"Oh yes!" said Maria with the enthusiasm of a child. "And please allow me to congratulate you and wish you many happy returns." The difference between this confident woman and the frightened supplicant who'd come to him in the summer was marked. Intrigued, Vlad teased her.

"Thank you. I think you must find your estates very dull."

"Very," she agreed frankly, then, as she realised what she'd said, her eyes flew back to his. "That is, I'm so grateful to have them, only living on them…"

"…can be tedious," Vlad sympathised. "Nothing, I imagine, like your old position with Countess Hunyadi. How *is* the countess?"

"Well, I believe. Though devastated by the loss of her husband."

"It must be a comfort to her to have your understanding."

Maria looked blank. She may have picked up his hint of sarcasm.

"Having lost your own husband," Vlad reminded her gently.

"Oh! Well, it *might* be…"

"Then what do the two of you talk about in those long letters?"

Maria blinked with incomprehension. "Countess Hunyadi never wrote to me in her life! But then, to be fair, I think I only ever wrote to her once, after I was married. Ilona writes to me, though, which is how I know the countess is well."

For some reason, that annoyed him. His half-formed plan to take Maria to bed tonight—it was unfinished business, after all, and part of him rather liked the idea of suborning the Hunyadis' informant by seduction—died before it was born.

In the end, he took an older lady, a widow like Maria, and quite as passionate and urgent. She had the advantage of lacking Maria's connections.

Chapter Nine

Visegrád, Hungary, 1474

Ilona woke to birds' song and the knowledge that things had changed. For a few moments, she lay still and let it wash over her.

Last night's conversation through Vlad's prison door had the quality of a dream. It was more than possible she'd fallen asleep here and dreamed of going in search of him, dreamed of the things he'd said and the things she'd agreed to.

What *had* she agreed to? And what did it matter if it was only a dream?

Was it?

In the years following Vlad's exile and imprisonment, she'd dreamed of him a lot. Not wild or sensual dreams—or at least not very often. Most of them had been rather like last night's—quiet conversation after coming upon him unexpectedly. In those dreams, talking to him had made everything all right. She'd been happy. And waking, knowing it was merely a dream, had broken her heart all over again.

"Real or not real?" she whispered.

"Beg your pardon, lady?" said Margit cheerfully.

"Nothing." Ilona sighed, pushing back the covers and reaching for the grey dress.

"Oh, madam, not that one," Margit begged. "Half the court will be watching...!" She bit her lip. "Don't look like that, my lady, you know what this place is, how public everything is. Wear *this* gown. It will look beautiful."

Ilona tugged indecisively at her hair. She hadn't dreamed that he'd been here in this room. The assignation under the auspices of Aunt Erzsébet was real enough. She picked up the dull, grey gown. She didn't care about the watchers.

People would make fun of him, tying himself to her for the sake of an unstable principality on the Ottoman border.

No one looks down their noses at Szilágyis.

Yes, they do, Father.

But no one must disrespect *him*, so which dress...?

"Here we go again," she whispered, pacing around the room, dragging her fingers through her hair. "Back on the sleigh ride, up and down, turned this way and that, churned up like snow beneath its blades. All because I don't know which wretched dress to wear? For God's sake, what is wrong with me? *It doesn't matter!*"

She snatched the new silk from Margit's stunned hands.

Unsure why, Margit began to laugh.

Vlad made sure he was early. There was no way he'd subject her to the stares of the curious alone. Of course, she probably wouldn't be alone. She'd have the countess in tow at the very least.

Because he hated to be idle, he brought a book—one of Matthias's fine collection—and some letters to answer. Accompanied by Count Szelényi, he entered the gallery, inclined his head to every eye he caught, and settled down on a carved bench with his book. He remembered to turn the pages, but he didn't read them.

A faint rustle of activity alerted him before even Count
Szelényi's murmured, "Sir."

He glanced up and forgot to breathe.

Countess Hunyadi was nowhere in sight, just Ilona's attendant
of last night, more gorgeously attired. But Vlad barely noticed her.

Ilona was beautiful.

Her shining dark gold hair was braided, pinned up, and
veiled as was appropriate for a mature lady, but with such discreet
artifice that it covered only the streak of grey. Her crespine was
light but jeweled. The dark red silk of her gown intensified the
pale roses in her white cheeks and soft lips, emphasising the taut
skin over her high, delicate cheekbones. Heavily brocaded under
her breasts, the gown was cut into a low V at the front, showing the palest pink of the underdress. The wide oversleeves were
folded back, revealing brocaded cuffs, and the pale pink sleeve
beneath. And on her fingers, she wore two rings. One of them,
he'd given her.

Vlad's throat constricted because she'd taken such care. Or, at
least allowed it, surely, for the right reasons.

She walked quickly, not with pride but with a certain distance
that gave a false impression of self-esteem to anyone who didn't
know her. Ilona was still held together by a thread, but she'd made
the effort, and he wanted to laugh and weep at the same time. She
was the only person in the world who'd ever had that effect on
him.

He rose quickly, dropping his book on top of the letters, and
went to meet her. She let herself see him then, and he could have
sworn some more colour entered her cheeks before they paled.

"Countess Ilona," he said formally and bowed.

Ilona curtseyed. "Prince."

She was shaking. He could feel it. He lifted his arm and offered
it to her. Her breath caught. Then one slim, still elegant hand lifted
and rested on his velvet forearm. It did tremble, vibrating his skin,

stirring memory and desire and a need to protect that had become urgent.

They began to walk.

She said, "I can feel their eyes like a thousand pinpricks in my back."

"They're admiring your beauty."

"Oh, please..."

"As am I."

"Vlad..."

"Yes?"

She glanced up at him uncertainly. And slowly, the tiny frown between her brows smoothed out. Her eyes seemed to clear. She said, "We talked last night."

"I remember."

A sound like a laugh came from her, quickly choked off. "I wasn't sure *I* did. I—sometimes—I'm confused."

Sharp as nails, Ilona. His gut twisted, but he said only, "I spoke to you often in dreams."

Her step faltered. No wonder—she'd closed her eyes. He stopped and, for the benefit of watchers, turned her to face a painting—some garbage purporting to depict the birth of the Hungarian nation.

She whispered, "How awful has it been for you?"

"Not so bad. Even amusing in places. They wheel me out to frighten Ottoman embassies and other foreign dignitaries they want to impress."

Ilona's lips twisted. "On the assumption that a king who can keep the Impaler imprisoned must be powerful indeed?"

"You always had an incisive grasp of politics."

"Of my cousin Matthias. And do you?"

"Frighten the dignitaries? I do my best to scowl and look fierce. I think it actually frightens the Hungarians more, but I can live with that."

"Shh-shh!" Ilona looked around for eavesdroppers.

"Countess Hunyadi promised us privacy, remember? In fact, where is she?"

"I haven't seen her this morning. I expected to, but she didn't appear."

"So you came anyway?"

Again that faintest of flushes that reminded him unbearably of the girl she'd been. A girl too honest and too serious to flirt, though never too serious to laugh.

"I felt I should. I didn't know if you'd be here. Even if I hadn't dreamed…our last conversation."

"You haven't changed your mind? You're still content with this betrothal?"

She gave the strange, choking sound again. "Content? That's a strange word."

"You once thought happy was a strange word."

"No, just your interest in its connection with me." The light in her eyes dulled and vanished. "I don't know what you want, Vlad, but I know I can't give you it anymore."

He reached with his free hand and covered hers on his arm. It jumped at his touch and was still.

"Ilona," he said, low. "Ilona." It was a plea, to keep her there with him, but words had deserted him. A tear began to form, trembling at the corner of her eye. "This is impossible," he said intensely. "We can't do this here… Ilona, you are the only gift I want. Then together we can make it right."

"Make what right?" she asked in despair.

"Whatever is wrong."

She brushed impatiently at her eye before she would look at him. She swallowed. "I—I am not the—help—to you I'd once hoped to be."

"With you beside me, I'll defeat the world single-handed. Wielding nothing more deadly than a wet fish."

A tinkle of laughter broke from her. Encouraged, he smiled into her eyes. "It's good to talk to you, Ilona Szilágyi."

She held his gaze, searching. Then her eyes dropped and her head bent, and he thought with despair that he'd lost her again. Then he realised she was still moving. In front of all eyes, she laid her forehead on his arm, and when she lifted it again, she was smiling.

"There you are!"

So much for privacy. Not only Countess Hunyadi but the king himself.

"Renewing old acquaintance, I see," said Matthias with false indulgence. "How wonderful. I have summoned another old friend for you to meet."

"Stephen," Ilona blurted, as if reminded she should have warned Vlad before. As if he hadn't known the moment Stephen arrived. "Stephen is here."

"So he is," Matthias agreed. He smiled at her with open affection. "I mean yet another old friend, my sister. Do you know, Ilona, in view of your reluctance to enter the matrimonial state, I think a convent would suit you best. My sister shall marry the Prince of Wallachia."

Erzsébet Hunyadi's heart smote her. For an instant, gazing into the violent storm of Vlad's furious green eyes, she wondered if they were doing the right thing. All very well to rescue Ilona. She owed Ilona. But to save her niece, only to throw her *daughter* to the Impaler?

"He'll give my sister all the respect that's her due," Matthias had said impatiently. "And she won't care about his temper or his wild starts. It's the perfect solution for all of us. Vlad gets a better deal—sister instead of mere cousin. We get someone into his household we can trust."

"She won't be able to influence him!" Erzsébet had objected, instinctively protecting her daughter.

Matthias blinked. "And you imagine Ilona will? At least my sister can tell what's going on. These days, I doubt Ilona knows what day it is."

But it seemed the soon-to-be-Prince of Wallachia did not appreciate the honour done to him. Erzsébet was not fainthearted, but if looks could kill, she was well aware that both she and her son would be dead. And he had a nasty tongue. When his full, sensual lips parted, she prepared to sustain herself against whatever verbal vitriol was to come.

However, before he could speak, Ilona had jerked free of him, and he was distracted. Her hand clutched her veil as though to drag it off.

"Not *again*," she whispered, and without another word began to walk away from them. Fiercely, Erzsébet signaled to the waiting woman, Margit, to go with her. She, Erzsébet would follow in a few minutes, and at a more dignified pace.

Vlad dragged his gaze away from Ilona's back. Almost between his teeth, he said, "We have already given our words. I have contracted to marry Ilona."

"My sister is better. Younger, fitter for childbearing, closer kin to me." Matthias smiled. "And she wants to be Princess of Wallachia."

As a warning, it wasn't very subtle. Vlad must have understood it, and yet he continued to stare at the king as if waiting for more. Erzsébet found herself frozen, unable to move away. Even Matthias began to grow uncomfortable in the silence.

Matthias said, "You cannot insult…"

And Vlad interrupted him, leaning forward to say in that dangerous, soft voice that still made Erzsébet shiver, "I will not play, Matthias."

And he turned and walked away. Troubling no more than Ilona had with the bad form of turning one's back on the king.

Matthias called angrily after him, "Then I'll find someone who will!"

"You want Vlad," Erzsébet reminded him dryly.

"Yes," Matthias admitted with an angry little shake. "And Vlad wants Wallachia. He won't give that up by holding out for *Ilona*, will he?"

But it almost seemed that he would.

Ilona wouldn't speak to her. By the time Erzsébet caught up with her, she was back in her own apartments, sitting curled up on a corner of the bed, her veil askew, gazing blindly out of the window, merely smiling faintly, abstractedly, if either she or the woman, Margit, spoke to her.

Eventually, Erzsébet gave up and went in search of Vlad instead.

He too was in his own apartment, but alone, with the door wide open. There was no sign of his servant, or of Count Szelényi. Perhaps he was deliberately reminding them that he stayed because he chose to, not because he was imprisoned.

It was tempting to slam and lock the door on his infernal insolence, remind *him* who had the power to make his incarceration considerably less comfortable. But he knew they wouldn't do that. Not if they were planning to give him the sister of the king.

Like Ilona, he sat by the open window, letting the breeze stir his thick, still-black locks. But unlike her he was busy, writing furiously.

"Come in, Countess," he said as her shadow fell across his doorway. He put aside his paper and pen and rose to his feet. "I was hoping to talk to you."

"Now that you've recovered your temper?"

His smile was so thin it was barely a smile at all. "You are mistaken. My temper is far from recovered."

"Then perhaps I'll wait until it is."

"No," he said quickly, gratifying her that at last she had got to him. "Please, sit. Despite my temper, I promise to be good and not shout or scream. Countess, in your own way, you care for Ilona."

"As my own daughter. She was my brother's favourite child."

"I know."

She condescended to sit in the chair he placed for her, but annoyingly he stayed looming over her. He knew exactly how intimidating he was, but perhaps he considered her beyond that. She'd thought she was too, until now.

Then, with rare difficulty he said, "You can't keep doing this to her. It's tearing her apart, you must see that."

"I see that she needs peace," Erzsébet said stiffly. "Which is why the king and I have followed her wishes and released her from the obligation to marry you."

"I do not release her."

"Then *you* are tearing her apart!"

"No," Vlad said. "No. Countess…" He drew in his breath, and she wanted to crow because this was so difficult for him. He didn't want to ask, his pride forbade it, and for a moment, she was sure pride had won. Then he said abruptly, "What happened to her? Why is she so…frail?"

Erzsébet raised her eyes to his face. She refused to feel guilt. The greater good of the family always came first. And yet she wanted another reason. She *needed* one, and surely it lay in Vlad himself. "You tell me."

"I can't."

"Oh, I think you can. She came to your castle, she and her mother, Countess Szilágyi. Before they left, my sister-in-law was dead and my niece no longer herself."

"You're wrong. She wasn't like this when she left me."

Erzsébet stared. "You deny that she was upset? Over her mother? Maria? *And whatever else you did.*"

Vlad stared at her, at a rare loss for words.

She said, "You'd lost to the sultan; your days as prince were numbered. The Ottomans were practically at your castle gates. Would you really have noticed what state she was in?"

Having reduced him to silence, the silence, surely, of guilt, Erzsébet was triumphant, and struck home. "What did she see there? *What did you do to her, Vlad?*"

She was aware of the risk of riling him. She'd calculated on it. But she never anticipated the thoughtful, almost quiet look that entered his eyes.

He crouched down at her feet so that he could look directly into her face.

"Oh no," he said softly. "That isn't it, is it? She left me distraught, grieving, frightened, but *strong*. I'm beginning to think the question is rather what did *you* do to her?"

Chapter Ten

Wallachia, 1457

If Ilona had ever been in any doubt as to her welcome, it vanished before they even entered Maria's house. As she stepped out of the carriage, a luscious female figure in bright blue flew down the front steps, careless of the blustery March wind, and hurled itself into her arms, squeaking out her name in uninhibited joy.

Laughing, Ilona hugged her back. Then, thrusting her a few inches away so that she could look at her old friend properly, she exclaimed, "You haven't changed a bit!"

"You have," Maria said frankly, looking her up and down with approval. "How very elegant you are! And that gown…!"

Ilona wrinkled her nose. "Court fashion," she said deprecatingly. "We've just come from Buda."

Maria's expression changed quickly. "Oh, Ilona, I'm so sorry about your cousin."

Ilona turned away quickly, unwilling to face that grief yet, or the consequences. "Yes. Thanks." With relief she found her father, dismounted and walking toward them with a tolerant smile for their nonstop chatter. "You remember my father, Mihály Szilágyi?"

"Of course I do! I'm honoured to welcome you to my poor home, sir. Come inside out of the wind. We baked honey cakes this afternoon…"

A little later, gathered in Maria's hall, sipping wine while they watched her stepson play hide-and-seek with two larger cousins, Ilona said warmly, "You have a good home here, Maria."

Unaware of her faint twinge of envy, Maria said doubtfully, "Yes…though it gets a little dull. There's nothing much to do."

"Apart from the honey cakes," Mihály interjected, toasting her with his second.

Maria laughed. "Even honey cakes get boring if there's nothing else. When it all gets too tedious, I go to court."

"To Tîrgovişte?" Ilona said quickly. "My father is bound there tomorrow to see the prince."

"Aren't you going? Oh, you should, Ilona, you have to see the prince now!"

"Why?" Ilona asked lightly. "Has he changed so much?"

Maria opened her mouth, then closed it again. "Actually, I suppose not. He just seems to have. Because he's found his proper setting perhaps. But the court's a much more entertaining place to be than it was in Vladislav's day. Now we have music and art, and you're as likely to come upon learned men as soldiers…"

She broke off, flushing as she registered too late how insulting that could sound to Ilona's father. Mihály, however, had wandered off to speak to the boys, and Maria turned back to Ilona with relief.

"You'll love it," she said happily. "Although perhaps it will be too provincial for you after Buda."

Ilona, unused to being considered so worldly wise by her friend, only laughed.

"We should both go," Maria said eagerly. Leaning forward, she took Ilona's hand and squeezed it. In a whisper, she added, "Seriously, Ilona, he'll turn even your knees to jelly now. As a boy, there was something about him. Now—he's magnificent, I promise you."

Something churned inside Ilona, a powerful urge to see him, a twist of doubt as to Maria's relationship with him, an echo of the

old, childish jealousy. She wondered if she'd regret staying away.
After all, curiosity usually won her over.

In the end, she had no choice. Her father decided she would
accompany him. And Maria, anxious not to lose her friend again
so quickly, went with them.

Lifting the paper Vlad had just signed, Carstian said, "And Mihály
Szilágyi is here."

Vlad glanced up quickly. "Where?"

"Since his daughter's with him, they have the house next to
the palace. But in the immediate, he's in the outer chamber."

"Damn it, Carstian, why didn't you say?" Vlad shoved back his
chair, and although his doublet was not fastened, falling open to
reveal his shirt unlaced at the throat, he strode to the door as he
was. Wrenching it open, he said, "Mihály?"

He barely registered the other occupant—a shadowy figure
in shades of amber—for his eyes sought and immediately found
Mihály Szilágyi, who seemed to be pacing the room. At the sound
of the door, he paused and smiled.

He looked tired, fresh lines of anxiety around his piercing eyes
and stern mouth, and yet Vlad's heart lifted immeasurably at the
sight of his old friend. While Mihály swept off his hat and bowed
in the manner appropriate to a prince, Vlad strode to him and
embraced him without formality.

Vlad said, "Damn it, it's good to see you here!"

And Mihály gave his lopsided grin. "Not as good as it is to see
you here, at last. I'm honoured to be able to congratulate you in
person. As is Ilona."

Vlad glanced with him to the window. A shimmer of sunlight
on amber silk temporarily dazzled him. Then the figure moved,
walking toward them with quick, graceful steps, and he beheld a

slender, beautiful woman with luxuriant red-gold hair. A wispy, trailing scarf barely touching her head, served as its only covering. Something about the way she moved, all understated, or even unconscious, sensuality stirred his body into wakefulness.

He felt his lips curve involuntarily, even before he saw her smile. Then something thudded in his chest, almost depriving him of breath. Not just because her smile was an enchanting mixture of shyness and genuine pleasure, but because he knew that smile, he knew those dark, melting eyes, at once secretive and perceptive and just waiting their moment to fill with laughter.

He remembered to move forward, to take her hand as she curtseyed with a grace he didn't recall her possessing before. But he couldn't take his eyes off her as he raised her fingers to his lips.

"You grow more beautiful each time I see you." As soon as the words spilled out, he wished he'd said something cleverer instead. It was too late to withdraw them, but at least they brought that delightful flush to her cheeks. But her hand didn't tremble in his as he was sure it had done once before. Somewhere, she had learned to deal with flirting. The same place, no doubt, she had learned to dress and walk with such style. They had made a lady of her at last.

She said flatly, "No, I don't." And Vlad laughed in delight, because she was still Ilona after all.

"Ilona!" exclaimed her father, only half-amused. "One does not argue with princes!"

Her hand gave a flutter in his, a faint tug, and he gave in and let her go. "Besides, on this subject, I claim to be a better judge. As always, you are an unexpected pleasure. Please, sit down. Have you broken your fast?"

Carstian, who'd been lurking by the inner door, took the opportunity to bow to the room in general—although his eyes, Vlad, noticed, seemed to be fixed on Ilona.

"You may go," Vlad informed him.

"Thank you," said Carstian. Only as he walked did Vlad realise Carstian was carrying the princely belt, which he'd failed to put on before dashing to meet Mihály. Vlad glared at him, and Carstian's eyebrows twitched once before he dropped the belt onto his prince's arm in passing.

So much for princely dignity. With difficulty, Vlad refrained from aiming a kick at Carstian's retreating rear. Instead, opting for blatancy, he discarded the belt onto a vacant chair and held the one next to it for Ilona and then sat down opposite her and Mihály.

His eyes wanted to gaze at Ilona, but she was too distracting. There were things he had to say to her father.

He began at once, meeting the older man's eyes steadily. "I was shocked as well as saddened to hear about László. I never thought it would go so far."

Mihály nodded curtly. "Perhaps it was inevitable after what he did at Belgrade. But before God, to deprive so young a man of life shows a lack of compassion and understanding beyond…" He broke off. "But perhaps you disagree. I can only assure you the charges against László were entirely false."

Entirely? Vlad wasn't sure. But mostly, certainly. Although, the king undoubtedly wanted to teach the Hunyadis a lesson, with the Cilli faction at his ear, flattering him and baying for blood, Vlad suspected there was a grain of truth in the young king's fears. Exactly how it all affected his position, he was not as yet certain.

He said diplomatically, "The countess must be devastated."

"She is, of course."

"And Matthias?"

"Still under arrest—a hostage to our good behaviour."

Vlad, who'd spent a good part of his youth in the same uncomfortable position, felt a twinge of sympathy for the child who had once admired his sword in a sunny Transylvanian garden.

He said, "What will you do?"

Mihály shrugged. "Reach some sort of rapprochement with the Cillis and watch our backs till Matthias is freed. Which is one reason I've come to you. I'll need to spend most of my time in Hungary, and I'm afraid the Cillis will foment rebellion in Transylvania behind my back."

"I'll do everything in my power to support your position as governor."

His wayward eyes strayed from Mihály's watchful face to Ilona's. The girl was gazing at him fixedly. He felt a frisson of awareness, a discomfort at being so closely observed that was, curiously, far from unpleasant. Her hands lay still in her lap, not fidgeting like the child he remembered who wouldn't be still. He wondered if he could make her lose this new self-control.

"And if," he added, intrigued that she didn't look away, "you come across my half brother or any of the other pretenders to my throne beginning to crawl out of the woodwork in Transylvania, I'd be grateful if you kicked them in my direction."

"Consider them kicked, arrested, and delivered."

"Thank you."

For decency's sake, he dragged his gaze away from Ilona, just as she said, "What will you do with them?"

Vlad let his eyes move back, let the half smile tug at his lips. "Another of *those* conversations?"

She knew what he meant at once, for a flush rose up from her slender neck at last, suffusing her face with new colour. It gave him a fierce satisfaction he didn't want to understand. But she didn't back down. Instead, her chin lifted, and she spoke aloud the words in his head.

"*Kill them all?*"

"Probably," said Vlad steadily.

Mihály stirred. "One cannot govern a country while others undermine it. Rebels and traitors must pay the price. You must have grasped that much, Ilona."

Now her gaze did fall, because she'd let Mihály down. Riling Vlad instead of…what? Why *had* he brought Ilona?

"Forgive my daughter," Mihály said gruffly. "Her heart is too tender."

That drew a flash of her eyes, as if she knew she'd been insulted and had no idea why.

Amused, Vlad said, "But the world needs tender hearts. Without them, no one would be afraid of men like me."

"I'm not afraid of you," Ilona said at once. Just a shade too quickly. Vlad's stomach twisted.

"I don't mean you to be," he said lightly, while he searched wildly through all their past dealings to discover where and when he could have made her afraid. Just by *Kill them all?* Or was the subsequent sleigh ride to blame? Certainly, he deserved to be flogged for that one.

But it wasn't just those things. He looked frightening. He *was* frightening, because he'd cultivated the image since boyhood. Perversely, perhaps, and certainly unacknowledged, he'd valued Ilona Szilágyi because she'd never been afraid of him. Until now.

He let a faint smile twist his lips. *I should have dressed properly.* Swinging away from the eyes and the thoughts that churned him up, he said to Mihály, "You should speak to my cousin Stephen while you're here. I'm sure he too will support your cause."

"Stephen?"

"He's about to embark on his own adventure—a bid for the Moldavian throne."

Although he spoke directly to Mihály, he felt the change in the girl's attention too. He remembered that she'd always got on well with Stephen, had seemed at ease with him, and was disgusted to recognise the twist in his gut as unworthy jealousy.

What is the matter with me?

Mihály said uneasily, "Is that wise right now? The king has little time for the present incumbent, but he hasn't sanctioned Stephen's…"

Vlad said dryly, "He doesn't need the king's approval. He has the sultan's."

Mihály blinked. "The sultan's? But the sultan supports Petru Aaron..."

"Now he supports Stephen more."

"How...?" Mihály began, then broke off, understanding.

Vlad smiled with deliberately false modesty.

A servant came in, carrying a jug of wine and some decent goblets. Mihály waited until the man had set the tray down before them and departed. Then: "*You* spoke for him to the sultan? Your word carries weight at the Porte these days."

"Actually," said Vlad, reaching for the wine jug, "it always did."

Mihály exhaled heavily. "You play a dangerous game, my friend. Sometime, you will have to swallow your pride and accept Hungary's protection—or be swallowed up by the infidels."

"I hope not," said Vlad. He stood and walked the few paces to Ilona to give her the goblet. She took it without taking her eyes from his face. There was no sign there now of any fear. "I've sworn allegiance to both but submit to neither."

Vlad turned from her gaze with reluctance and gave the other goblet to Mihály. "It's my belief that Europe's security depends on the autonomy of border states like Wallachia and Moldavia. In other words, I must compromise with the Ottomans so Hungary doesn't have to. On the clear understanding, of course, that the Christian states must cooperate in emergencies."

"Emergencies?" Ilona pounced. "As defined by whom?"

Vlad raised his cup to her in a toast. "That," he said, "is the vital question. *Salut*."

"So what did you think?" Maria demanded as they walked arm in arm into the prince's hall. "Was he very splendid?"

The table, although not set for massive numbers, looked magnificent. Delicious smells had been assailing Ilona's nostrils since before they'd entered the building, and now, at the sight of the elegant dishes of soup and fish and poultry, all set among bright fresh vegetables and fruit, her mouth began to water. It gave her an excuse to look at the table rather than her friend.

"Not splendid," she murmured. She'd expected a prince, stiff and proud in velvets and jewels, and instead found a supremely casual man in little more than his shirtsleeves who had the charm of immediately welcoming her controversial father to his home. "But you're right; he is *different*."

"How?" Maria asked eagerly while she nodded several greetings to acquaintances among the gathered noblemen and women.

Because he stared at me like that. *Because wearing less, he somehow looked more. Because he couldn't take his eyes off me, and God help me, I wanted that.*

Impossible to say this to anyone, let alone Maria, who still seemed to carry a torch for the man who rejected her as a youth. To give it words was to trivialise it—*trivialise what?*—when she only wanted to hug it to herself, feel the secret, overwhelming excitement of his attention.

"I don't know," she said hastily. "Perhaps because he seemed at ease. In his own setting, as you said."

"Look, there's Stephen of Moldavia with your father!"

Ilona followed her gaze across the room. Stephen glanced up and smiled. And then the door near the head of the table opened, and the Prince of Wallachia emerged.

Here at last was Maria's magnificent prince. As precisely dressed as he had always been, only now with the wealth to indulge his taste for opulence without vulgarity. Here were the velvets, the gold, the jewels, and yet they did not swallow the man; they enhanced him, emphasising the breadth of his powerful chest and shoulders, the sheer strength of his distinctive face.

"Deny it now," Maria whispered in her ear. "Is that not splendour on legs?"

As it often did in Maria's company, a surge of laughter threatened her hard-won dignity.

"Go on." Maria gave her a little push. "You're being summoned."

Vlad Dracula, it seemed, was according Mihály Szilágyi every honour, placing him on one side of the prince, while Ilona was seated on the other. On Ilona's left was Stephen of Moldavia.

"How wonderful to see you here!" Stephen exclaimed.

"Thank you! But I hear you won't be here long yourself—adventure beckons?"

"Indeed it does. To be honest, you've only just caught me. If you'd come next week, I'd already have gone."

Ilona regarded him with curiosity. He had the backing of the sultan but no Ottoman troops that she knew of. And no Hungarians, since the king was not involved in this enterprise. He was unlikely to have a massive native army, since in most challenges for the throne in the Romanian principalities, the people sat on the fence to see which way the wind would blow. There was really only one possibility.

"And does the Prince of Wallachia go with you?"

"Ah, no. It wouldn't be good for Vlad to leave Wallachia this early in his reign. But he's lending me Wallachian troops—brave veterans who should get the job done!"

And if he lent his best troops to Stephen, even for one season, did that not leave Vlad dangerously exposed?

"He's fulfilling our boyhood oath," Stephen explained, as if he read her mind. "But I know Vlad, and he wouldn't do it now if he didn't judge it was safe. He has things well under control here."

Was that true, or did Stephen just need to believe that for his own reasons?

"Don't you, Vlad?" said Stephen, and Ilona felt the hairs on the back of her neck rise up. Worse, it wasn't even unpleasant.

Feeling as if she was taking some huge step in her life, she turned her head and met Vlad's dark, almost blazing gaze.

"I hope so," said the prince. "Besides, it's a small price to pay to get this troublemaker out of my hair."

Stephen laughed, and Vlad spared him a flickering smile before returning to Ilona. "So, what do you think of my capital city?"

"I've barely seen it, to be honest. We arrived after dark last night."

"I'll show you it myself, tomorrow."

Her heart beat like a drum. "Thank you," she managed. "But more to the point, what do *you* think of it?"

"I think it's closed in, incestuous, and rife with intrigue."

Ilona blinked. "Then it isn't worth all the waiting after all?"

"On the contrary. Tîrgovişte is only a tiny part of the country, and one easily cured of its ills." His gaze slid beyond hers, and he smiled at someone farther down the table. That smile made her shiver. And since he followed it up by turning politely to Mihály on his other side, Ilona cast a hasty glance down the table too.

Roughly in the direction aimed at by Vlad's smile, two noblemen were exchanging uneasy words.

"Who are these gentlemen?" she asked Stephen bluntly.

"Ah. Radul and his son. Once supporters of Vladislav who've come into the fold."

Ilona lowered her voice. "Does he trust them?" Would she? The men certainly looked uneasy, but then so would she at the receiving end of that smile.

"He doesn't trust anyone until they earn it. The question should rather be has he forgiven them."

Ilona let her gaze stray back to Stephen. "For what? They must *all* have supported Vladislav at some time."

Stephen lowered his voice. "But they didn't all murder his brother."

Ilona blinked at the soup, which had materialised in the bowl before her. "Did *they?*"

"I don't know. But he does."

"What will he do?"

Stephen picked up his spoon and began to eat. "That's what worries me. It worries them too. He appears to have forgotten, if not forgiven, but I know that's not true. He plays with them and with others, like a cat with a mouse, convincing them he's won over and then resowing the seeds of doubt."

"As a punishment, it could be worse," Ilona pointed out.

"That's what worries me. I'm sure it will be. Especially when I'm not here to—*moderate* him."

"Can you?" asked Ilona, distracted in spite of herself, and Stephen laughed.

"No," he admitted.

The following morning, unable to stay away, Mihály Szilágyi went off with Stephen to inspect his troops and talk about war.

Ilona, summoned by a knock on the front door of their house, and by the squeal of the maid who opened it to discover the prince leaning down from horseback, found herself out riding around the town with no escort but the prince.

Though initially dazed and unnerved because of the way he'd looked at her yesterday, Ilona quickly relaxed. Although they weren't on the open road, surrounded by soldiers, she was reminded of that journey home from Sighisoara last Christmas.

Beyond the palace compound, they rode among narrow streets of large houses into an area of pleasant gardens that made Ilona exclaim with pleasure. Vlad pointed out the cathedral where he'd been formally invested as prince, another rather charming church, and the busy market square. The people didn't pay them a huge amount of attention. Beyond bowing as their prince rode past, they got on with their lives. Noblemen and women made more elaborate obeisance, smiling and waiting to be addressed, but Vlad merely nodded and rode on.

A moat and the inevitable walls surrounded the city. Vlad led her across the bridge, then turned to face his horse back toward the town. Ilona did likewise and enjoyed the view he showed her. A charming town of spires and turrets and flowers, nestling among the surrounding, vine-laden hills and sparkling blue lakes.

"It is a beautiful city," she observed. "You should appreciate it more."

"Perhaps." His gaze flickered up to the hills. "I'd take you farther, show you the real Wallachia, but perhaps not today. You have no escort, and Mihály would kill me for risking your reputation."

Ilona, who hadn't been aware he even noticed such mundane matters, blinked at him. For an instant, she imagined something vulnerable, almost wistful in his strong face, and knew an insane urge to touch it with her fingertips. Then his head turned, and he met her gaze. Unexpectedly and without reason, he began to smile, and his constantly veiled eyes softened.

"And so you're still waiting," he observed. "I thought some dashing husband would have snapped you up in Buda."

Ilona shrugged uncomfortably. "Things are too uncertain."

"And no one wants to *waste* you on a lesser man."

"You make me sound like a flagon of wine," Ilona said wryly. In truth, she often felt like one. She expected most women did.

"A very fine wine," Vlad assured her, and she laughed, urging her horse forward once more onto the drawbridge. Vlad came alongside her. She felt his gaze on her face, hotter than the spring sun.

He said, "But what of you? Is there no one you wish to marry?"

She shook her head. "Wishes are unwise. It will never be up to me."

"It might be. Mihály listens to you because you perceive things he doesn't."

Ilona smiled with a trace of cynicism. "Perceiving a man's beautiful soul would not sway Mihály Szilágyi."

"Is that what you want? A man with a beautiful soul?"

"To be honest," Ilona confessed, "I'm not perfectly sure what that is." When he laughed, she gave another quick smile and apologised. "I was only babbling."

"Then you haven't encountered one?" he teased.

"A beautiful soul? I expect they're only beautiful after death."

"Don't be morbid. Does no living man stir *your* soul? Set your pulses racing and make you long for love?"

Astonishment pulled her gaze back to him. He didn't appear to be laughing at her. But his intense, long-lashed eyes looked straight into hers. She had no breath, no words.

Oh God, help me, please…

Struggling to avoid the question, she countered shakily, "Why? Do you ever feel like that?"

"Not until recently."

Pain twisted through her, causing her hands to tighten on the reins. Confused, her horse, sprang forward, and she had to haul it back before it broke into a dangerous gallop through the narrow streets.

Vlad's hand seized her mount's bridle, holding the animal soothingly but implacably. Ilona kept her gaze on that hand.

"What will you do about it?" she asked, striving for lightness.

"I honestly don't know yet."

"I wish you well," she muttered, urging the horse forward. Vlad released it, and for a time, they rode on in silence.

Until recently, Ilona thought miserably. When he met Maria again? Maria had made it clear she'd fallen for the enigmatic prince, had told her every word, every gesture he'd made toward her, and it did sound to her as if Vlad had been flirting. Perhaps held back from anything else by his previous knowledge of Maria as Countess Hunyadi's protégée. And there had been times yesterday, after the banquet, when as she'd sat with Maria, she'd felt his gaze and watched Maria blush.

He didn't know what to do about it yet. Marry her or take her as his mistress. Maria, she suspected, would be delirious with either arrangement.

He said, "Do you never believe anyone is looking at you?" His voice, unexpectedly harsh, broke into her unhappy reflections.

"What?"

"Are you really not aware of your own beauty?"

At a loss, she stared at him, feeling the colour mount high into her face and hating it. He looked almost…angry. "It's the court dresses," she explained.

And Vlad's hard eyes suddenly laughed. "Ilona—" He broke off as someone on horseback bowed right in front of them. A priest, who clearly knew him. Vlad spoke civilly to the man, asking after his health as well as briefly discussing the progress of some new monastery, and then they moved on.

But the small interruption had crystallised some observations in her head.

"They're not afraid of you," she blurted.

"The priests? I flog them if they're not polite."

"No, you don't. And I don't just mean the priests. Everyone. The townspeople. The nobles. They bow, they hope, no doubt, for preference, but they're not afraid of you."

"Should they be?"

"Yesterday, you implied you ruled through fear. Or would do. But you ride among them openly as prince without fear, and they treat you the same way."

"I haven't been here very long," he excused.

She regarded him with, no doubt, her mingled amusement and frustration clear in her face, for he smiled faintly in response.

"Fear is an extremely powerful weapon," he observed. "And the most useful one a ruler will ever have. Take the Ottomans, whose very name inspires terror throughout Europe. How many Europeans would believe that the Ottomans are a warm, gentle, generous-hearted people? All they need are a few atrocities from the past and an occasional military victory, and they can hold together an impossibly far-flung empire while the rest of the world shivers in its shoes, afraid to attack, terrified of the moment the monster advances."

Fascinated, Ilona began to make sense of it. But she couldn't resist challenging, "*All* they need?"

"Well, a massive army helps too."

"You don't have that."

"On a smaller scale, I do. If necessary, every peasant will rise up and fight."

She smiled. "You're a mass of contradictions, Vlad Dracula."

"I'm a successful mass of contradictions."

"So far," she provoked.

He closed one eye. "Keep watch."

Chapter Eleven

Tîrgovişte, Wallachia, 1457

"Of course you have leave to depart to your estates. They are not so far away, which will make it easy for you to return for my Easter banquet. I can promise you unprecedented entertainment."

The prince's voice travelled the length of the great hall, where before the prince stood the nobleman Radul and his son, whom Stephen suspected of involvement with Mircea's murder—or at least suspected that Vlad suspected.

Ilona, who'd just strolled in with Maria, suddenly heard the blood singing in her ears.

I will take my revenge on those who murdered my father and my brother. No mercy, Ilona Szilágyi. I will kill them all.

Grabbing her friend by the hand, she pulled her back outside, into the passage.

"Maria," she whispered. "Your husband was Vladislav's man."

"Right up to the end," Maria confessed sadly.

"And before? Did he help to oust Dracul? Vlad's father?"

"I think he probably did. The family were always Danesti supporters."

"Did he...?" Ilona broke off, struggling for words, casting a quick glance around for eavesdroppers. "Maria, was Dragomir involved in Mircea's death?"

"Oh, I really don't think so…"

"Think, Maria, was he here in Tîrgovişte when it happened?"

Maria stared. "How should I know? Ilona, what's the matter with you?"

Ilona straightened, reaching up to tug at her hair. Maria tutted and immediately began to rearrange it. "I don't know, to be honest…"

"Well, it doesn't matter anyway, does it? Dragomir's already dead."

But you're not. The boy is not.

Mary, Mother of God, what am I thinking? Why do I have to make him either a hero or a monster? He's just a man in pain. A wounded man, perhaps even a damaged one…

Ilona clutched her head again. "I'm going mad… But I don't think you should be here at Easter. Something bad is going to happen."

Maria laughed and hugged her. "Nonsense! Easter is wonderful in Tîrgovişte, and this year, with him, it will be even better!"

Dusk was falling on the gardens, lengthening and intensifying the shadows of the beech and the willow by the ornamental lake, dulling the brightness of the spring flowers and drawing the eye to the pink and gold of the setting sun instead.

It was a fine night, mild and fresh, and it drew Ilona farther on until, nearer the palace building itself, she saw a familiar figure standing very still in the shadows.

She couldn't make out his face, but she knew it was Vlad Dracula, savouring his moment of solitude. God knew he didn't get many of those. But although she meant to turn and tiptoe away from him, something far more powerful than tact drew her on like invisible ropes until she stood beside him. He didn't turn, but she saw him smile.

After a moment, something touched her hand. Before she could properly register what, his fingers had curled around hers and held. Astounded, Ilona didn't move. She barely breathed. She'd no idea why he did it, but she knew even then that she'd treasure it long after he'd forgotten.

From somewhere close by, the birds sang their final evening song. The gold changed slowly to a dusky, darkening pink. Vlad's strong fingers held hers without moving.

He said, "I thought if I touched you, you'd disappear like a desert mirage."

She could think of nothing to say to that. So she just gazed at his peaceful, averted profile.

He said, "Why are you afraid of me, Ilona Szilágyi?"

"I'm not," she protested, finding her voice at last.

He turned his head slowly toward her. "You never used to be. But I saw it in your eyes when you first came here with Mihály."

"Oh, that." Stupidly, she felt relief, before she considered trying to explain it to him. She felt the blood seep into her neck and face. "That was just…because of the way you looked at me."

His eyes seemed to darken further between the long, almost womanly lashes. "And how was that?" he asked softly.

"I don't know, but it wasn't you I was afraid of." She broke off, biting her tongue, dragging her gaze free of his too perceptive eyes. His thumb stroked the soft skin between her thumb and forefinger, just once. Slowly, his fingers uncurled and released her.

"You'd better go inside, Ilona. Before I look at you that way again."

She flickered a glance at him, but he was watching the last rays of the sun and didn't seem to notice. There might have been the faintest smile on his sensual lips; but equally, she might have imagined it.

"Good night," she murmured and walked quickly back toward her own quarters.

She'd almost reached the path before he called, "Ilona?"

She paused and glanced back over her shoulder.

He said, "It's not the dress."

Laughter bubbled up and spilled from her lips as she ran the rest of the way home. It felt like pure happiness.

In the end, Mihály's need to return to Hungary cut their visit short the day before the prince's planned Easter celebrations. And since Maria offered her house once more as a staging post, she elected to miss the Easter fun and travel with them.

Of course, her disappointment was mitigated by the soiree thrown by the prince to mark Mihály Szilágyi's departure. Musicians played during the sumptuous feast, and afterwards, the tables were cleared away and gypsy musicians brought in to encourage the guests to dance.

Ilona, in high spirits that amounted to exhilaration, realised she much preferred life in Tîrgovişte to the confusing hugeness of the Hungarian court. Although she didn't want to leave tomorrow, she couldn't contain the burgeoning happiness that glowed within her and kept growing. Because that strange interlude with Vlad in the gardens had made her wonder if he wasn't regarding her at last as a woman, even a desirable one.

She couldn't think beyond that, but surely it was possible that all those glances she'd almost intercepted had been aimed at her and not Maria? And he *had* noticed her; he had looked at her like *that* when she'd first arrived. It had thrown her utterly because she hadn't known what it meant, for him or for her, apart from the fact that it made her own secret burden harder to bear. But now...

Now surely there was warmth in his profound green eyes whenever they rested on her. And they rested on her often. It made her whole body flush but in a manner that was far from unpleasant. In fact, it was strangely exciting. And though he didn't speak directly to her on many occasions during the feast, when he did, his deep, soft voice felt almost like a caress.

She wasn't even surprised when, as the gypsies struck up a lively tune, the prince stood and offered her his hand.

Since she and Mihály were guests of honour, he was merely observing etiquette. And yet, when she looked up into his face, her breath caught. With the oddest feeling that she was giving over something of vital importance, she laid her fingers lightly in his, and he led her in dignified silence to the centre of the newly cleared floor.

His fingers curled strongly around hers. He bowed, and a smile that was almost wicked gleamed in his eyes. And the dance began.

It was a dance of the people rather than the nobility, but everyone knew it, however seldom practised as the stately Italian dances replaced it in noble entertainments. It didn't surprise Ilona that Vlad knew it. It surprised her how good he was.

Unexpectedly light on his feet, he stepped and whirled and spun her until the sheer fun of it held her completely captive. Breathless and joyful, she savoured secretly every touch of his hands, every brush of his powerful body against her own.

The gypsies were clearly an inspired choice, for the floor was soon full of spinning, leaping dancers. And whether from a sense of fun or cruelty, the musicians went without pause from one tune to the next. Most of the dancers didn't even notice. Ilona wouldn't have if Vlad hadn't suddenly dropped his arm around her waist and swept her to the side.

"You'll drop from exhaustion," he observed, and Ilona laughed. She'd never seen him so relaxed, so dedicated to simple fun. It was a beguiling and dangerously attractive side to him.

"I'm fine," she assured him.

"Come, a little fresh air will do us both good."

They were close to the inner door that led to his private apartments. And since it was open, it seemed natural enough to go through it. A staircase led upward, but it was to another door Vlad led her, and this opened onto the garden.

Stepping out, with her hand still in his, Ilona inhaled the scents of the night, delicate spring flowers, a hint of herbs drifting over from the kitchen garden, the fading remains of the splendid dinner. She lifted her face into the cooling breeze and breathed deeply as they walked toward the formal flower beds.

As if making a discovery, she said, "That's the first time I've danced with you."

"I hope it won't be the last."

"I can't remember ever having so much fun." The words spilled out because they were in her head. Once said, she realised they were probably unwise, but she couldn't and wouldn't take them back.

"Even among all those fine young suitors in Buda?"

"Some of them were old," Ilona confided.

"Who found the most favour?"

"With me? None of them." She was already spoiled, because her heart had been given long ago to a strange, driven man with a hard face and profound green eyes you could drown in. Those heavy-lidded eyes that seemed to leap now at her flippant comment. A smile played around his full lips.

"You are a difficult woman to catch. Elusive...You slip through my fingers like..." He broke off, pausing in midstride to lift a lock of her hair, letting it trickle over his palm and between his fingers. "Like that."

Though she'd recovered her breath, her heart still beat like a drum. She said, "I don't know what you mean."

The smile tugged his lips higher and faded. "I know you don't." Gently, he pushed the captured lock of hair behind her head and rested his hand lightly on her shoulder. The butterflies in her stomach fluttered so hard it was almost painful. He bent toward her until his hair fell across her neck and she forgot to breathe.

His lips touched hers, brushed once, and sank into her mouth. Ilona closed her eyes, let the happiness consume her. It was a brief embrace, yet one so longed for and never imagined that it shook her utterly. When he released her lips, she opened her eyes and gazed up at him. In wonder, she lifted her hand and touched his rough cheek with her fingertips, pleading, though for what she barely knew.

"Again?" he asked huskily.

"Again," she whispered, and he took her mouth once more, this time in a longer, much more thorough kiss. She felt his tongue slide along her parted lips and delve into her mouth, exploring, caressing. Shattered, she pushed one arm up around his neck and kissed him back while her free hand clung to his velvet mantle like a drowning woman to a rope.

He drew back at last, staring at her from eyes so dark they looked opaque. "Now it's changed," he whispered. "Whatever happens, it's all changed."

"What do you mean?"

"Life is like our sleigh ride—do you remember? Rushing up and down over bumps, striving through the fear and exhilaration to find a safe way to the end. You may know you've done wrong, made mistakes, but you can't change them, and you never know quite how or where it's going to lead you… Am I babbling?"

"Yes."

He smiled and reached up to take her hand away from his neck. He kissed the palm before curling her fingers over it as if to hold a precious gift. "Then it's time I took you back before your reputation is ruined beyond repair."

I don't care.

It was a moment of sweetness, undeserved but impossible to forego, before the ugly realities of life intruded once more. This feeling for Ilona Szilágyi, which seemed to have sprung up fully fledged from nowhere and yet had been growing unobserved and unacknowledged for years, was in danger of obsessing him. But a man could handle only so many obsessions, and before he could allow this one, he had to deal with another, far less palatable one.

So, with the echo of her warm, passionate kisses still on his lips, he bade her and her father farewell early the following morning. She blushed adorably when he kissed her hand, and he drew the memory around him like armour. When all else was done, for a few minutes on a warm spring evening, Ilona Szilágyi had loved him.

He handed her and Maria into their carriage in person and turned to embrace Mihály and wish him luck. In the coming struggle with the wayward young king, he was going to need it.

Then he stood back and let himself wonder, just for a moment, what it would be like never to watch her leave. To have her at his side as his partner in governance, his conscience, his lover, to share laughter and comfort.

It was a sweet, warm ambition, but one that would have to wait. For tonight, the dish of his revenge would finally be cold enough to taste. And Mircea could rest in peace.

Their souls as shriven as they could be by religious ritual, the prince's carefully chosen guests trooped back from church and gorged themselves on his food. Bright, almost exotic in their finery, Vlad imagined those rich nobles, ladies, and merchants as rare animals and birds in some distant, tropical location, squabbling for every last piece of whomever or whatever they'd slaughtered last. Even though they each had more than enough.

But it was human nature too, to always want more.

His food untouched, Vlad sat back in his chair at the head of the table. "So, my friends—this is my first Easter here as your prince."

"And a most notable one it is too," said some sycophant near the middle of the table.

"Indeed? I'm honoured to stand out, since you must have known many Easters, with many different princes."

"True," said Radul with a nostalgic sigh.

They were all drunk on his wine, full of well-being and good cheer.

Vlad said, "Exactly how many princes *have* you known? In your lifetime?"

Radul thought. "Maybe thirty."

"No, no, just twenty," said the peacock next to him.

"Well, you're younger than me. I count thirty. Listen…"

"What of you?" Vlad interrupted, addressing Radul's son.

The young man shrugged. "Maybe seven or eight?" he hazarded.

"Certainly a lot," Vlad agreed. "I could recite them to you, one after the other. Some names appear more than once, as you know. It would take a long time, just to enumerate the princes of the last fifty years. So how do you explain that phenomenon, gentlemen? Or ladies. How is it that there have been so many princes throughout your single lives?"

For the first time, a flutter of unease seemed to pass round the table. A few surreptitious glances were exchanged, a few buttocks shuffled on their seats.

Radul smiled and spread his hands deprecatingly. "Your Highness…"

"I'll tell you," Vlad interrupted. The harshness of his voice broke through Radul's response, silenced every whispered conversation around the table. He stood up and leaned forward to gaze into each face in turn while he spoke with all the hate and contempt festering inside him since boyhood.

"This is *your* land, your country, and yet you destroy it. The guilt for that, for the murder and destruction of so many striving princes, is entirely due to your shameful intrigues."

The faces blanched; each pair of eyes slid away as soon as he released them. He felt like a puppet master. He felt sick. Worse, he knew most of them would never even understand. Disgusted, he slammed the table once, making them all jump. Several women squealed.

"Well, it's enough," he uttered. "It ends here, now."

Straightening, he pushed over his chair and strode to the door. It opened before he even got there, and several soldiers entered as he'd bade them.

"Take the six at the top of the table and execute them. The rest can start walking."

"Walking?" one woman wailed, as if it was a worse punishment than execution. "Walk where? Home?" she added, optimistically.

Vlad paused to glance at her over his shoulder. "Oh no. You'll walk to Poenari," he said. "I need a castle built."

"What's going on?" Ilona asked in confusion.

Their departure from Wallachia seemed to be littered with obstacles. Having spent the night with Maria and departed later than planned, due to a minor domestic crisis, they had then been forced to halt to repair one of the carriage wheels, thus wasting even more time in Mihály's eyes.

And now, a dejected line of people were being moved to the side of the road by soldiers to let her and her father, together with their coach and escort, pass. The people were clearly prisoners of some kind, but very bizarre ones. Their garments were brightly coloured, expensive silks and velvets, although some were torn and all were spattered with mud and dust. Some, especially the women, even wore jewellery dangling from their ears and necks.

As Ilona edged her horse nearer her father's, one woman caught her eye and implored, "Have pity, my lady, have pity and save me…"

"Save you from what?" Ilona asked, panicked. "Who are you, where are you being taken?"

A soldier dragged the woman away, pushing her roughly back into line.

"The prince's orders," he explained. "They're all traitors and murderers, bound for hard labour—namely building His Highness a new castle at Poenari."

"Murderers? Whom did that poor woman murder?" Ilona demanded.

"The prince's brother. Prince Mircea. They all did."

The blood sang in her ears. Understanding swamped her. "I thought he would kill them," she whispered.

"Killed some of them," said the soldier laconically. "The rest, as he says, can work for the first time in their lives."

"Shut up, Alex, he's coming," hissed another soldier, coming up behind. "Keep moving there!"

As the bewildered line of torn beauty trudged onward, Ilona became aware of a solitary rider coming up fast behind them. Unmistakably, the proud, arrogant figure of Vlad Dracula.

Ilona couldn't look at him. She continued to gaze after the sorry line. But Mihály halted to wait for him, blocking her escape as well as Vlad's swift passage. The prince reined in only feet from them. His horse snorted. Still, Ilona kept her face averted.

Vlad said, "I'm sorry you've been inconvenienced. The road parts not far ahead."

"An odd, cruel sort of punishment for the nobility," Mihály observed, and Ilona heard the mingled admiration and disapproval in his voice. "You intend that even the women should work?"

"Why not? Peasant women work all the time, in the fields, in the home. It could be worse," he added brutally. "They could be dead. Like my brother."

"They might wish they were," Mihály said ruefully, and Ilona realised that that would be the verdict of the world. This was one of Vlad's "few atrocities" in the name of peace, and no one would understand that in his own eyes, he was being merciful.

Slowly, Ilona turned and looked at him. After an instant, his eyes widened. As if he didn't see what he expected in her face. Then the hooded lids came down.

She said, "Be at peace," and didn't know if she meant Mircea or Vlad. She urged her horse forward, following the slowly moving coach.

Behind her, Vlad said, "Mihály? I have another proposition for you. I'll write to you."

"I'll receive it with pleasure." There was a pause while Mihály's horse danced. Then, more abruptly, "Take care, Prince."

Ilona shivered. The best of Vlad's troops were out of the country, winning Moldavia for his cousin. If the nobles revolted at this unusual punishment of their own kind or flocked to one of his rivals already hiding out in Transylvania, would he be able to survive?

But he only said, "You too."

Chapter Twelve

Visegrád, Hungary, 1474

It was inevitable that one day Stephen would come face-to-face with Vlad Dracula. The king's prisoner seemed to roam largely at will during the day, although he was generally accompanied by the watchful Count Szelényi, and the castle and grounds were not so huge that they could miss each other forever.

However, it was the day Stephen prepared to leave hurriedly for home that the dreaded and looked-for encounter finally occurred. And of course it had to be when Vlad's fortunes were once more up in the air, and the exiled prince had no cause whatsoever to feel gratitude toward the man who had betrayed him.

Stephen was hurrying through the gallery on his way to make a hasty farewell to the king, when he saw the figure striding toward him. Unmistakably Vlad. The sun beamed in through the high windows, momentarily dazzling him, and for a moment it was if the years rolled back. Nothing seemed to have changed about Vlad—he had the same lean but powerful frame, the same devastating dark green eyes and luxurious black hair. As he moved beyond the direct beam, Stephen could see that of course he had aged. There were more lines around his eyes and mouth, a fuller moustache and, surely, a wealth of patient pain in those fathomless eyes.

For a moment, Stephen thought he hadn't been noticed and wondered cravenly if he could pass by without a word. But although the other prince didn't break his stride, he did see him. And it seemed Vlad was the one who would pass without a word.

Stephen said, "Vlad," and was annoyed by the ridiculous huskiness of his own voice. Vlad halted almost abreast of him and regarded him without expression.

"Stephen," he returned, as if they'd parted only yesterday and he counted him of no more importance than a dog.

Stephen blurted, "I'm sorry things have turned against you again."

"I'll survive. I'm sorry things have gone badly for you too."

Stephen stared. "They haven't."

"I heard you married my niece. It's not good blood. And of course, the usurper Besarab Laiota has betrayed you."

"No, he hasn't," said Stephen, more annoyed by that than the slur on his wife, Radu's daughter.

Vlad smiled. It wasn't a pleasant smile. "He will."

Stephen knew it. As soon as he'd put Besarab on the Wallachian throne, the ungrateful bastard had started grovelling to the Ottomans. It was why he was here, negotiating with the king to try to restore Vlad, who alone had the right touch to keep a proper balance and resist the sultan. But he hated that Vlad knew it.

Vlad nodded ironically and passed on.

"Vlad?" Stephen said to his back. He paused but didn't turn. "Marry the king's sister and take Wallachia back. It'll be like the old days."

Vlad turned his head slowly, and Stephen was amazed to see an expression of total disbelief on his face. Pain and guilt smote him so hard he couldn't breathe. Then Vlad turned back and carried on his way.

So the betrothal would not happen tonight after all. Margit rather thought her lady had had a lucky escape and should probably thank God, fasting. But perversely, Ilona seemed even more upset by this turn of events. She wouldn't speak to Countess Hunyadi, and when Margit tried to cheer her up, she simply laid her cheek on the pillow and closed her eyes. Margit knew she wasn't asleep, but she couldn't force comfort upon her.

Sighing, she left her in the inner chamber and decided to go in search of her own amusement. There was, for instance, a very nice young nobleman with a charming smile who'd spoken to her in the gallery this morning. She wouldn't be averse to running into him again, although there probably wasn't any point now if they were going to pack their bags and head home to Transylvania.

Opening the door, she stepped into the passage and almost bumped into Count Szelényi.

"Lady Margit," he said, bowing, and Margit couldn't help preening at the title. "The Prince of Wallachia begs a few words with you, if it won't distract you from your care of Countess Ilona."

Margit blanched. "The Prince of… Oh dear, what does he want with me?"

"He's anxious for your mistress," Count Szelényi said severely.

Margit squared her shoulders. "We all are," she said with hostility. "And if you ask me, he's the cause of all her troubles."

"I don't ask you. You may tell the prince," said Szelényi maliciously.

Well, she would! Terrified or not, she wouldn't let Ilona be further upset if she could avoid it.

Count Szelényi led her into the formal gardens, where she saw the prince almost at once, seated on a stone bench with an open letter in his hand. He laid it down and rose to his feet as they approached.

"Thank you for coming," he said before she could speak. "Shall we walk?"

Deprived of words, Margit obediently walked beside him.

"How is your lady?" he asked abruptly.

"Distraught."

He nodded once, as though he expected that. Then, surprisingly, he said, "You have attended the countess for a long time?"

"Eleven years. Since her husband died."

He frowned. "Her husband... Did you know him? Was he a good man?"

"I believe so. He died only months after they married."

"Did she grieve?" If she didn't know better, she'd have thought the words were wrung out of him. But although they sounded slightly strangled, no doubt because of his excessively formal speech, his facial expression never altered.

Margit said, "It's my belief she's still grieving."

He glanced at her. "Why?"

"Because..." Margit struggled with something she'd never put into words before. "Because in all the years I've known her, she's never shown any desire for anything. She is sweet, kind, considerate—and completely indifferent to everything. Except her garden, which she nurtures like her own child."

The prince frowned. If he'd been looking directly at her, her knees would have buckled. As it was, her heart jumped in her breast so that she could barely breathe.

"And in all those years, she's never changed? She was like that when you met her?"

Margit nodded. "Yes." With conscious bravery, she added, "But she never once wept until she came here."

His gaze came back to her, and she made ready to run. But unexpectedly he said, "Is that a bad thing?"

"Is it good to weep?" Margit demanded.

"I don't know. It's better to laugh, as I recall, but at least either means you're alive... Your family lives near Horogszegi?"

Margit, as baffled by his change of subject as by his previous words, could only nod.

"Then do you remember when she first came home from Wallachia?"

"I remember. Her brother brought her."

"Miklós... How was she then? Just as you remember her?"

"I didn't see her then. It was said she'd had a terrible fright escaping the Ottomans and was alive only through God's intervention. I think she was very ill. Countess Hunyadi visited. They say even the king came, though I never saw him. Then she married György Baráth..."

"Who the devil is Baráth? I've never heard of him."

"They are an old family. Of the same stock as the Szilágyis. And my own family. Although neither of us rose as high as the Szilágyis."

"A curious marriage for the king's most marriageable cousin."

"She needed peace. He gave it to her."

"Did she tell you that?"

Margit bit her lip. "No," she admitted. "It's what we all thought."

"We being all the concerned neighbours around Horogszegi?"

When she nodded, he stared broodingly into the depths of a large bush before reaching out and pulling the head off the nearest flower. Margit swallowed.

He said, "I suppose there is no one in her train—servants or attendants of whatever station—who have been with her for longer than you?"

"No," said Margit with satisfaction.

The Impaler said, "Thank you for your time, and your help." And, turning on his heel, he strode back toward the palace.

Margit gazed after him with her mouth open. It was some time before she remembered to shut it.

"There *will* be war," Stephen told the king during his farewell audience. "I've invited it by not paying Moldavia's tribute to the sultan. A gesture from you could stave it off or enable a notable Christian victory."

Matthias sighed and went back to staring out the window onto his formal gardens. Today there was precious little enjoyment in them, let alone peace.

"I'm aware of it," he said at last. "As I told you before, everything possible will be done to preserve the principalities."

"And Vlad Dracula?"

Matthias lifted one annoyed hand as if to wave that name away. "I have offered him my sister—apparently that is not enough for His Mighty Majesty."

He sounded petulant, and he knew it. Vlad always brought out the worst in him. But he was damned if he'd pander to the Wallachian's every whim. In fact, if he was honest with himself, he had to admit that continuing to withhold Ilona had less to do with his mother's request and more to do with his desire to show Vlad who held all the cards. After twelve years' incarceration, it should have been obvious.

Stephen smiled slightly. "You never saw them together much, did you?"

Unbidden, a vague, half-forgotten vision flashed through Matthias's mind. His brother and cousins tense before an oddly magnificent stranger with a fabulous sword which he showed especially to him. And Ilona, taking his attention in a wild game of tag that somehow excluded everyone else. His small self had been resentful, glad when his father and Mihály had come to break it up…

Matthias frowned. "Not much, but enough," he said dryly.

Stephen said, "I always thought of them as two halves of the same whole. I told her that once, although I never told him…"

Matthias stared at him as the words sank in. He remembered Ilona when he'd seen her in the garden shortly after her arrival; and Ilona with Vlad in the gallery this morning, the vagueness falling from her like autumn leaves under his attention. Two halves of the same whole that it seemed he really couldn't afford to unite. Not for Ilona's sake, or even his mother's. But for his own. For the sake of his dynasty. His mother's scruples about Ilona had probably saved him from a disastrous decision.

Stephen's eyes fell before his, as if he sensed Mathias's new determination.

"You could," Stephen said delicately, "leave the matter of his marriage for future negotiation. Vlad's usefulness does not depend on his marriage to anyone."

Matthias glanced at him. "Meaning?"

"Meaning he's more than a prince. He's a military commander with considerable skill and genius. He inspires confidence and devotion among his own men, and among the Ottomans, as you know, he inspires a terror second to none that can only count in our favour."

Matthias tugged thoughtfully at his upper lip. "This confidence and devotion may no longer be so great."

"He'll win it back," Stephen said with certainty.

Matthias regarded him. "You are a man full of ideas, suddenly. Is this your reparation to your cousin, or are you helping yourself?"

Stephen's gaze didn't waver. "I hope I'm helping all of us."

When Count Szelényi reentered the room, Vlad turned from his desk and said impatiently, "Well?"

"Countess Ilona is resting."

Vlad smiled sourly. "You didn't get past the dragon, did you?"

"No," Szelényi confessed with a sheepish smile. "She is a very determined, if comely, dragon. However, I believe she is entirely devoted to her mistress."

"Devoted and misguided is a difficult combination to deal with."

"I don't believe she'll keep your message from the lady," Szelényi added with a shade of anxiety. "She just won't disturb her in order to deliver it."

Vlad nodded thoughtfully. "However, a note she may leave by her side without disturbing her. Would that offend our dragon's protective instincts?"

"It might work…"

With sardonic amusement, Vlad drew a piece of paper toward him and began to write swiftly, conscious always of other eyes that might read it. In fact, it was Szelényi's duty to read it. Vlad was fairly certain it would be beneath his honour to do so now, but then it was not really Szelényi's prying eyes which concerned him.

"Ilona," he wrote. "I will not give up. Give me something, anything that might aid me." It might, he thought, be taken as a request for a love token. Although he was pretty sure Ilona wouldn't see it that way. The old Ilona would have understood immediately that he was asking for information, for anything, to use as leverage to change the king's mind. Whether this frail, vague, and distraught version would be able to read between the lines was another matter.

He sealed it with unnecessary force, as anger invaded him once more. But all his life he had schooled himself to put the anger aside before it prevented his brain from working and brought about disaster and even now, he forced himself to remember courtesy and common sense.

"Forgive me for treating you like a messenger boy," he said ruefully to Szelényi. "It is a matter of honour to me, and you are the only man I trust to act for me."

A tinge of colour spread into Szelényi's cheeks. "I am glad to. And please know, it is also an honour for me."

Then, taking the brief note, he departed. Vlad watched him go, then turned back to the letter he'd been previously writing to Carstian. That too was a difficult task. It had taken Carstian a long time to become reconciled with Radu, and Vlad didn't want to endanger his old friend or the man's family by speaking out of turn.

He still had friends in Wallachia, good people who had never deserted him in their hearts, however necessary the physical submission to his enemies had been. He would reward that when he went home. In the darkest of days, when hopelessness had engulfed him, their loyalty had been all that kept him going.

The words he'd written danced in front of his eyes. It was Ilona's face he saw clearly. Ilona as a girl, laughing and lively and insatiably curious. Ilona on their first sleigh ride, berating him. Ilona dancing in his arms, glowing with such happiness that her beauty dazzled him. Ilona now, thin and faded perhaps, but still beautiful, still his...

How long did it take to walk to Ilona's apartments and back? Where was Szelényi?

Vlad pushed his letter aside. He was in no state to concentrate on it, let alone do it justice. He rose from his chair, stretching prodigiously. He needed to be in the open, he needed to ride for miles, to run on his own legs for miles, to best someone, anyone in sword play. Or in a straightforward, unarmed fight. He slammed his fist into the nearest cushion.

When Szelényi got back, he'd make him take him out of this closed-in hell. It was worse than Tîrgovişte.

Hurry, damn you.

Szelényi's familiar knock sounded at the door, heralding his slightly breathless entrance. To Vlad's disappointment, he still carried the letter to Ilona in his hand. Striding to the prince, he held it out like a prize.

"The lady answered."

Vlad's heart soared. Seizing the letter, he shook it open and read the single line she'd written under his:

"There is nothing you can say."

What in hell does that mean?

Frustrated, he tossed the useless note on to his desk. "Count, would you care to ride out with me?"

"Of course. I'll have them ready the horses."

As Szelényi left once more, Vlad picked up the letter and gazed at it harder, as if willing it to reveal something more. Like what had happened to Ilona between her escape and her first marriage. *Yes, her first marriage. I will make another for her!*

Her writing was just as he remembered it—hasty, almost to the point of a scrawl, and yet perfectly legible, free of elaborate loops. Firm.

He realised there was hope in that line. Perhaps not the hope he'd been looking for, but surely it told him she wasn't sinking back into indifference and vagueness.

"I stopped paying attention, Vlad, but I was never stupid."

Vlad had the feeling that, distressed or not by the king's infernal procrastination and wavering, Ilona was paying attention again.

All he had to do was find a way to make Matthias change his mind, to make their marriage possible.

Chapter Thirteen

Transylvania and Wallachia, 1457-1458

"He's coming, he's coming!" The servant gasped, collapsing in a breathless heap on the floor. "Save yourself, lady, take your lady mother and run! Everyone must run!"

"Stand up and explain yourself," Ilona said severely. Although the man's hysterical fear could not but communicate itself to her, making her stomach lurch and twist, she knew better than to act on his fear without any facts.

She was alone in the comfortable hall at Horogszegi. Her mother, recovering from some fever that had laid her low all summer and autumn, was in her bedchamber, resting. Mihály, inevitably, was in Hungary, and Miklós and his wife absent as usual on one of the larger estates. And so it fell to her, peacefully embroidering a shawl as a gift for Maria, to act on this new crisis.

"Who is coming?" she demanded as the man hauled himself to his feet, still overexcited but with a touch of the sheepish behind the wildness in his eyes.

He uttered, "Dracula!"

Before she could prevent it, one arm closed across her leaping heart. Her other hand nearly made it as far as her hair before she forced it to drop back to her side. The needle fell, dangling from her work.

"Vlad Dracula? The Prince of Wallachia?" she said, to remove any possible doubt.

"Of course!"

"Don't be silly," Ilona reproved. "The prince will not harm us or anyone on this estate! He is my father's friend and ally. You are spreading stupid fear where there should be none!"

All the same, she had to admit that the man's behaviour was at least partly Vlad's fault. He'd led several punitive raids into Transylvania, to help Mihály quell Cilli-inspired revolts and to punish the German towns for their fickle harbouring of pretenders to Vlad's throne. The German towns had long played that game, of course, and the princes had been forced to put up with it, doing no more than writing strong letters of protest or curtailing the town's trading privileges in Wallachia.

Only Vlad went a step further, using military intervention, and if the carnage he left behind was ridiculously exaggerated by the towns to evoke the sympathy of Hungary, well, it was still horribly efficient and thorough.

Mihály was back in control of Transylvania, thanks largely to Vlad's help and the fearsome reputation he was accruing—much according to plan, Ilona thought cynically. But his raids had never come close to Horogszegi before. There was no need.

"Are you sure it's the Prince of Wallachia?" she asked the man doubtfully.

"He's not as easy man to mistake!" was the indignant answer.

Ilona frowned at him for insolence, and he tried visibly to pull himself together. "It's him," he said firmly. "And a huge, wild army. Oh my God, he's at the gate! My lady, what'll we do?"

"Let him in," Ilona said dryly. "With all respect. He is a welcome guest in my father's house!"

Not entirely convinced by her calm good sense, the man seemed inclined to dawdle, to debate the sense of allowing such a man entrance, but before he could go and obey her, Ilona heard the sound of voices below. Something thumped loudly, and booted footsteps sounded on the stairs, leaping up them, surely, two or more at a time.

Ilona and the servant stared at each other, each wondering if somehow Ilona had got it wrong.

The door burst open, and Vlad Dracula strode in.

At once the room filled with his size, his presence. Though he wore no armour, there was something unmistakably martial about his dark clothing and long boots. His father's sword and several daggers clanked at his belt. His long, black hair flowed over his leather-padded shoulders.

Ilona stood up, immediately drawing his gaze. His furious dark eyes slammed into her like a blow.

"Prince," she managed. "You are most welcome, though you take us by surprise."

The fury darkened, retreated enough for a gleam of sardonic amusement and, perhaps, shame. "Forgive my—sudden—entrance. Your people denied any of the family was home, and I knew they were lying."

"That's the price you pay for *a few atrocities from the past*. May I know why you've come?"

A smile had begun to play around his lips and eyes. "I suppose I must have come to be chastised again." He hesitated. "You must know there is no danger from me. Neither I nor my men will harm anyone or anything of yours."

"I'm aware of it. They"—she indicated the servants now gathering in the doorway, staring at Vlad with popping eyes—"are not."

"I'm sorry," he said abruptly. "I need to speak to Mihály, and this seemed the easiest way."

"He's in Buda."

Turning away, Vlad looked as if he would slam his suddenly closed fist on the table. With an obvious effort of will, he relaxed his hand.

"I understood he would be here."

"He was detained in Buda. He still plans to come home, but we don't know when. Jakob, have them bring wine for the prince, then go about your business." The man bolted, looking back over his shoulder as if unsure whether it was right to leave her in the company of the terrible prince. Vlad kicked the door shut in the faces of the other servants and walked towards Ilona.

She regarded him in what she hoped was a sensible and mature way. "Why did you need to speak to my father so urgently? Can I help?"

A short laugh escaped him. "I don't know—can you?" The smile was back, teasing about his lips and eyes, but she had the uncomfortable feeling that the anger hadn't left, was merely controlled—for the time being.

He said, "Perhaps you know I have been in correspondence with your father."

She nodded. "Of course."

"About you."

Her breath caught. The unwelcome colour began to seep into her face as she turned away.

He said, "You didn't know?"

"I know there was a letter from you."

A letter proposing a marriage between the prince and Ilona. Mihály had told her that much, sending her into a state of blissful shock. She hadn't dared to hope that those few moments in his arms, his kisses, would lead to anything further. Men flirted with attraction; they married politics and power. And Mihály's position in either was still uncertain. Though that fact hadn't made her father grab at the offer. Instead, he'd told her about it, brooding, frowning at her without really seeing her.

"Historically, Wallachia is not stable," he'd mused with regret. "Vlad might change that. If anyone can, it will be him. But a marriage for you… Interesting. I'll discuss it with your aunt."

In an agony of anticipation she'd waited and waited for anything further to be said on the matter, and nothing ever was. Gradually, the fever of longing died to a dull ache, because she imagined Vlad had lost interest, found a better marriage to pursue, although she heard nothing about that either. Maria kept her informed of court intrigues from time to time, but even she had said nothing.

And so Ilona went back to waiting.

Vlad said, "I came for an answer." His implacable voice reached deep inside her, filling her with hope once more, because he hadn't forgotten, had, in fact, cared enough to come riding furiously out of his way with an army at his back just to get his answer.

Ilona repeated, "He's not here," and it came out as a whisper.

"What did you say?"

She cleared her throat. "I said, he's not here."

Vlad took a step closer to her. "No. What did you say to your father? I know he cares for you deeply, would be reluctant to give you where you didn't want to go."

Perhaps, Ilona thought ruefully. But she'd have to make a spectacular fuss and have the reasons listed in writing with evidence. And even then she doubted it. She tried to drag her wayward thought back into line, to remember the question he expected her to answer.

She said, "I didn't say anything. He didn't ask me."

Her head was turned away from him, gazing at the door, willing the servants to come with the wine, terrified in case they did before... *before what?*

She felt his fingers under her chin, gentle, yet shocking and impossible to resist as it turned her face up to his.

"I'm asking you now," he said softly. "Do you want this marriage, Ilona Szilágyi?"

Heat flamed under his fingers, flooded her. "Don't make me answer that," she whispered.

"Why not?" His hooded eyelids swept down on a flash of something that looked like pain. It wrung her heart, forced her to blurt the truth.

"If I admit it, I admit so much more that I couldn't live with if…"

The long, black lashes snapped upward. "If what?"

She took hold of his wrist, trying in vain to dislodge his fingers from their hold of her chin. He said, "If I don't love you?"

Her hand fell away, leaving her helpless. She closed her eyes, afraid once more, not of him but of herself.

He said low, "Tell me, Ilona. If you don't want it, I'll never trouble you with it again. If you do, you have to tell me. Do you want it?"

She gasped, forcing her eyes open to meet the blaze of his. "I want it," she whispered, and the light in his dark eyes seemed to flare. His lips curved upward. The fingers on her chin moved, caressing, making her shiver. He bent his head, and her lips, remembering, parted for him of their own accord.

The door whisked open, and abruptly Ilona was free. Vlad stood in front of her, instinctively protecting, which made her want to laugh and cry with pride.

Especially when her mother's voice said, "Ilona? I hear we have a guest… Why, Prince, how wonderful to see you again."

"He's *dead*?" Ilona stared at her aunt in disbelief.

"I just said so," snapped Erzsébet, but not in temper, merely to get it out of the way so that her mind could race ahead, thinking, planning.

King Ladislas, known as the Posthumous because his father— *"If it was his father!"* Erzsébet always said cuttingly—had died before his birth, had suddenly died himself.

"But he was so young…"

Erzsébet's lips twisted. "László was young too." It was a grief neither forgotten nor forgiven, but overwhelming it was, clearly, the future.

"What will happen now?" Ilona said. But she knew the answer. Her father and Erzsébet would fight to make Matthias king far sooner than anyone had expected.

And if they won, if Matthias was elected King of Hungary, then she, Ilona, would be the king's cousin. It was, no doubt, the least of anyone else's concerns, but that couldn't stop her own personal, wayward thoughts—that at last she would be a worthy wife for the Prince of Wallachia.

And from Mihály's point of view, surely now of all times, as he struggled against the next inevitable Habsburg candidate, he needed to cement his alliance with Vlad Dracula.

Carstian and Stoica glanced at each other, then back to the prince, who was still gazing at the letter as though stunned. Stoica, who had spoken for Vlad at the recent peace negotiations between the town of Brasov and Mihály Szilágyi, had been reporting the favourable outcome for all concerned—except, of course, for Dan, the most troublesome pretender to the Wallachian throne, who'd finally been evicted from his refuge in Brasov—when the messenger intervened.

"Bad news?" Carstian hazarded at last.

"Bad?" Vlad dropped the letter. "Damned if I know. Ladislas is dead."

"The king? Dead? How?"

"Apparently of natural causes. Last month, in Prague." Vlad reached for the wine jug and rattled it on the table. At once, a servant appeared and poured cups for each of them.

"I don't see that it's bad," Stoica said judiciously. "If the Habsburgs gain the throne again, we've lost nothing."

"It may lose us Mihály Szilágyi's favourable influence," Carstian pointed out. "But I don't believe the Habsburgs *will* win. If you ask me, the Hunyadi boy will be elected in a wave of glory because of his father's memory."

"If the Szilágyis have anything to do with it—and they will—that's exactly what will happen," said Vlad.

"But that is the best thing possible for us!"

Vlad knew it. It would give the German townships in Transylvania less excuse and less cover for troubling him. And he would have the greatest friend possible at the Hungarian court in Mihály Szilágyi, who undoubtedly would govern in the name of the king until Matthias came of age.

He just prayed that Mihály had sent his messenger with the marriage contract before the king had died. Because if he hadn't, he would inevitably start looking ridiculously high for Ilona. Always in search of more power or even security should anything go wrong with Matthias.

Vlad understood that. It was what he would do himself. And that made him fear the worst.

Rightly, as it turned out. When a messenger finally came from Buda, bearding the prince in his hall at Rucăr as he held audiences with petitioners, he brought not the contracts but a letter from Mihály Szilágyi excusing himself from entering such negotiations at this busy juncture. Although he valued nothing more highly than Vlad's continued friendship, his first concern had to be matters of state.

"Negotiations?" Vlad raged, sweeping everything off the table in one violent sweep of his arm. Abruptly, the room fell silent. "We'd done all the damned negotiating! Several times! And now…"

He broke off, reining in the full force of his vile temper for the benefit of the others in the room waiting to speak to him. And yet he wanted to maintain that anger, that fury, because it kept out the despair.

Ilona was further from his reach than she'd ever been. His stupid, childish dream of a life partner who was also his friend and his lover should never have been allowed to exist. He was a prince with a country to rule, not a snivelling boy to weep over lost love.

And yet all he really wanted to do was weep and howl all his pain away. Preferably in Ilona's arms.

He laughed harshly. "Happy Christmas. Bring the next petition."

The boyars hadn't forgotten Easter. They knew his generosity was occasionally barbed. It was why he made a special effort to make the Christmas feast enjoyable for all. Not to curry favour after his cruelty but to remind them of the difference. Under his regime, the rewards for loyalty were as great as the punishment for betrayal.

And so, after being the perfect host, eating, drinking, dancing with his guests, he had left them to it and retired to his lonely quarters to get blind drunk.

He succeeded in that too, as he discovered when he rose to his feet and stumbled to keep his balance. Perhaps he should just fall into bed and finish the flagon there. At least that way, no one would find him sprawled unconscious on the floor.

On the way to his bedchamber, he became distracted by the moon, beaming in through the narrow window, and paused to admire it. He hoped Ilona gazed at it too and thought of him. What was she doing? Celebrating with her family...if they took the time away from advancing the cause of Matthias's election.

Vlad sprawled on the bench beneath the window and rested his burning forehead on the wall's cool stone. Once he'd been naïve enough to hope for Ilona by his side this Christmas. Missing her was like an ache he could neither lose nor assuage. Not with work, not with wine.

Maybe he should go out in disguise to some low tavern and pick a fight. Grimly amused by that idea, he grabbed the jerkin he wore for hard riding and left the room. Not that he'd any real intention of carrying through his drunken fantasy. But the fresh cold of the night air called to him.

By the time he reached the stairs, he had better control over his wayward limbs and was able to walk down with almost his normal pace. Annoyingly, the first thing he thought of at the door was that in the spring, he'd taken Ilona out this way and kissed her in the moonlight.

He hadn't really thought she'd let him, and her response had both surprised and delighted him. And knowing Ilona, he'd believed then there was more than the thrill of dangerous flirting in her heart.

He still believed that. Was she suffering as much as he? He couldn't wish that for her, and yet anything else maddened him.

Hauling the door open, he wanted desperately to be rid of this feeling, this agony, before it consumed him.

A faint, fluttering behind him made him turn his head. Someone slid under his arm and for an instant, he thought, incredibly, that it was Ilona. He could swear she smelled of Ilona.

But it was quite a different pair of eyes that peered up at him, half-anxious, half-teasing. "Your Highness? Is everything well?"

Maria, he recognised. Maria Gerzsenyi, Countess Hunyadi's little spy, Ilona's friend. What business did she have smelling of Ilona?

Drawn, he lowered his head and located the distinctive scent to her shoulders and lower—a rather beautiful embroidered shawl pinned over her breasts for modesty, yet still revealing enough to set a tortured man's blood on fire.

"Your shawl is beautiful," he observed. He didn't even slur his words.

"Thank you!" she said breathlessly. "Ilona sent it to me as a Christmas gift. She does such lovely work."

Vlad laughed and placed his hand over the shawl. Beneath its soft texture, he felt her heart beating like a bird's. He put his lips to her ear. "What do you want, Maria? To come to my bed?"

Her breath came quick and uneven. "To serve Your Highness any way I can," she managed.

"Oh, good answer." He bent his head and pressed his lips over the scarf and the wildly beating heart beneath. He closed his eyes and imagined it was Ilona. The woman began to speak, but he hushed her, inhaling before he raised his head and claimed her willing lips.

"Don't talk," he said into her mouth. "Don't talk."

She didn't.

It took the letter some time to find her, since she was in Buda with Countess Hunyadi. Matthias, duly elected as King of Hungary, was everybody's darling. And Mihály Szilágyi, his uncle, was appointed governor for five years to guide the young king's first steps in ruling his domain.

To Ilona, it was almost amusing to be treated like royalty. To *be* royalty, even if only on her little cousin's account. She wondered if Vlad would come in person to swear allegiance to the new king and felt her breast constrict with longing. Mihály, however, whenever he mentioned her marriage, never did so in conjunction with Vlad's name. With more than a hint of indignation, Ilona realised he was too sure of Vlad now. Vlad was his ally with or without the marriage, so Ilona was a far more useful bargaining tool elsewhere.

And when she tried to broach the subject with Mihály, she realised he was no longer listening to her. Both he and his sister had bigger issues to consider than her opinions of lesser men. So, frustrated at every turn and still, interminably, waiting, Ilona was delighted to see Maria's ornate if slightly childish handwriting among the letters from home. It was always a joy to hear from Maria, and now, sometimes, her letters gave her the added secret pleasure of domestic news of Vlad.

She waited until the countess went for her afternoon rest. Then, enjoying her brief gift of solitude, she took the letter with her to the fireside and settled down to get warm among the wintry draughts of Buda Castle to enjoy it.

She even smiled at Maria's opening rush of words. Something, clearly, had happened to excite and please her volatile friend. But because Maria tried to tell her so many things at once, it took Ilona some time to decipher it. At first she thought she'd misunderstood completely and went back to the beginning. But slowly, horrendously, the truth began to form in her mind.

Something cold pinched around her heart. It hurt. That must be what hurt. Maria's happy words faded into blackness before her eyes. Ilona lifted the letter and dropped it into the blinding flames.

Vlad Dracula took the tiny baby into his arms and gazed down at him in wonder. It didn't seem possible that any living creature could have fingers so small. He became fascinated by the child's perfect, miniature ear.

"Your son," Maria murmured. Vlad spared her a smiling glance—she too looked tiny and exhausted in the huge bed, yet happy enough to be purring like a cat—before returning his attention to the baby.

"Mihnea," he uttered. "That is a good name in my family."

Reluctantly, he surrendered his son to the waiting nurse. Mihnea made a tiny, grunting sound that tugged at his heart.

Maria said, "You are pleased with our son?"

He sank onto the bed beside her and smoothed the damp hair from her face. "I am well pleased," he admitted. "And grateful."

Maria smiled and turned her head to kiss his hand. "Thank you," she murmured. "I am so lucky, so blessed."

Vlad rose to his feet and left her falling asleep. The euphoria of his son's birth lingered and with it the surge of affection for his mother. In many ways, taking Maria as his mistress was not the cleverest thing he'd ever done. She was sweet and good-natured, but though far from stupid, she had no interest in the things that mattered. Like governance and alliances and balancing power within the country and without. Besides, Vlad was well aware that he couldn't have chosen a mistress more guaranteed to wound Ilona Szilágyi.

He hadn't done it for that reason. In fact, after the drunken night in Tîrgovişte, which he could barely remember—beyond a shawl and the aching smell of Ilona—he had resolved not to repeat the experience. He had taken Maria for the wrong reasons, and his best excuse was the desperation of his body, which, for some romantic reason of honour, he'd kept pure during all the protracted negotiations for Ilona. But he was an intensely physical man, and he'd been unable to stop himself from finally seeking release when opportunity offered. And this child, Mihnea, was the result.

He didn't think he'd set eyes on Maria for the next two months, until she came to him privately one day and told him she was pregnant by him. Cynically, he'd doubted that—until he looked into her eyes and read a genuine love he'd done nothing to inspire.

Startled, he'd swallowed the words with which he'd meant to dismiss her and asked her instead what she wanted to do. She didn't ask him to marry her, which, fortunately, saved him the trouble of refusing. Instead, she fell into some inarticulate story of her youth and how she'd been misled by a man before and given birth to his child, which had been taken from her. And again, the grief and misery in her face had been genuine. Further questioning had elicited the information that Ilona and Countess Hunyadi had helped her then, and how Ilona had kept her secret and been her only friend.

But the point of her story was she couldn't bear to give away another child, nor suffer the shame of a nameless birth. And so he'd acknowledged the child and made her his official mistress. God knew it was no hardship to make love to her.

In fact it would be hard to force himself to leave tomorrow morning for his new castle at Poenari, but there were matters to attend to there before winter set in.

Returning to his hall to announce the birth of his son to the waiting court, he found a familiar messenger skulking in the doorway.

Wordlessly, Vlad held his hand out and received the document. He clapped the man once on the shoulder and nodded to the boyar Iova to pay him. Then, striding to the table amid the expectant silence, he swept up his cup and raised it high in an enthusiastic toast.

"To my son, Mihnea! May he have a long and happy life!"

They roared out their approval and drank deeply. His line had an heir, to keep out his Ottoman-dominated brother Radu as much as the hated Danesti clan.

Satisfied, Vlad sat and opened his letter—which cast rather a blight on his happy day. Mihály Szilágyi had been dismissed from his position as governor and the young King Matthias had taken up the reins of independent government himself. Worse, he'd arrested Mihály and imprisoned him.

"That," Vlad said with a shiver of prescience, "is not good."

Chapter Fourteen

Tîrgovişte and Poenari, Wallachia, 1459

Mihály Szilágyi said, "Come with me to Wallachia."

And here she was. Although it was the last place in the world she wanted to visit, she couldn't refuse her father, especially not after he came home from prison, a changed and chastened man. He had endured prison before, of course, and escaped none the worse for his ordeal, but somehow it was different to be turned on by your own nephew, the boy you had brought to power. And so Ilona didn't even try to talk him out of it. Part of her was even touched that he wanted her company again.

All she did do was suggest her mother came too—but, still low from last year's illness, Countess Szilágyi remained at home. When Ilona remarked casually that she would prefer to avoid the court and perhaps spend time with Maria, Countess Hunyadi snorted.

"She is not a fit companion for an unmarried lady of the royal family."

"I believe she is considered perfectly respectable in Wallachia," Ilona returned calmly. "Her son is just as acceptable as an heir to the prince as the child of any woman he actually marries."

Erzsébet sniffed. "Maybe. In Wallachia. Besides, if you ask me, Maria will be wherever the court is."

Mihály's purpose, now he was again in Transylvania, was to discuss with Vlad the parameters of their alliance. Matthias, in an attempt to cow the prince or to replace him, had again sent the pretender Dan to the Transylvanian town of Brasov, to act as a focus for Wallachian discontent and rebellion. Vlad would not be happy about that.

Ilona's purpose, if she had one beyond restoring the spark of enthusiasm to her father, was to avoid Vlad. But if she couldn't, then she knew she would deal with that too. A year and a half without him or the hope of him had returned her to full strength and common sense.

Despite that, she couldn't help her profound relief when they discovered Maria to be alone in Tîrgovişte. Vlad, apparently, was in the south, organising the construction of a new fortress around the villages of Bucharest.

Mihály set off at once after the prince, leaving Ilona with Maria. They watched from the rain-spattered window as he rode away. Then, almost gleefully, Maria tugged at her arm.

"Come and meet Mihnea!"

Prepared, Ilona went with her gladly to the nursery where the seven-month-old baby sat amid a collection of bright toys, gurgling happily while his nurse watched over him. When they entered, he reached up his arms immediately to Maria, and something constricted Ilona's throat.

Not jealousy or pain. Just simple longing.

The child put his arms round his mother's neck and from that position of smug safety smiled at Ilona.

Her heart melted.

She was twenty-one years old. She would have to marry soon and have a baby of her own to love. It was, Aunt Erzsébet said, the consolation of many women given in marriage to unpalatable husbands, and for the first time, Ilona understood her. Now that she was over her youthful passion, she still hoped for a palatable husband but was realistic enough not to rely on it.

Kneeling on the soft rug, watching Maria with the baby, Ilona said with genuine warmth, "You're happy."

"Oh yes," Maria agreed, dropping a kiss on Mihnea's bald head. She cast Ilona a wicked smile. "I don't think I'm cut out to be a nobleman's wife. I prefer the excitement of being a prince's mistress. Well, this prince's mistress." Her smile faded, and, after glancing at the nurse, she said in Hungarian, "You don't despise me, do you? For what I've done?"

"Of course I don't." As the old pain threatened to grip her heart again, she strove to drive it off.

"I'm treated just as a wife here," Maria said anxiously. "The prince shows me every respect, and if he isn't…"

"Isn't what?" Ilona prompted, against her better judgment. God knew she wanted this conversation over with.

"If he isn't faithful, I know he loves me best."

She supposed the jealousy was inevitable. She was prepared for that. Even for the indignation on Maria's behalf. What she hadn't expected along with them was the fierce surge of satisfaction that Maria couldn't make him faithful either.

Unworthy, Ilona…

"I'm glad," she managed to say as she jumped to her feet. Impossible to stay still. She added dubiously, "He doesn't flaunt other women in front of you, does he?"

"Of course not," Maria said, shocked. "I never know anything about them, except that they exist. Otherwise, he would be in my bed more often."

I can't hear any more of this.

"I'm sorry I haven't written recently," she said, plucking from the air one of the many things she had to say to her old friend.

"Of course, you've had so many troubles! I'm so glad to see your father free and powerful once more."

Powerful? Mihály's trouble was at least partly that he felt himself completely powerless and at the mercy of the child he'd intended to guide. They all were.

Vlad reined in his horse at the top of the hill and gazed with satisfaction out over the many lesser hills and valleys. In the distance, he could make out Tîrgovişte with its spires and turrets, nestling among the fertile hills and bright blue lakes.

The wind blew his hair out behind him, and he lifted his face into its sharp coolness. Mihály's horse snorted beside his own.

Vlad said, "We'll go fishing tomorrow, if you wish."

A smile flickered across the older man's lined face. "A day of leisure. How extraordinarily appealing."

"I wondered if you'd had too many of those just recently," Vlad said, alluding to his imprisonment.

"Forced inaction is not the same thing."

"True," Vlad agreed with feeling.

For a time, they sat in silence, letting their horses rest while they gazed out over the countryside. Vlad never tired of looking. He loved this land, from the tiniest blade of grass to the tallest mountain.

Mihály said, "It's like a drug. Like poppy juice."

"What is?" Vlad asked. Though he knew, he needed Mihály to keep talking.

"Power. It consumes you, uses you up, and yet you can't bring yourself to lay it down. Being without it is like a physical pain. Like watching someone else violate your wife."

Vlad reached out and slowly pulled his horse's black ear. "She isn't your wife. She's Matthias's."

Mihály smiled into the wind. "I know." He sighed. "I put his son on the throne. I made John Hunyadi's son King of Hungary. Is that enough to secure my place in history?"

"A mere trifle," Vlad said. "You put *me* on the throne of Wallachia."

Mihály laughed, as he was meant to do. Then, turning to look at him, with the smile dying in his eyes, he said, "You are generous to remember any small part I played in that."

"I will always remember."

Mihály drew in his breath. "The marriage. With Ilona. I behaved ill, drawing back at the last minute. It was never meant to offend you or show disrespect for you or what you've achieved here."

"I know."

"God help me, I just wanted to keep all my bargaining power where I could use it."

"And you still haven't," Vlad observed.

Mihály urged his horse forward over the ridge of the hill, and Vlad followed.

Mihály said, "And now it's not in *my* power any more. The king controls all royal marriages. There will come a time, I know, when he wants to buy your loyalty."

Vlad's lips twisted. "My loyalty is not for sale. Ever."

"Then you are a rare man indeed. For what it's worth, Vlad, if you still want her, I'll do what I can to speak for you. When it won't do you more harm than good."

Vlad couldn't suppress the stab of bitterness. If Mihály had only acted on this two years ago... But he wouldn't waste his time in recrimination or regret. The game was not over yet, and the prize could still be won.

Delighted with her purchase in the market, Ilona went directly to the nursery, where, at this hour of the afternoon, she fully expected to find both the child and his mother.

"Maria?" she called, opening the door and walking in. Though she could hear the baby laughing, his usual place on the rug was empty. In her chair close by, the nurse still smiled at her and continued sewing. Before the woman could speak, a movement by the window caught Ilona's eye. Dazzled her.

Mihnea sat on his father's naked shoulders, held firmly under the arms while he held on to Vlad's curls with his stubby little hands and crowed with laughter.

Vlad stared at her, unmoving.

Ilona wanted to die.

His arms and chest were naked, his shrugged-off white linen shirt dangling upside down over his belt, hanging over his hips to his knees. As if he'd just arrived, thrown off the worst of his travel-stained clothes, and come straight to see his son because he couldn't wait any longer. It was the worst of all possible scenarios and one she had never envisaged, to come upon him in the midst of so domestic and private a scene.

That he was as stunned as she provided no consolation.

"Ilona." His husky voice drove straight through her. "I didn't know you were here." He lifted the boy down from his shoulders, moving him into a more conventional hold. "Mihály didn't say."

"I was looking for Maria," she blurted and at last made her feet move toward the door. "I didn't know you were here either."

"I rode in with Mihály only minutes ago. Ilona."

She was forced to turn, her hand already on the latch. He was walking toward her, shaking her with unreasonable panic. His arms were thick with the muscles of a swordsman. His gaze was on her hands.

"What do you have there?"

The toy she'd bought for Mihnea. With relief, she held it straight out to the baby, regarding it as much as a weapon to ward off his father. It made the odd rattle that had first attracted her attention in the market.

Vlad took it with unexpected interest and turned to deposit both son and toy on the floor. He crouched down with the baby, and Ilona couldn't take her eyes off his naked back. Not because it was beautiful—although it was, rippling and golden in the sunlight—but because it bore a mass of long, deep scars, like the marks left on snow after a hectic day's sledging.

Mihnea grasped the small, carved stone toy, which was shaped like a horse and painted white with brown eyes and black lashes and nostrils. As he lifted it, gazing into its eyes, it rattled faintly again. Mihnea frowned and shook it, and the beads within made a noise almost exactly like a horse's whinny.

Vlad laughed. Mihnea screamed with delight and jiggled up and down on his bottom to the constant wninnying of his new horse. Vlad looked round over his shoulder. "What a beautiful toy. Thank you."

"I just saw it in the market," she muttered.

Again she turned to go, but the old curiosity, the old need to understand him, held her captive. She glanced back to find him still crouched with the baby, still watching her with eyes so veiled they looked black.

She blurted, "What happened to your back?"

A lady shouldn't have seen his back. She certainly shouldn't have seen or commented upon the scars. But he didn't seem to mind.

Rising to his feet, he said only, "A legacy of my stay with the Ottomans."

"They beat you?"

He shrugged. "Sometimes."

"Many times!"

His smile was twisted. "I never took well to discipline."

Emotion churned inside her. It might have been pity. "You said they were a gentle people," she whispered.

"They're not all gentle."

His eyes held her, and with despair, she felt herself drowning all over again. He took a step closer. "Ilona…"

The door on the other side of the room, the one that opened onto Maria's bedchamber, flung open, and Maria bustled in.

"Vlad," she crooned, walking toward him with both hands held out. Then, taking in the vision of his seminaked form, she dropped her arms in horror. "Vlad!" she exclaimed in quite another voice. "That is a most improper state in which to greet Ilona!"

Vlad's lips quirked. "Oh, I don't know. Ilona is quite used to being greeted by me in an improper state."

Then he remembered. He remembered looking at her *like that*. Thank God she was older now and wiser.

"I'm sorry," she got out. "I'll leave you alone." And finally she fumbled with the latch and opened the door. She fled.

"I admire what you've done here," Mihály said. From the tower where he stood between Ilona and Vlad, he gazed out on the village of Poenari, at the dramatic cliff that dropped in an almost sheer line from the castle walls to the River Arges. It was one of five towers which guarded the Transylvanian border, commanding views over vast swaths of mountainous land—harsh, spectacular, and curiously beautiful. This was, apparently, Vlad's favourite.

"I'm fond of it," Vlad acknowledged. "I come here as often as I can."

Beyond the prince's stern profile, Mihály turned his head. "I meant this new prosperity, the land you've opened up, the safety of your roads and your towns."

Vlad inclined his head without either pride or modesty. It was only what he had set out to do.

Mihály added, "I didn't mean the castle. Though it's very fine, I'm still not convinced of the morality of your building methods."

From Vlad's faint, twisted smile, Ilona surmised that not many men would have had the courage to state such an opinion to him.

Of course, he had a deserved reputation for harshness, not least because his most frequent form of execution was impalement, a barbaric cruelty admittedly still practised in many other countries too. Ilona didn't like to think of it, though she had heard his subjects speak of it with both relish and perverse pride. Vlad's policy of "a few atrocities" appeared to work. In all their travels here, Ilona had seen no evidence of crime or of punishment.

Vlad said, "The castle was an interesting experiment. Of course, they couldn't build it alone. I still needed engineers and experienced builders, but the prisoners made reasonable labourers, in the end."

"In the end?" Ilona couldn't help repeating, and then could have kicked herself because as Vlad turned to her, she saw in his eyes that he had expected, even wanted her, to pounce on those words. Never one to refuse a challenge, she asked, "Did they all die?"

"Surprisingly, no," Vlad said. "Some did. They weren't used to hard work or to living rough, and it told on their health. And there were accidents, of course, carrying such large stones over such dangerous ground, but those would have happened anyway, killing people who were innocent of any crime."

Ilona, who'd heard plenty of rumours since her return to Wallachia, wouldn't let that pass either. "The children were not guilty. You had children here too."

"I had children here," he acknowledged. "Rebellion runs in families. If I had left the children free, what would they have done? Grown up, hating me even more for punishing their parents, and from places like Brasov and Sibiu they'd have worked against me."

"And now?" Ilona asked, fascinated in spite of herself. Mihály, presumably leaving them to fight it out, stepped back and moved to another window for a different view.

Vlad said, "Now at least, there's a chance. They saw at first hand what it means to oppose me. And they saw that I can be merciful. And their parents now live useful lives as farmers or builders. Some of them," he amended. "At any rate, they no longer have the wealth or the will to intrigue against me."

"You broke their spirits," Ilona murmured aloud, gazing sideways at the massive walls of the castle. Such an outcome seemed incredibly sad suddenly, taking away what made the person who they were.

"Considering the spirits in question, they were no loss."

If they had been in a sleigh, Ilona thought with dark amusement, he'd have pushed it out of the window and ridden straight down onto the rocks. But there was more to it than that. There was the unbearable pain of his brother's murder and, she suspected, his long-planned revenge hadn't given him the release he expected.

"My brother," he said without warning, "was afraid of the dark."

Ilona's heart twisted. Mircea's murderers couldn't have found a crueler death if they'd tried. Without meaning to, she reached across the space between them and clasped his hand. His head snapped round; his eyes stared into hers. Hastily, realising her mistake, she tried to snatch her hand back, but his rough fingers moved, gripping hers strongly before he released her and turned away.

Mihály said, "My daughter feels for everyone, good and bad. It isn't always an advantage."

Vlad shrugged. "Maybe not. But if I had a conscience, I'd give it to Ilona for safekeeping."

Unaccountably angry because he was still trying to perpetuate the myth, even with Mihály, even with her, she snapped, "It isn't detachable. That's what troubles you."

Again, Vlad stared at her. His eyes looked like some boiling storm in a dark green sea. His breath hissed out between his teeth. It might have been a laugh.

He began to move toward the steps, saying to Mihály, "Never give this woman a dagger."

Abruptly, he swung back to the window as if something had caught his eye. Instinctively following his gaze, Ilona saw what it was. A single horseman, riding furiously along the road to the castle gates.

"Something's happened," Vlad said. He sounded more annoyed than fearful.

They returned to the castle's great hall: a spacious rather than a gigantic room, more or less completed to the prince's satisfaction, with some decorations already adorning the walls—a painting depicting a somewhat excessive feast, a pair of ancient crossed swords, the stuffed head of a wolf above the door.

Vlad's visitor was a boyar Ilona recognised. Turcul, slumped against the table, was already gulping down wine straight from the jug when they entered. His clothes were almost caked in mud.

On their entrance, he lowered the jug at once and straightened, giving a low but hasty bow.

"Turcul, you ride as if all the fiends in hell are after you," Vlad observed, going forward with hand held out, a casual gesture of friendship that Ilona hadn't expected from the formal prince. It was part of his charm, though, and how he had won so many of even the more reluctant boyars to his side. He used formality to the point of magnificence to impress and overwhelm, yet with those who had begun to win his trust, he relaxed enough to show normal human friendship.

Begun to trust. Ilona, remembering Stephen's distant words about the few men who had ever won Vlad's trust, wondered how far that process had gone with Turcul. The boyar accepted the hand with an unexpectedly warm smile, as if the gesture already made up for the awful journey which had clearly exhausted him. After which he remembered to bow to Ilona and Mihály.

"Sit, my friend," Vlad encouraged. "Food is on the way. Now, why were those fiends after you?"

"I don't think they're after *me*," Turcul replied ruefully. "You remember my cousin Cazan? He doesn't come to court, but he has land on the Transylvanian border."

Ilona exchanged glances with her father. Surely there wasn't trouble there again?

"I remember him," Vlad said. His voice and his face were expressionless. As if already preparing secretly to deal with another betrayal. "He does not like me."

"He doesn't like anyone very much. He avoids princes and politics. Like those monkeys of legend all at once, he neither sees, hears, nor speaks any evil. However, after wrestling with his conscience, he finally sent me word at Tîrgovişte that Pardo had passed through his lands."

"Pardo…" Vlad repeated.

"Who is Pardo?" Ilona asked curiously.

"One of those who betrayed my father," Vlad said. "And one of those I will never forgive. He shelters in the German towns in Transylvania, which occasionally, under duress, agree to expel him. But even then he goes into hiding and eludes me, and during the next squabble with Brasov, he generally turns up there again."

"With Dan back in Brasov, it was inevitable he'd reappear," Turcul added with a quick glance of reproach at Mihály. Since Mihály had nothing to do with the king's decision to support Dan, it wasn't an entirely fair reproach, but as the representative of Hungary, he had to accept it.

"Where is he now?" Vlad demanded.

"That's the trouble—we don't know. None of our spies have reported sighting him anywhere. So he's not inciting open rebellion or even conspiring. I think we'd know if that was the case."

Vlad, who clearly had a vast network of spies, merely nodded at that.

"In fact, he's gone into hiding like he does when he's kicked out of Brasov, and we know he's very good at that. Because Cazan is notoriously untalkative, he didn't trouble to hide from him, and that is the only reason we know he's in Wallachia."

Vlad frowned at his boyar. "Why did Cazan open his mouth to you?"

Turcul gave a lopsided smile. "I suppose he likes you after all. He likes that the busy road through his land is no longer beset by bandits, and he likes the increased prosperity that comes to his people from that safety. Our troops passing into Transylvania did him no harm either." Turcul took another drink—from a cup this time. "And, to be honest, I suspect he also likes that your justice never wavers or distinguishes between the great, the poor, and all those in between."

Vlad said flippantly, "I love vindication." But watching him closely, Ilona rather thought he did. He'd chosen a harsh, unwavering road, and perhaps the benefits did not always balance in the conscience she'd accused him of still possessing. Whatever, he didn't linger over the self-congratulation. His mind moved on, pursuing Pardo.

"So what is he doing here? Now?"

"Travelling incognito with only one servant, who," Turcul added, "could easily be mistaken for his companion."

Vlad's gaze locked with Turcul's. "Ah."

Turcul nodded. "Your beggars' feast."

"Your what?" said Mihály, amused.

Turcul said, "The prince decided there was no logic in constantly feeding at his table those who already had plenty. He said it made more sense to provide a meal for the poor and the hungry and the sick."

"Actually, I'm just bored with their conversation," Vlad said. "And feel the need for some earthier chat."

Turcul grinned before continuing. "At any rate, there is a huge feast arranged in Tîrgovişte, and word spread around the country to invite the destitute. The city is already filling up with beggars and gypsies who keep the sluji—the prince's civil security force—run off their feet."

"But who," Vlad added, "provide a perfect cover for Pardo. A city full of strangers, in which to hide…"

"To do what?" Ilona asked. "Conspire against you?"

Vlad shrugged. "Assassinate me, probably."

Something cold and heavy seemed to land in the pit of Ilona's stomach. She stared at Vlad, who gazed back, half-amused, half-searching. As if to see if she cared.

Turcul said, "I've told no one, apart from Carstian and Stoica. Stoica wanted to cancel the feast, eject the beggars, and flush Pardo out that way."

"No," said Vlad.

"Carstian thought you'd say that. He wants to flood the city with sluji, which will either scare Pardo off or catch him."

Vlad shook his head again. "He's in hiding. If he doesn't want to be recognised, he won't be. He's also in the unenviable position of not being able to trust anyone. So…we go ahead as planned. And we'll be ready when he strikes."

He frowned. "And in the meantime, the guard must be doubled on the palace. Security for my son—"

"—is already taken care of," Turcul assured him. "And the lady Maria understands she can no longer take him out unattended."

For the first time since they'd left Tîrgovişte, Ilona wished Maria had chosen to accompany them.

Vlad said to Mihály, "I have to go back."

Mihály nodded. "I know."

"Turcul will look after you. Accompany you back to Tîrgovişte or wherever else you wish to visit, at a more leisurely pace than I can afford."

The ache Ilona had learned to live with intensified. This quiet, delightfully pretty place would lose its charm without his presence.

With despair, she recognised that without him, her whole life would seem flat.

She wished she'd never come to Wallachia. She wondered how long it would be before she and Mihály returned to Tîrgovişte too.

It seemed a good idea, in keeping with her ambivalent attitude to the prince, to go quietly back up to the top of the tower, from where she could watch him ride away from the castle. With a little care, he'd never even know she was there. No one would.

But her plan was ruined when, about halfway up the stone, spiral stairs, she heard the unmistakable clatter of boots thudding swiftly downwards toward her.

She glanced up in alarm, prepared to flee ignominiously. All she could see was a beam of sunlight boring into a point above her head. Within it, stone dust danced and whirled.

It needn't be him. It could be Turcul or a servant or one of the builders who still haunted the castle carrying out finishing touches to the prince's exacting specifications. She refused to be so cowardly as to run from anyone. Even him.

She took two more determined steps into the light, just as the man descending swung round the corner and cannoned into her. Half-blinded, almost winded, she felt his hands on her waist, catching her before she fell. With an effort, he pulled back his body's own forward rush.

It took only an instant before their balance was rectified. And yet he didn't remove his hands. Long black hair flowed in the dazzling sunlight until his head shifted, blocking the light, and she could gaze into his face.

"Ilona." He didn't sound surprised.

She muttered, "I was going back to admire your view."

"I just have. It's become a farewell ritual to my haven."

Still his hands didn't release her. She knew she should make him and yet couldn't find words that didn't sound silly or childish. Or didn't betray her utterly. *I can't bear it if you touch me.*

He said, "I'm glad you came."

"My father wished it."

"Didn't you?"

She shook her head.

His hands moved on her waist like a caress, awakening her whole body. "I had hoped we'd be married before this."

She gasped, holding herself rigid. "On the contrary, it's just as well we're not!"

A frown flickered across his brow. "Maria."

She said nothing, merely stared in what she hoped was a haughty manner at the centre of his chest, waiting to be released.

He said softly, "I did not marry Maria. I never will."

"That is an entirely different crime. She deserves better."

"Crime?" he pounced. "What crime have I committed against you?"

Raising indignant eyes, she glared at him. She should have known better than to bandy words with him, and now the conversation had gone all wrong.

"Dishonesty," she threw at him.

"No," he denied.

"No? Then what would you call it? I always expected an advantageous marriage arranged by my parents. You pretended something else entirely."

Unable to endure more, she tried to pull herself out of his hold and instead was held faster against him. The shock of his hard body made her gasp, then stilled her, silenced her as she tried to suppress the betraying thrill.

He said flatly, "I pretended nothing. If it makes you feel better, I was celibate as a monk until Mihály refused the contract. But I'm *not* a monk, and Maria was there. It was never done to hurt you."

"I am not remotely hurt," Ilona flung at him with such palpable untruth that she wasn't surprised by the upward tug of his lips. Infuriated, she plucked at his immovable hands. "Let me go," she raged. "Or have you really become a monster?"

Something flashed in his eyes. She knew a twinge of fear even before he pressed harder against her, making her stumble back against the wall. For an instant, she hung there, helpless, trapped between the hard stone curve and his powerful body. But there was more than anger in the green flame of his eyes.

He said, "Do you know why I took Maria? Because her shawl smelled of you. I wanted to be *your* lover, *your* husband. But Mihály rejected me as the latter, and without that I could not be the former. Do you understand?"

Through her own body's yearnings, she understood more than he knew. He touched his forehead to hers in a gesture of unexpected tenderness.

She whispered, "I understand you should have asked."

And was instantly appalled by her own words. Any desperate hope that he'd fail to grasp their meaning vanished at the stunned expression on his face. Astonishment loosened his hands, and at last Ilona whisked herself free, stumbling hastily down two steps away from him.

She barely heard his sudden movement as he leapt past her and again stood facing her, this time from the step below, breathing as heavily as if he'd just run all the way up. In agony, she laid her hand flat against the curved wall for support and waited for his next words, which could only humiliate her further.

He said, "Mihály told me he'd speak to the king for me."

She felt her eyes widen. It seemed he could still surprise her.

"About our marriage," he added, as if to remove all doubt from her mind. Hope leapt in her like fire, yet was quickly squashed by her grasp of reality. Emotion swamped her. From the maelstrom, she plucked the warmth of his persistence and hugged it to her for the future.

"Don't," she begged. "Matthias won't agree, and I can't bear that sleigh ride again."

With a gasp, she spun away from his hot, determined eyes and ran up the steps as fast as she could. Behind her, she heard his soft laugh, but she couldn't, wouldn't pause. She almost burst into the cool sunlight at the top of the tower, where she stood, gasping, her back against the wall as her breasts rose and fell with the erratic rhythm of her breathing.

For several moments, she thought he might follow her, wondered wildly if she felt more fear or longing. But when she heard his boots thudding on the stone steps once more, they were heading downwards and away from her.

She didn't move, just stood there, leaning heavily against the supporting wall, gazing outward through the window at the woods and hills. Only when she heard the sounds of his departure did she move forward, unable to help herself, to see him ride out with the small escort, which spoke volumes for his rule here.

He turned once, as if he felt her avid gaze on the back of his head, and lifted his hand. It could have been to anyone, to Mihály and Turcul who moved together in the courtyard below. But she wanted to believe it was only for her.

Chapter Fifteen

Tîrgoviște, Wallachia, 1459

*I*t was a free meal. Vlad knew with his native cynicism that far more than the disabled and the destitute passed inside his doors. Among the old soldiers with missing limbs, the cripples, the beggars, and the homeless, came able-bodied gypsies with only temporarily bent backs, working men in clothes they would have thrown out but for the occasion. Vlad didn't mind. They were all his people, and if he could turn any of them toward being productive members of his community, then he counted the effort well worth it.

Of Pardo, his most persistent and elusive enemy, there had been no sign. But, still convinced that the beggars' feast was the event he'd be waiting for, Vlad welcomed each of his guests individually with his piercing gaze. After which they passed between Carstian and Stoica, two of his most trusted boyars who knew Pardo well.

Since the number of beggars had grown well beyond the ability of the palace hall to accommodate, Vlad had bade them all to a warehouse he'd inherited from a Wallachian merchant who'd been seized and murdered by the citizens of Brasov during their previous disagreement with him. He hoped Pardo would appreciate the significance. All the doors and windows were already boarded up, so Vlad had only one door unblocked for the occasion. There was only one other exit, one he'd had made specially and secretly.

Otherwise, he treated the event as if he was welcoming foreign dignitaries and his own boyars. The vast room was scrubbed and clean. Rugs and pictures adorned the walls, covering the ugliness of the boarded windows. The tables were decorated with flowers and set with as much silver as he could beg, borrow, and steal. It would be interesting, he reflected, to see how much of it remained tomorrow, or if his fearful reputation for punishing wrongdoers would deter would-be thieves. For their own sakes, he hoped the latter, for dining with a man would not deter Vlad from killing him.

And so, for what seemed like hours, they counted all the "beggars" into the feast, and when the places were all full, another table was set up. And Vlad could swear Pardo was not in the room.

And so it would be when the feast was finished and he left the building. Pardo would hope to escape among the departing guests. Fair enough. He could deal with that too.

Vlad took his customary place at the head of the first table and toasted his ragged guests, who set up a cheer for him in response. Under cover of the noise, Vlad nodded dismissal to his boyars. But at his side, Carstian bent and murmured in his ear, "I admire your courage, sir, but at least let us stay."

He'd said it before and as then, Vlad shook his head. "No, go and keep watch on my son. I've been misdirected before."

"Sir, what if it's not Pardo but his servant who is in the room? None of us would know him…"

"Even if he is, he isn't armed. Before they even stepped over the door, they were all searched by the sluji. Have faith in me, Carstian."

As Carstian gave up and left with Stoica, Vlad reflected that though he'd used logic to convince them, his own feeling was far more instinctive, that though Pardo wanted him dead, he wanted to do the deed himself. He too was looking for vengeance, for his equally traitorous friend Michael, whom Vlad had killed last year.

Vlad spread his hands. "Eat, my friends," he invited. "Enjoy."

Ilona suspected it was no accident that they arrived back in Tîrgovişte on the evening of Vlad's beggars' feast. While doing his duty by the guests as the prince bade him, Turcul was clearly determined to return in time to protect his lord if it became necessary. A devotion that rather contradicted the criticisms voiced by Vlad's detractors.

They found the city quiet but full of sluji, Vlad's police force, watchfully patrolling the streets. The palace itself was surrounded by soldiers, who looked carefully inside the carriage before permitting them to enter the palace.

There was even a guard placed outside the nursery, Maria told them with nervous amusement as she welcomed them back. At Maria's request, Ilona ate quietly in her friend's private chamber. The unusual security in the palace made Maria uncomfortable. Ilona, though used to living under more martial conditions from time to time, understood how she felt and did her best to soothe.

Although all the while, she thought of Vlad, her stomach twisting with fear for him. Like Maria, she would be glad when this night was over.

Later, watching Maria struggle over some embroidery work—she was sure it was the same cloth she'd been sewing during her last visit—Ilona said abruptly, "What will you do if he marries?"

She was aware of guilt as well as concern in her question. Maria had no idea, she had *never* had any idea, how Ilona felt about Vlad. And perhaps this convoluted situation would not exist if Ilona had just been open when they were younger.

Maria sighed. "I've asked myself the same question many times." She laid her needle down. "I think—at least I like to think—that I won't mind, providing he still loves me best."

It felt like a stab in her stomach, whether of jealousy or of anger she didn't know and didn't much care. All she knew, instinctively, was that she could never share as Maria seemed prepared to. And yet Ilona had so much less of him than Maria already possessed.

Or do I? If he loves me, is that not more?

If what he had told her was the truth…but then, she knew in her heart that Vlad did not love Maria, not as she deserved to be loved, and that broke Ilona's heart all over again.

Her eyes strayed restlessly to the blackness of the window. Surely his feast was over by now? Had they found Pardo? Or had Pardo found the prince?

Vlad sat back in his chair, sweeping his gaze around his guests, who, by now, were well and truly drunk. Several were snoring into their food. Others sprawled across the table to address friends on the other side. Some had fallen down altogether and lay helpless on the floor. One or two had vomited.

With distaste, Vlad had bade the servants clean it up, but he ejected no one. In all, it had been an interesting experience. He'd learned from his lowliest subjects, and he trusted they had learned something from him. If they remembered it in the morning.

Of course, they weren't all inebriated. One or two more comprehensible discussions could still be heard, including those on either side of him. No doubt his presence had imposed a certain constraint there. Well, it was time to remove all constraints.

Quietly, Vlad pushed back his chair and rose, moving to the back of the room, where a rickety staircase led upward to the loft.

If anyone watched him go, they would assume he had private facilities for relieving himself.

In the loft, Vlad found his sentry still alert beside the newly installed skylight. He should be the only guard left inside or outside the building. The sluji had all been dismissed in order to draw Pardo out.

"All quiet?" Vlad asked.

The soldier nodded. "Not a thing. I glanced out a couple of times, but there was nothing. The men at the door have gone, as you ordered. But I've heard nothing since except the occasional footstep in the street outside."

Vlad nodded, signalling to the soldier to open the window and pass him the rope already firmly tied to the roof's stout beams.

"Take care, sir," the soldier said anxiously as he climbed out of the window. Vlad didn't pause, just ran forward across the roof, pulled the rope tight, and walked backwards off the edge.

Lowering himself foot by foot, Vlad listened carefully, looking constantly around for observers. But he saw no one, and the only sound was his boots bouncing softly, rhythmically off the walls as he went down.

Landing on the street, he moved quickly farther into the shadows, then stood perfectly still. Nothing moved in the darkness.

He moved to one corner and glanced around. Nothing and no one. Vlad ran back the way he'd come and on to the other corner. The narrow passage down that side of the building was empty too.

However, he could hear something, some movement close by. His heart began to beat with excitement.

Pardo…at last.

Swiftly, lightly, he ran the length of the passage, his hand on his sword hilt to stop it clanking against the wall. But as he moved, he realised they were hardly the noises one would expect. Not pacing, surreptitious rustling as someone hid in ambush, no whispered conversation or instructions. There was a low scraping sound, followed by gentle tapping, Then more scraping and tapping which grew louder. Like a hammer on nails and wood.

Vlad began to understand.

He paused for an instant at the corner, listening to the hammering, which had become more speedy than silent. Then, ready to meet the last of those who'd betrayed his father, he walked round the side of the building.

He saw both men at once, by the door, one holding the wood in place, one hammering in the nails. They'd done a pretty efficient job of barring the door, he allowed. What a pity for them that the prince they'd planned to trap was already on the outside. Whether they'd meant to set it on fire or unblock a window and shoot arrows at him, they'd misjudged him again. He'd learned long ago always to leave himself two exits.

He strolled toward them and drew his sword. At the scraping of steel, they both whirled round. And gaped. Even in the moonlight, Vlad could see their stunned expressions and almost laughed aloud.

Pardo, a broad man of medium height with a dark, drooping moustache and a large nose which had obviously been broken at least once, recovered first and reached for his sword.

"Good evening, gentlemen," Vlad said. "Are you looking for my Majesty?"

Just in case they didn't know him. Just in case they were in any doubt as to who killed them.

The servant scrabbled for his dagger, but before he even drew it free, Vlad was upon him, stabbing him cleanly through the heart with his own dagger while with his sword he parried Pardo's powerful lunge.

Once, Vlad might have drawn it out. Having gauged the level of his opponent's skill, he might have played with Pardo, inflicting pain as viciously as he knew how before the final blow. But he'd grown tired of long revenge. Now, he just wanted it over. And so he slashed him twice across the chest and hacked the sword from his numb fingers. For an instant, he stared into the stunned, desperate eyes of his enemy.

He said, "For my father, Vlad Dracul." And, just as he had with Vladislav, he swung his sword high and cut off Pardo's head.

Vlad stood back, his breathing only a little quickened, and surveyed his handiwork. A distant smell of smoke tickled his nostrils, reminding him of wood fires and home. And Ilona, whom he'd hurt and whom he longed for all the more because of her admission.

Bending, Vlad bent and wiped his sword on Pardo's deliberately tatty clothes. Then, sheathing sword and dagger, he began to walk home.

Perhaps because he'd had enough of ugliness, he let his mind dwell on Ilona, on memories of her shy, passionate kisses and the feel of her body melting in his arms. On the physical pleasures he would so enjoy teaching her when she became his companion, his lover, his wife. They were sweet fantasies, and he had every intention of making them reality. Even without Mihály's offer of support, he'd planned to pursue the matter with the king. When the time was right.

Vlad stopped. Smoke. He could still smell smoke, more strongly than ever. Like a bonfire rather than a campfire.

"Oh Jesus Christ," he whispered. He turned, facing the rising plume of smoke above the rooftops. "Oh, please, no…." He began to run back to the warehouse, his footsteps echoing in the empty streets and then blending with the sounds of other running feet, of cries of "Fire!" and "Help!"

He could hear their screams long before he got there and began tearing at the wooden barriers with his bare hands. But the whole building was already a mass of flame and the heat intense enough to have thrown back all other would-be rescuers.

His soldier, the one from the loft, tried to pull him away, but Vlad shook him off furiously, even while he acknowledged gladness that he at least survived.

His foot kicked at something—Pardo's hammer. Seizing it, he swung it twice at the largest strip of wood and dislodged it. With another mighty swing, he broke in the rest of the door. The fire sucked the air into a torrent. A huge fireball exploded in front of his eyes, and something blasted him across the street.

When he could see again, he rose to his feet and stumbled across to the burning warehouse. He waited, watching them douse the blaze. But he already knew that all his guests were dead. All they would find were charred remains.

Ilona left Maria to sleep and was escorted back to her own house within the palace grounds. Mihály had already retired. Without taking off her cloak, she went straight outside into the garden. Perhaps because she'd once met him there.

But everything was different tonight. Tonight she churned with fear for him, not fear of her own feelings. And tonight soldiers patrolled the garden perimeters, and their effect on her was the opposite to that intended. They prevented any peace.

There was a smell of burning in the air. When she looked out between the trees, she saw a faint glow over part of the town. Unease multiplied as she recognised a major fire, though surely it was unconnected with Vlad or his beggars.

Close by, someone shouted. An order to the soldiers, who at once began running away from the garden toward the palace building. Ilona, unable to help herself, ran too, crying out to the first man she met, "What's going on? What's happened."

"Fire in the town, lady," he said grimly. "The beggars' feast."

There was a roaring in her ears. She knew it was blood, but it sounded like fire. With an inarticulate cry, she too began to run toward the glow.

She knew where the building was. Turcul had pointed it out to them as they arrived earlier—much earlier—this evening. But as she ran and walked and ran again and lost sight of the soldiers in the darkness, she also lost her precise sense of direction. She moved in the general direction of the noise and the powerful reek of smoke.

Although she could hear people, she saw no one, until finally, someone lurched around the corner she was aiming for, walking like a drunk. Stupidly careless of her own personal danger, she walked single-mindedly toward him to ask for directions, for news.

She was quite close before she recognised the drunk as the Prince of Wallachia.

"Vlad!" she sobbed and ran to him. When she hurled herself into his arms, he staggered back but held on to her from some instinct. His hand in her hair, pulling her head back, was rougher than she'd ever known it. His eyes, wide and terrifyingly blank, stared into hers.

"Ilona?"

"You're alive," she whispered, clutching his shoulders. He smelled of smoke and singed meat. "You're alive."

"And one more atrocity to my name."

A different fear for him rose up to replace the old. "What have you done? Where is Pardo?"

"Dead," he answered without any interest.

"Did you kill him?"

"Of course I killed him." It wasn't boastful, merely impatient. After a pause, he added harshly, "They're all dead too. All the beggars."

"The fire?" she whispered in horror. "Did Pardo burn them?"

His eyes closed. "No. I did." His hands on her elbows gripped convulsively, then slid round to hold her tightly. Numb with horror, Ilona tried and failed to speak. "I barred all the doors and windows. I killed him and walked away without a thought to them. I never thought—I never once thought—that he might have lit the torch before he barred the door. Jesus Christ, I even smelled the smoke, and still I walked away."

Relief mingled with the horror, weakening her limbs. She flung her arms around him. "Vlad. Vlad. This one isn't yours. It isn't."

His cheek pressed into her hair, he whispered, "It is. I take it as mine. Even as a sin of omission, it is mine in the eyes of God."

"God is not so unjust or so stupid."

Wetness trickled onto her hair, rolled down her cheek. She tugged at his head until he raised it, and she saw the streaks down his blackened face. They weren't her tears.

He said fiercely, "Don't look at me, Ilona Szilágyi." His arms tightened. "Just give me your comfort, because God help me, I can't do without it."

She tightened her arms around him in pity, reached up to press her lips to his cheek, but he moved his head and took her mouth instead. It was a strong, ravenous kiss, rough and desperate, full of at least as much pain as passion. She endured the assault, seeking only to soothe, to absorb his unbearable grief. Yet what began in compassion ended in flaring desire that left her just as helpless in his hold.

Only gradually did he become gentler, more tender, as some sort of sanity seemed to return to him. His arms moved so that he could touch her cheeks with his fingertips and slowly, reluctantly, detach his lips.

That was when she saw the blisters on his hands.

"You're burned!" she cried in horror.

"I couldn't get the damned boards off the door." He rested his forehead on hers. "Take me home."

Chapter Sixteen

Visegrád, Hungary, 1474

When Count Szelényi returned from arranging their horses and his own riding dress, he had with him a letter from Mihnea, which he handed at once to Vlad before departing under pretext of having forgotten something.

Although Vlad said nothing, he appreciated the other man's discretion and understanding. A letter from his son was a rare enough event to be savoured alone. And yet although he looked forward to them and seized them greedily, these missives always left him feeling vaguely unsatisfied, vaguely anxious, while that gnawing ache in his heart intensified.

Without taking off his cloak or his hat, Vlad sank into the nearest chair and broke the seal. It didn't take long to read. Mihnea's letters seldom did. As always, Vlad drank in the boy's evident affection, unwavering despite the years apart, the news of his doings and successes. But for the first time, he made himself look closely at the less savoury aspects.

The boy was not receiving enough education; his morality was as suspect as his view of his father. Vlad never doubted his love. What he did doubt was what was feeding it. It hurt to know that Mihnea was so excited by his father's appalling reputation. Not to put too fine a point on it, Mihnea was dining out on his relationship to the Impaler. The balance of his life was all wrong. He needed endurance, harshness, wiliness, yes, but tempered by justice and perception and honesty.

The familiar pain of parting swept over Vlad once more. He was doing what he had vowed never to do. Allowing his son to be reared among strangers, away from his parents as he himself had done. Not that Vlad had had much choice. When he'd left Wallachia in search of Matthias, he'd entrusted Mihnea to the care of Carstian. There hadn't been many options. Mihály Szilágyi was dead and Ilona hadn't believed her brother would accept Mihnea willingly. Carstian was a good man with an honourable family, but in the end he'd been forced to give the boy up to Matthias.

To his credit, Matthias had not imprisoned him. Instead, he farmed him out to favoured nobles who filled the child's impressionable mind with tales of his bold, bad father. Vlad could count the number of times on both hands that he'd been allowed to see Mihnea during his years of confinement. And those visits were never enough, either to assuage Vlad's longings or to keep his son on the right track.

One of his many plans, once his door was permanently unlocked, was to bring Mihnea back to live with him and Ilona. Now, after reading the letter, Vlad knew more than ever that he had to act. So much more than his own personal desires were at stake.

Vlad stood up and stored Mihnea's letter carefully in his desk with the others. He needed fresh air to clear his head, and then he'd seek another audience with the king.

From her bedchamber window, Ilona watched him ride out with Count Szelényi. Some emotion that was neither pleasure nor pain, yet contained something of both, rose up her throat and choked her. Without permission, her hand lifted and touched the part of the glass that covered him. He rode out from her fingers, then paused, glancing back over his shoulder as he'd done before.

She wondered if he could make her out through the glass. He made no sign, but his shoulders straightened, and he urged his horse into a gallop. Ilona smiled faintly. He had always been a fine horseman…

And he needed so much to be away from this confinement, this velvet-gloved torture.

Margit's anxious voice said, "My lady? Countess Hunyadi is here again."

Ilona moved her gaze to focus on her companion of many years. Because it crossed her mind, she frowned and asked, "Why do you stay with me, Margit?"

Because she provided Margit with a home and a lifestyle she would not otherwise enjoy coming from so very minor a noble family. But there were rather more disadvantages.

As Margit stumbled over mumbling about her duty, Ilona interrupted. "You're wasting your youth with a dull and difficult mistress."

"You're not difficult," Margit protested.

"Let it be written on my gravestone. Here lies Ilona Szilágyi, who wasn't difficult. It's a poor epitaph… I've never done a thing for you, have I?"

"I don't know what you mean," Margit said with genuine incomprehension.

Ilona swung away from her. *I'm ashamed.*

She didn't know if she spoke the words aloud. It didn't matter. They would only baffle Margit further. But she had to keep them there in front of her. *I'm ashamed.*

Margit sighed, clearly imagining she'd drifted off again. "I'll tell the countess…"

"I'll come now," said Ilona.

Margit's eyes widened as she climbed off the bed. Then, clearly cramming in as much as possible while Ilona was listening, she added, "Also a messenger came from the king, saying you have leave to retire from court. Tomorrow."

Halfway to the door, Ilona paused and drew in her breath. "Thank you." She walked into the outer chamber. "He's sending me away." She didn't trouble with a greeting, and Countess Hunyadi didn't seem to expect one.

"The king? He's fulfilling your request to leave. I passed it on to him."

Ilona frowned at her. "You don't want me to marry Vlad. You've never wanted me to marry Vlad."

Erzsébet said dryly, "My dear, it was you who said you did not want to marry Vlad when the king and I brought you here for that very purpose."

"There was no one else with whom to tie him to you. Now you have. And I'm being sent home. Again. In vague but unspecified disgrace. Again."

"You bring it on yourself, Ilona."

"And if I said now, I recant, I was wrong, I will marry Vlad. What then?"

"It's too late. The king prefers the other marriage."

"And you, Aunt Erzsébet? Which do you prefer?"

"It's not my place to oppose the king," she said with dignity.

"He's your son," said Ilona dryly. "You've opposed him since the day he was born—whenever you chose to." She gazed closely at her aunt, clawing back the layers of confusion and dragging out the memories to try to aid her understanding. "You spoke for me to Matthias. Before you knew your daughter was free, you tried to dissuade him."

Erzsébet nodded. "You've been through enough."

"Have I? Who decreed that my life should end? Who decreed that I should never live again? Did you speak for me, Aunt Erzsébet? Or for you?"

The king had agreed to see him for five minutes. Vlad was aware the minutes could stretch if he said anything Matthias wanted to hear. If he didn't, he'd be unceremoniously ejected and locked up by sunset.

As he strode to his chamber to prepare for the appointed time, he almost ran into someone, a woman, lurking at the corner of the passage.

Margit, Ilona's "dragon."

He lifted his eyebrows. "May I help you?"

"They're sending her away," Margit blurted.

Ignoring her informality, Vlad said only, "When?"

"Tomorrow."

Tomorrow! That gave him very little time to work in. Yet he couldn't resist wasting a moment of it to ask, "Why do you tell me this? Did she send you?"

Margit shook her head. "Because now it seems she doesn't want to go." And she melted back down the passage, leaving Vlad to go in the other direction, reciting repeatedly in his mind like a war cry, *Still with me, still with me…*

Matthias had the contract laid down in front of him. Vlad barely glanced at it.

The king said, "It's all we agreed on before. You convert to the true Roman Catholic faith, swear allegiance to me, and marry my relative. I give you my support to retake the throne of Wallachia when the time is right, and many gifts, including the aforementioned relative in marriage and a private house across the river in Pest. And this time, I even throw in a military command while we wait for an advantageous position in Wallachia. It's time we retook Bosnia from the Ottomans."

He meant his last words to catch Vlad's attention, and they did. In spite of everything, Vlad knew an upsurge of excitement, a spark of joy at the anticipation of such a battle. Apart from anything else, it would make Wallachia more secure.

Matthias smiled. "I knew you'd like that idea. It will be a bold alliance of the kind you recommended years ago."

He didn't even blush when he said it.

Of the type I recommended. Of the type I formed and you agreed to and reneged on in the most dishonourable manner possible.

Once, he would have said the words aloud. And got nowhere. Now, quelling his indignation without too much difficulty, he said only, "Your terms are even more generous. I am most appreciative. My only concern is the bride's name."

"This," said Matthias, "is a better bride."

Like a better horse or a better grade of gold. "I'm happy with the lesser bride."

Matthias's brows snapped together. "Damn it, man, why are you so stubborn?"

"Why are you?" Vlad countered. "You have an opportunity to give less. Save your honoured sister for a greater alliance."

Matthias wasn't even tempted. He'd thought it all out with perfect clarity.

Vlad leaned closer to the king, and softly, so that only the clerk standing closest could possibly hear too, he said, "You fear that together Ilona and I will make too much noise."

Matthias rose abruptly, glaring at the prince, and everyone present in the room, nobles, lawyers, clerks, all stood too.

He said, "Look, my lord, I am being more than generous here. I admit your value. I need a good ruler in Wallachia and your half–infidel brother does not suit me! Nor does that idiot Stephen insisted on putting on the throne—Besarab Laiota is about as trustworthy as a snake. But you are not the only possible choice."

"I'm the best choice."

"I'm beginning to doubt it!" Matthias flashed. "There is never a shortage of candidates in Wallachia—not least of them your own son."

"Mihnea is fifteen years old!"

"I can wait."

His triumph wasn't lost on Vlad, who could wait no longer.

He drew in his breath. "Your Majesty. Let us not quarrel. Truly, it is farthest from my wish. Give me Ilona and let the past be silent."

Matthias stared at him. His eyes acknowledged the threat, understood it implicitly. An unpleasant smile curved his lips. "We all know what you are, Vlad."

"I know what you made me and why."

"The world doesn't care. The world has moved on, and your reputation is *still* in my hands." He reached out and took Vlad by one shoulder, murmuring in his ear, "I can give you it back, Vlad, a second chance at glory."

Tied to another Hunyadi spy? Vlad let out an involuntary breath of laughter that clearly took the king by surprise.

Vlad turned his head so that now his lips were at the king's ear. "I'd make her name infamous, and through it, yours."

"The world understands politics and the lot of royal women. On the contrary, it's *your* name that is in *my* hands."

"I rather think my name has gone well beyond your hands or anyone else's. I ignore that, as I'll ignore the past. For Ilona."

Matthias's eyes, so close to his, dilated as they stared. And Vlad saw at last that it was useless. That Matthias feared his marriage to Ilona more than he wanted Vlad in Wallachia. But he didn't fear Vlad or what he could reveal. Anything Vlad said was immediately suspect because he was the insane Impaler. Matthias had already admitted as much, and he was right. It was Ilona he feared, not the marriage.

Ilona. Isolated in Transylvania, more cut off from the world even than Vlad, especially in recent years. Ilona, vague, almost entirely abandoned by her family until now. Perhaps it had seemed worth the risk when the proposed marriage was revived. A vague, indifferent Ilona, whose words would carry as little weight as Vlad's.

But married to Vlad, she was back in the public eye. Matthias could no longer bury her at Horogszegi, and perhaps he even feared that, with Vlad once more, she might recover enough to be a danger.

Jesus Christ, what sort of a danger? She couldn't pull down the monarchy, depose the great King Matthias Corvinus! All she could do was sully his precious name, besmirch it as rumours of the truth began to emerge.

"She threatens your place in history,"Vlad said softly, wonderingly. "Finally, after all is said and done and suffered, this is what it comes down to."

Matthias's eyes shut down like a slammed door.

"She'll never threaten anything. She'll go home and be happy where she belongs. For you, it's my sister or back to prison. Count Szelényi, show the prince to his chamber. It's sunset. Make sure his door is locked."

A furious pulse hammered in Vlad's head, pounding home the knowledge that he'd failed. That at the last hurdle, he'd fallen, and with him came Ilona and Mihnea and Wallachia itself, everything and everyone he'd ever cared for.

But he couldn't let it go; he couldn't just drift back into melancholy and confinement and the exchange of letters confirming old loyalties that mattered not one gypsy's curse when he lay rotting in this place.

Think, damn you! She's leaving tomorrow, and there's nothing you can do to prevent it.

No, but he needn't give up either. Tomorrow, when she'd gone, he'd try again. Convince the king that *no* marriage was necessary. Then, when he had his freedom and a military command, he could find Ilona, take her back to Wallachia with him…

It was fantasy. He recognised it with growing despair as he strode silently along the palace passages with Szelényi sympathetic at his heels. He ignored everyone who bowed to him, everyone who stared. He may have stared back at a few since he caught a few hunted or fearful expressions, but he hadn't been glaring at them, only at Matthias and the injustice of the world.

Uselessly venting his spleen, he kicked open his bedchamber door.

Count Szelényi said uncomfortably, "Shall I send your servant?"

"No. Just lock the door. Please," he added with difficulty. He glanced back at the man who increasingly seemed his only friend in this country. "Forgive my ill manners. I will be better in the morning." *I won't. I'll be a thousand times worse unless I can think of a way, any way to stop her leaving, to make this infernal marriage happen at last.*

As Szelényi smiled sympathetically and stepped outside, closing and locking the door, Vlad wondered if he should just agree to everything. Take Matthias's sister and lose her somewhere. Of course, he'd been down that road before, and his heart rebelled against wounding Ilona in this way a second time.

But this wouldn't be like Maria, taken for the needs of his body. Just for politics. And hadn't Ilona once said to him, *"I understand you should have asked."*

A faint movement behind him irritated. "Christ, are you still here?" Neither he nor Szelényi had noticed the servant, and now, adding to Vlad's annoyance, the man would have to sleep in his chamber.

Receiving no response, Vlad spun round and saw the still figure of a woman, standing in the middle of the room, staring at him. In the lamp's shadows, her dark eyes were huge, and her red silk gown vibrated to the trembling of her limbs.

"Ilona," he whispered.

Chapter Seventeen

Horogszegi, Transylvania, and
Tîrgovişte, Wallachia, 1460-1461

Welcoming Mihály back to Horogszegi almost had the intensity of Ilona's childhood. Only the time of year was wrong, spring instead of autumn. And instead of overwhelming relief at his surviving the latest battle, her relief was that he'd survived a visit to his nephew.

It spoke volumes for Mihály's fears that he'd insisted on going to court alone, without any of his family.

But finally, it seemed, there was some kind of reconciliation with Matthias.

"He's confirmed my appointment as governor of Transylvania," he told his eager family as they gathered about him, pressing on him wine and food and affection. "And I believe we understand each other better. I have to let him go his own way, but he won't imprison me for speaking my mind."

"I should think not!" Ilona said forcefully, and her father smiled at her.

"Forgive him," he advised. "I have. Also, it may please you to know we have talked about a marriage for you."

On either side of her, Miklós and her visiting sisters hooted. For as long as anyone could remember, they had been talking about a husband for Ilona, but here she still lived with her mother, unmarried. Only Ilona felt the thrill of anticipation, a rush of fear in case it wasn't the marriage she wanted.

"With whom this time?" her mother demanded.

Ilona held her breath.

"The Prince of Wallachia."

Ilona closed her eyes, letting the blood pound in her ears with relief and gladness, while all around her, questions and answers ebbed and flowed.

"Dracula?" sneered Miklós. "Has he stopped beating up Transylvania?"

"You know he has. He has made peace with the towns, who have in return delivered up Dan's supporters."

"Didn't the king mind, considering the supporters were on his side?"

"He couldn't really, since Vlad exterminated Dan and his invading army."

In fact, according to rumour, when the prince had captured Dan with his few surviving followers, he'd made him dig his own grave, had a priest read him the rites of the dead, and then personally cut off his head. It was a gruesome tale, like so many Ilona automatically discounted. But in this case, she thought it might just be true. It fitted Vlad's black humour as well as his ruthless quest to discourage any further pretenders to his throne.

Mihály added, "Matthias has other things to think about now. He needs peace with Wallachia."

"And our daughter is the price?" said her mother with indignation.

"It's a price we're all willing to pay." There was a touch of severity in Mihály's voice, which silenced any further criticism. Ilona, registering that the silence had gone on too long, opened her eyes to find everyone looking at her.

"Aren't we?" Mihály prompted.

Ilona swallowed. "Yes."

Of course, negotiations dragged on interminably. It wasn't until October, after Vlad had finished punishing his rebellious subjects in the duchies of Amlas and Fagaras—trouble also stirred up by Matthias's agents—that the marriage became part of the accord agreed between Wallachia and Hungary. And even then Matthias, piqued at having lost a war to a lesser prince, quibbled over details to avoid having to give his former enemy everything he wanted.

Ilona, still waiting, tried to be patient. Longing for a life with him, she wondered if Maria knew what was happening, how she would receive the news. Since it was still by no means certain, she didn't mention it in her few letters to her friend. And Maria, in her even less frequent correspondence, said nothing about it either.

Finally, during the long winter, Matthias agreed, but, no doubt striving to hold the prince to him by dangling the carrot a little longer, insisted on postponing the marriage for a year.

"To see if I'll behave myself," said Vlad sardonically.

He'd arrived with the thaw, almost chasing it across the mountain passes to spend one night at Horogszegi. He only just caught Mihály, who'd been about to leave on a military commission for the King in Bulgaria, where the Ottomans had recently made alarming advances. Naturally, the entire household had been thrown into confusion by the news of Vlad's imminent arrival, and Ilona, forced to submit to the grooming ministrations of her mother and visiting sister, had grown mutinous. Only the overwhelming need to see him, subduing all other instincts, kept her still.

And when he finally arrived with an escort little larger than that with which he'd first ridden into Hunedoara all those years ago, it felt to her like a dream. Larger than life, martially dressed, and formally mannered, his personality filled the castle. Even Miklós, who in his infrequent visits from the larger estates at Bistrita had been heard to deride the prince as being somehow inferior for not being Hungarian—how did he come to that conclusion? —was clearly overwhelmed.

He greeted her formally, barely brushing his lips against the back of her hand. If his eyes seemed to blaze like green flame, it might have been the fault of the poor light. So long anticipated and yearned for, the meeting stung Ilona with anticlimax. He barely spoke to her, concentrating on her parents. Her mother, clearly charmed, agreed over dinner to visit his principality in the summer, bringing Ilona.

"Why *is* His Majesty insisting on next spring?" Countess Szilágyi asked.

"To see if I'll behave myself."

"And will you?" Ilona blurted.

"Of course." His gaze shifted across the table to her, and he smiled. "I have to. He may have been worried because I renewed my peace treaty with the Ottomans last year." He shrugged. "That was something I had to do. I need time. But this year I'll pay the sultan no tribute, and when the time is right, I will help Hungary defeat the Ottomans."

It was a risky strategy. Ilona understood that. She also understood the huge gains Vlad could make out of its success. Having already won effective autonomy from Hungarian interference, he could, through military alliance with mighty Hungary, win the same from the Ottomans.

"You mean Hungary will help *you* defeat the Ottomans," said Miklós. It was the first thing he'd said since they'd sat down at the table.

"I mean all who agreed to the crusade and accepted papal money for preparations are honour-bound to help each other. To everyone's gain."

He could be a haughty devil when he chose to be, and the effect was clear in Miklós's painful flush. Perhaps Vlad recognised that. Rather more graciously than her brother deserved, he added, "Perhaps I do have more to gain than the king. But my country is on the frontier. I also have most to lose."

As the meal proceeded, Ilona tried to be content in his mere presence, but it was no longer enough. Her whole being churned in a maelstrom of vague but powerful desires, in fierce joy in his coming and premature grief at his leaving so soon. He would go home to rule and plan his fights, and she would go back to another year of interminable waiting. Although there was the summer to look forward to if her mother kept to her word…

But her mother was rising from the table, taking her away from him again. He and Mihály would talk long into the night, and in the morning, they would both be gone.

Her maid was late to her bedchamber when she finally retired. Ilona didn't mind. She wanted to be alone, to savour the lingering memory of his all too brief kiss on her hand, and the warmth in his eyes when he'd smiled his good-night. Staring out into the cold, blustery darkness, she wanted to *feel* that he was under the same roof.

When the maid finally did appear, she didn't notice at first, until the girl actually touched her arm. "My lady? I have a message from the prince!"

Ilona stared at her. The girl was clearly torn between outrage and delight that this first sign of romantic intrigue she'd glimpsed for her mistress concerned the man who was also her betrothed.

Smothering a breath of excited laughter, Ilona said, "What? What did he say?"

"He says he's on the stairs, waiting…"

Perhaps she had more to convey, but Ilona didn't hear it. She'd already flown across the room and out the door.

The stairs were in darkness. But below her she saw the blackness of a figure sitting on the stone steps. Modestly thanking God that she hadn't got around to undressing, Ilona ran lightly down the steps. The figure turned and rose.

Even in the dark, she recognised him, the straightness of his posture, the quickness of his stride as he leapt silently up two more steps to meet her. She tried to speak, but his arms seized her, crushing her to his chest. She gasped, inhaling his warm, distinctive smell of earth and horses, spices and good wine, and his mouth, hot and urgent, captured hers.

She couldn't breathe and didn't care. Throwing her arms up around his neck, she kissed him back, welcoming his tongue and teeth as well as his devouring lips.

"Ilona," he whispered into her mouth. "Ilona." And then went back to kissing her. "I have yearned for you… Sometimes, I'd sell my soul for one night with you… But I can't do that. I'm playing for it all, for everything, forever."

His words washed over her in a tide, feeding the gladness and the passion that held her helpless and trembling in his arms.

He swept one hand down the length of her body from shoulder to thigh, eliciting involuntary responses from her every quivering nerve.

"There isn't even a formal betrothal. I can't make you gifts. But God help me, I need to know that you're mine." His hand delved inside his tunic, tugging something free. "Will you wear this, for me?"

By the pale moonlight filtering through the opposite window, she saw that he held a small golden ring. In wonder, she gave him her hand, felt the ring slip over her knuckle, and gazed almost blindly at the single white pearl that adorned it. Somewhere, she recognised that it was a very fine one, but mostly her heart was singing because he'd given it.

He said, "It was my father's. A love token from a lady who was not my mother, but I know he treasured it because it came to me with his sword and his Dragon. If you don't care for it, I'll buy you new ones."

"I don't want new ones." It came out as a husky whisper. She brought her hand to her face, touching the ring with her cheek, her lips, and saw him smile with relief, as if he hadn't been sure at all that he was doing the right thing. Enchanted by this rare sign of vulnerability, it took her a moment to drag herself out of her daze and remember.

"Wait," she said abruptly. "One minute." And slipped out of his reluctant arms to run back upstairs to her bedchamber. Ignoring the maid who gazed at her from huge, wide eyes, she went straight to the chest under the window and rummaged till she found the tiny box. Tearing it open, she grabbed the golden ring inside and bolted back out and down the steps to where he still waited in the darkness, though closer now, as if drawn ever nearer to her bedchamber.

"I bought you this," she whispered, pressing it into his hand "Just in case…"

He pushed it on, holding it up to the faint glimmer of moonlight.

"It's not rare or expensive," she excused, afraid suddenly that he would find her gift tawdry, or, worse, silly. "It was all I could see in Bistrita…"

When he dragged his gaze away from the ring to her face, she saw with relief that he was smiling.

"Even in the darkness, I can feel its beauty. Rare because you gave it, and priceless." With the hand that wore the ring, he touched her cheek in a gentle, tender caress. She turned her face into it, kissing his palm, Then, daringly, she stood on tiptoe and kissed his lips. His eyes closed as if he savoured her touch, and in wonder, Ilona thought that perhaps he valued her kiss even more than the ring.

The idea was so intoxicating that she gave him another. His arms crept round her again, and soon they were both lost once more in kissing and caressing.

At last, Vlad groaned softly and lifted his head as if by brute force. "Go to bed, Ilona Szilágyi, before I find myself taking you here on your father's stairs."

Ilona burned. She managed to say shakily, "I can't. You're holding me too tightly."

"One more kiss," he said and took it, thoroughly, before releasing her. Dropping his arms to his sides, he stepped away from her.

Across the darkness, their eyes met and held. Ilona's heart beat and beat; she wondered what she should say to keep him with her. If she should say it.

Vlad lifted his hand to his mouth, kissed the ring she'd given him. Then, with a flicker of a smile, he ran down the stairs, away from her.

Joyful and aching, Ilona walked back upstairs to her bedchamber and let the maid undress her at last. She closed her eyes and wished it was him.

"You can't go there! Not now!" Miklós raged.

"On the contrary," said Ilona, "now is exactly when we agreed to go."

"That was before. My father is not two months in his grave!"

At that, Ilona felt everything erupt in fury. She'd had little enough to do with Miklós since they'd grown up, but even before that, from the time she'd decided she no longer needed to pacify him for every childish tantrum—because he was, in fact, too old to be having them—they'd grown apart. She was tired of his criticism and his whining. But to use Mihály's death as an excuse not to do Mihály's own bidding was the last straw.

She took a deep breath, ready to annihilate him.

"I forbid it!" he announced, thus saving himself from Ilona by provoking their mother.

"*You* forbid it? *You* cannot forbid what your father, what the king himself has ordered. You stand in Mihály's shoes and had best learn to fill them. Go to the king! Ask what his commands are for you. Our duty is already clear. We leave as planned and will probably stay through the winter to prepare for the wedding. Who knows? We may even manage to bring it forward by a few months."

Miklós slammed out the door, only to throw it back open a second later for a parting shot. "He isn't even a proper Christian!"

Countess Szilágyi sighed. "Well, he's right there. Since the prince clings to the eastern rite, I suppose you will have to convert and follow him."

"I don't fear for my soul," Ilona assured her with some irony. "We both worship the same God."

"Yes, well, the Ottomans worship God too," the countess said tartly. "It doesn't make them Christians."

And rumour said the people of the Romanian principalities would rather welcome the tolerant Ottomans than their fellow Christians who followed the Roman rite. Miklós made her understand why. But the issue didn't matter to her. Getting to Wallachia mattered.

Unexpectedly, her mother had become her most valuable ally in that cause. Perhaps because it was one of Mihály's last acts to promote the marriage. Perhaps because in a moment of weakness that came with the interminable talking after Mihály's awful death, she had confessed to her mother that she loved Vlad.

It was a secret she had told to no one before, and the mingled horror and pity in her mother's eyes had made her laugh at the time—her first laugh since Mihály had been taken in Bulgaria by the Ottomans. But she understood that her mother wanted a peaceful and contented life for her, not the erratic sleigh ride of being in love with a husband like Vlad Dracula.

And for her part, Countess Szilágyi seemed to decide that Ilona had waited long enough, even for so ill-fated a marriage. With that, Ilona heartily agreed. Grief for Mihály had only strengthened her longing. When she woke in the night, crying for her lost, tortured father, it was the comfort of Vlad's arms she needed.

Astonished, Ilona let the warmth of delight seep into her grieving, angry soul. This time she entered Tîrgovişte as the prince's promised bride, escorted from the drawbridge by smart, mounted soldiers, and the people came out to cheer her. They threw flower petals at the carriage, running along beside it to shout blessings and good wishes.

Her mother was enchanted, instantly divested of all remaining doubts concerning Ilona's marriage in such an unstable country. Ilona shared her delight in the uninhibited welcome of the people, their obvious gladness in her arrival. Beyond that, she understood Vlad had encouraged it. By letting the marriage plans be known, by publicising her arrival and allowing the public welcome, he was making it happen. To all intents and purposes, he was presenting Matthias with the undeniable, irreversible fact of the marriage. And that pleased her too.

At the palace gates, he was there to welcome them in full princely regalia. She saw him from the carriage window, straight backed and splendid in white silk and red velvet, fine jewels encrusting his round hat and the brooch which fastened his mantle.

"He is," Countess Szilágyi allowed, "a very fine figure of a man. There was always something about him, even as a boy. I was never sure whether we should fear him or encourage him…"

She spoke in Hungarian, in case the people who still surrounded the carriage overheard. Though she seemed to want to
say more, she closed her mouth on it as a soldier moved the crowd
back and opened the carriage door.

"I wish I'd worn the other gown," the countess mourned,
preparing to descend. "But at least you look nice, dear."

Ilona had meant to, not for the welcoming crowds which she
had never even imagined, but for Vlad.

The prince himself handed her mother down from the carriage, where he embraced her, a more gentle version of the greeting he'd always accorded Mihály. Without warning, Ilona's throat
closed up. Stricken, she saw his lips move as he murmured something in her mother's ear that made her nod. Then the countess
stood aside and he looked into her eyes.

The bolt of awareness was a relief. As she stepped down with
her hand in his, the cheering of the crowd intensified. And this
time there was no distant salutation brushed against her tingling
hand. He took her in his arms and kissed her lips. A formal kiss of
greeting, but one which clearly proclaimed her as his bride.

As before, the touch of his lips shocked her, delighted her. He
smiled faintly, then laid her hand on his and led her into the palace.
She felt his gaze on her face, but, suddenly shy, was reluctant to
meet it. Instead, she smiled and nodded to the people who'd been
allowed to line the path to the entrance.

He said, "I have no words for this, to make it better or easier,
so I'll speak now, and then it's done. Mihály was as my brother, my
father, and no loss has affected me so much since boyhood. That
your pain is even greater, I know only too well. I would take it
from you if I could."

She whispered, "I don't want you to," and smiled at a child
who threw rose petals in front of her feet.

"Remember his life, not his death."

Not that the Ottomans took him prisoner to Constantinople and tortured him before the sultan to make him betray Belgrade's defences and other military secrets. Not that when he would not speak they killed him by sawing him in half. How do you set about forgetting those things?

As if he heard her, Vlad said, "You won't forget. But his life is more important. I have learned that."

The people had grown too blurred to see. Still she wouldn't look at Vlad, but her fingers curled around his and squeezed.

Chapter Eighteen

Tîrgovişte, Wallachia, 1461

"Where is Maria?"

She asked Vlad the question with reluctance. Living here, in the house beside the palace, as his acknowledged bride-to-be, seeing him every day, riding with him, talking with him, dining with him in considerably more freedom than she'd enjoyed in any of her previous visits, it was easy to lose herself in happiness and forgetfulness.

But her old friend wasn't in the palace and neither was Maria's son. And Vlad was planning journeys around the country—necessary journeys which he intended to make use of to introduce Ilona to the people of the other regions. She didn't want to face Maria, but she had to, and common sense told her it should be sooner rather than later.

And so she asked Vlad as, along with several of his court, they took a stroll in the palace gardens in the cool evening air.

"At her husband's estate. With Mihnea."

"How is she?"

Vlad smiled faintly. "She is Maria."

Do you still make love to her?

The question almost spilled out, but she bit it back, knowing she probably couldn't bear the answer. When they were married, he would sleep in *her* bed. Until then…men were men.

240

"I need to visit her," Ilona said. "She's too old and good a friend to ignore and I...I need to know how she feels. About me."

He glanced down at her. "She loves you. And she knows that you come first."

Unreasonable guilt rose up, along with sympathetic pain. "This can't be easy for her. She loves *you*."

"I'll never know why. She is the mother of my son, and as such will always be accorded every respect. You are my wife."

He seemed to think that dealt with the matter. Only half-amused, she glanced at him. Unexpectedly, he laughed. "I know that look. Visit her tomorrow, then, but be sure to come back, because I leave for Rucăr the day after."

When Maria ran into the hall and hugged her, Ilona felt such relief that it took her an instant to raise her arms and return the embrace. Fortunately, she didn't need to say anything, since Maria's words tripped over themselves in their hurry.

"You came! I never thought you'd come to me... Oh, Ilona, I've been so afraid! I thought this marriage might end our friendship!"

Ilona, who still feared the same thing, drew back a little, searching her friend's eyes.

"You don't hate me?" Maria asked, rather like a wheedling child, but her eyes twinkled.

"Why should *I* hate you? It's I who've usurped your position."

Maria shrugged. "We have no choice in marriage, do we? I was sent to Dragomir. You were sent to Vlad. You do know I would never slight you?"

A hint of genuine anxiety in Maria's words caused Ilona to give her another quick hug. "Of course you wouldn't. But I know how you feel about Vlad, and I don't want you to...resent me."

Maria sighed. "I always knew it would come one day. I knew he'd never marry me. For Mihnea, that's unimportant. To be honest, I'm glad it's you, because you will never try to cut Mihnea out or destroy his future."

"Of course not!" said Ilona, shocked.

Maria smiled. "I would like our children to be friends."

"So would I. How is Mihnea?" She couldn't have said anything to make Maria happier. Immediately, she was conducted into the garden, where the toddler was playing in the sunshine on a wooden hobby horse. A much bigger boy of around thirteen was climbing through the branches of a tree for his entertainment.

"Dragomir's son," Maria explained. "He dotes on Mihnea."

Ilona smiled. "So the Danesti preferences of Dragomir's family end here?"

"Even before Mihnea was born," Maria said. "Vlad looks after him, takes him hunting and play-fighting, talks to him. He's devoted to the prince."

It wasn't the first such story she'd come across. Vlad was building future stability just by paying a little attention to the young. They, together with the new and loyal boyars whom he raised to power, were slowly replacing the self-serving and untrustworthy older families as the mainstay of his regime.

Later, when the boys had been introduced to their "princess" and Mihnea had climbed all over Ilona—an honour he insisted upon when he was told she'd given him the much-favoured horse rattle—they sat in the shade with cool lemon drinks and watched the children play.

Maria said lazily, "You *are* content with this marriage?"

Ilona drew in her breath. Now, if ever, was the time to tell Maria the truth about her feelings.

"Not," Maria added wryly, "that it would make any difference if you weren't! But I wouldn't like to think you were unhappy. I know the prince can be a bit—daunting. Not to say downright terrifying…"

"I've never been afraid of him."

"I know." Maria smiled nostalgically. "Even when I was, you weren't. Marriage is different, of course. But don't be frightened of…*intimacy* with him. He likes intimacy."

Intimacy. There were times over the last few years, waiting for Vlad, that she had thought of little else but intimacy with him. Her original impression of such doings, drawn from her observations in the country, had been that this was an animalistic way for humans to procreate. Yet her body's reactions to Vlad's kisses, the bold caresses of his hands, made her yearn for the greater pleasure she knew awaited her.

A pleasure with which her friend was already only too familiar. "Maria…"

"Oh dear," said Maria, standing and hurrying across the grass toward Mihnea, who'd tripped over a fallen toy and was crying with rage.

Distracted, Ilona wondered if Vlad had looked just like that when he was an angry three-year-old.

Ilona reined in her horse beside Vlad and gazed at the scene before her. Men, some in working smocks belted over their rough trousers, others bare backed under the boiling sun, wielded axes, enthusiastically cutting down trees.

A large area had already been cleared, and beyond it, the same again already under cultivation. A few women and children pottered in the fields, hoeing weeds. Some houses formed a village in the centre.

"You said you would do this," she remembered. "Clear more land for crops."

He nodded. "We're doing it all over. Several new villages are thriving already. In time, it will make a huge difference."

She smiled at him. "You really were born to do this, weren't you?"

"What? Watch other men work?"

"Rule."

"To rule this country," he amended. "I used to dream of it, in exile. Which is funny, because I don't remember thinking anything very much of it when I lived here as a child. I wanted adventures then, to travel to Italy and France—anywhere was more interesting than Wallachia."

"We all take home for granted."

"Not anymore," said Vlad, watching her with a gloriously warm smile in his eyes. And she knew he meant more than his country; he meant her living in it as his wife.

She flushed with pleasure, and, because they were alone, he edged his horse closer to hers, leaned from his saddle, and kissed her mouth. Butterflies danced desperately in her stomach, fluttering lower as she opened to him.

The sounds of birds' song, of the men labouring and calling to each other melted into the distance. The horses, restive, moved forward, forcing them to break apart.

"Christ,"Vlad said unevenly. "How am I to wait another nine months for you?"

She smiled. "Well, I've waited nine years for you."

"Really?" He looked stunned. "Since we first met? That was ten years ago."

"Who's counting?"

"You, apparently." He smiled, just a little predatory. "You loved me when you were a little girl?"

"Yes," she admitted. "Only I didn't really know it then."

"When did you know it?" he pursued.

"Later. At Hunedoara."

"I wish I'd known…"

"I'm glad you didn't!" Ilona said with feeling as they turned their horses to move back to the road and rejoin the main party. "I always expected the feeling to have disappeared the next time we met. Actually," she confessed, "I still expect that."

"Why?"

"I don't know. I think about you so much, I don't see how the reality can ever live up to my expectation. I'm always sure the disappointment will cure me, but it never does."

His warm gaze clung to hers. "I love your honesty, Ilona Szilágyi."

"Because it flatters you?" she teased.

"Of course. I wish I'd kidnapped you from Hunedoara and married you by force."

Something thrilled inside her at that, but, laughing at herself, she argued, "You never even noticed me until I'd been to the Hungarian court and acquired the outer polish Aunt Erzsébet had always wanted for me.

"Yes, I did. I liked you. I used to find myself thinking of you at odd times, looking forward to seeing you as much as Mihály. But perhaps I always thought of you as the girl playing tag, not as a woman."

She shrugged philosophically, and he added, "A girl with eyes that saw and knew too much for my own comfort. But still I liked you. I still wanted your company."

"And now?" she prompted, hoping unworthily for a compliment.

"Now I want all of you."

He spurred forward, muttering something under his breath that made her burn from the inside out. It sounded like, "In my bed."

The summer progress through Wallachia, or *Tara Romancu* as the natives named it, was a revelation to Ilona. Not just because she learned about the country and the people who were to be her own, or because she saw sights of great beauty, although that was part of it. But much of her wonder was in learning about Vlad through his feeling for places, through his people's feeling for him.

From fortresses such as Rucăr and the new one he was creating at Bucharest, to monasteries such as the fortified island community at Snagov, she saw what he had done and how the people greeted him. He wasn't always loved. In many places, where he'd had cause to visit the full force of his implacable justice, he was truly feared. But everywhere, she saw respect. In many places, there was appreciation for the improved prosperity or safety that the prince had brought about. And in a few places, where he'd spent some time, such as the monastery at Snagov where he sometimes retreated for peace and contemplation, she found a genuine love.

She began to understand that he shone in the eyes of others beside herself, that his brilliance drew people to him, fascinated them, and held them. And strangely enough, his people, the ordinary peasants, seemed as proud of his cruelties as of his greatness. Perhaps they recognised his courage in looking always toward the greater good.

Although seeing the country in his company was a delight for Ilona, she was glad to rest at the castle at Poenari on the River Arges for more than one reason. Her mother was showing signs of fatigue at the constant travel of the last few weeks, and, besides, despite its controversial beginnings, the castle felt curiously like home.

So, while her mother recuperated, Ilona rode out in the sunshine every day, sometimes with Turcul's wife and an escort, sometimes with the prince. In the more relaxed formality of Poenari, sometimes she even rode out alone with Vlad, and those were the days she secretly liked best, when he would talk to her about great matters as well as small ones, and they had the opportunity to know each other better and grow closer.

Sometimes, as their horses rested, she wanted to take his hand as they walked along forest trails. She wanted to kiss him in the sunshine and feel him crush her in his arms. But he rarely took such advantage of their time alone, and she couldn't help feeling disappointed. Especially when she knew the desire was there, simmering so near the surface.

Once, as he helped her remount and settled her in the saddle, without warning he buried his face against her thigh and seemed to inhale her. His breath burned through the fabric of her gown, shocking and thrilling in equal measure. Her hand trembled as she reached down and touched his hair.

He spoke into her thigh, muffled and uneven. "I should separate us, send you away from me. I'm no saint, and I cannot bear this…"

"What?" Ilona asked in distress.

An extra breath of laughter burned her leg, and he raised his head. "It doesn't matter. I can't bring myself to let you go out of my sight."

For the rest of that day, it seemed he meant what he said, literally. Riding home, eating dinner in the castle, she kept looking up to find his gaze upon her, curiously dark and predatory. It made her uncomfortable, yet it thrilled and excited her too. She wasn't quite sure what to do with such feelings, so when her mother retired early to bed, she used the excuse to go too, not long after her.

In the end, she didn't go to bed, though. She was too unsettled to sleep in the same chamber as her mother. She went to the top of the nearest tower instead and cooled her burning body there.

Perhaps she'd known he would be there. Certainly, when she heard the soft, approaching footsteps, she didn't expect anyone else.

Wordlessly, he took her in his arms and kissed her more deeply than ever before, while his hands, bolder than ever before, roamed over her hips and breasts. He pressed his lips to the pulse beating frantically at the base of her throat and with his hands on her rear, pressed her into his body. Their clothing preserved few secrets now. Devastated, shocked, yet completely given over to physical sensation, Ilona could only cling to him and wait with delicious joy for whatever would come next.

When his mouth took her breast, she thought she would die of pleasure. Throwing her head back, she gasped and gasped again. He pulled her head back up and returned to kissing her mouth, while his hand covered her breast's nakedness instead.

Trembling, awash, she felt the cool stone against her back. His hand tangled in her skirts, and then he paused and lifted his head. Through the hot, friendly darkness, his eyes glittered.

"What am I doing?" he said shakily. Slowly, he lowered his forehead to touch hers. "What am I doing?"

Ilona, who was more concerned that he keep doing it, had no answer to offer.

"Kiss me," he whispered. Without hesitation, she lifted her mouth to his. He accepted her kiss with grace and tenderness, but it was his sigh of relief that made her understand he'd been asking for forgiveness.

When his hands touched her, it was to draw her gown and undergown up over her breasts and shoulders. "Good night," he murmured. And Ilona, feeling like a dismissed attendant, could only walk numbly away from him.

Although Ilona thought she understood some of the reasons that made him do it, what she chiefly understood was that she'd been rejected. She'd made her offer with words the last time they'd been together in this castle. And now, surely, her body had made an even more blatant invitation. And still he sent her away.

She felt like the eighteen-year-old Maria, setting out to seduce him in Hunedoara and being sent back to her room like a naughty child who was beneath him.

Wildly, she began to imagine that she'd got it all wrong, that this was merely a political alliance after all. He'd never said that he loved her. Dear God, had she mistaken *politeness* for love? Was she really so naïve?

Since she'd tossed and turned for most of the night, and since her mother was complaining about it, she rose early and went down to the kitchen in search of food. She would avoid him today. And if they met, be strictly formal from now on. She would invite, would *allow*, no more such scenes as last night's.

Her determination was put to the test rather sooner than she expected. For as she emerged from the kitchen with a laughingly presented piece of new bread, she almost ran into Vlad, informally dressed in an open shirt with his doublet dangling unfastened over his shoulder.

Wordlessly, she stood aside to let him pass. His eyes searched hers.

"Good morning."

"Good morning," she managed.

Something flickered in his eyes. It might have been a smile or understanding. He said, "Will you ride with me?"

No! I will not ride or walk or stand still with you.

"Please. I'd like to talk."

She swallowed, knew she would regret it. She nodded once.

The smile grew stronger. One of the cooks emerged from the kitchen with a grin and an apology and edged past them.

Vlad warned, "I won't be good."

Her heart turned over in her breast and seemed to fall with a clunk. She said haughtily, "I will," and brushed past him.

She vowed to ride in silence, but Vlad made up for it with a flow of charming and often funny conversation that almost made her forget. She couldn't help smiling sometimes, and once she laughed out loud, though she cut it off again quickly.

They rode along a forest trail for some time before he veered off it between two large beech trees. Ilona wanted to ask where they were going but refused to open her mouth.

I'm being childish.

I don't care.

The sun glinted in ever-changing patterns between the trees. The horses' hooves made soft, muffled thuds on the forest floor, aiding the illusion that they were the only two people in this world. Birds sang and fluttered among the branches, and occasionally some small animal rustled in the undergrowth. It felt warm and cosy and isolated. Sweet forest scents filled her senses, melting her anger and humiliation.

Vlad reined in his horse, dismounted, and tied the reins loosely around a branch. Lifting the pack from behind the saddle, he unloaded a blanket and spread it on the ground while Ilona watched. Then he turned and reached up his arms to her.

Since she didn't want to appear churlish, she permitted him to lift her down, but she held herself stiffly and wasn't surprised when he released her as soon as her feet were on the ground. In the past, he might have stolen a kiss, or at least lingered close to her.

"Please, sit," he invited.

She knelt on a corner of the blanket and sat back on her heels. Vlad lowered himself to the ground, leaning his back against a tree and drew one knee up under his elbow while he watched her.

"Before I say anything else, would I be right in assuming your displeasure with me this morning has more to do with what I didn't do last night than with what I did?"

"You are impossible!" she burst out. "Self-satisfied, arrogant, overweening…"

When he laughed, it fuelled her anger even further so that she barely noticed he'd moved until he pushed her onto her back. When she lashed out at him, he caught her hands, holding them on either side of her head while he straddled her body, looming over her.

The words dried up in her throat. Her heart hammered like a bird's in the jaws of a cat.

"I'm all of these things, and worse," he confessed. "But not with you. Ilona Szilágyi, I want a perfect world to live in with you. I want a priest to marry us and the world to recognise me as your husband before I take you to my bed and keep you there. But the world is not perfect, and neither am I. Part of me refuses to give in to my body's lusts until we have that perfection. And part of me…"

"What?" she asked hoarsely when he stopped.

"Part of me wants to take, and to give, what happiness I can in the present and save my sanity if nothing else. And so…and so, I have come to the conclusion that all I can do is lay the matter before you and let you choose the way for both of us."

She felt her eyes widen. Yet when he would have released her hands, she gripped his fingers so fiercely that he stayed where he was.

"What way are you talking about? What do you mean?"

"I mean do we justify our abstinence over the years by continuing to cling to it until the spring? Or do we make love now and face the wrath of whatever aspect of God you believe in?"

Ilona gulped in air. "I don't believe He cares about such things."

"Nor do I. So we come down to our own choices. Your choice."

She stared at him, trying to read the expression in his strange, green eyes and made a discovery. "You think I'll choose abstinence and that will strengthen your own resolve."

A smile flashed across his face, brief and blinding. "You know me well, too well. Before you decide, let me just say two things. I can love you without giving you a child to shock the world. It would be our own, private matter involving no one else. And if you choose to wait, as the world and your family expects, then I will respect that completely. My erratic behaviour is largely due to uncertainty. Make me certain, Ilona, one way or the other. And one way or another, I will be good."

She believed him. But there was never really any choice to make. If there was, she had made it years ago, long before there had been a possibility of carrying it through.

For the first time, she relaxed under his constricting hands.

"Kiss me," she whispered, as he had done last night, and slowly, he lowered his mouth to hers, gentle, tender, holding everything in check. Even when she urged him on with her tongue and teeth and devouring lips, he kept it controllable. He held her hands, held her pinned, so that she couldn't move.

A choke of laughter that was half sob broke from her throat. He raised his head, and she gasped, "You're going to make me say it, aren't you?"

"Yes," he agreed. "I'm going to make you say it." But his eyes were already blazing with a victory he'd never thought to win.

"Then love me," she pleaded. "Love me now."

"I do," he whispered and lowered his body until it fitted perfectly to hers, making every nerve ending and every pulse leap in response. At the same time, he brought his mouth down on hers, and this time kissed her in earnest.

It was a curious bridal bed, but Ilona could have hoped for none better. Instead of the forbidding formality and even more terrifying licence of wedding guests, their only companions were the birds and animals, who ignored them. He released her hands at last to remove her clothes one by one, and worshipped her virginally shrinking body with words and hands and lips, coaxing and arousing her passion with caresses that grew increasingly intimate.

When he slid his hand between her thighs, she accepted it with wonder and delight, pushing herself onto it. More daring now, she burrowed under his tunic and shirt, searching for his warm skin. He helped her, tugging off his clothes and letting her explore his muscled shoulders and chest with awed fingers.

She splayed her hand across his heart, feeling its strong, violent tattoo.

"Your heart beats so fast," she whispered.

He pressed his lips over hers. "So does yours."

He moved, and she cried out at the loss of his magical hand between her legs. But then she felt what replaced it, and was silent. He lifted his head, his eyes wide open to watch her every expression as he entered her body.

Her breath caught with the unexpected discomfort, but he held his body still, continuing to arouse her with the long, slow caresses of his hands and lips, all the time gazing into her eyes, until she relaxed back into the sensual pleasure once more. Only then, his body trembling with the mighty effort of self-control, did he begin to move, with slow, rocking motions that thrilled her anew. And so, blending care and passion, he took her as his wife before God and showed her how to reach the joy locked in her own body.

Withdrawing from the body of Ilona Szilágyi at the instant of climax was the hardest thing Vlad Dracula had ever done. But because he'd promised, he did it, and having done it, felt even more triumphant.

There had never been anything sweeter than reviving from lovemaking with her in his arms, pliant and still trembling from the pleasure he'd given her. Unless it was giving her that pleasure in the first place. She was such an intoxicating mixture of instinctive sensuality and wonder, as desperate to give as to receive, that there had been many times he'd almost lost his self-imposed, rigid control.

In fact, looking back, he was sure there had been several times when his mischievous love had deliberately provoked him to do just that. Well, there would be time for those wilder encounters too.

Shifting his weight, he turned with her still in his arms to lie on his side and stroked her hair. She smiled, tracing the outline of his moustache with one finger.

"Thank you," she whispered, taking him by surprise yet again.

"The gift was all yours."

She shook her head and pressed her cheek against his, her arms tightening around him. He said in her ear, "You understand about last night? I wanted you so badly, but I couldn't take you like that, a quick fumble in the dark. Not the first time."

He felt her smile against his skin. "Then there's still hope?"

Laughter shook him. "Minx." He sat up, reaching for the end of the blanket to wrap around them both. But as he gripped it, he felt her hands on his back. He paused, shivering at the butterfly caresses, unexpectedly sensual. It took him a moment to realise that she was tracing the lines of his scars.

His fast-returning lust dissolved into the old shame, the old memories that never really went away. Perhaps she felt his rigidity.

At any rate, her mouth kissed his shoulder, and her arms wound around him from behind.

"Whoever did this to a child must have been a monster."

Vlad swallowed. "I was a difficult child. But yes, he was a monster. I used to lie awake at nights inventing more and more gory ways to kill him."

"And did you?" she asked.

"No." He gave a deprecating smile. "Not yet. I still, occasionally, fantasise about meeting him on a battlefield, but men like him don't fight in battle."

"Who was he?"

"My jailer for the first two years, when we were held in close captivity. Beyond keeping us alive, he had no instructions for our welfare."

Her lips glided up his shoulder to the back of his neck, and desire began to twinge. She said, "Stephen told me you protected Radu in those years. Was this the price?"

"No. Well, partly, maybe. But beating a tearful child is less fun than lashing an angry adolescent. And when Radu really needed protection, he didn't want it. Why do you make me talk about this now?"

"Because you don't like me to touch you there." Her fingers skimmed across the scars and left them.

He turned into her arms, pushing her back under him and rejoicing fiercely in the excitement that sprang into her melting dark eyes. He said, "I like you to touch me anywhere and everywhere. Even there. But especially here, and *here…*"

For the rest of their time at Poenari, Ilona's heart sang. Her love for Vlad, already intensified by his close companionship, seemed to grow wildly out of control. Sometimes, her own feelings actually frightened her, but she couldn't and wouldn't draw back from the physical relationship they'd begun.

Their early morning rides became a fixture, accepted even by her mother who may or may not have suspected that Vlad took her into the woods to make love to her. Either way, she didn't object, and Ilona was free to enjoy her life at last. It really did seem that the waiting was over, that even if Matthias postponed the wedding for another year, it didn't matter, because she and Vlad were already husband and wife in every way that mattered. Fully awakened and alive as never before, Ilona was lost in love.

But of course she knew it was an idyllic interlude. With the conversations and debates that formed another part of their relationship, she knew that rough times were ahead for Vlad and his country. Politics, even war, would interfere with their idyll soon enough, but the love would remain, and she had every confidence in Vlad to find his way through it. With pride, she even relished the part she would now play in those matters as his bride-to-be, his companion and friend whose thoughts he genuinely valued.

Interruption came late one morning as they rode back into the castle after an interlude of particularly blissful loving. The boyar Stoica waited for them in the main hall, with the news that an Ottoman embassy had arrived in Tîrgoviște.

Vlad didn't look remotely surprised. Instead, his lips curved and a glint of quite different excitement entered his green eyes.

"Asking where the tribute is?" he hazarded.

"Precisely."

"Well, we'll let them stew for a bit," said Vlad, striding across to the table to find the wine jug which had already been brought for the weary traveller. Over his shoulder, he called, "Whom have they sent? Someone important, I trust?"

Ilona didn't really register the strange, Ottoman names. But she saw Vlad's expressive face turn blank with shock.

Chapter Nineteen

Visegrád, Hungary 1474

"Ilona." Vlad started across the room to her. "I didn't know you were there!"

"No…"

"Szelényi's locked the door."

"I know."

He stood in front of her, gazing helplessly down at her anxious face. Though he couldn't prevent the warm gladness seeping through him because she had come to him to talk at last, he racked his brains for the means to save her the embarrassment of discovery.

"Someone will come if I shout, and let you out, but you know it will be all over court tomorrow that you were locked in here with me. If I call immediately, perhaps it will save you the worst. Szelényi himself…"

"Vlad," she interrupted, and he saw with amazement that her eyes were full of amusement as well as frustration. "That is the point."

He heard his own breath falter as understanding flooded him. She tore her gaze free of his, beginning to pace as she spoke. "If you want this marriage, we can force his hand. Make sure everyone knows. He may be so angry, of course, that he keeps Wallachia from you, but I gather there aren't many options, and he will come back to you, whatever you've done. And after all, you'd still be allied with his family as he planned in the first place."

He said, "You'd do that. You'd really do that…"

She shrugged, still not looking at him. Her pacing became faster, more agitated. "It doesn't matter. If you call now, they'll just think I wandered in here in my madness. It might make them a new myth—Dracula's kidnapping and ravishing gentlewomen— but it will make no real difference. This time, the choice is yours."

She stopped talking and drew in her breath. Vlad caught her in midpace, gripping her shoulders to still her, and at last she lifted her gaze to his. Anxiety blended with determination and uncertainty in almost equal measure in her soft, dark eyes.

He whispered, "I cannot take your reputation just to force my will on the king."

"You needn't touch me," she said vaguely. "Your private honour is the only one that matters, after all. For the rest…it is, I think, our last chance. For it all. Other bits may be left to us. I don't know. It doesn't matter. It was the only idea I had, but you needn't go through with it…"

"Ilona."

She stopped talking and swallowed. Because he had no words of his own, he bent and kissed her lips for the first time in twelve years. Her mouth opened in a silent gasp, and the salty wetness of her tears trickled from her face onto his lips.

Lifting his head, he touched the taut skin over her cheekbones, traced the line of her tears. "Your beauty still breaks my heart."

She closed her eyes. "Because I have none left. But I can make myself think again. Perhaps I can still help you."

He brushed his lips across the fresh tear drop. "Everything about you is as beautiful as it ever was. Together, I think we could shine again."

A smile trembled into being on her lips. She opened her eyes but remained silent. Understanding, Vlad began to laugh with soft delight. "You're going to make me say it, aren't you?"

"Yes," she said happily. "I'm going to make you say it."

"Then stay with me in secret tonight, and in the morning we'll shock everyone. I'll twirl my moustache most villainously, and you, the outraged princess, must hold out for marriage."

Vlad brought her wine in the elegant Venetian glass goblet, then dragged his chair closer and sat almost at right angles to her, his knee close to but not quite touching her silk gown.

He said, "Does your dragon know you're here?"

"Margit? She isn't a dragon... For some reason, she's been protecting me. She seems to love me, though I don't know why. I've let her serve me all these years and given her nothing. I should find her a husband before she withers like me."

"You're not withered," Vlad objected. "You've just been... resting."

"Resting," she repeated doubtfully, and since he was afraid she would drift back off into vagueness, he brought her back by returning to the question.

"Does Margit know you're here?"

"Oh no. She thinks I'm asleep. She won't wake till morning, when I have hopes that she'll raise a really loud alarm..."

"If she does, you'll owe her a very fine husband."

Ilona brightened. "Is your Count Szelényi married?"

"Unfortunately, yes."

"Pity. I like him."

"Why?" The unexpected twinge of jealousy took him by surprise, but at least he could laugh at himself.

"He seems to care for you... And he troubled to be civil to the king's dowdy cousin. Beyond lip service." She frowned. "Although he shouldn't be intriguing with that woman. She's beneath him, I think."

"Have pity on him," said Vlad, amused. "He's been apart from his wife for some time."

She began to say, "Do *you*...?" and broke off. From the clear gaze with which she began, to the rising flush when she realised the impossibility of continuing, it was so reminiscent of the old Ilona, blurting out her curiosity before considering the consequences, that he smiled.

"Do I intrigue?" he finished for her. "No. In recent years, they allow me to assuage my baser instincts with court whores, but you wouldn't dignify such passages even as intrigues."

She looked into his eyes. She didn't appear hurt, and, ruefully, he didn't know if that was a good thing or not. So he added, "Since our marriage was revived, I've returned to celibacy."

That didn't get quite the reaction he'd expected either. She smiled as if at an old joke.

"You always did that," she remembered, and he realised that it was true. A sop, a nod in the direction of honour and fidelity that he had chosen from some only half-understood instinct. The rest, even Maria, had been some almost mundane necessity, like eating.

She said, "I wasn't faithful either, in body."

"You were married." He kept it neutral, no accusation—how could there be when she would have had no choice? And hoped she understood that it was also different from his demeaning couplings. When she said nothing, just absently sipped her wine, he added, "I heard he was a good man."

"I heard that too."

Vlad still knew her very well. He ducked his head down to catch her eye again before he pursued, "And was he?"

Her breath came out unevenly. "In his own eyes, in the eyes of the world. I didn't like him. I was glad when he died. I don't want to think about him."

He reached out, covering her suddenly agitated hand with his. He took the wineglass from her and laid it on the table.

"Ilona. We're fighting together again, and I need to know what we're up against."

"Not him. He's dead."

Her voice was flat, uncompromising. If it hadn't been for her fingers clinging almost involuntarily to his, he would have thought she was slipping away from him again.

He said, "What does Matthias fear about us being together? That you'll deny his Impaler myths?"

Her lips curved slightly. "Oh, I don't think anyone can deny those now, can they? They have all the authority of the new printing. Which doesn't mean Matthias doesn't fear it."

"Perhaps he fears we'll be too strong for him together."

"It doesn't matter if we're on his side."

"Are we?"

"I really think we'll have to be. The Ottomans are no longer an alternative."

Vlad sighed. "I made a huge mess of that, didn't I?"

Ilona lifted their joined hands to her cheek. "No. The mess was Matthias's fault."

"I didn't even see it coming. Not that. And not Stephen."

"We can't undo the past," she said sadly.

"But I think, if we're to move on, that we'll have to."

Chapter Twenty

Tîrgovişte, Wallachia, 1461-1462

"Who is Zafer Bey?"

She'd waited for him to tell her why the presence of this man in Tîrgovişte shocked hm. With all the confidence of their new closeness, she knew he would. And yet the princely train had already set out for the capital, and still he hadn't so much as referred to it.

As if that blank look had never been, he talked about pacifying the ambassadors, playing for time because he wasn't yet ready to face an Ottoman invasion. The alliance was not yet ready, despite the papal crusade declared in Mantua two years before. Hungary, who'd received forty thousand ducats from the pope for the purpose, was to lead the crusade, just as in the great days of John Hunyadi; and Matthias had to be kept up to the mark. Internally, the massive popular army of Wallachia had to be organised and armed and trained to augment Vlad's regular troops of nobles, professionals, and mercenaries.

All this he discussed openly with Ilona. And it jolted her, because it forced her to realise the dangers to Wallachia and to Vlad himself that an open breach with the sultan would entail. Somehow, she'd imagined he would never let the war touch his beloved country, but that was naïve, and Vlad was nothing if not a realist. It would not be Matthias but Vlad who drove this crusade forward. Ilona understood that and still she had every faith in him.

But his silence on this one point disquieted her. Until, finally believing she understood that too, she asked the question outright as they rode together along the muddy road south.

"Who is Zafer Bey?"

Almost to her surprise, he didn't turn the subject. He didn't even look irritated. He said, "Interesting question. The answer is, I think, that he is the man with whom the sultan means to frighten me."

Ilona, knowing now she was right, asked steadily, "And does he?"

Vlad dragged his upper lip between his teeth. "I don't know," he said at last. "That is one of the many interesting things we'll discover when I meet him."

Ilona wanted to weep because of all that was admitted in those words, but more because of the storm of shame that whipped through his eyes before the heavy lids and the long, thick lashes veiled them.

With difficulty, she said, "Some childish fears we never get over, no matter how irrational. There is no shame in that, especially not when your monster is real."

He turned to her, the hoods lifting from his eyes to reveal them bright and speculative. "Zafer's monstrosity is not in question—or not by me—but the really interesting thing is how the sultan knows it."

Ilona frowned. "If this Zafer is a fearsome man…"

"Mehmed doesn't believe I fear anyone. Or at least he didn't. It's one of the reasons he's backed me for so long. And yet now he sends me Zafer. How does he know now? Zafer himself would not reveal such abuse."

Gazing at him, Ilona blurted, "*You* know. I can see you know how."

"Radu," said Vlad. "My little brother, whom I once protected from Zafer himself, is the only one who knows."

"He betrayed you," Ilona whispered in pity. The boy he had risked reimprisonment to go back for. But that didn't appear to be what was concerning Vlad.

"He means to supplant me," he said flatly. "When the Ottomans come, it won't be to swallow Wallachia into their empire. It will be to put Radu on my throne."

Vlad received the sultan's ambassadors from his princely throne in the great hall of the Tîrgovişte palace. Leaving out only his dragon collar—which would have been too much an open insult at this stage—he wore his most magnificent garb. Jewels glistened on his velvet mantle and silken hat. Fine ostrich feathers stretched upward from his headgear, adding height and splendour. He was surrounded by his greatest and wealthiest nobles, also very finely dressed, and an array of scribes and clerks sat at a finely polished and intricately carved table below his dais. At a greater distance milled the lesser courtiers, together with the upper rank of court ladies.

The entire hall shone, from painted ceiling to floor, with highly polished wood, with decorative gold and silver plate, with extravagant candlelight to augment the sun streaming in the windows on either side. Vlad clearly meant to impress.

Ilona, accompanied by her mother, sat among the court ladies, aware that Vlad would not have considered it proper to receive foreign dignitaries in any less a manner. Even Mihály, though greeted informally as a friend on first arrival, had always been subjected to a formal reception when he came as the king's representative.

Trying not to be anxious, she watched surreptitiously for signs of disquiet in Vlad—and found none. Not even when the visitors from the Sublime Porte were announced and walked the full length of the hall to his throne. Was that a trick he'd learned from Countess Hunyadi?

Dividing her attention, she let her gaze focus on the ambassadors. Both were richly robed, their turbans jeweled, and their moustaches and beards luxurious. The taller, stouter of the two walked with a subtle kind of strut, like man aware of his own importance, his dark eyes unwaveringly on the prince. The smaller, thinner man was older, but with fierce intelligence still gleaming in his eyes. Both looked proud, and neither, she suspected, were strangers to cruelty. But she could not guess which was Zafer, which the man who had beaten the boy Vlad so badly.

Approaching the throne, both men bowed low, their noses all but touching their knees.

Vlad Dracula looked haughty and not best pleased. As they rose, he waited in silence, then lifted one interrogative eyebrow. "You do not uncover in the presence of a great ruler?"

"Your Highness is aware of the customs of my people," said the tall man smoothly in acceptable Romanian.

"Your Excellency is aware of the customs of mine," Vlad countered. Ilona knew then that Zafer was the taller man. For a moment, she wondered if Vlad would force them to uncover their heads, but he said nothing more, merely held out his hand for the document carried by the smaller man. He stepped forward to the dais, but at once a clerk rose, bowed, took the document from his reluctant fingers, and jumped up to present it to Vlad.

Vlad opened it and read it thoroughly. It took a long time. The courtiers grew bored and began to murmur in low voices or to stroll among the throng to find particular friends. The Ottoman ambassadors stood perfectly still. After a while, the smaller man cast an anxious glance at Zafer, who gave an infinitesimal shrug in response, as if completely unconcerned.

He thought Vlad was taking his time just to rile them. He may have been right. Ilona murmured an excuse to her mother and rose to change positions, moving closer to the throne so that she could see the faces of the ambassadors.

Zafer continued to watch Vlad as he carefully perused the document. She'd been right earlier. There was no anxiety whatsoever in the Turk's face. In fact, she thought she read a faint, cruel amusement that bordered on contempt. He imagined this excessively careful reading was Vlad's last attempt at dignity before he gave in. And in that Ilona knew he was wrong.

But why should a man who knew Vlad so well imagine such an unlikely outcome? Because he knew Vlad's secret fear of him? Because he imagined Vlad would do anything to get him out of his country as fast as possible? With a new spurt of dread, Ilona began to suspect she didn't after all know all the facts, that she was missing something vitally important here.

Vlad sighed, closed the document, and passed it to Carstian on his right-hand side.

"His Sublime Majesty the sultan does me too much honour, gives me too much credit for the wealth and well-being of my country. I shall write to him to explain that although I acknowledge everything I owe him, I cannot pay the tribute this year because I and my country are both bled dry through constant war with our enemies here and in Transylvania. Nor dare I leave to bring any part of the tribute in person, as His Sublime Majesty wishes. If I did, the Hungarians would seize my throne before I could wink, and that would not be good for His Sublime Majesty."

"I am sure," said Zafer, sounding bored, "that His Sublime Majesty would be open to receiving Your Highness and Your Highness's tribute at some place nearer to home for you than Constantinople."

"Then when I can gather the money, I shall arrange it," said Vlad smoothly. "This matter of the children, however. I am duly honoured that His Sublime Majesty so admires the quality of Romanian manhood that he wants our boys for his janissary corp.

But Wallachia has never paid a child tribute. It was never part of any agreement between His Sublime Majesty and either myself or any of my predecessors." Vlad smiled into Zafer's eyes. It was not a pleasant smile. "I believe I have had frequent cause before to—er—push that point home."

Since Vlad had ruthlessly captured and impaled several Ottoman recruiting commanders trying to steal Wallachian children, his meaning was abundantly clear. One or two of the Wallachian nobleman grinned openly, as proud of their prince's wit as of his cruelty in defence of his most vulnerable people.

Although the smaller Turk's lips tightened, Zafer didn't bat an eyelid.

"But that is why His Sublime Majesty sent me. As Your Highness knows, I push my own point very effectively."

Ilona's gut twisted. For an instant she thought she would vomit and had to swallow down her own bile. The ambiguity of Zafer's words was more lewd than Vlad's, but by everyone else they were taken as a feeble boast to try to rival Dracula's reputation. Only Ilona picked up the sexual allusion, and that because she saw Vlad's involuntary twitch. And at last she understood the nature and extent of Zafer's abuse.

The beating he could and did endure. The other assault was the one he had longed to rip out Zafer's heart for. The one he had saved Radu from. Although rumour said Radu was not immune to manly charms and had given himself willingly to none other than the sultan himself. The protection he had not wanted from Vlad.

And Vlad, face-to-face with the unrepentant, the boastful abuser of his childhood, merely smiled.

"Not as effectively as you imagine. Your courtesy, whether as host or guest, leaves much to be desired. However, since you feel you know best, let me help you keep your own customs in my country." His eyes flickered, in some lightening signal to the soldiers who guarded the door. They strode forward.

Vlad stood and said disdainfully, "Kneel."

And for the first time, alarm truly did cross Zafer's face. The other ambassador gasped out, "You cannot kill the representatives of His Sublime Majesty!"

"Of course not," said Vlad, stepping down from the dais. Turning to one of the soldiers, he tossed something into his hands. "Make sure these gentlemen's turbans remain well attached to their heads."

The soldier looked down involuntarily. Several carpenter's nails lay in his palm. He grinned.

The Ottomans fell to their knees unaided, crying out for mercy, crying out the sultan's anger at such an insult and much more in their own language that Ilona couldn't understand.

Ilona had seen enough. Moving quickly, she returned to her mother and led her silently out of the hall. They didn't quite make it before the screaming started.

As the palace grew quiet and her mother retired for the night, Ilona continued to gaze out into the darkened gardens. Unless he didn't want to be found, she knew where he would be. Even in the summer storm. With sudden decision, she seized her cloak from the back of the chair and walked quickly to the door. Once there, with her hand on the latch, she paused. For the first time, she felt uncertain of her ability to deal with Vlad Dracula. Those agonies of their relationship that had once eaten her up now seemed completely trivial in the light of today's revelations. Learning to know the Prince of Wallachia was not unmitigated pleasure.

But her path was chosen and couldn't be abandoned, even if she wanted to. And she didn't. There was nothing he could do to make that happen, God help her.

Lifting the latch, she hurried out into the rain, crossing into the palace section of the gardens and hurrying down to the willow tree near the pond.

But no figure leaned there against its branches. There was no Vlad-shaped bulge against the trunk. It seemed he didn't need the fresh air—or herself—as much as she'd imagined he would. What had she expected? Vlad had learned to live with this long ago. And his acts of cruelty, his "minor atrocities" were not so few that they could be allowed to eat him up. He was a strong ruler, unafraid to take the road he'd chosen.

It was she who needed the fresh air, to remind her of the goodness in the world. Who needed to see him, to assure herself he was still the Vlad she'd always thought him.

And so, gasping, she grasped at the willow branch and let the rain run into her mouth and trickle down her hair into her neck and down the front of her cloak. She looked down slowly, her gaze drawn by invisible strings to the ground behind the tree.

He sat there, in his shirt and doublet, soaked through without any further protection from the rain, his back pressed against the tree trunk, his knees drawn up under his chin. Her heart gave two powerful beats before she realised that his eyes were turned up to her in the darkness.

Without thought, she slumped down beside him. She thought he smiled, but she didn't look.

She said, "Are they dead? Is Zafer dead?"

"No. He was right. I can't go around killing the sultan's representatives. Or at least not yet. But their headaches should keep them from going home too quickly."

"You always meant to do it. You had the nails with you."

"The carpenter left them lying in the hall. It struck me they were miniature stakes. It appealed to my sense of humour. And so I picked them up, although I wasn't certain what I'd do with them."

She leaned her head back, turned her face up into the rain. "Why didn't you tell me? About Zafer?"

He was silent. The rain pattered down on the ground, splashing up over her hand, cascaded onto her face in a thousand tiny blows.

He said, "There are things I don't tell you. The blood of battle, the harshness of justice and punishment. They are my cross, my burden. Not yours. And not fit to be yours."

She turned her head to look at him. "But this is *you*, Vlad. Not what you did, what was done to you."

He gazed straight ahead, his black hair plastered against his face and shirt. "Still my cross, my burden."

"But not your shame."

She thought his breath caught. She couldn't tell where, if anywhere, tears mingled with the rain on his face. She reached out and covered the hand which lay clenched in his lap. It turned in hers and gripped.

"I know that. And yet to cover it, I took on another. I shouldn't have done it when you were there. And yet you know what I am. You've always known."

"No saint," she whispered, turning into him. "And no monster."

His arms closed around her, holding her hard to his sodden chest. The rain continued to fall, but still they sat there, soaking it up like comfort, like love.

Winter closed in on Wallachia, partially stemming the flood of letters from Miklós and from Countess Hunyadi recommending Ilona's and her mother's return to Transylvania, if not to Hungary itself.

By spring, Ilona had been granted a foretaste of what her life with Vlad Dracula was likely to be: risky, exciting, exhilarating, punctuated with alternating periods of total fear and utter bliss. Like the sleigh ride Vlad had once described it.

With the colder weather and longer residence at Tîrgovişte, there were fewer opportunities for physical intimacy. But Vlad still made it possible, taking her on horseback through the snow to a cave he'd discovered as a boy beneath the overhanging roots of a willow. There, wrapped in cloaks and horse blankets, to the rippling sounds of the lake that threatened to flood them, he made exquisite love to her before leaving for Giurgiu and another meeting with a very different representative of the sultan, the soldier and chief falconer, Hamza Pasha.

No one was happy about this meeting. Originally, it was planned for Tîrgovişte, but at the last moment, Hamza requested the prince come instead to a place nearer the Ottoman-held fortress of Giurgiu. Presumably to help allay any fears of an Ottoman trap, a Greek-born Ottoman scholar called Thomas was sent to escort him.

"I don't care that the actual meeting will be on Wallachian soil," Carstian said firmly, when Thomas—who'd made a point of removing his headgear well before entering the princely presence—had been duly greeted and sent away to refresh himself. "It's a trap."

"Of course it is," Vlad agreed.

"So don't go," Ilona commanded, stung by his lighthearted response. To her, the matter was simple.

"Forewarned is forearmed," Vlad said. "This way, I find out more—and put the Ottomans firmly in the wrong if they do try anything. Carstian, I need the cavalry to follow us at a discreet distance. With the usual scouts. But stay out of sight."

There were no fond farewells. The interlude in the lakeside cave that morning had to serve as that. With no more than a formal hand kiss for herself and her mother, Vlad rode off with Thomas and their very few attendants.

By nightfall, messengers returning from the cavalry unit had confirmed the ambush. After a wretched night of fear, Ilona learned that Vlad had survived it and that both Thomas and Hamza Pasha were on their way to Tîrgovişte as prisoners. But still there was no sign of Vlad, and Ilona, discovering partial news to be worse than none, feared for life-threatening injuries instead.

Eventually, Vlad descended on the palace without warning, sweeping into the hall in a wave of euphoria and plans. Although he spared Ilona a quick smile of apology and comfort for herself alone, it was clear that his mind was elsewhere.

"It's begun," he told his boyars, who scuttled from all over the palace in his wake to sit at the table informally with him. "I've taken back Giurgiu."

"With so few men?" Turcul stared at him. Everyone stared at him, except the officers present who had been with him, who grinned with pride in their prince. "How did you manage that?"

Vlad winked. "I speak fluent Turkish. When I commanded them to open the gates, they imagined I was one of their commanders. By the time they discovered their mistake, it was too late. We were inside, and they, taken by surprise, were easily defeated."

"Was that wise?" asked one of the older boyars uneasily. "A bold move, I agree, but it alienates the sultan beyond..."

"The sultan is already alienated. Some letters of mine to the King of Hungary fell into Ottoman hands—so the sultan knew I wasn't negotiating in good faith. That much I learned from Thomas. The sultan knows about my marriage and my commitment to force this crusade against him. So, taking Giurgiu is a first and necessary step."

His gaze swept round the assembled boyars, glittering but deadly serious. Ilona, still partially numb from relief at his return, felt her stomach begin to churn all over again.

"Because he *will* come against us now," Vlad assured them. "Between now and the spring, I want all the Danube crossing points destroyed, and all the river fortresses in our hands. It gives us a head start. And with the sultan busy fighting in Trebizond, it's likely we'll have a few months' grace."

His excitement was infectious. Ilona felt it, rose with it. And yet she wondered if he even remembered now that spring was to be the time of their wedding. Instead, it seemed likely to be the time of a major war.

Chapter Twenty-One

Wallachia, 1462

Timing, Vlad knew, was everything. Familiar prebattle excitement galloped in his veins, urging him to immediate action, to assuage the battle yearning of his restive soldiers. But through the darkness, his eyes and his mind still operated with crystal clarity. They had to if he and his men were to survive this night. And so he held them back and made them wait in total silence until the time was right.

From the hill forest, he watched and listened until the sultan's busy camp drifted slowly into the same silence as his men. The village of tents was a mere blur in the night, but the pattern was already carved in Vlad's mind.

He'd hoped never to let them come so far, had hoped to frighten them from ever crossing the Danube by a show of force made up of his own and the Hungarian army. But Matthias had dragged his feet, and the sultan had managed to cross the river by night several miles away from where Vlad watched.

There had been an inevitability about that. Sultan Mehmed, the Conqueror of Constantinople, having earlier sent a lesser force against Vlad and seen it easily defeated, had come in person with a vast army to avenge the humiliation. And so the two forces had glared at each other across the mighty river, the Ottomans unable to cross because Vlad had destroyed all the major crossing points over the winter. Not well enough, it seemed, for the Ottomans had secretly moved position, crossed by boat, and surprised him by night.

Well, now it was his turn to do the same. And if he succeeded, there would be no more retreating, no more burning of his own country, his own crops, no more poisoning his own wells and rivers to keep them from sustaining the invaders.

The time was right.

Raising his hand high and holding it there for a count of ten, he thrust it forward, and without further invitation, his horse began to move under him.

Exactly as planned, they began slowly, silently, picking their way free of the forest cover. The sky was on their side: a new moon and plenty of cloud made the night as dark as possible, veiling the attack until the danger of being spotted by lookouts was just too great.

Vlad gave the order, low voiced, heard it repeated among the men following. In an instant, it seemed, the torches flared into dazzling light. The path to the sultan's camp was clear, and when his bodyguard raised his torch high, he knew with relief that it could be done.

As planned, the slow advance turned into a gallop. Even before the sentries were properly awake, they were dead, and Vlad's cavalry stormed into the sultan's camp. Now the shouting began, not just the panicked screams of the Ottomans, but the deliberately blood chilling cries of the Wallachians, the blare of trumpets and drums.

Vlad wielded his sword with efficiency. He knew he did because it dripped dark red in the torchlight. But the slaughter was almost automatic. His real attention was on maintaining the tight formation of his men—if they spread out, they were more likely to be killed by the wakening Ottomans—and on leading them unerringly to the sultan's own tent.

Vlad knew his enemy. He knew he already inspired terror in their hearts. Although his force was far smaller, they never knew where he would attack next, and his raids were always devastating. Because he had killed Hamza and Thomas, they called him Kazugli Bey—the Lord Impaler. He played on that, leaving them other such "presents" whenever he attacked and captured anyone of importance. He knew its effect on his impressionable enemy.

But more than that, he knew the probable layout of their camp, and observation had confirmed the sultan's whereabouts.

"Here!" he yelled in triumph. It had to be. The biggest and best-guarded group of tents in the camp. At once, his men formed up, and the real killing began. Using every weapon they had, from swords and daggers to rearing horses' hooves and the vilest war cries, they attacked the terrified guards. As planned, torches were thrown onto the tents as people spilled out of them, and Vlad, galloping from tent to tent in the searing heat, searched desperately for anyone resembling Mehmed. They'd been boys together once, not friends perhaps, but there had been a certain guarded respect amid the fierce rivalry. It made no difference. None of that would stop Vlad killing him.

But Mehmed also knew Vlad. By the time the prince realised his mistake, the best of their advantage had vanished. The sultan had swapped tents. Vlad knew it when he became aware through the smoke of the Ottoman soldiers forming thickly around one of the lesser tents close by.

Probably, Mehmed hadn't really believed it would happen, but he'd taken the precaution anyway. Now Vlad's task was more or less impossible, but it wasn't yet time to give up. Yelling orders above the din of battle and the crackle of fire, he wheeled around and led the charge on the sultan's protectors.

The battle waged for hours. Several times, Vlad glimpsed the petrified face of the sultan behind the rows of fallen and fighting soldiers. The man for whom Ottomans and Romanians were dying. He even sent his dagger flying straight and sure into the melee, but a soldier took it in the breast for him.

Another glance at the sky told Vlad it was time to go before the failure of his task turned into a rout of his soldiers. He called the retreat.

"What now?" gasped Gales, who had become one of his most trusted commanders, as they withdrew speedily back to the forest, still in good order.

"Now?" Vlad repeated. "The war goes on. We will harry them out, with or without our allies. For the moment, you hold the men here, stay in cover. Do *not* attack without my order. I ride to Tîrgovişte, to do what I must before the sultan arrives."

Ilona, still not Princess of Wallachia although many of the lesser people had begun to call her so, didn't feel that she was still waiting. Matthias had again postponed the wedding until the war was over, forcing his decision by adding a new insistence that Vlad change his religion rather than Ilona hers.

Which was a wily trick. At a time of national crisis, with the Ottomans at his door trailing his brother as an alternative prince in their wake, Vlad could not afford to offend his people by renouncing Orthodoxy in favour of hated Roman Catholicism. But almost to her surprise, Ilona found it made little difference to her. Living in a country both torn and lifted by war waged against a cruel invader, she adopted that country fully as her own. She made her own tasks, organising hospitals in Tîrgovişte for the wounded who drifted in from the surrounding countryside, making sure the available food in the city was evenly and continually distributed.

In the beginning, Maria had been a huge help in this work, but as time went on and the Ottomans grew closer, she became increasingly less use. Instead, she bent all her energies on persuading Ilona and her mother to flee into the mountains with her.

Though Ilona refused without a struggle, she did agree that Mihnea should be taken to a place of safety. And so Maria took her son and stepson into the latter's mountain lands to wait for the end of the war.

Maria wasn't the first to advise her to leave. In the spring, Countess Hunyadi paid an unexpected visit to Tîrgovişte. Officially, she brought Vlad Matthias's love, encouragement, and support. Unofficially, she told her sister-in-law and niece to come home with her immediately. And when Ilona refused, she had simply taken the battle to Vlad.

"You were too eager in this," she told Vlad severely. "The king's first priority is to bring home the Crown of St. Stephen from the Emperor Frederick. Until that happens, I doubt he'll be able to give you the help you want. Countess Szilágyi and Ilona must return with me for their own safety until this matter is resolved."

But Vlad, even as a boy, had never been the sort she could influence by intimidation or her own brand of good sense.

"I have every faith in the king to do what is right," he'd said smoothly. "As for the countess and Ilona…"

"We will be staying here," Ilona had interrupted flatly. Her presence in Wallachia, after all, might force Matthias to intervene against his will. Aunt Erzsébet's presence here proved the possibility.

"That is entirely a matter for your mother," Vlad said coolly. "If she wishes to depart, I can spare a small escort to the Transylvanian border. For myself, I can only assure you that when the Ottomans come, I will be ready. They shall not have Wallachia, and from that one circumstance, Hungary will remain free."

While Vlad and Erzsébet had stood glaring at each other, Countess Szilágyi had glanced uncertainly at Ilona, who shook her head imperceptibly.

"We will remain until the wedding," she said.

And so Countess Hunyadi had departed alone. And Matthias, still negotiating for his crown, had been no help whatsoever. Vlad and his people fought alone, a war that involved huge sacrifices from everyone. Masses of people had been evacuated into the mountains to keep them safe and to keep them fed, for Vlad burned everything as he retreated, leaving neither food nor clean water nor people. It broke Ilona's heart, as she knew it broke his, for he was destroying much of what he had achieved for his country. And yet he did it without regret, because the alternative was unthinkable.

Ilona hadn't so much as laid eyes on Vlad for weeks. Carstian was in charge of Tîrgovişte's defences, which had been massively strengthened over the winter and spring. He'd prepared for a long siege, which everyone had hoped would never happen, though with every passing day, it seemed more likely that it would.

And then, when she least expected it, Vlad rode into Tîrgovişte with a substantial part of his army. Emerging from the hospital one morning, she saw them trot smartly past in a long, bristling line. If Vlad was among them, she'd already missed him, but a quick search of the thin, exhausted faces closest to her told her much of what she needed to know.

Hurrying by backstreets and alleys, she arrived at the palace as the soldiers made their way to stables and camps. Anxiously, she dodged through them. Once, recognising a face, she couldn't resist asking, "Is the prince with you? Is all well?"

"Yes, the prince is here. And it could be worse," was the laconic response. A smile of some pride in the exhausted face gave her some relief, some hope that all was not yet lost.

Even before she entered the hall, she heard his voice. It might have been sheer relief or the fact that she hadn't seen him in weeks, but her heart began to beat faster. And when she saw him, her legs suddenly stopped working.

He stood with Carstian and some of the other boyars and commanders, accepting a cup of wine from a servant. Others were scurrying to put food on the table. While he talked with all of his old energy, giving news and demanding it, Ilona stood still and gazed at him.

Still in half armour, as if he lived in it these days, he'd uncovered his head, letting his hair flow around his powerful shoulders. Like his men, he looked tired and lean, but there was no defeat in his glittering green eyes and only humour and mild regret in the story he was telling of a night attack on the Ottoman camp, which had only just failed to kill the sultan.

"It's a pity," he allowed. "Because even now they'd have been on their way home if we'd got him. But still we achieved something, and all is not well in the Ottoman ranks. They're starving and thirsty and completely demoralised. Unfortunately..." Uncannily, he glanced away from Carstian and saw her.

At once, the glitter of his eyes melted into something much warmer. He didn't smile, but his gaze continued to hold hers as he continued. "Unfortunately, they are heading now to Tîrgovişte. It's time to put our plan into action, Carstian. We may yet avoid a siege here."

"And you, sir? Are you staying?"

Please stay. Please.

"I'm better employed with the cavalry," he said after a significant pause. "What news here?"

"More messages of support and admiration from all over Europe," said Carstian wryly. "From England and the emperor, from the pope himself. Nothing from the King of Hungary."

Like the others, he had found the direction of the prince's gaze, and with their joining it, the spell was broken. Vlad took a step nearer her, and her own legs managed to move forward again.

His fingers were warm on hers. Stupidly, she felt them tremble in his light grasp. And yet it was a formal greeting before his people. He raised her hand to his lips and kissed it. Perhaps it was imagination that felt secretly ardent pressure.

"I have missed you," he said softly, and having no words except to repeat his own, she could only blush. He began to smile. But, remembering where he was, he added, "However, it is time for us to bid farewell. You and your lady mother must go now into Transylvania until the war is over."

She'd known it would come. And yet it struck her like a blow.

"Mihnea and Maria must go too," he ordered relentlessly.

"They're already in the mountains. Let us go to Poenari," she asked in a rush. Because she'd thought it all out already. "We'll be safe there, surely, and if the Ottomans do come, it's closer to the border for escape into Transylvania."

Something changed in his eyes then, a leap of emotion that went beyond gladness that she wanted to stay; it was almost recognition, though of what she didn't know, only that it warmed to her toes.

Then his heavy eyelids came down, and he said ruefully, "That one I must leave up to your mother…" What more he would have added, she never found out, for the clattering of horses' hooves and a shout in the courtyard outside distracted his and everyone else's attention.

Ilona shivered, for no reason except it seemed no news was good news. Unless Matthias…

Slowly, Vlad's hand fell away from hers. The door swung open, and Turcul strode in.

"Sir, thank God," he uttered as his wild gaze fell at once on his prince. "I thought I might have to ride south to find you."

"What's happened?" Vlad snapped. But he knew. He must have known, because Turcul had been in command of the troops at the Moldavian border.

Turcul drew in his breath. One of the few admitted into the inner sanctum of the prince's friends, he knew the blow he was about to deal. Ilona could see it in his eyes.

"Prince Stephen has attacked Chillia. With Ottoman help."

He'd been expecting it. Otherwise he wouldn't have divided his forces as he had and left Turcul to watch his back. Stephen had allied with Poland, accepted Ottoman suzerainty, and was therefore the enemy of Vlad's new friend, Hungary. Worse, Matthias was sheltering and supporting the unspeakable Petru Aaron, who had slain Stephen's father. Such politics made it difficult for the cousins to remain allies.

But they had remained friends. Stephen had been to Tîrgovişte in May, to discuss their differences, including the strategically valuable fortress of Chillia, held for Vlad by a Hungarian garrison that was Matthias's only contribution so far to the fight.

Once, during the formal banquet, she had found the Prince of Moldavia watching her with a strange expression on his handsome face.

Stephen had changed from the open, friendly youth she remembered. He had lost his hero worship of his cousin and learned a little wisdom and a lot of native cynicism of his own. In short, Stephen had matured and learned to stand alone.

He said, "I'm jealous, you know. But I believe I'm glad he has you." He lifted his recently refilled glass and took a sizeable swig of the rich, bloodred wine.

"Why?" Ilona asked, because she wanted to know.

Stephen shrugged. "I don't know." He drank some more and laid the glass down too precisely for an entirely sober man. "I could see something. Even at Hunedoara. You were like—two halves of the same whole." He smiled at that, pleased with himself. "No wonder I loved you both. I still do, God help me."

And yet, when it mattered, he would not stand by that love. He'd chosen Moldavia first, as perhaps a prince should. All she knew was Vlad would not have done so. And now Vlad had to fight his cousin as well as the sultan.

He left at nightfall, taking his exhausted troop after the briefest of rests to march to the relief of Chillia. Ilona stood by his stirrup to bid him farewell, wishing futilely that there had been more time, that she could reach and soothe the storm of emotion behind his blank, determined eyes. When he remembered to turn to her and reach down to take the cup she held, she said, "I'll be in the castle at Poenari."

And he managed to smile. After a quick sip, he gave her the cup back and touched her cheek instead with his gloved fingers. He whispered, "I'll find you there."

And then he was gone in a cloud of dust and noise.

Ilona and her mother left in the morning. Already Vlad's preparations for repelling the siege were well under way.

"Don't look," she urged her mother, but it was too late. Countess Szilágyi's gaze was riveted on the forest of stakes which had grown around the outside of the town walls. Several men and women worked feverishly, hanging bodies onto the sharpened sticks any way they could. Skeletons, foully rotting corpses, people of all ages and sizes who might simply have been asleep.

"Dear God…"

"They're dead," Ilona explained. "They're dead already. Dead prisoners, the battle dead from both sides, homeless dead. The rest are exhumed skeletons from unconsecrated graves. They're impaling the bodies to frighten the Ottomans, who'll believe this is what he does to his own people…"

The countess dragged her eyes away and swallowed. "I don't know about the Ottomans, but it certainly frightens me. Can you really marry this man?"

Ilona stared. "He's saving his capital city."

And, in fact, he did. When the sultan came in sight of Tîrgovişte, he was so appalled by the huge forest of rotting corpses impaled before him that he turned his troops east and headed for home.

By then, the news didn't make so much impression on Ilona as it should have, for the sultan had already defeated Vlad's main army under Gales. Against the prince's orders, Gales had attacked in Vlad's absence and suffered huge losses. In short, Wallachia had lost most of its army. Vlad, having ensured possession of Chillia, abandoned the fight against Stephen and chased after the sultan instead.

But too late. The sultan hastily invested Radu as Prince of Wallachia, left him a contingent of Ottomans to protect him, and turned his own nose toward home. And there was nothing left for Vlad to do but harry the Ottomans' miserable departure. They were already dying of hunger, thirst, and plague, but still triumphant, because they'd done what they set out to do—put Radu on the throne.

The war hadn't changed Poenari or the prince's castle on the Arges river. Here, gazing out over the forest where Vlad had first made love to her, Ilona could put the horrors of war to one side, forget her fears for the future, and daydream of the previous summer when all that had concerned her was her next assignation with Vlad.

While her mother rested in bed, recovering from the arduous journey and the threatening return of the illness which had laid her low a few years earlier, Ilona rode out in the countryside and spent hours at the top of Vlad's favourite tower, just gazing along the road in the hope of finally seeing him.

In the end, he took her by surprise once more, arriving after dark, unannounced and unexpected as she finished eating in the hall with the two ladies who'd accompanied them from Tîrgovişte.

A blast of cool night air hit them as the door was thrown open, and abruptly their quiet, feminine companionship was invaded by maleness. Vlad and two officers all but fell into the hall, bringing Ilona to her feet in alarm.

"Forgive us," Vlad said at once. "We're just exhausted."

But Ilona was already across the floor to him, and it seemed no restraint in the world could prevent his arm from circling her waist. For an instant, she thought he would simply crush her in his arms and kiss her, but though he pressed his cheek hard against hers, he drew back almost immediately, calling for more food and wine.

Then, seated, he spilled out the latest news. That although Radu was crowned prince, the boyars stayed away from him. He could not form a council, since the only nobles he had were the handful of exiles he'd brought with him.

"What will you do?" Ilona asked.

He shrugged. "Wait it out. The country is exhausted by war. I have few enough soldiers left to fight Radu's Turks. I could do it, but God knows I don't want to lose anyone else if it isn't necessary. When the Hungarians come, I'll just walk in and Radu will flee."

Ilona bit her lip. "*Will* the Hungarians come?"

Vlad nodded once, and finished his wine in one draft. "Apparently the King is finally on the move." His smile was twisted. "To rescue me."

Ilona frowned. "Do you know, I wish I'd *smacked* Matthias when we were children."

Vlad laughed aloud, and when she glanced at him in wry appreciation, his eyes were much too warm for company. Flushing, she looked away. It struck her that she'd never eaten with him under so little chaperonage.

As if he heard her, though, Vlad said, "Where is your lady mother?"

"Asleep. She hasn't been well since we came here. Travelling isn't good for her anymore."

"I'm sorry to hear that," he said with civil but genuine concern. His gaze was too intense, lingering on her too long before it flickered across the other women. "I know you have finished your meal, so don't let us detain you. We are poor company tonight in any case, fit only for sleep."

One of his officers was asleep already, facedown in his plate. Vlad and the other pulled him out, and he jerked awake, crumbs and grease trickling down his dazed face into his moustache. Vlad gave a lopsided smile and stood.

"I think the feast is over. To bed, men. We'll eat tomorrow."

The ladies curtseyed and scuttled away, giggling at the unfortunate soldier, whose friend was already dragging him away to their own quarters. Ilona gave Vlad her hand, smiling. She felt bold yet safe, knowing that tomorrow, at least, they would be together. It added a curiously calm contentment to the excitement of being all but alone with him now in this precious instant.

Perhaps he felt it too, for when he took her hand, he closed his eyes as if imagining a different world, a different setting. Or perhaps just falling asleep…

He said, "It's madness. I'm so tired I can barely walk, and yet all I can think of is loving you."

He opened his eyes, gazing into hers like a man drowning. "Come to my bed," he whispered. "Please."

She nodded, once, unable to say more, and he smiled, touching his forehead to hers. "I'm covered in travel dirt and fit only for sleep."

"Is that how you seduce all the girls?"

He kissed her, still smiling. "Of course; but for you, I'll bathe, tomorrow."

It seemed neither his tiredness nor his dirt mattered. He led her by the hand to his dark, deserted private chamber. He didn't light a candle or even undress. Instead, he tumbled with her onto his bed, fully clothed, and fell instantly asleep.

Ilona cradled him in her arms, consumed with love, and watched him until, finally, sleep claimed her too.

Chapter twenty-two

Poenari, Wallachia, 1462

When Vlad awoke at dawn, he was naked. Which was curious because he distinctly remembered falling asleep in all his clothes, in Ilona's arms. Smiling, he opened his eyes. She was gone, leaving only a depression in the pillow. Vlad shifted and laid his head where hers had been, inhaling the scent that was uniquely Ilona.

He remembered a sweet dream of wakening in the dark and making sleepy love to her… In the light of his nakedness, he could probably assume it had been no dream. His smile widened as his body stirred all over again.

Sometimes, when he was at his lowest, the prospect of "coming home" to Ilona had been what kept him going. This curious mixture of contentment and excitement that he found only and always in her presence…

His body, his mind, his very spirit needed her healing to enable him to return to the fray. Although he acknowledged the selfishness of that, of letting her stay here when his life and his position were so uncertain, he still could not forego this time with her—not least because it seemed Ilona needed it too.

Turning onto his back and stretching, Vlad Dracula thanked God for the woman who was still not his wife. Then he rose and shouted for a servant and some bathwater.

After he'd bathed and dressed, when he went down to the hall, it was empty, although someone had been there before him. The loaf had been neatly cut, and the jug of water was half-empty. Vlad tore what was left of the bread in half and wandered restlessly about the hall while he ate it. He wanted to relax, to let his mind go blank and think only of Ilona, but his thoughts were wayward, still relentlessly going over what had passed and planning for what was to come.

He knew her footsteps before he turned and saw her. She was beautiful in the morning sunlight, a faint flush rising through her pale skin, which seemed to be stretched taut over the fine, delicate bones of her face. Her thick auburn hair was tied loosely behind her head for convenience, her gown clean and pretty, but plain enough to be scorned by the ladies of his court. If he still had a court.

Her murmured good-morning sounded husky, as if she was having trouble dealing with his presence. That would have bothered him if he hadn't read the gladness in her eyes.

He walked toward her, asking after her mother's health.

"She seems better this morning," Ilona answered. "Glad that you are here."

"Good," said Vlad, and, because they were alone, he took her in his arms and kissed her mouth. Any lingering, foolish doubts vanished in her instant response.

He released her with reluctance. "Have you eaten?"

"With my mother."

"Come, then. I want to show you something."

He led her outside into the central courtyard. From one of the towers, he could hear his soldiers laughing. Another, angrier voice shouted orders in the kitchen. Vlad walked across to the well, and rested his hip on the wall as he gazed down into the watery depths.

Ilona gazed too.

"It's a wishing well?" she hazarded.

A memory stirred, associated with Ilona. But no, it was Maria who had sat at his side at Hunedoara and talked of wishing wells. He pushed it aside.

"It could be," he said ruefully. "If you're ever in a hurry to escape. Look."

He pointed to the narrow iron ladder that lined the wall of the well and stopped some yards short of the water.

"At the bottom of the ladder is a door. It's disguised so you can't see it from here, but when you get there, it will be obvious. It leads into a secret passage."

"Really?" She sounded excited, like a child discovering a new adventure, a new game. He hoped that was all it would ever be to her. "Where does it go? Your secret passage."

"Down to a cave on the river bank."

"Did you build it?" she asked curiously.

"I caused it to be built. After my noble work force departed. Remember it's there, if you need it."

She glanced at him with clear, penetrating eyes. "Am I likely to?"

"No," he admitted. "But especially when I'm not here, I want to know that you're safe. From now on, we post permanent sentries on *all* the towers—including our own." At that, a flush of memory suffused her cheeks, but even more delightfully, she didn't break her gaze. "That way," he finished, "we'll have plenty of warning of any visitors. Either from Transylvania or from my little brother."

For Ilona, there was a feverish intensity about those days. Since her mother kept largely to her own chamber and the other ladies preferred to stay out of the prince's way, there seemed little to keep her and Vlad apart. They rode and walked together in the local village, where she had already made friends with some of the families, including the large and helpful Dobrin clan, and where they greeted Vlad with every respect due their prince. And very often, since nobody cared, they didn't trouble about finding discreet places to make love. Vlad simply took her to his bed, whether it was morning, afternoon, or night.

And Ilona couldn't get enough of him. Parting and uncertainty had added obsession to love, and she felt alive now only when she was with him. In her heart, she knew this interlude would be a short one, and she grabbed at it with both desperate hands, aware that fate would part them once more.

Then, one morning, at dawn, she rose from Vlad's bed, escaping his heavy, imprisoning limbs, to scamper back to her own chamber before her mother awoke and questioned her absence. It wasn't that she wished to lie to her mother or in fact had ever done so, but she didn't want to upset her or have this most private aspect of her relationship with Vlad under moral scrutiny.

Countess Szilágyi's eyes were open, startling Ilona.

"Mother?"

The countess was silent. She didn't even blink.

Oh Jesus, oh God, oh Mother...

Ilona touched the cold face as fear and shame and horror gathered within her, stifling the grief that she knew would never leave her.

"What have I done?" she whispered and laid her face against her mother's, as if trying to wake her with her own warmth.

"I let her die alone. I didn't even notice she was so ill. I took my own pleasure while my mother died."

"She died in her sleep, Ilona. She didn't even know you weren't there."

"I should have been," Ilona whispered. "I should have been there."

Vlad knelt at her feet, taking her hands. "There's nothing you can do about that now. Grieve for the very fine lady who was your mother. Don't warp it with guilt."

Without her meaning to, she grasped his hands, holding on to them hard. "I'm afraid, Vlad," she whispered. "So afraid. When Mihály died, I almost recognised the grief because we'd been through the fear of it so often before. This is like…the world has gone. My mother, the rock I never even realised was there, is gone."

Vlad pressed his cheek to her hands. "I know."

There was no Roman priest in the village, so after a short service in the little castle chapel beside the well, Countess Szilágyi was buried according to Orthodox rites. Ilona didn't think she would mind. She knew God wouldn't.

If it hadn't been for Vlad, Ilona thought the yawning chasm that was life without her mother would have swallowed her. She knew it would pass as the sharp edges of her grief for Mihály had passed, but you couldn't *make* them blunt. You had to get on with life and wait for it to happen. And so she devoted herself to Vlad and the people of the castle and the villages who called her their princess and seemed to truly believe she was.

Once, as she stood quietly in the chapel, praying for her mother, she became aware of Vlad beside her.

He said, "We could ask the priest to return and marry us now."

Ilona dropped her head onto his arm. She found herself smiling for the first time in days. "Our wedding is for the world," she said at last. "For your family and mine and everyone else who's affected by the politics of it. If they don't want it, they'll only annul it. But in the ways that matter to me, we're married already."

She felt his kiss on her hair, soft and tender. "And you're living with me without an effective chaperone. If this was Tîrgovişte…"

"It isn't. And the world isn't here yet."

Their first visitor from the world was, unexpectedly, Maria, who arrived with her son, his nurse, two maids, and several men-at-arms.

With all her old impulsiveness, she threw herself into Ilona's arms. But there was a strange desperation in that hug that Ilona had never noticed before.

"I'm so glad you're here," Maria gasped.

"What is it? What's happened?" Ilona demanded, trying to peer into her friend's face.

"Oh, just this wretched war…"

"I thought you were safe in the mountains!"

"I was. But I can't live like that, cut off from the world. It drives me insane. And I can't go to Tîrgovişte because it's full of Ottomans."

Vlad, who'd lifted the delighted Mihnea onto his shoulders, curled his lip. The Ottomans were almost Radu's only companions. The boyars still stayed away.

And the world was back in Vlad's eyes. Ilona couldn't help the sinking of her heart. But she knew it had to be.

"I'm glad you came here," he said to Maria. "You can keep each other company. I think it's time I tickled Radu again."

But that night, as she lay in Vlad's arms, Radu tickled him.

A shout went up from one of the sentries, who'd seen movement on the hills across the river. With the dawn, it became apparent that Radu's Ottomans were approaching.

"They followed *me*?" Maria squeaked in horror.

Vlad shrugged impatiently. "They might have done. It doesn't matter. They've set up camp across the river, and they've brought cannon. Perhaps they were coming anyway, in which case you were lucky to avoid them. The point is, they'll never take this place. But they will make leaving difficult. I'll shoot a few of them, see if it scares them off, but I doubt it will. Radu is desperate. He needs me out of the way before the boyars will go to him."

While Maria inexplicably hid in the guestchamber with her head under the pillow, Vlad led an attack from the castle, fording the river lower down and indulging in a quick skirmish with the enemy before returning with the news that he'd encountered an old friend among the Ottomans.

"He came with me the first time I took the throne," he mused.

"Did you speak to him?" Ilona asked, wondering what, if any, difference this would make to the situation.

"No. But he saluted me once. Before he called off his men."

"Perhaps they'll go away now," Maria said optimistically.

They didn't. Instead, they crossed the river and set up camp under the castle. Vlad scoured them with a hail of arrows from both facing towers, but, undeterred, they stayed where they were.

"I think," he said, "it's time to leave."

"Where will we go?"

"Transylvania," Vlad said reluctantly. "It will take you home and let me find Matthias. I need his Hungarians and quickly."

"But we can't leave," Maria wailed. "The Turks are down there!"

"There's a secret passage," said Ilona.

"It will avoid them," Vlad explained. "The Dobrin brothers will help us down the mountain, and then we're free."

"And if we're caught?" Maria stared at him as if he was mad.

"We won't be."

"You're insane," Maria whispered, burying her face in her hands.

Ilona frowned, touching her friend's hair in pity. "No, he isn't. Really. He isn't."

Vlad said implacably, "We leave tonight. The servants should come with us for their own safety, but the choice is theirs. Bring only what you can carry in one hand."

Maria moaned and ran from the hall.

"She's overwrought," Ilona said, rising to her feet, torn between following Maria and the need to speak further with Vlad. "Something's wrong with Maria."

"She'll be fine in Transylvania. She has a morbid fear of the Ottomans."

Unworthy jealousy flickered through Ilona's mind. She hadn't realised how much she would dislike being reminded of the domestic intimacy which had once existed between Vlad and Maria. He knew things that even Ilona didn't.

But she said only, "Will we be able to take Mihnea down that ladder?"

"And down the mountain. I'll strap him to my back. Ilona?"

He crossed the space between them, his eyes dark with sudden, unmistakable lust. Her heart began to hammer.

"Yes?"

"Before I organise the men…come to bed."

"For the last time?" she said, trying to smile as the tears closed up her throat.

He kissed her. "For the last time in this castle, for this month. That's all."

Maria had never liked this castle. Even after so many of her late husband's friends had finished building it, she'd hated coming here. She would be glad to leave it, only she was running out of places to go. As darkness threatened, the blackness in her soul crept higher, catapulting her from her own chamber in search of the security that always eluded her now. Along with the peace she never found. And the fun that seemed to have slipped away when she wasn't looking.

Maria, who'd always lived surrounded by people, couldn't escape the inner isolation that consumed her. She knew that. It was something else entirely, something beyond thought, that brought her to Vlad's door. She didn't even knock when she went in. In truth, she would rather not even find him there. It was a ritual farewell for her, not for him.

But he was there. Kneeling on the bed in all his glorious nakedness. In the fading light, Maria couldn't even make out the mess of scars which marred his back. But she recognised the beautiful woman he was with. As naked as he, her face raised to his, full of love while he wiped a single tear from the corner of her eye with his thumb.

Ilona, Maria thought with sudden, blinding clarity. *He loves Ilona. This was never a political marriage…*

Ilona's head moved, and Maria found herself caught in that dark gaze like a wild animal unable to flee.

"Maria," she whispered. And Vlad's head snapped round too.

Laughter caught in Maria's throat. At least, she thought it was laughter. Whipping away before they lost their dignity altogether, Maria left the room and closed the door. She hurried now, back to her own chamber.

The lamp was still burning, casting shadows up the bare, stone walls that Vlad had never troubled to decorate. Though she was afraid, Maria forced herself to go to the window, to look out on the fearful sight of the Ottoman camp to her right. They had cannons set up. Maybe Vlad was right and fleeing in secret was safer than being locked up in here…

Of course, Vlad's agenda was different. Vlad couldn't waste the months of siege. He needed to oust Radu before the boyars started coming in to his brother from necessity and boredom.

Something whizzed past her ear, and Maria fell back with a cry of horror. She was almost surprised to discover there was no pain, that she was still alive. An arrow had buried itself in the bedpost. And from the still-vibrating arrow hung a sheet of paper.

Slowly, as if in a dream, Maria walked toward the arrow and reached up to tear the paper free.

The paper was torn over the first words, but she read the others without difficulty.

"Escape if you can. All is lost."

Escape. The lure of the word was irresistible.

Maria, curiously unafraid now, walked back to the window. There was no sign of whoever had sent the message. Vlad's old acquaintance, presumably. Below her, the river flowed relentlessly over rocks and stones, past castles and soldiers, oblivious to the wars and politics that occupied men. It simply made its way to the sea, and nothing could stop it.

I won't be taken by the Ottomans. I won't be killed unspeakably like Ilona's father or see my son taken into captivity. I won't run anymore, and I won't listen to the guns.

No one needed her. Not even her children. There was no guilt in this. It was simply for her.

Maria hitched up her skirts and climbed onto the seat under the window. She opened the window wide and stood in its frame. The wind caught at her hair, whipping it free of its confines. Below her, the river swirled and rushed over the rocks.

Maria smiled, closed her eyes, and floated.

"I think—at least I like to think—that I won't mind, providing he still loves me best."

"What?" Vlad stared at her as if trying to find the meaning in her wild words. Ilona was throwing on her clothes, dragging her fingers through her hair as if they were a comb.

"That's what she said to me," Ilona said impatiently, "when I asked her how she would feel about your marriage. She never resented me because she didn't know I loved you. I tried to tell her once, but Mihnea cried, and the moment passed, and somehow… She didn't know, Vlad! And suddenly she's so…frail!"

She took a deep breath. "I have to go to her."

Vlad nodded once. "Make sure she's ready. And Mihnea."

Ilona didn't wait for more. She ran all the way to Maria's chamber and found the window open wide. The wind had sprung up.

From somewhere, she could hear shouting. Her blood ran cold. But the window drew her as if by invisible bindings.

Maria's broken body lay on the rocks. The river rushed over her legs and torso but missed her head. By the light of Ottoman torches and lanterns shone from their own side, she was sure she could see Maria's beautiful, peaceful face.

Another guilt, another failure. She had recognised Maria's frailty and distress and still spent the time with Vlad. It was like her mother's death all over again.

"It would have made no difference," Vlad said grimly. "Whether she'd seen us or not. Whether you'd been there or not. Her mind was made up. If anything, *this* pushed her over the edge."

He dropped the scribbled note onto Maria's bed.

"We *were* escaping," Ilona raged. "We *are* escaping!"

Vlad grasped her by the shoulders. "That's not the escape she wanted. Ilona, put it aside. Grieve later. Help me care for my son. His safety must come first."

And so she'd shouldered that burden too.

The Ottomans took Maria's body from the water and laid it out for them to claim. They had to leave her for the villagers to bury, while they climbed down the ladder into the well and crawled along the secret passages that led down to the riverside cave.

It was full of people. After a moment, Ilona recognised them as the seven Dobrin brothers.

Patiently, the Dobrins guided the little train of exalted nobles and their servants and soldiers down the difficult, treacherous mountain to safety.

And then came the hardest part of all to bear. The parting.

Instead of leaving Wallachia altogether, Vlad had decided to take the soldiers to the little mountain fortress of Konigstein—built by John Hunyadi—where he'd organise resistance to Radu and wait for the slowly advancing King of Hungary. Mihnea and his nurse would go too, there to meet up with loyal Wallachian boyars, possibly Carstian, who would care for him in Vlad's absence.

"Unless you think your brother would take him in?"

"Miklós?" Ilona blinked.

They stood apart from the others, sheltering from the rain under the branches of an old oak, and Ilona found it hard to think of anything but the unendurable parting only moments away.

"If Mihály were alive, I wouldn't hesitate. For I can think of no one I would rather care for Mihnea than you. But I don't know your brother."

Ilona swallowed. It was so tempting to keep his child by her. "Take him with you," she managed. "God bless him. And you."

"Are you weeping?"

"It's just rain," she whispered, and he bent and kissed the "rain" from her eyes and cheeks.

She threw her arms around his neck, wondering how she could bear it now that he was her whole life.

"It's not forever," he said intensely. "We married each other a long time ago, remember?"

He showed her the pearl ring on her left hand, the one he'd given her at Horogzegi, and as he'd done then, he pressed it to his lips before kissing hers.

She clung to him, uncaring who watched. "I love you," she whispered. "Please live."

"For you. I'll find a way."

From nowhere, a twist of laughter curled through the tears. "Do it quickly," she ordered, and while he was still smiling, she pressed her mouth to his, hard, one last time, and stepped back to watch him leave.

Although she hadn't expected it to, the sight of her brother waiting for her so close to the border lifted her spirits out of the pall of grief that had settled on them after parting from Vlad. Encountering Miklós so conveniently felt like an omen.

As she and her escort rode up toward the house of the nobleman with whom they hoped to lodge that night, she discovered Miklós there before her. His strong, stocky figure was unmistakable, his dirty blond hair blowing in the wind. He looked nothing like Mihály, and yet something in his posture reminded Ilona of her father. Memories of childhood flooded her.

Like a breath of home, Miklós came out onto the front step and watched her dismount and run toward him. As always his boots and his cloak and the tunic visible beneath, were modest and yet spotless.

All quarrels with him forgotten, she embraced him with enthusiasm and felt his arm close hard around her waist. He must have been so afraid for her, and they had still to share their grief for their mother…

But these were private matters, and so, as he drew her inexorably into the house, she said only, "Where is our host?"

"Visiting." Miklós closed the door firmly in the face of the faithful Dobrin brothers. "We have his permission to use his house as our own."

"Thank God," Ilona said. "I don't feel fit for company."

"You aren't," Miklós said and hit her full across the face.

Ilona staggered back against the wall, her head spinning with more bafflement than pain. Covering her stinging jaw with one hand, she stared at her brother as he advanced on her with fists clenched. His face contorted in contempt and a determination she'd never seen there before.

"You've ruined us," he uttered. "Whore. Traitor." And struck her again.

Chapter twenty-three

Visegrád, Hungary, 1474

As the last of the remaining daylight faded from Vlad's comfortable prison, Ilona looked more ethereal than ever, like a ghost who'd disperse in a puff of air. Vlad rose and lit the other lamps, then returned to sit with her by the dying embers of the fire. Her gaze followed him. "We harried Radu a little," he said, "just to show that I was still around, but even then some of the boyars began to trickle in to him. I could have raised another army, but the people, the country, had had enough. They needed time to recover. I chose to wait for Matthias so that I could simply frighten Radu and his Turks away. It never entered my head that having finally got to the Wallachian border, Matthias would change the game and recognise Radu instead."

"It didn't enter anyone's head," Ilona remembered. Afraid she'd drift away again, Vlad took her hand. She didn't withdraw it. She said, "They kept it from me for a while, but even by the time I learned of it, people were still scratching their heads over it. He went to rescue you and fulfill his part of the crusade—and returned with you as his prisoner and an Ottoman alliance in his pocket."

"He 'negotiated' with me for weeks. I knew something was wrong, but even after he'd actually recognised Radu, he was still offering me an alliance that included you. Eventually, we crossed back into Wallachia, where I was separated from my soldiers by trickery and taken prisoner. By then, they'd managed to collect a fine array of forged letters and stories of atrocities, largely from the Transylvanian Germans, with which to convict me. And here I am."

Ilona whispered, "They told me that you'd made a secret alliance with the sultan, offered to deliver Matthias himself up to him. They said you were in league with Stephen too. I told them that I was there, that none of that was true. They told me you'd impaled most of your people and just about the entire German population of Transylvania. They said *you*'d burned the beggars in Tîrgovişte, even when I told them it was Pardo. They told me vile, disgusting things that you'd done to women and children and priests and when I told them it was all lies, they began to show me books, as if they made it any truer. So I stopped talking to them."

"To whom?" Vlad asked.

Her gaze flickered up to his. "I didn't believe it. It was as if they were talking about somebody else. At first it distressed me, until…"

"Until what?"

"Until I realised *they* didn't believe it. They just wanted me to."

"Who?" Vlad asked again.

Ilona sighed. "Everyone."

Vlad tried again. "The Dobrin brothers came back to me. They said they'd given you into the care of your brother, only just over the Transylvanian border."

"Yes," Ilona agreed. "They were good men. I hope you rewarded them."

"I gave them more land then they'll ever be able to hold, but I'd like to see any lawyers take it away from them. Did you go home with Miklós?"

"Eventually." Ilona swallowed. "He took me to Matthias first."

"To Matthias? Why?"

"I think…I think because I insisted I was already married to you. In the eyes of God."

Delighted in spite of himself, Vlad asked, "What did they think you meant? Deflowering you is the one crime they never accused me of!"

"Well, they couldn't, could they?" Ilona said reasonably. "To have had a member of the king's family so close to you while you betrayed Christendom would not have suited Matthias at all. Anyway, I didn't mention deflowering, just let them think we'd gone through some kind of formal betrothal. I insisted it was as good as marriage."

Her lip curled. "That was when they decided it would be best if I'd never been to Wallachia. But they couldn't pretend that, so they said I'd *barely* been, just for a few weeks, and had been saved from this horrendous mistake by the timely invasion of the Ottomans, from whom I had only just escaped with my life."

"That's what they wanted the world to believe," Vlad said slowly.

She nodded. "With the implication that you and not the Ottomans were in fact the greater danger."

"So they gagged you by tying you to the husband you didn't like."

She nodded once and dropped her eyes. Taking her chin in his hand, he lifted her face again.

"Are you ashamed of that?"

She seemed to think about it, then: "No. That didn't feel like betrayal. I didn't want it, but I couldn't prevent it either."

"Did something else feel like betrayal?"

"I didn't betray you," she whispered. "I didn't."

"I know." He put his arms around her, very gently, felt the trembling of her silent sobs against him. "I know, Ilona. I just want to know why…how…you…*stopped paying attention.*"

She closed her eyes as if she couldn't bear to see him, but at least she didn't pull away from him.

"They just went on and on, every day. And when I wouldn't listen, when I defended you and stuck to the truth, and refused to disown the marriage, they began to…to revile me."

She gasped. "They said things that were true to make me believe things that weren't. That I was responsible for my mother's death, for Maria's, that I was a worthless creature who'd almost brought about the fall of John Hunyadi's family. That you would never have married me unless you had to for political gain, that you had a hundred mistresses besides Maria. Everything was cast up, from my clumsiness, to my stupid tongue, to the fact that I had no husband and had done nothing for my family. Aunt Erzsébet came specially to ram those points home."

Her eyes opened again suddenly, staring into his. "I wouldn't have cared, if only I'd been able to make them listen about you."

"Ilona…"

"But I couldn't. That was my betrayal, my final failure. I waited and waited for you to come, to send me some word. I tried to reach you by letter, by messenger, but heard nothing back. They said you never asked the king about me, had requested a different match. And then I found out that you were in prison. And all that was left was my worthlessness. My sisters were appalled that I defended you, couldn't believe that I had changed so much that I was opposing my own family. They seemed to hate me too. It wore me down, wore me out. So that now when Miklós beat me, I knew I deserved it."

Vlad couldn't prevent the convulsive grasp of his fingers. She gasped but didn't cry out at the pain, and he kissed her head in pity and horror. The quiet, systematic destruction of her as a human being, a sensitive, compassionate woman, by all the people who were meant to love her, appalled him beyond belief.

"Miklós was my brother. We didn't get on, but I'd cared for him. And he struck me."

"Because *he* was worthless, not you!" His instinct was to hug her too tightly, to rage against her brother to the point of breaking everything in the room as if it was Miklós. He heard his own breath tremble with the effort of restraint. "How often?"

"I don't know. At first, when we went to Matthias, he let everyone believe my bruises were your fault, not his. Later, no one noticed them. Sometimes it's good not to pay attention. When I was away from him, I thought it probably had more to do with the fact that I'd gone to Wallachia in the teeth of his opposition. Perhaps even because my father had trusted me more than him. It doesn't matter now. They all lost interest when I did. And for good measure, they married me off."

He was torturing himself, and by stripping away some of her protective coating, he knew he was torturing her too. But he had to ask.

"Did your husband abuse you?"

She looked surprised. "*Can* husbands abuse wives?"

Oh yes. As families abuse their daughters. The savage words rang in his head before he caught the hint of sardonic humour in her eyes. And he smiled as if he'd discovered some new beauty in her. Ilona, his Ilona, was still there.

She whispered, "I didn't regard it as abuse. My own family, my own brother, gave me to that man. It was all part of the same... I deserved it because my family reviled me, because I couldn't change them about you. I couldn't bear myself. I had to...step away. I drifted, I suppose, and the years fell around me like autumn leaves." The faintest smile flickered across her lips, as if she liked the image. Then she swallowd hard. "I couldn't bear to go through it all again. Not with you. They'd reduced it all to pain and betrayal and suffering and *longing*, a waiting that never ended. And I knew when you saw me, you wouldn't want me anyway—how could you? —and that would be a million times worse."

"I will always want you."

Her lips parted in a gasp that was half sob and half smile.

He said urgently, "We played for everything, and we lost. But the game is not over. It was never over."

"Can we really win this way?"

"I think so," Vlad said. "The last time, we waited and let him prevaricate. We played by his rules. This time, we have to strike quickly."

Another smile flickered over her lips. "I like being with you again, Vlad Dracula." Unexpectedly, her lips touched his, like the caress of a butterfly wing. Even so, it stirred his blood, and he knew he'd be fighting another enemy before the morning. He'd dreamed for years of making love to Ilona Szilágyi again. But he'd never imagined a frail and damaged Ilona. She needed to be cherished and cared for, not taken in blind lust.

He said, "Then come, sleep in my bed, and I'll watch beside you until the spectacle begins."

She let him raise her from the chair, walked with him to the bed. Her fingers fumbled with the fastenings.

He said gently, "You don't need to. The scandal is in your being here with me."

"I'd be more convincing in my shift."

Gown and underdress fell to the floor between their feet in a shining red puddle. Then, in her shift, she climbed into the bed. Vlad couldn't take his eyes off her. Though thinner than he remembered, her body was still young and shapely, her breasts prominent and alluring. She was still the woman who'd lain in his arms so often, surrendering to the passion that consumed them both. It was consuming Vlad again now. Memory was in danger of blending with the present.

He drew the sheet over her too hastily, saw her quick frown as she searched his eyes. Whatever she saw there cleared her brow. She shifted over against the wall.

"Lie beside me," she pleaded. "Just once."

Just once. Because she didn't really believe their desperate plan would work? Or because she didn't believe he loved her still?

Vlad took off his clothes without a murmur, leaving only his linen shirt, and climbed into the bed beside her. That was when he saw the pearl ring on a narrow ribbon, nestling between her breasts. Almost as if she'd hidden it there from her family, from everyone, all these years. She'd worn it on her finger in the gallery, but she must have hidden it again as soon as the king forbade the marraige. It broke his heart. When she looked at him with uncertain, almost frightened eyes, he took her gently into his arms, kissed her hair and her cheeks and her lips.

"Go to sleep," he whispered.

Her arms closed over his. Her eyes shut, and she lay perfectly still. He had the feeling she didn't want to sleep, but she did. He could tell by her breathing. He didn't think he'd be *able* to sleep, tortured as he was by his own bodily lusts. But old memory and new contentment washed over him, soothing him as he lay beside her. His last coherent thought was that she still smelled the same.

Ilona woke in the darkness. A man's body pressed close to her, his unmistakable erection hard against her thigh.

Vlad.

Her heart beat loudly in her ears. It was no dream. She'd really come here. She was really lying in his bed beside him, his body moving instinctively against hers, although when she opened her eyes and gazed at him by the starlight gleaming palely through the unshuttered window, she saw that his eyes remained closed in sleep.

Right now, it didn't matter whether it was general or specific lust. All that counted was that he was here with her. She moved her head on the pillow to bring her lips closer to his, brushed them against him. His mouth opened, drawn to hers, where it fastened in the first kiss of passion she'd known in twelve years.

He moved, throwing his thigh over hers, and she pressed closer, urging him on. His hands roamed her body, finding her breasts and hips. An inarticulate groan came from deep in his throat, and he woke suddenly, staring deep into her eyes.

"Ilona."

For an instant, they rocked on a cusp of his misplaced honour and her sense of inadequacy. But because his eyes, still struggling into wakefulness, betrayed his need, she pushed him back and rolled onto him. Beneath his shirt, she laid her palms flat against his naked chest. Then, without releasing his wondering gaze, she moved and took him inside her.

"Ilona," he whispered again. "Ilona." And then he rolled her beneath him, and if there ever had been, there was now no possibility of turning back.

Dawn was breaking. Naked in her lover's arms, Ilona wanted to sing with the birds. She felt as if she was awakening with them after a very long but disturbed sleep.

Vlad said, "That's the first time I've ever left my seed in you."

She smiled into his shoulder. "Perhaps I've conceived. Or perhaps I'm too old."

"Either is fine with me," he assured her.

"It will have to be now. I wonder if Margit's awake? When does your servant come?"

"When Szelényi lets him in. Are you hungry?"

In fact, she couldn't remember when she'd last eaten, and her stomach rumbled audibly at the mention of food. In wonder, she watched him pad across the room and return with bread and watered wine. They sat together in bed, eating and talking while the castle woke up. For modesty's sake, she put the shift back on but rejected the gown in favour of the bedsheets. Vlad, still bare-chested, smiled at her with delighted approval and cut her another slice of bread.

The knock, when it came, almost took them by surprise. As they exchanged glances, it came again. Then the key turned in the lock and Szelényi's voice said, "Sir?"

"Szelényi?"

The count needed no further invitation. The door opened, and he came in, followed closely by the servant. They both stopped dead, their jaws dropping. When Ilona turned her face into the pillow in embarrassment, it wasn't all acting.

Vlad slid out of bed, reaching for his shirt, and, the damage now complete, stood protectively in front of her.

"You shut her in," he said mildly. "Peter, go away. Count Szelényi, I wonder if I might ask you a favour?"

The servant bolted. Hopefully to spread the gossip as far as he could. Count Szelényi swallowed.

"You know you can rely on my total discretion, sir." Studiously, he didn't look at Ilona.

"I'm delighted to hear it," Vlad returned. "But not what I was going to ask. Do you think you could possibly bring Countess Hunyadi here? To protect the lady Ilona, obviously."

Szelényi goggled at him. "That would be a *favour*?"

Vlad grinned. "I suspect it's the only way you'll dance at my wedding. Oblige me, Szelényi. Get her here, and don't trouble about how much noise you make doing it. They'll hush it up afterwards, but the damage will be done."

Understanding dawned in Szelényi's face. He looked as if he didn't know whether to laugh or complain. In the end, he waved his hand wordlessly and left.

Ilona got up and padded across to the mirror by the washing bowl and made use of Vlad's hairbrush. As if he couldn't help it, Vlad came and stood beside her, watching her face in the mirror while he ran a few strands of her blood-gold hair between his fingers.

"It's not all grey," Ilona observed.

"Hardly any. Why did you hide it?"

She shrugged. "It's less trouble to be old and dowdy and invisible. But you will *not* impale my dressmaker."

Laughter sprang into his eyes, just as the door swung open and Countess Hunyadi sailed in, only to halt so suddenly that Count Szelényi only narrowly avoided bumping into her. She glared at the intimate picture presented by Ilona and Vlad at the mirror. By this time, Vlad had covered his nakedness, although he looked uncharacteristically informal in his shirtsleeves, but Ilona, still wearing no more than her shift, felt blissfully unashamed.

She turned to meet the countess's horrified gaze. Feeling no urge either to smile or rush into apologetic speech, she simply waited until the fierce old eyes snapped up to Vlad instead.

"You *are* a monster! How could you do such harm to this poor…?"

"I have never," Vlad interrupted with perfect clarity, "done any harm to Ilona Szilágyi. Nor would I. I devoutly wish I could say the same for those in her family who have had the duty to care for her."

The countess's eyes narrowed.

"Oh, I know what you've done," Vlad said softly. "And whatever you imagine, so does she. I don't know what your motives were, whether you imagined you were somehow helping her or just your son…"

"My family," the countess interrupted in her turn. There was a whiteness around her lips that Ilona had only seen on very rare occasions, a kind of desperate defiance in her hard eyes. "Family must always come first, before any one individual, before any personal affection. Submitting to your family should not have done this to you, Ilona."

Erzsébet wanted, even needed, to believe the prime cause was Vlad. That was why she'd tried save Ilona from him, because in spite of everything she'd done, she still cared for her neice. Maybe Ilona would value that one day. Maybe.

"It wasn't Vlad," Ilona said clealry. "It was never Vlad."

The countess gasped, as if short of air. "The name of János Hunyadi's family will never be sullied," she uttered.

"Then perhaps," said Ilona thoughtfully, "Matthias should simply have paid the forty thousand ducats back to the pope."

"It was already spent."

Unexpectedly, the king himself stood in the doorway. Having gained all eyes, he made his entrance as magnificent as it could be without his usual escort and into a simple bedchamber that was fast becoming overcrowded. Vlad bowed with incomparable if ironic grace.

Ilona rose to her feet, but not as an obvious mark of respect. Standing before the king in her shift, she said vaguely, "I never understood why, in that case, you didn't simply send the troops you'd promised. You got as far as the Transylvanian border. One week more, maybe two, and you would have had the glory of defeating Radu's Ottoman protectors."

And no need to make up elaborate lies to justify his actions. And lack of actions.

"You have no understanding of state matters," Matthias said loftily. "The little country that is so important to him was a very small part of my concern. For Hungary's security, I needed the friendship of Emperor Frederick, and I needed him to release the Crown of St. Stephen to me. You know that.

"But," he added, sweeping his displeased gaze around the chamber. "I am not here to discuss ancient history, let alone justify my actions. I have forgiven the Prince of Wallachia."

Ilona laughed.

Ignoring that, although a flicker of his shoulder betrayed his surprised irritation, Matthias continued, "Which is why I cannot understand his shocking act of what I can only assume is rape!"

"It was not rape," Ilona said quickly.

Vlad said, "John Hunyadi's family cannot be associated with anything so squalid as rape."

Matthias and Erzsébet looked at him in quick suspicion. As if unaware of it, Vlad moved to lift his cloak from the back of a chair and placed it carefully around Ilona's shoulders.

Matthias gave a sigh. "My dear prince, I am the king. I can cover anything up. Especially with you back in close imprisonment and my cousin back in the country—preferably in a strict convent I have picked out especially for her. Did you really think you could force my hand with this...crime?"

Ilona felt the familiar churning of fear. She wanted to grab Vlad's hand for reassurance, and yet instinct told her to show no sign of such weakness.

The silence stretched. Vlad was smiling faintly.

At last, reluctantly, Countess Hunyadi said, "Ilona's woman has been shouting her disappearance all over the castle since dawn. Search parties have already left to look for her."

"Not a problem. She will be found somewhere else."

"Count Szelényi is, of course, the soul of discretion," Vlad observed, drawing attention to the stunned and not best pleased nobleman. "But I think you'll find the castle already knows exactly where she was found." He waved one supercilious hand. "Servants gossip."

Matthias snapped. "Servants' gossip does not concern me! Did you imagine you could defeat me at my own…"

He broke off. Vlad smiled into his eyes.

Ilona said innocently, "At your own game? No one can deny your mastery there. You have destroyed a prince's reputation with the world, with history itself, by massive distribution of rumour. To say nothing of imprisoning an innocent man and causing unspeakable suffering to a Christian people you were sworn to protect. Just because you'd spent the pope's money and didn't want to earn it. We cannot fight you with rumours of such magnitude. But little rumours of the salacious kind are much more…insidious. You may be able to create counter-rumours, but you'll never squash this one."

Matthias looked stunned. No doubt because no one had spoken to him like this since childhood. No one, let alone his supposedly fading, unimportant cousin standing before him in nothing but her shift and a stranger's cloak. Perhaps he was taken back to their shared childhood, for there was something of the childish retort in his blurted response.

"It won't matter when you're back in obscurity. When he is. Again."

"He'll never be in obscurity. You made him a monster, and the world can't help being interested."

Furious, Matthias opened his mouth again, but before he could speak anymore, Countess Hunyadi intervened.

"They're right," she snapped. "There will be no scandal. Marry them. In one week."

"Oh no," said Vlad. "Tonight would be best. A quiet ceremony."

"Tonight is impossible," Matthias objected. "There are no arrangements…"

"There were arrangements for a formal betrothal," Vlad reminded him. "A wedding is little different."

"Do you imagine you can live here, married to my cousin?" The king waved a contemptuous hand around the room.

Count Szelényi coughed. "Your Majesty, I believe the house in Pest is ready."

Matthias stared at him. "The house in Pest?"

"Your gift to me," Vlad reminded him. He smiled. "As part of our alliance."

Matthias stared at him. Then without a word, he turned on his heel and stormed out. He didn't trouble to close the door behind him.

Countess Hunyadi said stiffly, "You will need to work hard for the king before he allows you anywhere near Wallachia."

"I know," said Vlad. He didn't sound rueful. He wanted to work, to fight, to live again. Even if it took him from Ilona. His hand gripped her shoulder, soothing whatever panic she felt at the prospect of yet another parting.

Countess Hunyadi nodded once to him, and once to Ilona. Oddly, there was no anger in it. She accepted the situation, she accepted defeat by an unexpectedly worthy opponent. And, perhaps, in this solution, the guilt she refused to acknowledge was assuaged.

"Also," Szelényi said beneath his breath, "when you do get to Wallachia, you'll need to watch your back."

"I know," said Vlad. He held his hand out to Szelényi. "Thank you."

Although Szelényi bowed over his hand formally, he smiled as he left.

Dazed, Ilona glanced over her shoulder at Vlad Dracula. "Is that it? Is the waiting finally over?"

Vlad drew her slowly against him. "Do you know, I believe it is."

Epilogue

Snagov, Wallachia, January 1477

Through the deep, freezing blackness that enclosed the Vasia forest, a motley group of people could be faintly discerned, making their way on foot across the ice to the fortified island monastery of Snagov. Several silent men in armour, surrounded a monk, a youth, a woman, and two children, one of whom she carried in her arms while the youth led the other by the hand.

From the monastery side, two more monks waited and greeted their visitors with grave faces and respectful bows. The profoundest bow was given to the woman and her round-eyed son. The baby slept in her arms, as oblivious to the cold as to the solemnity of the occasion.

The monks then led the way along invisible paths which only they could see. The monastery gate opened silently to admit them and closed behind them almost immediately, after emitting only the dimmest, briefest of lights.

Once inside, they lit more torches and the group made its way between two lines of grave-faced monks, some of whom were openly weeping. The woman lifted her gaze as she walked, looking into the face of one such grieving man. Her own stricken eyes were dry as she smiled at the monk, who whispered, "God bless you, Princess."

Inside the beautiful Chapel of the Annunciation, the abbot awaited them. He stood in front of an open crypt at the door, no doubt to prevent anyone falling into it.

Bowing, he murmured a solemn greeting to the lady. Then: "Have they told you how this happened?"

She said, "I know he was attacked by Besarab and his Ottomans in the forest." Her voice was quiet, faintly husky. Though unbearable emotion lurked somewhere below the surface, it remained steady, almost forceful. "I know he was not the only one to die." Here she looked directly at the Prince of Moldavia and inclined her head. Without smiling, Stephen nodded to accept her acknowledgment, and the never-crowned Princess of Wallachia finished with commendable steadfastness. "And I know that thanks to the Ottomans, his body is not whole."

The abbot bowed again. "Besarab ordered his body to be left in the forest as carrion for the crows, which is why we must move so quickly. For the sake of this house, we cannot be seen to bury him. I tread a fine line between what is right and what is safe for my house."

"I understand. And I am grateful."

"My house owes much to the prince. On a personal level, many of us feel his death as a greater grief than any that has yet befallen us."

The princess dropped her eyes, as if this admission weakened her more than the talk of her husband's grisly death.

The abbot said hastily, "I've discussed it with the Lord Carstian, and we decided this was the safest way to go. We have laid a memorial stone at the altar, engraved with the prince's name. We will deny his body is there, and if anyone is mistrusting enough to look, they will not find it. They will find only an apparent insult

to the prince's memory which I hope you will forgive in the circumstances. Instead, we propose to bury him here."

He stepped to the side and turned to reveal the crypt. Inside
lay an open coffin. And a rich mantle and cloak that the princess
knew well. It did not look like a man, let alone like Vlad Dracula,
because there was no head.

Ilona got through the burial ceremony as she had got through the
whole night, because it felt like a dream. The freezing mist around
the lake had fuzzed the edges of her consciousness, helping her
remain calm and steady throughout the journey, and the abbot's
unspeakable revelations, most of which she already knew from
Stephen and the others.

And as the liturgy was read over the strange, headless corpse
who wore Vlad's clothes, she found herself concentrating not on
the words but on her own memories.

Their victory may have been short, but it had been total.
Married late in the same day they had confronted Matthias with
their scandal, they had moved immediately into the hastily staffed
and prepared house in Pest. At the time it had seemed so natural
that it was only later, looking back, that Ilona was astonished by
how quickly they had settled into married life. Almost as if the
twelve years between had never been.

Almost. In Vlad's company, the remaining veils of her "inatten-
tion" had gradually lifted. Vivacity returned with the love she now
had for her life. She'd picked up her responsibilities with increasing interest and enthusiasm, ensuring her household ran smoothly,
defusing trivial problems as they arose among her staff. She'd even
promoted Margit's desired marriage to a visiting nobleman and
seen her faithful attendant suitably settled at last.

By the time her first son, Vlad, was born, Ilona was secure enough to bear her husband's imminent departure for the war in Bosnia with equanimity. She had rediscovered her own place in life, was able to revel in her own long-awaited happiness as well as in the eccentricity they often presented to the world.

Like the occasion Vlad had killed a rude official for daring to enter the house without permission to pursue a felon.

"I committed no crime," Vlad had said dismissively when confronted about the killing. *"It was the officer who committed suicide. If he'd troubled to ask me first, I would have killed the felon myself, but anyone who invades my house without permission can expect a similar fate."*

It had been shocking, and unfortunate for the poor—if stupidly misguided—officer concerned, but there had been a certain black humour about the whole situation that had tempted Ilona to guilty laughter. In fact, it had made everyone who heard the story laugh and had been the single most important factor in finally reconciling Matthias fully to his new "cousin."

Vlad's often-reported words had also served as a warning to Besarab in Wallachia.

Busy with her son and absorbed by her new pregnancy, Ilona had easily filled the days of Vlad's first long absence with her own necessary and self-imposed duties. And when he returned, victorious in battle once more, Ilona had felt more whole than at any time in her life before.

After John's birth—he was called for John Hunyadi, not as a sop to Matthias, but because Vlad wished it—they had moved to Vlad's old house in Sibiu, from where Vlad continued to fight in the king's name. And from where he again fought alongside his cousin Stephen, who had himself been deposed by the Ottomans because of his new alliance with Matthias. This time, the cousins took back Moldavia first, and with Stephen restored, they'd attacked and retaken Wallachia.

Ilona let her eyes wander to Stephen. Undeniably a lesser man than her husband, but yet a better prince, because he didn't let little things like loyalty, revenge, or temper destabilise his policy. Vlad, her Vlad, had, perhaps, been a flawed man. Certainly a flawed prince, and yet he shone, he had always shone with a brightness that eclipsed Stephen and Radu the Handsome and Besarab Laiota and even Matthias Corvinus himself.

She was biased, of course, because she loved him. But there had always been something about him, some brilliance that drew others and held them. Not just Stephen, who had made such amends, but Carstian, Stoica, Turcul, and his cousin Cazan… Her eyes moved from grieving face to grieving face as she thought their names. The boyars had taken a long time to accept Radu, and when Vlad had returned, these men had led most of the others back to him. The monks here at Snagov were motivated by affection as much as by righteousness and gratitude in risking the new prince's wrath to bury the old.

And yet despite all that loyalty, he'd been given no time. Barely two months after he'd retaken Wallachia, he'd been ambushed and attacked by Besarab. Maybe he'd mellowed too much. The old Vlad would have ensured Besarab's immediate death.

Her eyes flickered back to Stephen. The Prince of Moldavia had left him a bodyguard of two hundred Moldavians, who'd been with him when he was attacked. They were nearly all dead now. Another tragedy that spoke volumes for the loyalty Vlad could inspire. They had refused to leave him, even when ordered by Vlad himself when he'd seen there was no hope of escape. Only ten had limped away to bring the news to Stephen and to Carstian and the others.

The magnitude of this disaster struck Ilona all over again. The tragedy for Wallachia, and through that for all the free Balkan states, for Hungary itself. She wasn't the only one who could see it. All these men gathered here understood it. Statesmen all over

Europe would recognise the significance of the death of the last great crusader.

And perhaps, in Buda, her cousin Matthias would see it too, although he'd never admit it. At the moment, very few people knew that Vlad Dracula was dead. Officially, Stephen didn't know. Besarab kept it quiet because he'd allowed his enemy's head to be taken to Constantinople. That would not sit well with the Christian states. And Stephen's and Vlad's supporters kept it quiet so that they could bury him with honour and allow Ilona and his children time to come from Sibiu to pay their last respects.

Ilona almost jumped when Mihnea took the baby from her. Though he was weeping, he must have seen the trembling of her arm as exhaustion took its toll. There was so much hope for Mihnea, for her own sons, although she'd do her best to keep them from the poisoned chalice that was the throne of Wallachia. But they would go their own way. She would love them and guide them to the best of her ability, whatever path they chose.

The abbot had stopped speaking. The liturgy was over. Everyone was looking at her, expecting her to make some sign of farewell to the body that contained no more of Vlad than his crimson mantle. Not even the ring she'd given him so long ago, that he'd always worn. His assassins had stolen that too.

And suddenly that seemed more overwhelmingly sad than anything else. Because he'd died without her and was buried almost in absentia. Without conscious intention, she found herself kneeling by the side of the crypt, gazing at the corpse, searching for a sign that something remained of the great, unquiet spirit that had been her husband.

Be at peace, my love…

Oh, but they'd had a good sleigh ride, wild and ultimately satisfying. She refused to allow that they'd crashed at the final turn. It was just that the snow had stopped.

Reaching out, as if she couldn't help it, she touched the thick, red fabric of his mantle, the crown he'd had made for his final reign, which lay beside him. There were no dead lips to kiss, no cold face to touch. But she could no longer see that. She saw him full of life and excitement because he was returning to his own beloved country, winning a place for her and the children as well as for himself. She'd already had the only place that mattered to her, but she'd always understood that wouldn't be enough for him.

She gasped and snatched at the ring on her finger. Not the ornate gold wedding band, but the ring he'd first given her all those years ago at Horogszegi. Dragging it from her finger, she wrenched at the claws that held the beautiful pearl until the stone came loose. She held it tightly in her left hand while with her right, she laid the bare ring in the folds of his mantle, covering it because it had always been private.

Two parts of the same whole, Stephen had once said.

Mihnea bent beside her and laid his own offerings in the grave: the cup and belt his father had given him on his last birthday. Like Ilona, he didn't need objects to remember Vlad. It was a pleasing symbol of giving him something back. Of making him Vlad again.

Slowly, Ilona's fingers trailed up the stiff arm and shoulder, touched the place where his lips should have been. A single tear dripped onto the mantle, making Carstian say her name in pity. But Ilona smiled through the mist, for now, it was bearable.

Tag, Vlad Dracula.

THE END

Author's Note

A Prince to be Feared is my fictional interpretation of Vlad's life, based on the meagre documentary facts and what I personally take from the folk tales and legends which surrounded him.

Our knowledge of Vlad III Dracula, Prince of Wallachia, comes from a few contemporary documents and a mass of atrocity tales and legends, many of which were given apparent authority by the new-to-the-time printing. Others are from oral tradition, stories still told about him in Romania today. These sources give hugely contradictory impressions: a bloodthirsty psychopath with a terrifyingly black sense of humour; a hero who protected his people from the Ottoman Turks and resisted invasion on behalf of not just his own country, but the rest of Christian Europe. With difficulty, I might have been able to buy into both these sides of one character. But what made me look with really serious doubt at his accepted portrait was documentary evidence of him clearing forest land for farming, thus improving the economic lot of his people. For me, this just isn't the act of a power-crazed prince who slaughtered thousands of his own people on callous whims.

And in fact, evidence of such slaughter comes largely from folk tales, printed and oral. Although there is, generally, a grain of truth in folk tales, to find the grain, it helps to look at why they were told; and in the case of the printed tales, where and on whose authority. The novel suggests possible culprits and motives. The atrocity stories themselves are clearly exaggerated as to numbers – and so are probably not entirely trustworthy in other respects either. If they're analysed with a generous pinch of salt, I believe it's possible to gain a truer picture.

Where possible, I've surrounded Vlad with other known historical characters: John and Elizabeth Hunyadi, Mihály Szilágyi, Matthias Corvinus, Stephen the Great of Moldavia. The names of the Wallachian boyars mentioned in the novel, are also recorded in documents. Count Szelenyi, however, is entirely made up.

About Vlad's love life, almost nothing is known for certain. There are particularly nasty atrocity tales involving his mistresses, and one poignant story tells of a wife, or possibly a mistress, throwing herself from the castle at Poenari rather than be taken by the besieging Turks. I used this event in the novel, but since there seem to have been marriage negotiations between Vlad and Hungary for some time before this, I've made Maria his mistress, the mother of his son.

Ilona Szilágyi is generally regarded by historians as the most likely candidate for Vlad's wife, although she is variously described as King Matthias's sister and cousin. In truth, a woman's importance in those days depended solely on her family and the political alliances she brought to a marriage; no one was terribly interested in her personal details. Ilona's character in the novel is, therefore, entirely from my imagination, as is her long-standing love affair with Vlad. However, given Vlad's connections to Hunyadi and Mihály Szilágyi, I don't believe it's unreasonable to assume that they knew each other for a long time before their marriage.

What is known is that on his release from prison, Vlad married a female relation of the king's and lived with her in a house in Pest, given to him by the king, where he created more legends before returning to war and the recapture of his throne in Wallachia. The novel's epilogue is based on archaeological finds at Snagov, but again, is only one possible interpretation of the physical end of a man whose name never seems to die.

~ Mary Lancaster

About Mary Lancaster

Mary Lancaster's first love was historical fiction. Since then she has also grown to love coffee, chocolate, red wine and black and white films - simultaneously where possible. She hates housework.

As a direct consequence of the first love, she studied history at St. Andrews University, after which she worked variously as editorial assistant, researcher and librarian. Although she has always written stories for her own entertainment, she began to make serious efforts toward publication in order to distract herself from a job she disliked. She now writes full time at her seaside home in Scotland, which she shares with her husband and three children.

Mary is the author of three historical novels:
A Prince to be Feared: the love story of Vlad Dracula
And from Mushroom Publishing:
An Endless Exile - the story of Hereward, 11th century outlaw hero
A World to Win - a Scottish governess finds love in 1848 revolutionary Hungary.

Please enjoy this first chapter from **An Endless Exile**, available now in ebook and in paperback.

Chapter One

"*Hereward is dead.*"

Whatever I had expected of my husband's nephew, rousing my household in the middle of the night to throw his dripping person and its accompanying blast of cold air at my feet, it was not that. Even though there can have been few men who courted death more insistently.

Just for a moment, I could only stare at the bent, agitated head, watching the rivulets of water run down his hair to join the thousand others on his sodden cloak. By the trembling, almost sinister flame of my porter's lamp, I could even see the little pool of water forming between us. Just for a moment, that fascinated me too.

Hereward is dead. Was this news, then, already galloping and spreading under the night-stars? Northwards, perhaps, to York and beyond, to his erstwhile Danish friends of Northumbria. West too, to the old rebels of the Welsh marches. South, probably, to the King in London or Winchester or wherever he was, and whatever pity was in his heart today. And eastward—certainly eastward—among the fens which had always been his. Were his people, the lost and despairing, loud in lament for their last great hero? Wildly—or silently—inconsolable? Or did they close their eyes in peace, breathe a mighty sigh of collective relief and say, "Thank God it is over at last: Hereward is dead."

Perhaps, in the end, it would even be the Normans who mourned most for their newly won friend. Or were the present masters of this land too full of such an unexpected triumph over their one-time enemy? An enemy who could never, after all, have become one of them; only a dangerous rival. Perhaps they would be unable to believe their luck, passing on the news in superstitious whispers through the great estates and courts of England and Normandy, that Hereward the Exile, the Outlaw, was dead.

There is a dreadful finality about that word. Even through the detached ramblings of my mind, I was aware of it. Gradually too, I became aware of the pain in my hand where Siward, my husband's nephew, was pressing it into his face. He knelt still at my bare, icy feet as though begging forgiveness for the news he bore, and in his own torment of grief—or his completely misplaced fear for mine—gentleness was forgotten.

Still distracted, I began to draw my fingers free. They were wet. Releasing me, Siward dashed his hands across his eyes, and rose slowly to his feet, sword clanking dully at his belt and brushing against the fur cloak I had dragged around my chemise to receive him. In the dimly flickering light of the lamp that my porter held unsteadily above us, the skin of his still young face looked taut and sickly, the hollows around his exhausted eyes black. The tangled mass of fair hair, palely imitating his uncle's, fell damply forward over one cheek; then, impatiently, he pushed it back, the better to peer at me, I think, for signs of emotional disintegration. Baffled, I gazed silently back at him until in pity he lifted both arms for me.

Instinctively, I stepped backwards out of his reach, and as his arms fell again, a frown of puzzlement creased his low brow.

"Torfrida, he is dead," he repeated deliberately, as if to a child, or to an imbecile who could not under-stand simple words. "Hereward, your husband, is dead."

And at last the breath seemed to seep back into my body.

"Good," I said with satisfaction. "Then I can go home to Bourne."

In the first light of a grey, wintry morning, I prepared with some care for my ride from Lincoln to Bourne. I dressed in a warm woollen gown of bright, sky blue, over a fine yellow under-dress. Beneath my veil, which was circled with a braided ribbon of the same blue and yellow, my hair was as neatly and becomingly pinned as I could make it. I had no intention of being surprised by anyone at any time.

That done, I drew the sable travelling cloak about me and regarded my reflection in the sheet of polished bronze which was the one extravagance of my solitary, sterile bed-chamber. My face was too thin now, marked by life like the grey streaks in my once jet-black hair. I looked, in fact, disconcertingly frail. My eyes, too large and bright for that countenance, stared back at me, half-frightened, half-excited; and in my breast my heart beat and beat and beat.

"Stop it, Torfrida," I whispered. "Stop it."

Then, taking a deep breath, I rose and went to collect my children. I was thirty-two years old, and felt as if I were waking up after a long, expectant sleep.

The journey was accomplished mostly in uncomfortable silence, at least after we had drawn away from the children. Siward, torn between his own grief and an increasingly desperate, if covert, search for signs of mine, began to withdraw even further into his own private misery. I could not help that. It was not the time to try. For my own part, I think I sang a little, snatches of a merry French song that brought Siward's eyes round to me with an astonishment that was far from admiring.

I smiled at him, beatifically, and twisted back in the saddle to give one last wave to the children. They were riding two ponies—Frida on one, the two little boys together on the other – in company with their nurse and most of the men-at-arms. We had agreed that they would go directly to Folkingham, to Gilbert of Ghent, their father's godfather, while I insisted on riding ahead with Siward, to visit Bourne on the way. Siward said it was not fit for me. It was where Hereward had been killed.

"Do they know?" Siward asked.

"Know what?" I asked, straightening in my saddle, and adjusting the warm, soft cloak at my throat.

"That their father is dead, of course!"

"Oh no. I see no point in spoiling their treat. They are going to see their grandmother and Aunt Lucy at Uncle Gilbert's hall; and Aunt Matilda will spoil them mercilessly. Now, Siward, add to *my* personal well-being: *who* had the ultimate honour of killing Hereward?"

This time he did not even try to keep the accusation out of his face or voice.

"The *honour* of killing your husband? Some treacherous Norman knights, purporting to be his friends! They were dining with him—it was the lady Aediva's birthday feast—when their servants, who had hidden weapons under their clothes, fell on his men and—."

"Yes, so you told me last night," I interrupted, waving that aside. "But who were they?"

"I don't know," Siward said bitterly. "I was not there. The assassins had fled by the time we came to his rescue. But it was Deda who escorted Aediva and Lucy to safety at Folkingham."

My lip twitched as I regarded his averted face. "Deda," I said with blatant mockery. "*Deda* killed Hereward?"

"Hardly!" Siward snapped, displeased all over again by the flippancy of my tone. Well, what did he expect? "From all I can gather, Deda did everything possible to try and stop the fight. But I doubt the same could be said for that swaggering fool, Asselin!"

I had no quarrel with that description, but glancing up at him from under my lashes, I pointed out, "You told me they fled before you got to them."

Siward's pale skin flushed, but his eyes met mine squarely. "I heard from those who survived."

"Yes," I agreed evenly. "I expect you did."

"Torfrida!"

I lifted my brows at him, watched him take a deep breath. Then: "Torfrida, I know this is hard to take in; after all he has done, God knows I never thought he would die like that, foully, in his own home—."

"That's just it, Siward," I murmured. "It wasn't his home."

Siward blinked his pale eyes once. "Wasn't his—?"

"No. He gave Bourne to me, in trust for Frida."

Siward stared at me. In truth, the contempt in his eyes hurt me far more than it should. What in the world did he imagine I still owed to a troublesome and adulterous husband I had cast off four years ago? Bourne was all I had had of him, and that I had looked after mainly for his mother and widowed sister who still lived there! My own efforts, my own reviving of my father's trading ventures, had fed and clothed my children and me.

But Siward was angry. I tried to make allowances for his grief.

"Are you really counting property while he lies cut to pieces not twenty-four hours since?" he said harshly. "He may have behaved ill to you once, Torfrida, but before God, he was still your husband!"

There was a short pause. Then: "Was he?" I actually sounded amused. Mind you, I had not been, although I had tried quite hard, when I first heard the song linking Hereward's name to Aelfryth's, and calling her his wife. It had been yelled out joyously by a couple of drunks in imperfect harmony one market day in Lincoln. Well, being young and fair and Saxon, she made a better heroine for the story than I—well past my first flush of youth, Flemish, and endowed with rather dubious knowledge for a Christian.

"There seems," I remarked judiciously, "to be some doubt."

Hereward is dead. What would she do when the news got to her? Was someone else—one of the twins perhaps, or Leofric the Deacon—even now riding across the country to tell her what Siward had already told me? Would she come crashing into Bourne, claiming to be his widow? Well, Bourne was one place she would have no such rights. Bourne, as I had just reminded Siward, was mine. Mine and Frida's.

Avoiding the village and the monastery, and the wide, stricken eyes of the few frightened people we encountered on the road, I came home to Bourne. His presence there, unexpected and uninvited, had prevented me returning at all for the last month, even for Aediva's birthday, and I had missed it. I acknowledged that as my tired horse picked its way daintily across the stream which flowed from St. Peter's Pool, the natural fountain close by. Above the stream rose the earth mound and stockade that protected my hall.

Whatever occurred here yesterday, Hereward's people had not deserted his ancestral home. The gates were closed and guarded by a man I knew well: he had a sword-scar on his left buttock. I tried to bear that in mind as he greeted me, disconcertingly with tears rolling unchecked down his rough, pitted cheeks.

While I stared carefully between my horse's ears and urged it through the gates, I heard Siward quickly questioning the man.

"Where is he?"

"In the hall."

"Is he fit?"

"As he can be."

I rode carefully on, and my heart beat and beat and beat.

There had certainly been a battle here. The whole yard and the burned and damaged buildings around it bore unmistakable witness to that. For the first time, foolishly, I wanted to weep, because in all the years of war, for all the halls and towns and castles I had seen destroyed by one side or another, Bourne had never before been one of them.

But *they* were there, Hereward's 'gang'. Just as in the old days, they would have had word this last half hour and more of my approach. And as my horse picked its way into the devastated yard, they emerged from the hall and the outbuildings, pausing in their tasks of clearing and burying and putting to rights, to stand and move silently towards me, united as one in their enormous loss, in their pity, and in the great grief they assumed, despite everything, that I would share.

"Fools!" I thought, with a sudden fury that could never be free of affection. "Fools, fools!"

Forcing myself, I picked out with my eyes those of them I had known and loved best, marked with my mind those who were notably absent.

"In the hall," the soldier had said. And since I had no words to offer the men I had laughed with and suffered with for so long, I half-turned, till I could see the hall door. It lay open, half ripped off its hinges, and the twins, Hereward's cousins Outi and Duti, stood on either side of it, shoulders sagging with fatigue, mouths drooping with misery. And yet they tried to smile at me.

I did not know what was going on.

My limbs were trembling, and not just with the cold. Lifting my head, I drew the sable close around my throat and moved forward to the hall. Men moved aside to let me pass. Behind me, I was aware of Siward saying urgently, "Torfrida, wait a little. At least let me ensure…." But I heard no more. At the door, Outi embraced me, and because I could not stop it, I let him. And then I was past them, in the hall itself.

The battle had been in here too. They had made some effort to clear it up, but broken benches and tables lay piled on both sides and hangings had been torn down or shredded. The walls were scarred and pierced by weapons, stained by many liquids, some of which, at least, must have been blood. There was always blood. And at the far end, even the high table had been damaged: one of its legs was propped up now on a broken chair. I could see that, although I could not see what was laid upon it. In front of it stood Leofric the Deacon, a stained, ragged bandage askew about his head. From the footsteps behind, Siward and the twins had followed me inside.

For a moment, Leofric and I stared at each other. Then my gaze flitted beyond him, and around the hall, and back to Leofric. It was he, inevitably, who moved first, stepping down from the dais, and coming straight toward me, a thousand expressions chasing across his open, gentle face.

I decided to strangle the pity at birth.

"Very well," I said. "Where is the body?"

Shock brought him to a standstill. Beside me, I felt the movement of Siward's tired shrug.

Leofric said, "It is here; but I have to warn you, lady—."

"I have seen dead bodies before," I interrupted. "You must remember *that*, Leofric—you were generally there." And I moved forward, brushing past him. At the last moment, he reached out and caught my arm. He was strong enough to force me, but I did not struggle. Instead, slowly, I looked back at him over my shoulder. His dark eyes gazed at me, serious, intense, *pleading*.

"Torfrida, don't."

I laughed. "Don't what? Don't look? Why do you think I came?"

I think it was the laughter that shook him off. At any rate I was free, with no inclination, or time, to think about what was in his face. On the table, to his left, I could see someone's up-turned boots.

I took my time. There were the boots, and leggings, and a short tunic worn without armour, save for the red painted shield still slung around his body like his sword-belt. There was a black dragon on the shield, with fierce, jewelled, emerald green eyes. My lips parted.

For the first time, I acknowledged the stale smell of burning that came off the body. His hair and head had been badly burned, beyond recognition. That should not have surprised me. I think it was the isolated clumps of thick, golden hair clinging still to his shoulders and chest that threw me off balance. Siward was right: he had been hacked to pieces. Bits of limbs were missing, there were massive, gory wounds in his legs and body, and his face, dear God, was enough to make seasoned warriors cringe.

I had seen enough. Sickened, I was already beginning to turn away when something on the body caught my eye: something frail and small and stained, but once, unmistakably, yellow. It shone through the singed, filthy, bloody rags of his clothing, somewhere between his chest and his left shoulder. Involuntarily, my hand reached out and touched it.

A braided, yellow ribbon, sewn with tiny gems.

My mouth opened, soundless at first, then gasping, and gasping again. Another storm filled my ears, rushing, swelling, endless. "Jesus Christ," I whispered, twisting with the awful, unbearable thing I had found. "Jesus Christ."

Leofric said, "What—?"

And Siward interrupted him savagely, "She did not know! She would not believe me!" He strode up to the dais and seized me by both arms. "You didn't, did you? That is why you behaved so, said all those things! For God's sake, Torfrida, what do you take me for?"

A queer, animal noise burst from my throat.

"Leave her!" Leofric said sharply. And as soon as the fingers slackened on my arm, I was away, bolting for the door, away from the tragedy I had not foreseen and would never be able to run from. The dreadful finality of death was upon me at last, and now, *now*, I was lost.

Hereward is dead.

Connect with Mary Lancaster Online:

Email Mary: Mary@MaryLancaster.com
Website: http://www.MaryLancaster.com
Facebook: https://www.facebook.com/mary.lancaster.1656

Made in the USA
Coppell, TX
02 June 2025

50199837R00208